THE UNEXPECTED

THE UNEXPECTED

Nicholas V Taylor

Book Guild Publishing
Sussex, England

First published in Great Britain in 2010 by
The Book Guild Ltd
Pavilion View
19 New Road
Brighton, BN1 1UF

Typeset in Baskerville by
Ellipsis Books Limited, Glasgow

Printed in Great Britain by
CPI Antony Rowe

A catalogue record for this book is available from
The British Library.

ISBN 978 1 84624 451 3

Contents

1

The Present

The six rifle shots were almost simultaneous. There followed no echo or reverberation but a silence unpunctuated by the buzzing of insects or the song of the infrequent birds. Even the still air seemed more still and the oppressive heat stagnant.

I knew they were rifle shots from the sound; not the noise heard in the cinema or on television, which is manipulated for dramatic effect, but a sharp 'crack' as the high-velocity bullet twists its way clear of the barrel. Of course there could be no accurate count, but I also *knew* there were six shots – it was always so, from the mists of time. I could understand why more than one but why six? I was pondering upon this when:

'Why don't you have a look?'

The voice came from a large, round black face atop a tall, large, round, well-dressed body seated opposite me across a scarred wooden table. Receiving no response:

'Go on. I don't mind. I know you are curious, or are you afraid?'

Again I said nothing but forced my face into a resigned, accommodating expression accompanied by a resentful sigh as I slowly, very slowly, rose to my feet. Truth to tell, whilst I was not at all curious, I welcomed the opportunity of getting off the most uncomfortable chair in the world, especially designed to inflict progressive discomfort having a high, straight wooden back, a hard wooden seat, well polished by previous occupants, sloping down from the back to the front just sufficiently to transfer the bodyweight onto the legs, more particularly the thighs, which needed to be tensed to prevent sliding off. The effect of this dastardly design upon the sitter was to induce strain into the legs, which slowly but inexorably moved into muscle-burning sensations, then white-hot pain through to screaming numbness. Even the most resolute would eventually lose complete leg control and slump to the ground clawing madly at the table in an attempt to break the fall and salvage some dignity.

My legs were approaching the white-hot stage whereby my control over them was uncertain and, whilst my body language was one of resigned indifference, my mind was battling with my limbs reluctance to respond and fighting the urge to scream as movement exacerbated the pain.

Rising from the chair, steadying myself with the table, I paused to emphasise lack of interest but in reality to allow time for leg pain relief; then, shrugging my shoulders, I slowly pushed the chair to one side, turned around and nonchalantly, so far as my legs would allow, ambled towards the window. I say window but it was no more than a hole in a thick block-constructed wall allowing the oppressive heat of the day to drift through vertical bars cemented into the block work. Upon reaching the window I grasped the bars ostensibly to hold my head close to get a better view but in reality to steady my uncertain legs.

Outside in a large courtyard I was greeted by a sight that had become fairly familiar to me. Six soldiers dressed in a ragbag mixture of military garb and hip-hop clothing, with a variety of headgear, were haphazardly leaning on rifles and gazing blandly at a bloody figure slumped on the concrete courtyard against a stained and dust-splattered wall, which may well have once been painted white but had through neglect long since lost any semblance of distinctive colour. A seventh soldier of officer class, distinguished by wearing a complete set of sweat-stained army fatigues and a battered peaked hat, stood looking at the six with his hands in his pockets and a cigarette hanging loosely from the corner of his mouth. None seemed eager to leave nor really content to stay, appearing to be waiting to see if the blooded figure with six bullets in its body would somehow raise itself from the floor in defiance of nature and ballistics.

'You are privileged to be able to see your future,' said the voice from the table, followed by a deep guffaw.

I looked around and saw the flash of pearl white teeth in the laughing open mouth of my tormentor.

'Well, as may be,' I said, 'but I cannot say the appearance of your military or its demeanour strikes fear into the heart. We are not talking Guards regiments here and the fact they do seem to be able to hit a still target ten or so feet away does not demonstrate potential SAS abilities.' He did not respond but just looked at me in a blank, almost pitying way.

I turned back to look through the window, not to renew the sight but to allow more time for my legs to come back to life. The movement to the window and standing had shifted the pain into pins and needles rooting my feet to the floor. Gradually the blood in the legs pumped around the strained muscles, and as the soldiers outside sloped disconsolately away, leaving the bloody mass where it was, I felt control returning below my waist. I shuffled, turned to lean against the wall and looked at the man sitting patiently at the table.

Whilst he was a big, round man he did not overly perspire for there was little sign of sweat marks on his pristine white shirt, though in deference to the heat he had taken off his suit jacket and tie.

'Come and sit down. How can we talk if you are so far

away. I know you really want to talk to me even if hereto-fore you pretend reluctance.'

'Heretofore'. A word he deliberately used to emphasise or impress upon me his English public school education about which he regularly boasted. I did not doubt his family paid for his English education – his English was perfect with only an occasional African intonation – though he was remarkably evasive when questioned to identify the school, so I assumed it was a minor public school giving sufficient education to gratify the paying parents but little else. That said, I could not fault his courtesy, though from the occa-sional steeliness flashing in his eyes I suspected the courtesy was but a thin layer barely disguising a ruthless and, if his associates were any guide, a callous and violent interior.

I remained leaning against the wall to extend the pleasure of pain-free legs.

'It is true I enjoy conversation with such a well educated man as you undoubtedly are,' a bit of flattery I thought was going to do me no harm in what was an increasingly obvious lose-lose situation, 'but the topic you choose to concentrate upon is becoming wearisome simply because I do not have the information you feel I should be divulging. Difficult though it is for you to admit it, you have the wrong man.'

His face clouded for an instant to be quickly replaced by what I'm sure he believed was an engaging smile but came across more as the grimace of a predator before it eats its prey.

'Come and sit down. I can't talk to you if you are so far away. I insist.'

I slowly straightened up from my wall-leaning posture and equally slowly walked to the table, taking as long as possible adjusting the chair before I sat down. Not that this would make any difference. It was time I was really after.

'All I want is for you to be reasonable and understand my position. You have not been treated badly have you?

Since your arrest you have not been tortured, simply interrogated to give us the information we know you have.'

Whilst a thoroughly good beating and kicking by half a dozen soldiers over two or so days may not be viewed in his eyes as torture I was not so sure Amnesty International would have the same benign opinion and from a personal perspective it certainly didn't class as one of my better experiences. I prudently said nothing.

'Let me explain to you once again my position and your position. Being recently elected to Parliament and very unexpectedly put in charge of the anti-terrorist department I have to get results not only to satisfy the people who are sick to their stomachs with violence but also to justify my appointment. If I can show success I will progress in government and be able to use my English gentleman influence to curb the excesses of my fellow politicians and so make life better for everyone. I have many friends in influential places who feel the same way and will support me. But what we must first do is to achieve stability and stop terrorism. You must agree that it's a noble aim, which is supported by all the western leaders.'

I didn't think at this point it would be useful to suggest the reason for the existence of what he termed 'terrorism' was that his government was wholly corrupt, skimming off every penny possible into personal offshore bank accounts, taxing the people past the threshold of pain and enforcing unjust and totally unjustifiable laws with a ruthless military leaving the people cowed, often blooded and frightened.

'We know,' he continued, 'a group of these terrorists have a white man helping them and that this white man seems to have influenced greater dedication, certainly greater efficiency and effect. So when my men gallantly fight off an ambush and find you unconscious where the terrorists had mounted an attack, obviously abandoning you in their haste to escape, it does not take a leap of imagination to conclude you were a part of the ambush, not least because you were armed with an automatic pistol. Now your position as far as I can see is that you face overwhelming evidence of being a terrorist, a crime carrying the death penalty so at any time I can have you shot. But I keep you alive because I'm a reasonable person, educated in your ways, and believe I can convince you to cooperate to give me the names of your accomplices and where they are. If you do this then I have no reason to have you shot. I will deport you back to England in a blaze of publicity, which will help me and cannot possibly harm you. If you continue with your stubbornness I will have to hand you over to those who are more qualified and more experienced in interrogation, which will surely be unpleasant for you.'

I had no doubt his thugs would make it very unpleasant for me and I was not at all keen to verify this though could not see how I could convince my interrogator of my innocence. My death was inevitable so, short of finding a way to kill myself – not something I had really contemplated – or a means of escape – something I constantly but fruitlessly contemplated – I had to devise a way to stave off the inevitable pain and suffering.

'Look' I said 'during your extensive education and living in England you obviously became aware of our legal system and for sure watched cops shows on TV so you know full well that your evidence would not stand up to the most biased jury.' I didn't think it worth mentioning that the chance of me getting anywhere near a jury was slightly less than the fabled snowball's chance in the hot place, but if my interrogator was to maintain the facade of English respectability he could not point it out either. I continued. 'Let us look at the real facts. Your men say they were ambushed by what you earlier described as terrorists with a great dedication, efficiency and effect, and yet, according to the boasts of your commander who first interrogated me with his boot,

not one of his gallant men was injured or killed. A somewhat unlikely scenario. Even if the terrorists were half trained
and half baked, if they surprised a dozen or so men in an
ambush by first detonating a bomb it's unlikely these terrorists would miss them all.'

'Please sit down,' he said. I stretched and looked casual,
then slowly lowered myself into the torture chair.

He looked at me for a long moment and shrugged. 'It
might well have been our highly trained and efficient troops
foresaw the potential ambush and took evasive and effective
action before being fired upon.'

'Not only do I hear the flapping of pigs' wings,' I said,
and to give credit, the ghost of a smile crossed his face, 'but
it is not the story they have so far related to everyone who
would listen.'

'In the heat of the moment perception can become
confused but I'm sure when it is necessary, in the cold light
of day, memories will be sharp,' he replied.

I didn't doubt for one moment if push came to shove all
his men would be singing in harmony from the same hymn
sheet.

'Even assuming,' I said, 'there was a presence of terrorists somewhere, this does not mean I was any part of them.'
He said nothing. 'Moreover,' I could counter his 'hereto-
fore', 'although I cannot deny I was unconscious, I have no
idea how I became so and now have no memory of events
even before that. The gun could well have been planted on
me by those gallant troops.'

'But you cannot explain why you had no papers or visa
to enter my country,' he retorted.

I confess I was initially surprised when he first raised the
lack of these because I know I had passport, visa and papers
to give credence to my presence in his country. True, they
were not actually kosher but should have passed even the
closest inspection in this country. I assumed the soldiers took

the papers from me – they took my wrist-watch and planted the gun – to bolster their story of the white terrorist, and for some reason had not told him. I was as sure as I could be that he did not know, but if he did, he was making a very good job of hiding this fact.

'Well at best,' I said, 'and stretching the imagination to breaking point, this makes me an illegal immigrant but isn't it strange that when, as you say, I was arrested I had no personal possessions of any sort. I would assume it unlikely that anyone involved in coordinating and taking part in terrorist activities as you maintain would not have at least a watch to synchronise attacks. Perhaps if you were to interrogate your troops you might find my papers and the all-important visa and passport. There is also of course the clincher. Even you have to admit a person fighting alongside terrorists in this country would not do so dressed in a laundered shirt, trousers and city shoes.'

We were now going over well-trodden ground. He was still far from convinced by my loss of memory and was fast losing patience. He sat looking at me and I could see his mind churning. There was definitely a seed of doubt but he was not going to let it flourish and, perhaps for this reason, he was reluctant to turn me over to those who would interrogate me in a rather more forthright way. And of course by breaking me himself he could gain greater political kudos. I realised, as did he, there were few throws of the dice left.

'No, mister, whilst you are persuasive, you do not persuade. I do not believe your loss of memory at all. You give me no option. I must have a result. I cannot go back to the minister without, at the very least, a confession. You have one last opportunity to tell me the names and locations of your co-conspirators otherwise I will get this from you by less civilised means.'

He barked out an order in the local dialect and a soldier came into the room levelling his automatic rifle at me. My interrogator rose, towered over me menacingly for a moment and left the room to return a few moments later with several pads of A4 lined paper and a handful of pencils. He did this so quickly I could only assume he had anticipated we would get to this stage. Obviously a planner, reinforcing my impression of a man well prepared and organised. He'll go far in politics, I thought.

'I have to leave here to inspect my garrisons later today and I will be back in five days. During that time you will write a full account of your activities. Failure will mean many weeks of pain and in the end you will do it. Trust me, men far braver then you fold in the end. Do not doubt my determination.'

He barked out another order and the soldier walked behind me yanking me off the chair, inducing the return of white-hot pain in the thighs, poked me in the back with his gun towards the door and I stumbled out down the corridor to my cell. My interrogator followed with the pads of paper and pencils, dumping them on the flea-ridden mattress on the floor, which, together with a very unsanitary bucket, accounted for the totality of the furniture in the room.

'You have just five days so don't waste time.' He turned and left, followed by the soldier slamming the cell door behind him.

I lowered myself onto the mattress and leant against the wall, stretching my legs as the blood circulation went through the layers of pain and discomfort before settling down to a dull ache. The lose-lose situation had moved on to a place of no return. Either I spilled the beans he wanted and likely die, or possibly live and be deported, or suffered painful interrogation, confess to whatever they chose to make me say and definitely die.

I picked up a pad of paper and looked at it, hoping for inspiration, again tossing about in my mind my limited options, concluding that, in modern parlance, it was a no-brainer. I had to write something and make it look real. That is not to say I would pour out my heart. I learned long ago it was always best to tell the truth but not necessarily wise to tell all the truth. It would obviously be somewhat of a giveaway if I included a disclaimer along the lines of 'any bearing this account has upon person or persons living or dead is wholly coincidental' but to protect my family, friends, indeed perhaps country, the names of countries, places and people I was about to write down would have to be wholly imaginary; though, not knowing what my interrogator knew, the events themselves would be real if apparently unbelievable. I hardly believed them myself and I had lived through them. I hoped I would somehow be well away from this place before my interrogator found out the names of those whom he would take to be my accomplices were false. This was but a wishful thought but I was grasping at straws although underlying all this I had a strong feeling I would not necessarily be condemned by what I wrote.

Not knowing where to actually start, I looked around at the grey, dust-flecked concrete walls of my cell to concentrate my mind. I had noticed before that unlike prison cells in literature there was no writing on the walls; no graffiti; no words of wisdom or pleas of despair. Not even lines scratched in the concrete to delineate the passing of days, weeks, months. Not for the first time I pondered on this. Either the previous inmates had been totally illiterate and innumerate or their time here was short; a mere staging post to the great wall of countless executions outside. This thought focused my attention on the job in hand. I picked up a pencil, rested a pad of paper against my knees, which I could now bend without pain, and began to write quickly. Surprisingly my thoughts fell into order. What my interrogator would get would not be a simple list of people, places and events but a narrative of how I came to be here from the great city of London. I guessed from the number of pads and pencils supplied, my interrogator anticipated as much; he will certainly go far.

2

The Beginning

It all started with a telephone call; to be precise it was two telephone calls that got me into the mess. Now I am not a great telephone person and my later experience has confirmed the insidiousness of this invention. My dislike of the telephone does not stretch to not having one; indeed modern life is such that the failure to have and carry the mobile telephone would instantly disqualify one as being a person of substance. I make and receive telephone calls but they are made only when totally necessary and kept short and to the point. Indeed my telephone bill is but a fraction of the next contender in the office.

I was sitting at my desk in my office surrounded by law books of one sort or another completing my notes for an advice upon an intricate and fascinating point of law, which had arisen during the execution of a client's contract. I felt pleased with myself for I had not only identified the problem – contrary to popular belief the lawyer's most difficult job is to identify the true problem, not the problem which the client perceives – but I had also found the solution so I was eager to dictate this for my secretary, Catherine, to turn into a fax for the waiting and apprehensive client when the phone rang.

'It is David Robinson,' said Julie, the switchboard operator and receptionist. I inwardly grimaced. David was a long-term client come acquaintance, almost friend, who only called me if he had a really impossible problem or was in London and bored so wanted to spend an evening 'on the town'. I knew it was not the latter for I was still recovering from last week's thrash around the West End so I feared the worst.

'David, how nice to hear from you so soon.'

'Well,' he said, 'you were the first person I thought of to help on this little problem.'

'Which is?'

'We have a ship in Louta under arrest for carrying illegal immigrants and smuggling and she has been there a week with no sign of a release.'

I was a bit taken aback for he had not mentioned this last week though I suppose it was not a topic falling naturally between his favourite subjects of football and girls.

'Just a minute,' I said, 'first, is someone pulling my leg here? What immigrants, legal or otherwise, would want to get into Louta? Escape from there, I understand. Secondly, you didn't say anything about it last week.' I was irritated here for I impress upon all clients, and David has been particularly receptive, early involvement in the problem (on day one would be nice) almost invariably means an early and cost-effective solution. Letting a week or more pass allows people, particularly government and quasi-governmental officials, to get entrenched, and to move them from that leads to loss of face, which many simply cannot accept. I continued.

'Bank or similar guarantees to release the ship from arrest will take weeks in Louta and still leave the problem of facing the somewhat partisan courts so you're going to lose a lot of money with your ship being idle. What you want is one of your port captains out there with a bag of cash.'

'I know,' he replied, 'I've tried that and Theolatis is in jail.' I was dumbfounded. For Theolatis to land up in the poky he must have approached the wrong person or the right person with a wrong number of US dollar bills. What-ever the position, he who followed was not going to be met with open arms. I could see who that 'he' was likely to be so I immediately changed tack.

'Then it's obviously a local lawyer's problem now. Who have you got?'

'A guy called Odubby. He was recommended and seems on the ball but as usual has not done anything except acknowledge his retainer.'

I'd not heard of Odubby and punched his name into the firm's database, which contains all the names of foreign lawyers, surveyors, experts and correspondence known to us, getting back a 'not recognised'.

'I don't know him and he's not in our database. If you like, I'll get in touch with him to sound out the local legal expertise. Let me have his name and details.'

'We really do not have too much time. The ship has to leave in a few days otherwise she will miss her next employ-ment, which is particularly lucrative, so what has to be done is an experienced, trustworthy, innovative, entrepreneurial person of your standing and ability has to go there and smooth the situation. I would go myself but no one would take any notice of me, but a London City solicitor is just what is needed.' I was not used to such effusive endorse-ments and my uncomfortable feeling of potential doom intensified.

'Well the fact is,' I replied, my mind racing to find a way out of this, 'I am right in the middle of a really important opinion, which has to go out tonight but I could get one of my partners lined up.' My thoughts immediately latching upon one of my partners who could possibly do the job but more importantly whom I would have absolutely no conscience over if he landed in jail – solicitor partnerships being an amalgam of talent and ego which leads to barely controlled competitive dislike held together only by the base instincts that as a unit the rewards are greater than as an individual.

'No,' David said, 'I would like you to go. There's a plane direct at 20:30 tonight from Heathrow, which will give you plenty of time to finish your opinion. To my certain knowledge you rattle off opinions off the top of your head and it was not that long ago we were in a taxi together when you dictated, over my phone, about four pages of pure magic. Your secretary e-mailed the results to the meeting we were going to and you made hardly a change before sending it off to the client. So don't give me this "overworked" line; I just don't fall for it.'

I could not disabuse a client over my perceived expertise and realised I was backed into a corner.

'Okay,' I said, 'I'll go.'

'Excellent. I knew you wouldn't fail me. I have already booked you on the flight with an open return, first class.' First class. If I was uncomfortable before, that was warning in itself, because ship owners wanted their lawyers to travel economy; as baggage if possible. David must be really worried.

'And,' he continued, 'a package is being couriered to you with all the papers I've received from Louta, Odubby's details, the local agent details, a visa receipt – just give this to immigration and pay fifty dollars and they will stamp your passport with a visa – hotel reservation for five nights and ten thousand dollars in cash. The local agent has access to another twenty-five thousand and I will wire more if you want it. You can read everything on the plane and be well up to speed by the time you get there. Oh, by the way, I've let the local agent and Odubby know you are coming so they will expect you.'

I inwardly groaned. Not only game, set and match, but also nothing is worse than a client telling a local lawyer he was sending a London hotshot to sort out something the local guy was too incompetent to do. I had to build some bridges urgently to try and neutralise the resentment I was going to face when I walked into Odubby's office.

'Okay,' I said, 'I'll keep you posted. If anything else comes in after, say, six tonight, e-mail it to me and I will pick it up on the hoof.'

The telephone conversation ended and Catherine walked into my office.

'Where are you going?' She asked.

'How do you know I was going somewhere?'

'I spoke to Julie. A call from David Robinson. Need I say more?'

I grinned, brought her up to speed and dictated a fax to Odubby in conciliatory terms along the lines it would be a privilege to meet him and I hoped I could in some small measure assist him in placating a ship owner client who clearly did not understand the intricacies and difficulties Odubby faced. It was not the first time I had had to send such a message, nor the first Catherine had sent for me, so I only had to dictate the bare outline, knowing she would fill in the obsequious bits. She left me to do that, find Odubby's details from somewhere – I've long since given up trying to find out how she gets information – and I went back to drafting my opinion.

3

The Opening

I finished and sent off the opinion in good time, tied up the loose ends on cases which were chuntering along nicely, went to my flat and packed a suitcase in the usual twenty minutes or so and made the airport reasonably on schedule. Amazingly, the plane took off on time so I settled down to read the papers David had sent me, which did not take me very long. I quickly realised, as had David, the whole thing was a put up job to squeeze money out of a ship owner but it had got out of hand with Theolatis obviously going at it with hob-nailed boots rather than kid gloves. This was a case where the law and the courts were going to be no good at all. Even if right was on the ship owner's side, it would take weeks, if not months, to get a result, and unless I could convince a judge to substitute the ship for a bank guarantee or bail bond, the ship would remain there idle. No. Minor and major local officials had to be seen and gently persuaded it was in everyone's interests to find a satisfactory solution and I inwardly smiled to recall David had booked me in to a hotel for five days, knowing it would take a fair time to identify and see the right people. It is a fact of life, officials cannot attend meetings straight away and they are invariably late. I have ceased musing over what level of insecurity is required to be boosted by deliberately keeping people waiting.

The flight was uneventful; the food suitably bland. A gin

17

and tonic followed by two glasses of red wine, I sank back in the seat reading a trashy paperback purchased at the airport and gently nodded off to sleep away as much of the flight as possible.

At the arrival airport the usual chaos pervaded, with passengers streaming to Immigration, forming long lines, jumping lines to get quicker service and the interminable wait while the passports were scrutinised and stamped. The oppressive African heat was not allayed by any form of air-conditioning but languidly moved around by a number of slowly rotating fly-spotted ceiling fans. It was not helped by the fact I always travel in a business suit and tie. It is the dress expected of London lawyers and whilst the jacket and tie can be removed once one gets to know the people, it is a mistake to 'go native', as it were, immediately. I am well used to this. My suit was reasonably lightweight – a tropical suit creases just too much when travelling and gives the impression of a television journalist – and I found by not getting flustered no matter what the situation and breathing slowly to bring down the heart rate allows a great degree of heat tolerance.

I shuffled slowly to the front of the line, giving my passport with the visa receipt to the immigration officer sitting there. The black face which scrutinised the documents was impassive. The visa receipt pored over. His brown eyes looked at me for a long time then back to the passport as he flicked through the pages, seeing the impressive number of immigration stamps. A standard procedure to make me feel uncomfortable; it did not. He looked at me again and I smiled.

'Visas costs one hundred dollars.'

My smile widened and I inclined my head to one side, producing a bill and said:

'Visa costs fifty dollars and twenty tax," slipping a $20 bill on top of the $50.

His eyes held mine then he grunted, snatching the money and stamping my passport with an oversized rectangular rubber stamp, which covered the whole of the passport page in a single fluid movement more akin to the ballet stage than the immigration box. He handed back the passport and I moved away towards the baggage hall where the chaos of the immigration hall paled into insignificance compared with the heaving mass of people and luggage strewn hither and thither. Such luggage trolleys as there were were being fought over and I gained no little amusement watching an enormous African woman in full multi-coloured African dress wrest a trolley from the hands of a small and insignificant looking African man badly dressed in western clothing only to find after she wheeled it about three feet it only had two working wheels and was useless.

I ambled over to the only baggage belt that was moving, noted on a partially working electric board the number (or rather, part number) of my flight and awaited the arrival of the baggage.

Picking up my suitcase when it eventually arrived I walked through customs with no difficulty to be faced by the usual mass of people waiting for their friends or loved ones to emerge. I politely shouldered my way through towards the exit and taxi rank to be accosted by a large, tall man in a crisp white shirt and dark trousers with a beaming, welcoming smile.

'Mister Turner, welcome to Louta. Let me take your bag.'

The crisp white shirt and immaculate trousers over polished shoes immediately eliminated this man from being a ship's agent or agency driver so I assumed it was the local lawyer. 'Mister Odubby?' I asked. He nodded. 'Delighted to meet you. I didn't expect you to meet me at the airport, how did you know who I was?'

His smile broadened and he looked me up and down.

'The suit and tie a bit of a giveaway then?'

He laughed. 'Indeed, come. Let us get out of this hell hole. Call me Robyn. That is Robyn with a Y. No wise-cracks though. I know it's a girl's name. Enough to say my father had a sense of humour.' He laughed uproariously, grabbed my suitcase even though I protested, and led me out into the heat of the African day, which, after the arrivals terminal, seemed surprisingly cooler, certainly more relaxing. He led me to an old, scarred Mercedes, which appeared well maintained. He put my bag into the immaculately clean boot and we clambered in.

'I have truly authentic ethnic eco-friendly air-conditioning,' he said as he started the engine, 'individually controlled by each occupant. All you have to do is to wind the window up or down to achieve your desired temperature.' He laughed loudly. His laughter was infectious so I joined in.

'Look,' I said, 'I'm truly sorry I've been sent out here to tell you how to do your job. I'm really embarrassed.'

'Don't you worry one jot,' he replied, 'I know how the world works and I'm not in the slightest bit offended. At least they sent someone with a sense of humour.' He pealed with laughter again and I joined in. 'Let's go somewhere more pleasant and we can talk about things there.'

His Mercedes ran and sounded smooth, which is more than can be said for the highway leading from the airport, which had long since lost any claim to be tarmacadam, being at best a shiny ribbon of well-polished tar, mostly potholed and compacted mud. Robyn skilfully avoided the worst of the surface and piloted us for some forty-five minutes down this highway and off along a dusty tar-free track with smaller, if not fewer, potholes, all the while pointing out features of the countryside and regaling me with local anecdotes. It was a truly joyous ride and I felt more relaxed and content than I'd been for a while. I actually like the heat and his eco-friendly air-conditioning gave just sufficient breeze to make it comfortable. We arrived at a long single-storey building, which looked like a bar with rooms attached. Whatever colour it had once been it was not now and there was an insignificant sign over the door reading 'Rest Motel'. It all indicated past attempts at some grandeur, which had long since worn away.

Robyn saw me looking at the dismal exterior. 'Don't you worry,' he said, 'in this country the smart people have "worn down and scruffy" on the exterior so no one can be envious and cause problems. In the interior, things are different. Take my Mercedes, for example, it is in excellent condition – except, that is, for the air-conditioning, which can't be repaired because we can't get hold of the old CFC gas – but it looks shabby and attracts no particular attention.'

I smiled. 'How can I possibly doubt you.' He went off into a peal of laughter, lifted my case from the boot of the car and beckoned me into the bar.

'I'm sure you have a five-star hotel reservation.' I nodded. 'Well two things. There is nothing five-star in this country and wherever you have been booked is unlikely to perform any service you would expect even from a one-star hotel. Though this you will like. I do.'

As we entered, behind the bar was a skinny black woman of average height with thick, black, single-plaited hair down her back, wearing nondescript but smart African garb. She scowled as we entered.

'Let me introduce you to your hostess, Miserable Miranda. That's not her real name but we all call her Miserable Miranda as she is the most miserable and rude person you will ever meet. In twenty years I have never seen her smile and the only reason she still lives is because the witch doctors can't find a doll thin enough to stick pins in.' Robyn laughed and Miranda deepened her scowl.

He dropped my suitcase on the floor and walked to a table with two very comfortable looking open-basket-weave armchairs. As he said, the interior was nothing like the exterior. The bar was very large with basket-weave tables and chairs at the far end for eating and a number of basket-weave armchairs scattered about close to low tables. The bar itself was to the left, small with shelves behind sporting a reasonable number of bottles of recognisable spirits. The walls, ceiling and floor were of timber, which had weathered into a mellow hue, giving an ambience almost of a traditional English gentlemen's club. Overall, very nice indeed.

'Come, take your jacket and tie off and let's sit down, have a drink and eat something. It's past my lunchtime. Miranda,' he said, turning to her, 'the usual.' We sat and before I could take breath Miserable Miranda plonked (literally) two glasses of a milkish-pink concoction before us.

'This is non-alcoholic I'm afraid. Unless I'm really depressed I do not drink alcohol before the sun goes down and about the only blessing in this impoverished country is the fact we have early sunsets.' He chuckled again and then had a deep drink of the concoction. 'It is a fruit juice of sorts. I really don't know what's in it, old misery guts won't tell anyone.' He glowered across to Miranda who had returned to the haven of her bar. 'But it is rather delicious. Try it.'

I sipped the drink to try to identify the ingredients but it was totally baffling. It did though taste good and, after a mouthful was swallowed, turned out to be very refreshing.

'What we will do. Oh, I hope I'm not taking you over?' I shook my head. 'Good, what we will do is have a bite to eat and afterwards I will bring you up to speed. Is that all right?'

'Perfectly,' I said, 'I do have to say your English is quite outstanding.' He smiled.

'Thank you. The product of a somewhat misspent youth really. I was fortunate in that my father could afford to send me to England to a very minor public school and I was just bright enough to be able to pass exams with the most minimum of effort. So I spent my time socialising and speaking to all manner of English people; then and later when at an equally indistinguishable polytechnic. I believe you call these places "universities" now.' He shook his head in a manner indicating incredulity and disbelief. 'England had a fine grammar school and university system envied by the world and then your Labour Party decides that everyone should be equal so instead of bringing up the standard of other educational establishments they managed to drag down the best to mediocrity. I thought I understood the English but now I'm not so sure for they voted this Labour Party in again!' I felt it best not to comment.

The food then arrived. A dozen small dishes of I don't know what, to which we helped ourselves while Robyn and Miranda swapped insults, which seemed to be getting quite acerbic, but I did detect a twinkle in both their eyes, indicating that the banter was somewhat more light-hearted than it appeared and probably put on for my benefit. The food was good, very good, although I had no idea what it was and when we had finished Miranda cleared away the plates and produced an extremely palatable coffee. Robyn leaned back on his chair, lit a cigarette and looked at me seriously for a long time.

'I am normally a very good judge of character and I believe I can see in you a no-nonsense something tinged with reality and understanding so I will tell it like it is.' He took a long drag on his cigarette, sipped his coffee and continued. 'Your Mister Theolatis is a disaster. He would not listen to me at all and blundered his way into the Chief Immigration Officer's office, uninvited and unannounced, told the Chief Immigration Officer which side his bread was buttered and shoved five thousand dollars at him as a "consolation" on the basis the ship left within the hour.'

I visibly cringed. Robyn nodded in agreement.

'Big mistake. Indeed much bigger than even he could possibly realise. He was not browbeating the Chief Immigration Officer but the Minister of the Interior who happened to be in the port and was using the office for an important ministerial phone call.' I groaned. 'Not surprisingly, the Interior Minister was not a happy chappie to be interrupted and was insulted at the bribe.' Robyn paused and looked meaningfully at me.

'Not enough you mean,' I said.

'Precisely.'

I pondered for a moment and said, 'Whilst I knew it was bad when I heard Theolatis was in jail, I did not foresee the magnitude. He's done this sort of thing successfully before in other countries. I just don't know what he was thinking of.'

'Quite,' said Robyn.

There followed a long pause while I contemplated the impossibility of my task and started to think of options. The first rule is to ask the local.

'There must be an angle somewhere. Leverage to persuade has to be available if we can identify a weak point. Are there any skeletons in the closet? Do any of the players have a weakness we could exploit or an ambition we could help fulfil? My real fear is the now involvement of the Minister of the Interior though.'

Robyn stayed silent as if thinking then broke into one of his infectious laughs.

'Yes, I was right. I do like you.'

I smiled and tilted my head to indicate I was open for any suggestions.

'Well, the Minister of the Interior is not such a problem as it first appears. You see, he's my cousin and we get on extremely well.' My leaden heart lifted. 'Also, we do have a bit of luck. The Harbour Master, who also happens to be a relation of mine, has been working the smuggling scam, if I can call it that between the two of us, for years. Captains of ships have to fill in manifests for all the alcohol, cigarettes, food, etc. on board the ship and it is easy to make a mistake – or convince a captain he has made a mistake – which raises a fine of ten thousand dollars and sometimes twenty-five depending upon the ship. The fine is just enough to produce a nice little income for the Harbour Master and his staff so everyone is happy. The Chief Immigration Officer was insanely jealous, not the sharpest knife in the drawer, and so tried to horn in. He couldn't do anything along the smuggling lines as this was outside of his authority so he devised the scheme of illegal immigrants. Unfortunately the men paid to be "caught" on the ship were not paid enough and they squealed under interrogation by the local magistrate.'

'Don't tell me. Another relation?' I asked.

'Certainly not. Well, he just happens to be the godfather of my sister's eldest child.' A chuckle. 'So faced with the collapse of his crony's story, the Chief Immigration Officer tacked on the smuggling charge to try and cover his back, which infuriated the Harbour Master who spoke to his relation, the Minister of the Interior.'

I didn't move. The heat of the day was long forgotten as I hung on his every word. This was so bizarre you couldn't make it up.

'This was not the first time the Chief Immigration Officer had blotted his copybook. It's all very well having a hand in the till in this country but you have to be bright enough to ensure it is your till and not someone else's. And last year there was an almighty scandal when a deficit in harbour dues was discovered at the same time as the idiot of a Chief Immigration Officer took delivery of a new BMW. A coincidence no one believed, but heaven knows how he managed to wriggle free! Earlier this year though, the cardinal sin. No one likes you stealing their stolen money but there can be a bit of grudging respect that the kidder has been kidded, in a manner of speaking. But what can't be forgiven is if you steal their girl and when caught very much in the act with the Chief Immigration Officer, the girl later throws herself on the mercy of her unsuspecting lover in front of his wife.' Robyn allowed himself a steely smile. I was really warming to this tale. 'However, one can't get rid of someone for getting his leg over – not in this country at least – but the Chief Immigration Officer had his card well and truly marked so when his latest escapade with your client's ship came to light, he was doomed. Hence the reason why the Minister of the Interior "happened" to be in the port at the time.'

I sighed. A way out. A result on the horizon perhaps.

Robyn looked at me and continued. 'The trouble is how to get out of this without anyone else being affected. It's a bit of an international incident now. Lloyd's of London has obviously been informed – it may well be an insurance matter – and that scurrilous London maritime rag has written an article about the detention of the ship.'

He paused and looked at me expectantly. I did not disappoint.

'So far as what you call the scurrilous maritime rag is concerned, it feeds on feedback. If you ignore it the story will just fade away and be forgotten. Everyone knows it's a sensationalist paper and does not really take too much notice of it. Lloyd's of London you can forget. It could be an insurance matter but Lloyds would only be involved, if at all, when the first layer insurance is exceeded or if they are involved in reinsurance. Both are highly unlikely.' I decided to drive this point home and at the same time indicate as strongly as possible, without being too obvious, the solution would involve but a small amount of money.

'Indeed,' I continued, 'if the amount we have to pay is below the deductible, no insurance company will have to be involved at all.'

I could see he liked this and I guessed he was not too up-to-date on maritime insurance and he assumed the standard deductible was $50,000 whereas in fact the market had moved on and the likely deductible these days was some $150,000. I continued.

'On the assumption you can square the people here all we are left with is the ship owner and Theolatis. The ship owner will be far too grateful of your efforts to do more than moan about your bill – they always do no matter how good the service and I can fix that – and I reckon a quiet word into Theolatis's ear in the right environment will keep him quiet. We can provide him with a story everyone will believe and immediately forget.'

Robyn was clearly pleased. 'I was right. You are the man for the job and to steal a phrase from your former Lady Prime Minister, someone I can do business with.' He laughed uproariously and Miserable Miranda's scowl deepened, indicating she was less than happy the peace of the afternoon was being shattered by this jolly, outgoing man.

'So then,' he said, 'a plan of campaign. You will obviously have to see the captain of the ship to put his mind at rest so we will go there first. Then I suggest to the prison to see Theolatis. His morale must be low and I judge it is as good a place as any to convince him to tell the right story.' I smiled and nodded. 'When that is fixed, I can do my bit with the various officials.'

'Excellent,' I said. 'I am ready as soon as I take my suitcase to my room and have had a quick wash to get the grime of the aeroplane off me.'

I looked around and noticed my suitcase was missing.

'Don't worry, my friend. Your suitcase has been taken to your room and is unpacked so go and have a quick shower and change while I make some telephone calls.'

'Unpacked,' I said, 'but it was locked.'

He gave me an old-fashioned look and beckoned Miranda

over to lead me down a long corridor off the bar to a large double-bedded and extremely well-appointed room. It was not five-star furnished but everything was sparklingly clean and comfortable looking. True enough, my suitcase had been unpacked and its contents hung up and put away. I had a surprisingly good shower – the water was satisfactorily hot and there was real soap in the form of a man-sized bar, not the miniscule square normally found in hotels. In a clean shirt, suit and tie I returned less than twenty minutes later to find Robyn and Miranda in deep conversation over the bar. Miranda still had a sour look and Robyn was not laughing but the body language was easy and friendly, confirming my early impression that their banter and apparent hostility did not truly reflect their relationship. Robyn turned and saw me, smiled and said, 'Come then, let's go.'

We walked out to his car and as I passed Miranda I said, smiling my most engaging smile, 'Thank you very much. Excellent meal, excellent room, good service.'

Her face did not change but there was a barely percep-tible nod as she stared at me.

My comments didn't go unnoticed with Robyn for when we were out of earshot, he said, 'Smooth. For all her misery she is a good woman. You can depend on her for anything.'

We drove to the port passing ramshackle dwellings where inhabitants were either sitting in the shade or attending vegetable patches, through the suburbs where houses took on a more permanent look developing into the occasional brick but more often concrete homes with dust-stained glass in the windows rather than an open hole over which was draped on the inside a sheet of fabric for some privacy. The road was no better than before and Robyn drove as smoothly as could be expected.

There was no guard on the port entrance and we drove

through the open barrier, past silos and ships to the lay-by berth where the client ship was moored in a forlorn manner. No one was around it or on deck and the whole appearance was of neglect and abandonment. We walked up the gangway onto the main deck, then into the accommodation and on to the captain's cabin on the bridge deck. Here, we saw through the open cabin door a despondent Greek man sitting in shorts and a vest, with no shoes, at his desk, looking vacantly into space. He looked up at our knock, saw Robyn and said:

'Mister Odubby. What to do? It's more than a week and nothing has been done. My men are prohibited from going ashore and our foods are getting low because no one will bring us anything.'

Robyn introduced me and we went through the usual rigmarole of the captain relating, in great detail and passion, his side of the story. I was silent and let the captain pour everything out. I find the best way to get a rapport with and information from someone is to let them talk on until they feel they have unburdened themselves enough; then they can be questioned on the real issues. Here though I knew the story and hopefully had the solution so my role was sympathy and a line of hope that soon all would be well. Robyn sat silently. When all that could be said was said I got up to leave.

'Captain, the first and most important thing is to get stores on board. You have a list?'

He grabbed a paper on his desk and thrust it into my hand. I glanced at it and noted the usual things a ship requires and said, 'I will try and get this to you tomorrow. In the meantime Mister Odubby and I will be working closely to solve this unfortunate situation and you must ensure your ship is ready to leave within an hour, or two at the most, when the agent tells you to go.'

He visibly cheered up and mumbled thanks and gratitude as we left him.

Getting into the car. 'That was masterful,' Odubby said. 'You have allayed his fears and given him hope without actually committing to anything. When he relays this later you will be the hero.'

I was embarrassed. 'In fact I'll be doing nothing; it will be all you.'

'No,' Robyn said, 'we will both do our bit and my accolade will come from those in this country who are currently very uncomfortable so we will both be the winners.' He laughed. 'Now to the agent with the list you have.'

The ship's agent was very amenable indeed. He was already in funds from the ship owner and promised faithfully some of the provisions would be delivered that evening and the remainder tomorrow. I got the distinct impression the non-perishable items had been in his store for a week or more and that he was sitting on them using the excuse of the vessel arrest to somehow gain an advantage. Everyone seemed to have an angle! He understood with Robyn in my camp he had no leg to stand on.

Then to the prison. By that time it was getting late in the afternoon and the lowering sun did nothing to soften the bleakness of the single-storey concrete structure, which sat on top of the headland. The road, such that it was, ran along one side of a depressing 'U'-shaped grey concrete building where every window was barred and from which no sign of life was evident. Either the inmates were too familiar with vehicles passing to look out and watch the free, or relatively free, going by or were so depressed and cowed as not to have the curiosity. At the end of the prison block we turned left and left again to be greeted by a concrete wall with large, tatty, ill-fitting wooden double doors reaching almost to the top of the wall and to one side a sentry type box in which languished two armed soldiers draped out of the window as if to capture as much of the non-existent breeze as was possible.

Robyn leant out of the open window of the car – he had been using the maximum air-conditioning setting as indeed had I – and shouted to the two, one of whom a raised hand in greeting and shambled to the big double doors, pushing one open to allow us to enter. I got the distinct impression the doors were not locked. We drove into the courtyard formed by the three of the 'U'-shaped blocks, the wheels of the car raising a reddish dust from the compacted mud. I briefly thought this would be a quag-mire in the rainy season. We pulled up outside another equally tatty and similarly ill-fitting door to park alongside three or four well-battered cars whose origin was difficult to establish not least because of a generous coating of the reddish dust from the courtyard.

Robyn jumped out and strode purposefully through the door, with me trailing behind, going immediately to an open doorway directly opposite the front door and engaging the occupant in the local dialect. This dialogue continued for quite a while in an amicable sort of way and eventually the man sitting behind the desk wearing the most ill-fitting, brightly coloured shirt I've ever seen – how can a shirt not fit? – got up and ambled off. Robyn pointed to four plastic chairs against a wall.

'Let's sit down and wait. He will be a while.'

We sat in a silence punctuated only by the buzzing flies. There was no clang of iron doors or tramping feet upon concrete floor, simply a silence, which seemed to grow darker as the sun lowered itself into the horizon, casting ever length-ening shadows through the iron barred window. Eventually brightly coloured shirt returned and motioned us out.

We followed him down a lengthy corridor to a depress-ingly small room with walls retaining the original concrete finish though ingrained with the dust and dirt of many years.

31

The floor had clearly not seen a broom for a long time as it was littered with cigarette butts mashed into the dust. There was a metal table in the middle of the room and one plastic chair each side of it. Opposite where we came in was another door, which looked to be metal and through which stumbled Theolatis pushed by a guard in soldier's garb. I say stumbled for Theolatis could take only small strides due to his ankles being clad in iron cuffs joined together with a short heavy chain. He immediately saw me.

'Nigel,' he screamed and shot across the room at a surprising speed for a manacled man and clasped me to his chest crying unashamedly.

'You come to get me out.' I gently prised him off my body, making note that these several days in a Loutan jail had done nothing to improve his body odour and that the clean suit I was wearing would need a dry clean and me a shower to get rid of the stink.

'Sit down, Theo, sit down so we can talk.'

He shuffled to the plastic chair and sat. I looked at Robyn who motioned me to sit in the other chair as he crossed his arms and leant against the wall. The soldier guard stood against the other wall picking his teeth, totally uninterested in what was going on. I assumed, quite rightly as it turned out, his English was severely limited.

No sooner had he sat down than Theolatis poured out his heart, embellishing the events that had landed him here to put him in a good light and everyone else in a bad one, pausing only to request a cigarette, which Robyn provided and lighted. So impassioned and desperate was Theolatis that he ran out of words and breath the same time and sat there panting, drained. I patted his arm.

'Theo,' I said, 'how long have you known me?' I didn't wait for him to drag enough air into his lungs to respond. 'Years; and have I ever let you down?' I hurried on before he could reflect on this. 'So I have to give it to you straight, no beating around the bush. Okay?' He nodded. 'Let us start with the reality. The Minister of the Interior will say you assaulted him' – I thought a bit of embellishment wouldn't do any harm here – 'and tried to bribe him and although I believe your story' – like hell I did – 'the fact remains that before a local judge the local man, particularly a well-placed and respected local man' – I made a mental note not to go too far on this tack for 'respect' and 'politician' is a well-known oxymoron – 'is going to be believed.' I paused to let the obvious sink in. 'I don't know what the prison sentences are here for this sort of crime but I would guess you're looking at anything up to ten years.' It was indeed a guess but at least I didn't say they would throw away the key!

Theolatis sat there with the weight of this information confirming his worst fears and pressing down on him, slumping his shoulders all the more. He was silent for a long time.

'There must be a way,' he said, 'I am innocent.'

I looked hard at him.

'Well, quite innocent at least.' He mumbled. A good sign for he was admitting to himself he was in some way culpable and once this is mentally accepted thereafter it is usually all downhill.

I got up and took a cigarette from Robyn, lit it and handed it to Theolatis.

'Okay,' I said, 'there may be a way out but not only do you have to cooperate fully now but for evermore stick to the story. Agreed?'

He nodded energetically as he choked on the cigarette smoke.

'It is possible that Mister Odubby can get the charges changed to a visa violation and then dropped on further investigation that will reveal the immigration officer at the airport mistakenly entered the wrong data on your visa. This does two things. It ties in Immigration in whose offices you were arrested and secondly gives a very plausible reason for the arrest as mistakes do happen.'

'Oh yes, oh yes,' he said, 'I agree this is definitely what happened. I recall it clearly.'

He had tears running down his face and was almost smiling.

'I have no idea of the timescale,' I continued, 'as this will be very tricky so don't expect anything for another couple of days. Okay?'

'Yes. Yes, no problem.'

I got up, shook his hand and we left the room, passing brightly coloured shirt, to whom Robyn exchanged what appeared to be grateful thanks with a big smile, out to the ever lengthening shadows of the prison courtyard to the car where I took off my jacket to relieve me from the over-powering smell of the incarcerated Greek. Robyn turned the car, sounding the car horn at the gates, which opened to allow us to drive through. We drove for a full half mile or so in silence. I wasn't sure if I'd gone too far or set Robyn an impossible task so I waited.

'You think he will stick to the story?' he asked at last.

'Oh absolutely. There is no way a Greek is going to admit he bungled a bribe, and cocked up visas are a well-known hazard of the sort of travel we do so he can parade injured innocence whilst regaling his friends with an exaggerated story about his stoic stay in jail.'

Robyn chuckled. 'I agree with your two points about an explanation of where and why he was arrested. Bringing in the Immigration Department just enough to give a way out, masterful. I think we can fix that.'

He sighed and concentrated on his driving while I continued thinking.

'I liked the touch of the manacles,' I said, 'I take it that was your idea.'

'Well,' he said, 'it gives the atmosphere, and certainly seemed to do the job.'

I smiled to myself as Robyn continued to drive before he said: 'I do believe the sun has set, or nearly set at least, so let's have a real drink.' I agreed.

He pulled into a parking space outside an uninviting looking bar. By now my faith in Robyn's choices and abilities to know the right people and places was on a high and I walked into the dilapidated bar, sat on a scruffy chair at an even scruffier table. Looking around I saw the walls were covered in torn and faded posters of some sort or another and the spaces between them exposed peeling paint from timber-clad walls. The ceiling fan looked as though it had given up the ghost before I was born. To say this was a spit-and-sawdust place would be denigrating to spit-and-sawdust establishments. I was beginning to lose my faith in Robyn but I received a most excellent gin and tonic, perhaps the finest I had ever tasted. Appearances can indeed be deceptive.

We drank while we talked through the current options and actions. The upshot was that I would return to Miserable Miranda's place by taxi, have a shower (Robyn was polite enough not to actually suggest this) and await Robyn's return in a couple of hours or so while he saw certain people and made certain unspecified arrangements. Drinks finished, we walked outside. I retrieved my jacket from the back of his car and got into a waiting taxi sufficiently scruffy to have lost all identity of its make and any pretence of comfort or luxury.

'The taxi is paid for,' Robyn said as he saw me off, and with a smile, 'Miranda will take care of the cleaning of your suit.'

Upon miraculous arrival at Miranda's place, somewhat shaken from the pothole battering, I walked in to be greeted, if that is the right word, by the ever miserable face still behind the bar. I walked over to her and smiled with a greeting.

'I'll be down in minutes to pick up your suit and laundry,' she said, demonstrating either the telephone system worked or Robyn had priority use of the jungle drums though perhaps it might well have been the prison odour permeating across the bar. I smiled thank you and retreated to my room to remove my clothes, put them in a neat pile and prepare for the shower. No sooner was this done than there was a knock on the door and Miranda entered, picked up the pile of clothes, looking neither left nor right nor glancing in my direction. Her timing was impeccable, bordering on the weird.

A leisurely shower followed by a stretch out on the bed where I mused over the day's events, hoping Robyn could indeed fix everything. I automatically reached for my mobile phone to check messages and e-mails, anticipating, indeed hoping, there would be no signal as we were so far from the town but, amazingly, there was a strong and clear signal. No telephone messages and a few e-mails, the longest from Catherine giving an account of the important things that had happened in the office since I left and the action she had taken on my behalf. If she got any more efficient she would do me out of a job. Already half the clients ring her, even at home, before or instead of ringing me. I briefly acknowledged Catherine's e-mail, sent a synoptic e-mail account of my day so far to David Robinson – emphasising the difficulties and problems and playing down the chances of an easy solution, otherwise he would get too optimistic, and experience has shown things do go wrong – and continued vegetating for a while before slowly dressing in slacks and a leisure shirt, noticing that I had inadvertently packed a pink shirt instead of a white one. I made a mental note to stop packing on autopilot although it was a fact that probably later saved my life.

Having dressed, I ambled to the bar, asking Miranda for one of her juice drinks – I did not know what the evening would bring so stayed away from alcohol – settling down in one of the comfortable chairs and continued reading the trashy paperback that had so usefully sent me to sleep on the plane. An hour later Odubby arrived.

'Now then,' he said, 'let's go into the dining room and eat while I set out the order of play for tomorrow, report upon what I have done today and generally relax over a drink or two. I have taken the liberty of ordering food for both of us and I'm sure you will like it.'

I did indeed like the food. I have no idea what most of it was but there was a subtle blend of spices, herbs and sauces, which made a truly memorable meal. Similarly, that which we were copiously drinking was foreign to me, again a very pleasant blend of fruit with heaven only knows what alcohol.

The upshot of the conversation, between exchanged anecdotes over lawyer/client problems and the like, was that Robyn had arranged a meeting in the capital with his cousin, the Minister of the Interior early the next morning to formalise the way forward (use of the telephone for such a delicate matter was too risky). This would result in the Chief Immigration Officer signing a consent to release the ship from arrest against allowing him to resign with some dignity rather than being prosecuted for perverting the course of justice. The Minister of the Interior send an order to release Theolatis, without charge, from jail. The consideration for all this was Theolatis would keep his mouth shut over the real events (sorted already) and accept immediate deportation (I was confident he couldn't wait to leave the country as fast as possible) with various players being 'rewarded' for their efforts. Quite how much this reward might be was left a little vague though Robyn assured me it would be modest because the whole thing had raised considerable embarrassment for everyone and no one would want to be tainted by it. Robyn reckoned he would return by mid afternoon and I said I should go back to the port by taxi to ensure the agent had delivered all the stores on board the ship, see the captain again and make sure there would be no hitch in arranging pilots and tugs if and hopefully when the arrest was lifted.

It was surprisingly gone midnight when we had finished and I accompanied Robyn outside to wave him off in his car. It was a wonderful balmy evening and I stayed outside for a few moments gazing at the clear and bright stars. Standing there, I realised the concoction we had been drinking was somewhat stronger than I had appreciated and although I was not actually drunk, I wasn't sober either. Time for bed.

4

The Start

The next day Miranda arranged a taxi for me and I returned to the ship's agent to find everything was under control to complete provisioning the vessel, so I went back on board the ship to see the captain and assure him everything was in hand, emphasising the ship had to be ready to leave. No emphasis was needed for the captain was fairly buoyant with expectation.

All this took me longer than I had anticipated and it was late afternoon before I returned to the hotel. Odubby had not yet arrived so I spent a fruitful couple of hours catching up on e-mails and speaking briefly to Catherine in the office. I was beginning to be a little concerned over Odubby but he arrived at the hotel early in the evening. He had much to report. After a deserved gin and tonic he brought me up to date as Miranda prepared a meal for us. 'Cousin Minister of the Interior went along with our scheme and I have a letter in my pocket releasing Theolatis to my custody for deportation,' said Odubby. 'I've made arrangements with the ship's agent for a one-way ticket on a flight tomorrow back to Europe. After that he's on his own.'

I nodded, relieved.

'In fact I could have got him out tonight but he has been such a pain in the bum I thought another night in jail wouldn't hurt him.'

I laughed. I would probably have done the same.

'The Chief Customs Officer was an arrogant bastard. I really had to paint the picture in strong colours to make him understand. He thought he was invincible and at one stage challenged me to prosecute him. I had to remind him any prosecution would take place in the capital and the police there are too overworked to apply the gentle touch, and he started to see reason. I promised if he signed the release of the ship and resigned, he would in due course be given another post in another place as I'm sure he will. He is not without connections. So we are signed up to everything. The ship can go tomorrow after we have gone to court to do the necessary there and then the Chief Immigration Officer leaves at the end of the week. A result, I believe they say.' He smiled and I could see from his face he was exhausted. He had had a very busy day.

'What about payments, money?' I asked.

'Peanuts. We can sort that out tomorrow. I trust you so as soon as I have finished this meal I am going to bed. I will stay here rather than go home. Who knows. Perhaps Miserable Miranda will warm my bed!' He broke into a peal of laughter. 'Unless of course you want her.' Which sent him off nearly into hysterics. I somehow could not imagine Miranda with anyone, let alone either of us.

I awoke as dawn broke and showered.

When dry, I dressed and decided to telephone David Robinson. The mobile signal was good so I pressed the button. He answered very quickly, also very sleepily. With great apologies for disturbing him, I told him if all went well both Theolatis and the ship would leave today and for him to stand by to wire me more money if I needed it. He promised the earth, saying if the ship was indeed away today she would make it onto the lucrative contract before the cancelling date. I promised a full blow-by-blow account later in the day and hung up. E-mail checking revealed nothing that could not wait for a day or two.

I suddenly felt hungry and wandered towards the dining room to find Miranda fussing around the tables.

'Nice and early,' she said. 'Robyn is not up yet.'

Robyn, I thought. An unexpected intimacy. Perhaps he wasn't kidding after all. I looked at Miranda carefully but her face was an impassive mask.

'The full English for you?' she said and whisked away.

The full English was indeed that, brilliantly cooked and I was full before I finished it. Coffee in hand, I sat back as Robyn arrived, ordering coffee and lighting a cigarette. We did the 'sleep well' bit and he repeated the plan of action. The first was the court to get the arrest lifted. To the agents to make sure the pilot and tugs were on the way to get the ship out and pick up Theolatis's ticket. Send the agent off to deliver the necessary papers to the captain then onto the prison to get Theolatis and take him to the airport. Then back to the agent to sort out the money.

All went according to plan and the only reservation I had was actually letting Theolatis get on the plane before he had a shower. It can be bad enough in economy without a reeking man sitting alongside. I did suggest though immediately after take-off he should go to the toilet and wash down; have a Mexican shower at least – that is, splash himself all over with the provided aftershave.

Back in the agent's office we did the sums. I still had the $10,000 in cash (the agent would pay Miranda's hotel bill); the agent had $25,000 already wired to him for me by David Robinson; the agent also had a further $20,000 sent by David for anticipated additional expenses for the ship plus $10,000 for the captain for crew's jollies ashore (which was never given to him because of the shore leave embargo) plus his usual fees and expenses. A total of $65,000 after the agent had taken out his not inconsiderable fees. The agent left us

41

to divide the spoils, as it were. The less he knew, the better he would feel.

In short, Robyn's expenditure on various facilities was less than $25,000. A real surprise to me but, as he said, everyone appreciated the delicacy of the situation and did not want to be identified as greedy. His fees he reckoned were $15,000 on top of the money he had already received on account from David. I said not nearly enough, so we settled on $25,000. This left the $10,000 cash I had, which I would give to David when I got back plus the $5,000 or so the agent would remit back to David. Ship owners like nothing more than getting money back so everyone was a winner. I called the agent in and he handed Robyn $50,000 in cash and we left for Robyn's office so he could give me a receipted invoice.

Whilst Robyn was getting the invoice prepared at his office I lounged in a very comfortable leather chair and phoned David, giving him the good news and financial update. He confirmed that the captain had called to say the ship had left the port though he had not yet heard from Theolatis. I suddenly thought, did we give Theolatis any money to call David for onward transport when he arrived in Europe? I'm sure we did not. I told David Theolatis might not have any money and gave him the flight details so arrangements could be made to meet Theolatis who would be mightily cold in his dirty and tattered shirt and trousers when he landed in Paris.

'So you're all finished there?' David said.

'Obviously a few loose ends to tie up,' I said cautiously, 'but I will probably be out tomorrow, certainly the next day.'

'Ah right,' said David and hung up.

Robyn produced the duly receipted invoice and we went through everything to ensure there were no loose ends while his secretary checked flight availability to London tomorrow. All very gratifying and relaxing. Don't get cocky, Nigel!

Robyn's secretary came in with a sheaf of faxes, which she gave to Robyn. He looked at them.

'For you, I think,' he said.

Before I could take them, the second and really ill-fated telephone call. My mobile rang. 'Nigel,' I said into it.

'Ah, Mister Turner, you won't know me. My name is Anderson and I'm from Meagre Insurance here in London. I bumped into David Robinson last night who said you were in Africa doing a little job for him and he has just told me you very successfully completed it and were now free.' I feared the worst. Robinson was definitely off the Christmas card list. The voice continued.

'We have a reinsurance contract with Nigra Insurance in Wandaro and they are not paying on a very large important claim. There is a standard Follow Clause but they do not seem to understand how it works. We can bring them to court in England if necessary but the English government is courting Wandaro for business and any legal action would not be helpful. We were just wondering if you could pop across to see them; first class of course. I faxed the papers to Mister Odubby's office so you can see how simple it all is and we'll give you full authority to negotiate a settlement if you can't get payment in full.'

'Mister Anderson,' I said, 'I am really flattered by your faith in me but this isn't Europe. It's not a matter of popping anywhere in Africa. It's big logistics to get to the nearest pub.'

'Quite, but you are known to be a very resourceful man. Please read the papers and call me back. We really would like you to help us.' He cut off.

Robyn handed me the papers.

'I had a scan through,' he said, 'interesting one. You going to take it?'

'If I can possibly avoid it without losing face or a potential client, no. I do though like a bit of reinsurance negotiation. It can be fascinating.'

'Look, my friend, read the papers before you make a decision. It might be your potential new clients are wrong so you can just tell them a trip would achieve nothing and be off the hook, with the new client being ever grateful you saved them your fees. I've got things to do here while you go through the faxes.'

At that point Robyn's secretary came in with even more papers for me from Anderson. I settled down and started reading. When I had finished and was weighing up the pros and cons, Robyn's secretary appeared and handed him a piece of paper. He looked at it, then me.

'Unless you want to go back to Europe there is no first-class to Wandaro,' he said. I was not surprised. Trans-African flights are notoriously difficult. 'There is though a direct flight with our glorious local airline in economy with seats free the day after tomorrow.' He saw my sceptical expression. 'Oh don't worry. For an African airline it is really well maintained and all the pilots are English or European, enticed over by big money, so it will be as safe as any flight. You have been tentatively booked on it.'

'What!' I exclaimed.

'Come on. We both know you can't resist a challenge and as you said reinsurance negotiation is fascinating.'

I groaned. Robyn was impassive. I reached for my mobile, rang Anderson with the glad tidings, giving him my potential flight details (it made me look efficient even though my contribution to that was zero) and asked him to make sure the right people in Nigra Insurance were aware I was en route. I promised to phone him the next day to confirm everything. Anderson was effusively grateful but I detected a certain smugness that his judgment of me was right. I then telephoned Catherine, brought her up-to-date on everything and asked her to set the money laundering regulations wheels in motion by her sending a message to Anderson that unless he provided all the information and documentation to ensure the checks and balances were done before my flight I would reluctantly have to decline his kind instructions. Let him rush around a bit and wipe the smugness away.

Robyn offered me his computer to report back in full to David Robinson for both our sakes. I gratefully accepted.

When I had finished and sent the e-mail to David Robinson it was well after first drinks time and heading towards dinner time so off we went to an unpretentious restaurant which served excellent food. We talked and joked until Robyn took me back to the hotel and bade me farewell as he had meetings the next day in the capital.

The next day passed off very easily. I found the hotel had a small swimming pool and I spent the day lolling around it building up a bit of a suntan, eating, drinking the fruit drink with the secret recipe and catching up on my e-mail and phone messages.

So after my leisurely day the following morning, packed and relaxed, I bade Miranda farewell, and, expecting the usual check-in delays, took a taxi to the airport to get there early for my flight to Wandaro. Surprisingly, check-in went very smoothly.

With time on my hands and anticipating the departure side of the airport would be no less chaotic or oppressive than the arrival side, I decided to take a stroll outside of the terminal in air considerably fresher than inside. I noticed a side entrance so headed towards it, out into a shaded and fairly people free area. I say fairly people free for there were a few porters or similar moving languidly around and a middle-aged man and young woman in deep conversation to my right. I walked slowly towards this couple for no reason other than that was the way I was facing when I started to walk. They appeared completely oblivious of my presence and as I approached the conversation became somewhat heated. Suddenly the man snatched at the carry-on type bag on the young woman's shoulder and she started to wrestle with him. By instinct rather than plan I sprinted the few yards towards them, caught hold of the man from behind, around his upper chest and shoulders, and heaved him away from the young woman. He immediately released his grasp on the carry-on bag to wrench my arms away from him with surprising strength. I was expecting him to turn around and assault me but instead, once free of my arms, he ran off.

'Are you all right?' I asked.

'Yes. Thank you.'

'Shall we find a policeman and report this incident?'

'No, no. It is unnecessary. It was simply a personal disagreement. You need not trouble yourself.' With that, she turned and walked briskly away in the same direction as the man had run.

I was not surprised she did not favour involvement with the authorities, though bearing in mind I had saved her bag from being stolen I was somewhat miffed at the abrupt and dismissive way she treated me. Nothing to be done though so I continued my stroll.

Eventually I went to the departure area – it would be inaccurate to call it a 'lounge' – after waiting patiently in a long line to pass through Customs and Immigration. I did have a fleeting moment of apprehension on passing through the immigration channel, for the officer/soldier/policeman, I really couldn't tell which from the bit of uniform I saw over the cubicle desk, looked particularly carefully at my passport and visa, consulting, more than once, papers in a grubby ring binder.

On boarding I saw the interior looked clean and tidy if just a little worn and the female cabin crew cooperative and attentive to get people to their seats. I had been allocated a window seat over the starboard, I should say right, wing just forward of the emergency exit. I settled into my seat, strapped

on the seatbelt and adjusted my mind to the semi numbness which I found benefited any air travel. No passenger
sat next to me as the plane was barely a third full.

Once airborne two or so hours passed in the usual monot-
onous way, punctuated by offers by cabin crew to provide
drinks and food. I spent my time reading my novel and
looking out of the window. My area of visibility was a little
restricted by the wing of the plane and its single enormous
engine so I had to look forward. For once there was not a
blanket of cloud below, giving the false impression that the
plane was but a few feet above a fluffy and solid surface. I
could see all the way to the beaten red and yellow African
earth punctuated from time to time by smudges, which could
be vegetation or dark rocks. We were too high to tell. I
strained to see if I could detect animal movement but if
there were herds of something there, they blended into the
earth.

It was during one of these unfruitful inspections of the
earth below and ahead of the plane I saw a stream of smoke
coming from the ground and heading towards the plane. I
was fascinated and realised the speed of approach could not
indicate a natural phenomenon. I, like everyone else with a
television set, had seen too many news reports and films to
be in the slightest doubt as to what was heading towards
the plane. It was a missile.

It is said when facing certain death, past life flashes before
the eyes. Quite how anyone could actually know this has
always been beyond me for if death is certain no one would
live to tell the tale. My life did not flash anywhere. It must
only have been seconds but it seemed to be like hours. The
world slipped into slow motion. I was fascinated, watching
the missile closing in. I could actually make out its shape
and dirty white colour as it became larger; then, when still
quite a distance from the plane, it exploded; I assume prema-
turely. I felt no relief that it had not buried itself in the

engine on the wing below me – I assumed it was a heat-seeking missile – for the debris from the explosion shot forward into the right wing and engine, causing the plane to lurch to the right and immediately plummet downwards. I could see the engine had been shattered and the upper wing surface damaged, though mercifully the cabin did not appear to be punctured. I have no recollection of passengers screaming or indeed any panic or movement from those on board. I suppose they were all too numb, wondering what was happening. After a few moments the plane returned to an even keel and continued on its flight, rocking a little from side to side. We had clearly lost an engine. My limited knowledge of aircraft was enough to know planes can still successfully fly on one engine so I was not unduly perturbed, thinking that at worst we would deviate to the nearest airfield, wherever that might be.

After what seemed to be an age, during which the cabin crew dashed around assuring everyone everything was all right, the captain's voice came over the internal speakers.

'Ladies and gentlemen. We have experienced a mechanical problem in the right engine, which has damaged the right wing.' No mention of a missile. Maybe no one on the flight deck saw it. Then again it would hardly have brought peace and comfort to those on board to be told someone was shooting at us.

'It seems the damage has affected the way I can fly the aircraft but there is no immediate concern and we are continuing on our route. I will keep you updated. Please make sure your seat-belt is fastened just as a precaution.'

There was a buzz from the passengers and those on the right side of the plane strained to look out of the window at the damaged wing. Indeed I too was fixated on this piece of the aeroplane, wondering what effect the holes, which now seemed to be bigger, were going to have upon our continuing to defy gravity. One thing I did notice: we were considerably closer to the ground than we had been before and it was apparent altitude was being lost. I somehow doubted this was a deliberate pilot ploy to be able to handle the aircraft easier and a few moments later the internal speakers sprang into life again.

'The damage to the right wing is too great for me to get the aircraft to the nearest airport,' the captain said, 'so I have decided to land at the first convenient spot I can find. This will be no problem as the ground we are flying over has lots of big flat areas. It will be a bit bumpy on landing and I will ask you in a few minutes to take up the position my cabin crew demonstrated earlier. I have radioed the emergency to the authorities and they will send rescue helicopters to us once we land.'

I was not convinced by the 'lots of big flat areas'. Big they might be; flat they may be but strewn with rocks, boulders and vegetation of some sort they were bound to be. This was going to be a lot more than a bumpy landing and I was reminded of something said to me by a guy in a ship repair yard a few years ago. 'The reason they ask you to adopt the emergency landing position is so you can kiss your arse goodbye!'

I never had the slightest fear of flying, nor indeed dying in a crash. Either it happened or it didn't. I could do nothing about it so why worry? I did though have a fear of burning alive and when planes crash the highly incendiary fuel spills can be lit by the slightest spark. So, I thought, let's just hope the crash kills me outright.

The plane was now losing altitude very quickly and I was certain this was not because of the pilot's actions. The pilot was clearly competent for he was keeping the wings level with just the occasional rocking. I strained to look out of the window, trying in vain to identify a big flat area when I noticed an escarpment with a flat top, a hill in fact. Whilst it was small we were not going to get over it.

'Please adopt the emergency landing position now.' I watched the hill rushing towards us. I could see the pilot was going to attempt a landing on the flat top of this hill. He had just one shot at it and I was hoping the flat top was big enough and didn't allow us to plunge down the other side of the hill.

Landing gear was not deployed and the plane's belly flopped onto the ground, bouncing and sliding in a straight line. Somehow the captain had managed to keep the wings level and the main force of the landing was taken on the fuselage, which buckled and ripped as we slowed and came to a stop. The cabin crew, who had stationed themselves at the emergency exits, opened the doors and shouted.

'Everyone leave the plane, quickly and quietly.'

Alive, uninjured and with an apprehension of spilled aviation fuel suddenly igniting, I needed no urging and left my seat to go out of the door immediately behind me onto the right wing, then slide down it to the ground and walk away. My first thought was to run away from the area of potential fire but, surprisingly, I could not smell the pungent odour of Avgas. Looking at the right wing, I could see the engine had acted as a skid pad, similar to a seaplane float, and although crumpled and nearly flat, it appeared the fuel tanks had not been punctured. As the pilot had skillfully and miraculously landed a plane with both wings level, I thought it was possible the left wing fuel tanks were also intact, particularly as the left engine was not damaged by the missile so had more internal workings to take the brunt of the landing.

Others were leaving the aircraft and as it was not full there was plenty of room to evacuate without people getting into each other's way. I assumed there would be injuries and indeed a woman slid off the right wing and staggered about moaning loudly, blind from the blood pouring down her face from a gash on her forehead. I went to her and guided her away from the plane.

'Don't worry,' I said, 'you are safe. I will fix the cut on your head. I'm sure it's not bad. All head wounds bleed an awful lot.' I speak from rugby field experience. Even a small cut on a forehead will produce a curtain of blood which looks far more dramatic than it actually is. I sat her down, pulled off my tie – yes, I was travelling in a suit and tie though not wearing a jacket at that point – got my fairly clean handkerchief from the pocket of my trousers, made a pad and identified the position on the forehead of a large gash. I put the pad over the gash and secured it tightly with my tie, tying it at the back of her head.

'Do you have a tissue?' I asked. She had one – all women seem to be able to produce tissues from nowhere. I wiped her eyes so she could see and as much of her face as possible before the tissue became saturated. The handkerchief was becoming blood-soaked but I was confident the pressure from the tie I would promote coagulation.

'You will probably have a headache and a bit of a scar but otherwise you are okay. Just stay there while we get everybody off the plane.'

Her moaning stopped, she smiled and settled down under the partial shade of a large scrub type bush.

I returned to the fuselage, all the while sniffing for even the faintest odour of fuel. When I got there the crew was inside the aircraft at the emergency exit tending to a man who had what appeared to be a broken leg.

'Anything I can do?' I asked.

The captain, who was amazingly wearing his hat, looked up from his ministrations and said, 'Everyone is out of the plane. I don't think the fuel tanks are ruptured so if you could administer first aid to anyone needing it, I would be grateful. The crew is fully occupied at the moment with this man.' He leant down from the doorway and lowered his voice, 'The break is a little tricky. The bone has splintered and punctured an artery.'

He spoke to one of the female crew, trying to hold the man's head and upper body steady while others worked on the leg. She reached behind her, produced a large and unopened first aid box and passed it to the captain who dropped it down to me, smearing the handle with blood from his hands.

'There is morphine in there plus all the other necessaries. Do you know what to do?' I nodded. My extensive offshore sailing boat training and experience included an in-depth first aid course, which covered the use of morphine injections.

'But don't inject unless it is absolutely necessary,' he said, 'it can cause more problems than it solves.'

'Okay,' I replied, 'if I have the slightest doubt or concern I certainly won't use morphine.' He smiled and went back to his immediate problems with the broken leg.

Before flying, Robyn had said pilots were good, but this man was more than that. Not only had he managed to land a plane on the hard baked surface of somewhere in Africa in such a way that no lives were lost but also organised an orderly and peaceful evacuation. He exuded calm and cheerfulness and was now not in the slightest fazed by administering to someone with a complex and life-threatening injury. Whilst I had been taught the theory of pinching and securing a severed artery I knew in practice it was far from easy.

The first aid box was heavier than it looked so I reckoned it contained far more than civilian kits. I lugged it around the passengers scattered about the area of the landing and applied aid as and where necessary. Surprisingly, there were few injuries. A sprained ankle, shoulder or hand here and there, which I left alone for the moment, bruises which did not need attention, and a number of cuts and scrapes easily dealt with by the application of antiseptic, bandage or sticking plaster. Unlike the films, there was no screaming hysteria, nor was anyone on their knees offering up their thanks to whatever god they otherwise would not have worshipped. The passengers were calm, almost numb; they could hardly believe what they had actually been through and survived.

When I could do no more good I went back to the captain who by this time had stemmed the blood from the man's broken and punctured leg, applied a full-length splint and, with the aircrew, moved him to the ground on a stretcher where he was lying unconscious in the shade of the fuselage. The captain was pulling off blood-soaked surgical gloves.

'That's all we can do for him at the moment,' he said, 'how did you get on?' I briefly reported the state of the passengers and handed him back the first aid box.

'Okay,' he said, 'my crew will now get food and water from the plane and I'll go back to the cockpit to see if I can contact rescue by emergency radio to get help here as soon as possible.'

He said this with confidence but I detected a certain amount of hope over knowledge and suspected he didn't actually believe he would succeed in speaking to anyone. He clambered back over the right wing into the plane, followed by the aircrew, each to carry out their separate tasks in an almost drilled way. I was even more impressed.

With nothing more I could do, I wandered away from the plane to take stock of the surrounding area to see if there was any habitation. I suddenly needed to pee so I walked swiftly deep into the bushes to be well away from the view of those sitting, lying or walking around the aeroplane. As I was finishing I looked around me and through the bushes saw, past the tail of the aeroplane in the distance, a large cloud of dust. I remained where I was, tucking myself in, and watched from my vantage point to decipher what was causing the cloud. In a very short space of time I could see the dust was being thrown up by three vehicles driving at high speed towards the plane. My heart leapt. Rescue, help. So soon. How lucky can we be?

I continued to look as the vehicles came closer and ascended the slope of the hill, which was not as steep as it appeared to me when I saw it from the plane. The vehicles turned into three jeeps, or similar, with four figures in each. As the jeeps came closer, I realised they were soldiers.

I have no idea why I did not rush out to my fellow passengers to relate the glad tidings. Even now I cannot explain why I remained rooted to the spot, watching the jeeps drive over the top of the incline and draw to a dusty halt at the tail of the plane.

A very tall, skeletal thin man in camouflage overalls hanging on his frame got out the front passenger side of the leading jeep and stood staring at the plane and the passengers. He was much too far away for me to see any expression on the skull-like face underneath an officer's hat. He looked around and the captain of the plane appeared in the doorway of the emergency exit and waved a greeting.

The officer turned and spoke to his men who got out of the jeeps with automatic rifles. They walked slowly towards the passengers and opened fire. Everyone was mowed down in a hail of bullets with the officer standing and watching. When it was all over and all the passengers and aircrew in bloody heaps on the ground the soldiers walked around kicking the bodies to see if any showed signs of life, snuffing out that life with a single shot to the head.

Now in the movies our intrepid hero, being unarmed, would understand the odds against him were high and his presence would likely be detected, so would hurl himself to the ground, heedless of snakes, insects or other potentially poisonous beings and wriggle away, snakelike, camouflaging himself in the bushes. My thoughts were certainly that way; but the gunfire attack was so sudden and unimaginable that I couldn't not look. It was as if an unreal scene was being played out, so I remained where I was, standing in the bushes. Real though it was. After the protagonists had completed the body check for life they started looking around to see if there was anyone else. Luckily, their first glances were not in my direction, which allowed me to slowly sink to my knees behind the thickest part of the bushes, hoping that this sparse foliage would hide me from sight.

I did have one thing going for me. My pink shirt. That rogue piece of packing! Against the reddish earth around me, it was a sort of camouflage. So, a modicum of luck and no immediate detection; but the soldiers would not have to walk far into the undergrowth to spot me and therefore, poisonous beings to the wind, I would have to wriggle slowly and carefully backwards to put distance between me and my would be executioners. I looked around to plan a suitable route. The silence following the massacre was punctuated by a crackling babble from a radio in one of the jeeps. I cautiously looked back and the officer walked to the leading jeep, picked up a transmitting microphone and said something into it. The radio crackled back with the far away operator relating something at length, which the officer was considering while turning around and looking directly at me. I froze. Not a muscle moved. I held my breath as I watched. His whole face was even more skull-like, almost a death's head in appearance. How apt, I thought, ironically. The transmission ended. Death Head said something into the microphone, turned back to the jeep, stowing the microphone somewhere and barked an order. The men sprinted back to the jeeps, got in and, with bellowing engines and clouds of dust churned up by spinning wheels, shot back at high speed the way they had come. I had not been seen.

I remained, kneeling, where I was watching the jeeps speed away. When they were but a diminishing cloud of dust I started to get back to my feet but stopped. What if I had miscalculated? I thought I saw twelve men in three jeeps arrive, get out, get back in and drive away but I could be wrong. What if it was a cunning plan and they had left one soldier behind to watch for anyone they had missed, and through curiosity or driven necessity would come out from the bushes to the plane? I was getting paranoid but then again, having escaped death twice in but a few hours, I was entitled to a little bit of paranoia. I stayed where I was.

5

The Journey

'I suppose,' a voice said behind me, 'you might be thinking, Will this be the third time unlucky?' A cold hand squeezed my heart. I couldn't bear to look around but was drawn by the voice. I slowly swivelled from my kneeling position and saw a very tall woman in military camouflage overalls with an automatic rifle hung over her shoulder pointing vaguely in my direction. My first thoughts were that I was looking at an Amazon. A large Afro hairstyle sat atop a beautiful, powerful black face. She had broad, very broad, shoulders, a significant bust, what appeared to be a narrow waist with long legs finishing off in brown, scarred and dusty boots. She had a small knapsack on her back.

Immediately to her right was a man similarly dressed and armed and of equal stature, though more muscled, who could have been her twin brother, and behind them, six more in camouflaged overalls armed with automatic rifles pointed at me in a very relaxed sort of way. The whole ensemble conjured a picture of efficiency and control.

Remaining on my knees – truth to tell I just didn't have the strength to stand – I looked her up and down slowly and tried to convey a message of relaxed nonchalance rather than the abject fear gnawing in the pit of my stomach. The icy hand squeezing at the heart relaxed enough for me to say in a fairly measured, even voice:

'In fact, I'm thinking, if anything at all, that good things come in threes.' I smiled at her. Smiled! Where did that come from? She laughed. Not a forced, unmerciful laugh but with natural humour as though the completely unexpected had suddenly turned funny. I slowly rose to my feet and looked her in the eyes. She was a little shorter than my six foot two. Twin brother though scowled. Whilst his face was as handsome as Amazon's was beautiful it had less openness; more stony. Before I could say any more she turned and spoke to twin brother in the local dialect. He nodded and beckoned the other men. They left us and went to the aeroplane looking at the bloody mess of strewn bodies around.

'Who are you?' I asked. She took her hand off her gun and waved it in the air in a dismissive way.

'That's no matter at the moment,' she replied and I could not entice her into any further conversation.

The men continued to look around the area of slaughter then returned. A conversation ensued between the siblings and when it ended she turned and looked at me. She continued looking and spoke again to her brother in the local dialect. Whatever she said did not please him and he scowled again in a far more chilling way and shot back a short but meaningfull response, which conveyed deep dissatisfaction and disagreement. She did not reply and said to me:

'Opinions are divided. We can leave you, shoot you or take you with us.' A long silence from which I felt she wanted me to respond. I inclined my head towards Brother, feeling he had both feet in the 'let's shoot him' camp, smiled politely and replied:

'Quite obviously the shooting bit is not my favoured option. Being left here is certainly better than that. I guess there is enough on the plane to sustain me for quite a while.' I inwardly shuddered at what airline food would taste like after a week in a roasting fuselage. 'Though the risk of Death's Head and his merry band of slaughter returning is firmly on the cards.' She gave me a startled, knowing look when I said 'Death's Head'. I continued. 'At the very least there is loot there, which they surprisingly abandoned.' I was referring to the strewn suitcases that had spilled from the ruptured fuselage as well as the undoubted gold, jewellery and odd Rolex or two that probably adorning the dead. 'And the chances of more friendly rescue arriving is probably very slim. So if I was given a choice I would go with you. It's an adventure at least.'

She smiled at that. Slightly comforted and warming to my theme. 'Also, you don't know me and I may well have hidden talents that could be of use to you.'

Her smile turned into a humorous laugh. 'I cannot even think of what talent a skinny white man from, it sounds like cotton wool England, could possibly have that we would find of the slightest use.' I was a bit miffed. Okay, I was nothing like the muscled frame of Brother but I wouldn't class myself as skinny. Lightly muscled perhaps but not skinny. I decided not to press the point. She continued.

'I've made up my mind. You come with us. There has been enough killing for one day.' So she was in charge then. She slung her gun on her back and turned, speaking to the others who returned to the plane, looking around for, I assumed, anything of value to them. They did not touch the dead and no more than gave the scattered luggage a cursory look. Value for them was clearly not that which could be turned into a quick buck.

'There is a very good first aid kit under the right wing by the fuselage,' I said, 'and probably another one inside close to the emergency exit over the right wing.' She looked at me with, I felt, just a little respect and she shouted this information to the men who found both first aid kits and brought them over.

'Anything you want?' she asked. Even if I could find my suitcase I had nothing in it for what I assumed would be a trek across the baking African soil, but I was conscious my fair white skin had been exposed to the burning sun for quite a while, and short of finding sun block somewhere I ought to cover up a bit more.

'Quickly,' said Brother, 'we do not have too much time.'

Did he know something I didn't or was he still peeved his solution had not been accepted? I quickly walked across to the plane, picked up the captain's hat and put it on. This would shade my head. Then I turned the collar of my shirt up to try and protect my neck from the sun and took out my cufflinks, allowing the double cuff to open and so shield my hands from the sun. Not sun block but a valiant attempt at something without wasting the time Brother felt was so precious.

They all looked at me. I must have been a sight so I smiled and bowed then marched smartly back to where they were all standing.

'Come,' said Amazon and she started out with me behind and Brother behind me. The other six varyingly fanned out each side or ahead of us, staying some twenty-five to fifty yards apart; sometimes three each side, sometimes all six on one side. This was a well practised routine, no doubt designed to be able to spot any danger and prevent easy targets for an ambush. I was impressed. Whatever they were they were no fools.

We trudged on at a steady pace; not so slow as to waste any time but not so fast as to sap and burn energy in the heat of the afternoon. I say trudged but the reality was that it was me who did the trudging. They seemed to float across the ground with little effort, giving the distinct impression that this pace was a stroll in the park to them; it was no doubt adopted in deference to my skinny inability to last more than five minutes if they walked at their usual rate. If that were so, they were right, for whilst I reckon myself fit in relation to most deskbound workers, after a very short while my legs started feeling the effects of exertion over uneven ground. Luckily I was wearing a sturdy pair of shoes but not designed, and certainly not made, for an African hike. I dwelt not but counted my blessings. Whatever the discomfort it was better than a bullet in the head. After a while I tried to survey the route we were following. Our course went over dusty ground, rocks, parched grass ankle high to waist level, and up and down small hills. There was no single landmark from which I could get my bearings and the other features of the ground were too insignificant to stand out to me as a marker, though clearly my hosts did not think so. What I did glean was that we were not walking in a straight line. My small boat experience had given me an awareness of the position of heavenly bodies and their importance to any navigator. I never relied totally upon GPS; it is a marvellous system but in a sailing boat in the English Channel, prone to ship water over the deck and relying upon battery power, one never knew when the all-singing and all-dancing visual colour display would blink into blackness. So I watched the passage of the sun through the afternoon, realising that whilst it was never in front of us it was sometimes behind, sometimes on one side, sometimes to the other. I guessed the circuitous route was not adopted to confuse the 'cotton wool' Englishman but had a more practical, if worrying, significance. An avoidance of being followed or tracked perhaps.

As the sun began to set so we walked into a clump of trees, which were numerous enough to be called a wood. Without any command or even gesture everyone squatted down together, rummaging into knapsacks to produce large leaves in which nestled a brown/grey substance. Amazon picked a large leaf from the sparse undergrowth and each of them put a portion of their substance into this leaf, which Amazon handed to me.

'Eat,' she said and started munching at a small handful from her own leaf.

It tasted a good deal better than it looked and that is not faint praise; it really was quite good. Okay, not Michelin standard but more than edible and I would have gladly eaten more if more had been available. I tried to identify the ingredients. Maize-based, I assumed, with herbs of some sort but there was more which either eluded my taste buds or were completely new flavours. After we had finished, a water bottle was passed around and the six men got up and disappeared. Whether to keep guard or just keep a distance I could not establish.

'Time to sleep,' said Amazon, and Brother too moved a distance away, settling down for a slumber.

'Tell me,' I asked, 'where are we?'

'Later,' she replied.

'Okay then,' I said, 'at least tell me what country I am in and why we have walked such a circuitous route.' In the fast fading light she gave me what I can only describe as a very odd, telling look.

'Sleep,' she said and lay down.

Faced with no other option and, frankly, with no desire to keep my weary body alert, I also lay down ready to sleep. The ground was hard but before I knew it I was being roused by Brother as the sun was peeping over the horizon to herald a new day. I cannot say I leapt to my feet. My leg muscles, not used to the African trek, groaned and strained in protest as I heaved myself up. I tried to keep the effort and discomfort from my face but Brother spotted it and leered in a satisfactory manner. We ate a smaller portion of the same which made up the evening meal, and after a swig from a water bottle, resumed our journey. For the first hundred yards or so I had to drag each leg, one in front of the other, but after a while the legs seemed to accept protestations by way of pain and discomfort were not going to relieve them of their task, and I settled into the rhythm of yesterday.

Mid-morning a water bottle was passed around and at midday we stopped under a small tree for another portion of the brown and grey substance and a swallow of water. When finished, Amazon told me to stay where I was and they all drifted off to sit or stand about fifty to one hundred yards apart where we all remained for I guess about an hour. I didn't think to look at my watch. When the rest time had passed we were on our way again with my rested legs hardly protesting at all.

The sun continued to beat down without a cloud in the sky and although I felt its heat through my clothes and a slight reddening of my face, the improvised ray protection seemed to be working. I pulled the peak of the airline captain's hat further down to give more protection to my face and plunged on manfully.

It was towards the end of the afternoon when we walked up a somewhat bigger hill than usual and over the top, descending once again to the plain. Just before we reached the bottom of the hill we stopped by a very large and particularly dense patch of thorny bushes and undergrowth. Three of the men pulled out a section of the bush, which came away easily, and disappeared into the gap, emerging a short time later in African tribal clothing minus any sign of firearms. The next three then did the same and came out wearing trousers and T-shirt or, for one of them, just a loin cloth. Amazon and Brother did likewise with Amazon appearing in tribal clothing and Brother in trousers and a T-shirt. I observed later in their village, and another, clothing was a mixture of tribal and casual western. The section of bush was pressed back into place and we marched off, this time in a single file. Two of the men stayed behind us and, looking over my shoulder, I saw they were carefully obliterating any sign of tracks or our presence by expertly sweeping the ground with clumps of twigs and leaves. No doubt about it, these cookies were professional.

Less than half an hour later as the sun was setting and my legs sending messages of 'enough is enough' I spied a collection of huts ahead, which became a large African village with a fire burning in the centre of a large court-yard around which the huts were built. There were several men, women and children moving about but none, save the children, took any notice of us; the latter's curiosity aroused by the strange white man sandwiched between their coun-trymen. We walked into the village, skirting the fire, to the largest hut where in the doorway was sitting an old man, naked to the waste and below that wearing a coloured skirt-type garment. His close-cropped hair was nearly white, his face lined and his upper body showed the tale-tale wrin-kled skin of the not so young. We stopped, Amazon and Brother walked up to him and stood waiting for him to speak. After what appeared to me to be a short question from the old man, Amazon spoke at length followed by Brother whose address was a shade shorter though slightly vociferous. When he finished, the old man looked at me. Obviously a part of the conversation, probably all of Brother's address, had been about me. The old man, whom I took, correctly, to be the chief, had no expression in his eyes or lined face as he looked me up and down and then stared as if to get into my head. I kept perfectly still and returned eye contact.

The chief turned to Amazon and said something short, so short indeed it could have been 'okay' whereupon she turned and beckoned me to follow her. She led me past the inner circle of huts to an empty hut outside of the circle. Empty doubtless because I could see from the firelight it had long passed its first flush of new build and almost teetered on the brink of collapse.

'Go in and wait,' she said, so I stooped to go in through the low doorway and sat on the floor.

As my eyes became accustomed to the dimness, and aided by the rising moon whose light filtered through a hole in the wall, which I took to be a window of sorts, and the gaps in the straw roof, I made out a space of about twelve feet in diameter, totally bare save for the partial remnants of a fireplace in the centre. I knew it must have been a fireplace for the stones surrounding it were dark, probably blackened, and above it was a man-made, hole in the roof to allow smoke out.

After a short while two women came in grasping two blankets and armfuls of dried grass. They expertly placed the grass on the floor close to one wall, arranged it and put one blanket on top, leaving the second blanket at the side. Bed, I thought. Things are looking up. They were totally silent and as they left I smiled and thanked them. Whether they saw the smile or not I did not know but I'm sure they understood the thanks.

I stayed where I was sitting and, leaning against one of the wooden uprights supporting and framing the grass wall, contemplated whether I could summon up enough energy to try the bed and convince my exhausted limbs that they were functional enough to get me there. Before I could make that decision Amazon came in with a wooden bowl of something hot, with a wooden spoon and another bowl containing a drink of some sort.

'Eat, drink and sleep,' she said and went out.

I had no idea what the food looked like, the moonlight was hardly enough to distinguish shape and certainly not the subtleties of colour, but fortified by my previous culinary adventures with Amazon, I was quietly confident it would be good, as indeed it was. Again I could not identify the ingredients but somewhere in it was meat. I did not dwell upon the animal from which this meat came. The drink was a wholly different ballpark. Lightish in colour, so far as the moon rays could tell me, and a very odd, slightly bitter taste. I cannot say I liked it but as Amazon had given it to me and her vote thus far was to keep me alive, I drank it down, anticipating it would not be poisoned, crawled to my very inviting looking bed and immediately fell into a deep dreamless slumber.

6

The Learning

I was awakened by the sun shining through a hole in the roof and I immediately realised it was well after dawn. The interior of the hut looked even more decrepit and forlorn than in the moonlight. I looked at my watch, which was no help. I always kept English time on my watch when I was abroad for I have never had any problems adding or subtracting the local country time difference but I had no idea of the time difference in whatever country this was and for the life of me I couldn't remember the time difference between London and Louta, which would have given me an indication of the approximate time. I rolled off my grass mattress, which had proved remarkably comfortable, with protesting legs fell out of the entrance and slowly hauled myself to my feet, making staggering steps past the huts in front of mine to the main courtyard/circle of the village. My legs took a little longer than yesterday to function without my brain actually ordering 'left right, left right' but by the time I had reached the circle I was walking reasonably and less like a drunk. In the circle there were a number of naked or partly clothed children playing happily and on the opposite side half a dozen women drawing water from a well there. To my right were three men who appeared to be making or renovating a hut with grass, and a couple of dogs wandered aimlessly about. No one took any notice of me so I stopped and wondered what to do next.

'Awake at last.' I turned and saw Brother looking at me. Before I could speak he continued, 'I suggest you go to the well and take a drink. You have missed the morning meal.'

I nodded and walked slowly across the circle skirting the ashes of the fire in the middle, which had been burning so brightly upon my arrival. By the time I got to the well all but one of the women had disappeared carrying water on their heads back to their huts. One young woman remained and she hoisted a jar of water on her head and smiled at me, pointing to the well and indicating for me to help myself. I thanked her. Her smile broadened as she waved an acknowledgement of my thanks, then turned and walked towards a nearby hut. I watched her, marvelling at the grace she displayed in carrying a jar of water on her head, then taking it off and ducking effortlessly with it through the doorway into her hut.

I looked at the well and saw a crude but effective structure for raising water from the deep. A bucket on a rope wound around a log, in turn secured to two frames with a handle for lowering and raising the bucket. I wound the handle so the bucket descended and when the rope was slack, then tightened as the bucket filled, wound it back up again.

I put the bucket onto the ground by the well and spotted a wooden bowl alongside the well, which appeared to be a permanent feature to allow instant drinking, so I filled it and drank. Although conscious of tales of cholera and the like from drinking untreated or unboiled water in Africa I had no hesitation in downing a full bowl of the well's offering. The whole village gave off an air of order and efficiency, no one I had seen so far looked ill or malnourished so I felt the water from this deep well was likely to be clean and pure. It certainly tasted good and cool, if not cold. It really refreshed me and I took another cup and poured it over my head and face as a cursory morning wash. When I had finished I wandered over to the men working on the hut. Brother appeared again, as if from nowhere.

'Oh,' he said, 'I am glad you are interested in the work because you will be spending the day helping and if you can learn enough you will be able to repair your own hut. If not, it will surely fall down on you while you are sleeping.'

I was rather heartened by this. I certainly didn't mind hard work, I was always open to learning a new skill, and the fact Brother indicated a hut was mine gave me great confidence I was not going to die or be abandoned, in the near future at least. Brother spoke to the men who looked at me in some amusement as though this puny (lithe?) Englishman would not be capable of learning their skills far less be able to work in the heat of the sun. I gave them all a beaming smile.

'Good morning,' I said, 'I hope I can be of assistance to you and I would be very honoured if you would teach me how to repair a hut as mine is in some need of attention.'

They seemed not to understand what I said because Brother translated and it produced loud guffaws from all of them. Nonetheless one beckoned me over as another propped a very makeshift ladder against the roof next to another ladder of similar appearance. Brother disappeared again as if swallowed up by the ground. I decided to emphasise my fearlessness and cooperation so I held out my hand to each of them with a 'pleased to meet you'. Each shook my hand with warmth though not, I felt, conviction that I would be anything but a burden. One of the men picked up a big bundle of a long dried grass and climbed the ladder while the other two indicated I should go up the other ladder, which I did. The man on his ladder dumped the bundle of grass on the roof, stopping it from falling by resting it against the top of his ladder, pulled apart an area of the grass roof, which had become thin, took out a full handful of loose grass, swiftly lay portions in the area, tucking it underneath a patch of good grass above the newly inserted material and, pulling a cord from around his waist, tied the grass in place against a horizontal lath of the roof structure under the grass. The whole process was fluid and done as quick as a flash. The result was a perfect, almost undetectable patch blending into the roof of grass around it. It was similar to English house thatching I had watched with fascination on television at home but did not have the perfect lined up ends thatchers produced by patting the reeds with a large flat piece of wood. The African finish was far more rustic but sections of grass vertically overlapped with sections below whereby any rain falling on the roof would run down, off it, without collecting or penetrating. I was impressed, said so and gave him a round of applause, smiling all the time. Whilst he may not have understood what I said, he appreciated the gesture and actually looked embarrassed.

In the meanwhile the other two men were going around the lower walls of the hut testing the construction and replacing deteriorated or missing grass.

We moved the ladders around the roof to another area in need of attention and my teacher once again worked his magic but this time very slowly so I could watch every hand movement. It seemed straightforward. Then he beckoned that I should try. In an effort to impress, I theatrically grasped a handful of the loose grass resting on the roof against the top of my ladder and immediately the remainder of the grass slithered out and fell onto the ground, scattering across the dust. I gave an apologetic look to my teacher who shrugged his shoulders and motioned me to continue. With just one handful, I couldn't patch much and indeed although I was confident I laid the grass correctly, tucking it in under the layer above, when it came to tying to the horizontal lath top grasses of my new layer slid down and were no longer under the layer above. More to this than meets the eye! The workmen were right to be sceptical of my abilities.

After my instructor had corrected my feeble attempt we went down the ladder to get more grass and while I moved to the pile waiting to be used, he shouted something at me and pointed to the scattered spill from my theatrical beginnings. I took it he wanted me to collect it to be used, which, on reflection, I understood, for everything here was in finite supply and nothing must be wasted. In picking up the grass another lesson was learned. First, the grass was less than half the thickness of English thatching reeds so it was not easy to retrieve each stem from the ground without bending or breaking it, making it useless; second, there was a definite art in bundling it together so that the cut ends lined up, or nearly lined up, and the stems were not compacted together, thus allowing an even layer when put on the roof or wall. A steep learning curve indeed emphasising the fact that the higher the quality and skill of the craftsmen, the easier it looks.

By midday meal time I was getting the hang of actually handling the grass without breaking or losing it and come the end of the day my roof laying was bordering on half competent though I just couldn't get the hang of tying the grass to the roof laths. My offshore sailing had given me knowledge and skill with knots of all sorts but the binding technique by the African roof craftsman just kept passing me by. My apprenticeship with them could not be classed as hard physical work, as distinct from mentally frustrating in not being able to perfect the simplest of tasks, but when I eventually got off the ladder at the end of the working day I felt muscles that had not been stretched, twisted or compressed before, complaining gently. Would I never be free of pain?

I thanked the workmen who gave me broad smiles and I walked to the well, passing the fire in the centre of the circle, which was burning merrily. Women gathered around it with pots and pans. Arriving at the well, I took a big drink of water from the cup. Then, taking off my now filthy pink shirt, I used the remainder of the water in the bucket to slop over my upper body to get rid of the sweat and ingrained dust.

'Not wise,' Amazon said as she suddenly appeared beside me. Are these siblings real or what? They seem to arrive and leave like ghosts.

'We are lucky to have a good well with clean water but nothing in Africa is for ever. Water is a particularly precious commodity and cannot be used simply to cool the body. If you want to wash or bathe it has to be done with the minimum of water you have collected from the well your-self and carried back to your own hut.' I felt chagrin. How could I have been so unthinking.

'I am truly sorry,' I said, 'please forgive me, I have much to learn.' She inclined her head in an acceptance of my apology. 'Also,' I continued, 'I would really appreciate it if you could thank the men I was working with today for their generous help with an apology for slowing them down and making their tasks harder by my ineptitude.'

'Yes, I will do that but I hope over the next few days your skills will improve otherwise your hut will fall about your ears. Anyway, we are going to eat in a minute. Go to your hut where you will find a change of clothes, change and come back here. I will meet you and explain what is happening.'

I walked back to my hut and on entering saw folded neatly on the foot of my straw bed a pile of clothes, a floppy canvas hat similar to that worn by American troops on the front line at leisure and a pair of worn but serviceable brown boots. I took off my pink shirt and trousers, removing my underpants, shoes and socks and put on the provided clothes. Both shirt and trousers were a faded khaki colour. The shirt was rather baggy and would probably fit Brother better than it fitted me, but the trousers were surprisingly a good size. There were no underclothes or socks and I viewed with some trepidation wearing boots without socks. The socks I had just taken off were so dirty that I could not possibly continue wearing them so I bit the bullet and put on the boots without socks. Like the trousers, the boots fitted well. How someone could have known my shoe size was a mystery.

All dressed up, I picked up my dirty old clothes and hung them on peg protrusions on the wooden uprights of the hut walls – living on my own in London had taught me to be tidy – and walked back to the circle as the sun was setting to find Amazon helping with some of the cooking. I watched her for a while and marvelled at the grace and ease she displayed. Everyone seemed to be contributing in a friendly relaxed way with no sign of resentment or animosity; simply everyone working for the common good. Amazon spotted me and moved away from the fire.

'Dressed in your new finery I see,' she said, 'come with me.'

She took me towards the well but stopped outside the hut into which I had seen the graceful young lady go earlier in the day and said something in local dialect. The graceful maiden came out holding several items in her arms. Amazon took these from her and said to me:

'This is your bowl and spoon for your food and here is another bowl for your drink. These are yours for you to keep and also keep clean.' She handed me two wooden bowls and a wooden spoon. 'Also,' she said, holding a large vase type pot with a lid, 'this will be outside of your hut with water to use to clean your bowl and spoon. It is your responsibility to refill this pot but remember water is precious.' She handed the pot back to the graceful young lady who went to the well to fill it with water.

'We will eat in a minute and when the food is ready you

can take your bowl to the fire where one of the women will give you your food for the evening and also your drink. You will see various groups of villagers sitting around and you can join any of these groups. There is no discrimination here. You can eat with whoever you choose.' She then turned and walked away towards the chief's hut, leaving me to watch men, women and children slowly gather in the circle, bowls in hand, waiting for the food to be ready. Being the interloper I was reluctant to be first in the queue so I stayed where I was watching the villagers get their food and sit down on the ground in groups. Some groups were men only, some women, others children of various ages but there was no particular delineation. Except where it was clear very young children were sitting with parents, everyone else seemed to take this evening meal as an opportunity to talk with friends and neighbours.

Eventually I walked up to the fire and the food serving women, holding out my bowl with a big smile. I was given a very generous portion of food and the liquid poured into my drinking bowl looked very much milk-based. I looked around to find somewhere to sit. I thought it would be bad manners to sit by myself and yet if I did join a group uninvited I might well be invading their privacy, and although I was sure everyone would be too polite to say anything, I was keen not to offend. In the end I opted for a group of teenage boys who seemed somewhat more intent on eating than talking. I walked over to them and said 'Good evening, may I sit and join you?' and on receiving no response save for curious looks, sat down on the ground, crossed my legs, a position everyone else adopted, and started to eat.

The food was tasty and nutritious and I ate with some gusto. Halfway through my bowl I paused and looked at the boys, saying, 'My name is Nigel, your name is?' All the boys stopped eating and looked at me but said nothing. Their looks were again curious so I said, 'You must have names.

Me Nigel, you?' And I pointed to one of them. He laughed and said something to his colleagues who also joined in the laughter, shrugged their shoulders and went back to their eating. I somehow did not believe they didn't understand what I was trying to find out, nor did I feel that they were in any way hostile. It might be teenage embarrassment; then again, simply a reluctance to share intimacies of their names with a stranger. We completed our meal in silence although at the end I said, 'Excellent food. We should compliment the cooks,' which induced another peal of laughter as they got up and walked away with one slapping me on the back in a playful way. This cheered me enormously for I realised I had caused no offence.

I too got up and walked towards the fire intending to thank the cooks for my meal but they had gone and, looking around, I saw people drifting away to their huts. There was no sign of Brother or Amazon so I went back to my hut, undressed and went to bed.

I spent the following five days trying to perfect my hut-patching skills, aided, guided and assisted by my teachers who seemed to have endless patience. I talked to them on and off but apart from friendly smiles and gestures did not get a spoken response. This was a little frustrating although it didn't worry me too much. The evenings were occupied with the same routine of eating and then going to bed although I selected a different group each night to sit with but no matter how hard I tried to find out people's names or get any conversation going, I failed. Once again, I did not feel any resentment or aggravation, simply a desire not to communicate with this strange white man.

At midday meal time on the fifth day Amazon appeared, once again from nowhere, and said:

'We have now finished work for today and the rest of the afternoon you can do what you like. This evening's meal will be a small feast with several different foods, which I think you will enjoy. I suggest you spend a part of this afternoon washing down but remember what I told you about using water.' She turned and walked away.

It had been over a week since I had last had a shower and washed my hair and although in the African heat I had perspired I was surprised that my body was not dirt ingrained. My hair was certainly dirty and my scalp had been itching for days. How though to wash it and my body by using minimal water? I mused over this for a while and realised I would need two bowls or buckets. One for clean water and another for recyclable dirty water. I went to the well but there was just a single bucket to raise the water and it would not be a good idea to use this at all. I looked around for inspiration and saw Graceful Young Lady standing outside of her hut watching me. I walked up to her with a smile and said:

'I need to wash my hair and my body and I would like to have two bowls or two buckets but I do not know where to get them, can you help me?' As up to now I had never been sure whether any of the villagers actually really understood what I was saying I demonstrated with arm gestures the washing of the hair and the body and made shapes in the air to indicate the required containers. Graceful Young Lady laughed at my efforts and pointed to the side of her hut where there was a large jar similar to that which I saw her carry so effortlessly and gracefully upon her head. I picked it up, smiled and said, 'Do you have another one? One with a larger top?' Again gesticulating in a pantomime way to indicate what I was after. She frowned and shook her head but looking at me held up her hand as if I was to wait and she disappeared into her hut, reappearing in no time at all with a wooden bucket. In the bottom of the wooden bucket was a cloth similar to a flannel and with only one ingredient missing I was ready for my ablutions.

'Do you have any soap?' I asked mimicking a lathering motion. My antics sent Graceful Young Lady into a peal of laughter and she lent into the bucket lifting the cloth under which was a lump of grey substance, which I took to be soap, although it looked nothing like anything I had seen before; indeed I had my doubts that in fact it would perform the task required. Nonetheless I thanked Graceful Young Lady profusely and went to the well to fill the pot. This I did carefully so as not to spill any water I poured from the bucket and when the pot was full I lifted it above my head as though to balance it there to carry away. This prompted Graceful Young Lady, who was watching me, into another peal of laughter and I simply smiled and brought the plot down to clasp against my chest to carry it, with the bucket, back to my hut. There was no way I was even going to attempt carrying the pot of water on my head for not only did I have grave doubts about my balancing skills but also, filled with water, it was much heavier than it looked. These women are strong as well as graceful, I thought.

I got back to my hut to put into effect my plan of campaign for the big wash. I carried the pot and bucket to the back of my hut, away from anyone who might be walking around the circle or their own huts, and set them down on the ground. I took off my boots, my shirt and my trousers, poured a little water into the bucket, soaked the cloth and applied the grey lump to it to find it did indeed produce a lather, although not much of one. I then washed my face with this cloth, my neck and the rest of my body, occasionally refreshing the lather with the grey lump. Once soaped down I rinsed out the cloth in the water already in the bucket and then carefully soaked the cloth with fresh water from the pot, allowing any excess to fall into the bucket, and wiped off the soap from head to foot, wringing out the cloth from time to time and carefully re-soaking it. The finished product was a very clean me and rather mucky/soapy mixture in the bottom of the bucket. The heat of the day was such that towelling down to dry was not necessary. I then repeated the same procedure for my hair. All done, I threw away the water in the bucket and looked into the jar to find I had used barely a quarter of its content. I felt really pleased and quite proud of myself. I picked up my clothes, the pot, bucket, cloth and soap, turned around and walked back towards my hut to see a sea of black faces looking at me with big beaming smiles. My clandestine administrations were not so after all and although I was not too happy at being the afternoon cabaret the fact the faces were smiling was, I believed, a positive reflection my parsimonious use of water. Either that, I supposed, or my English manhood was the subject of some amusement!

There was much of the afternoon left and I didn't want to waste it simply lying around in my hut so, when dressed, I went for a walk around the village, which comprised a number of huts around the circle then other rings of huts behind them. The huts were very well sited for none of the single windows of each hut overlooked another hut window or door. This meant that although there were framed grass shutters for the windows and framed grass doors, neither needed to be closed to maintain privacy, so allowing both openings to be uncovered to allow air to circulate.

I noticed that the cattle, which were taken out each morning to graze, were corralled at the back of the chief's hut as were the goats. The land around the village was mostly grassland, withering and browning from the heat of the sun with a number of patches of dense low bushes. Obviously this fare provided sufficient nutrition for the village animals. Over on the other side of the village I inspected more carefully a large cultivated area I had previously seen during my thatching operations and noticed a large variety of vegetables growing; many of which I did not recognise. This cultivated area was very well tended and would be a credit to any English horticulturalist. With such ingredients available I understood why the food was of such high quality and the villagers well fed and happy.

Further outside the village was a pile of fresh earth, which turned out to be from a deep hole being dug. I later found out that this was the start of a new well. Although the well in the village showed no signs of drying up, nonetheless with water such an important commodity the villagers wanted to have another source if possible so they had engaged an expert water diviner from another village who indicated where water would be found. The hole was fifteen or so feet deep already and I wondered how much deeper it had to go before striking water.

Before I had finished my slow perambulations around the outskirts of the village some men had started the fire in the centre of the circle, erected a spit upon which a goat was speared and being occasionally turned by a young boy using the handle on the spit. A number of women were busying around the fire preparing pots of food ready for the evening meal. Everything was being done in a steady, measured and controlled way. There was no sign of haste but a strong aura of confidence and concentration. The women were joined by a few men who helped with the lifting of the pots onto and off the fire, gathered more firewood from a stack behind the huts close to the well and carried out any tasks directed by the women. The cooking was clearly the women's domain but the men were quite happy to assist. It was a harmonious scene and I stood watching quite content to see such community atmosphere until I was aware the sun was getting very low in the sky and a number of people, particularly children, were emerging from their huts, wooden bowls in hand, ready for the evening meal.

I returned to my hut, picked up my bowls and spoon and slowly went back to the circle. On this evening villagers were not sitting in the groups but formed a circle around the fire. Some were standing, others sitting and all talking to each other in a quiet way with an eye on the cooks waiting for the food. The goat on the spit reached its succulent level, was taken off and laid on a thick bed of leaves where two of the women cooks started to cut pieces off. When this task had been completed and but the bare bones of the goat were left, the villagers started to congregate around the cooks for their bowls to be filled with food from the pots steaming gently on the fire. On top of each bowl of food a generous piece of the goat was placed. With their bowls full of food, the villagers returned to their position in a circle around the fire, sitting down on the ground crossed-legged, and started eating. I was about to get my own food when Amazon and Brother appeared.

'Come,' said Amazon, 'get your food and sit with us tonight.'

I followed her to where the women cooks were dishing out the food and, after she and Brother had their bowls filled, I proffered mine to receive a generous helping of both stewed vegetables and goat. Amazon, Brother and I walked over to the edge of the circle of people and sat down to start eating. As we did so, the chief appeared and sat directly opposite us upon a slightly raised dais. He was given a bowl of food by one of the women and he started eating. Whilst I had to look at the chief across the fire, it had burned sufficiently low to offer up some light in the gathering dusk without impinging upon the line of sight. I was sitting next to Amazon, on her right, and Brother was sitting on her left. While we were eating she began talking to me.

'Once a week we sit in a circle to have a special meal. It signifies the end of a working week and everyone can relax knowing that although they will work tomorrow, no one will get up at sunrise but will spend the first hour or so in their huts with their family. It is a tradition that the chief addresses the people at this weekly gathering to report on what has been done in the village, any news of importance the chief has heard from outside the village and to map out the tasks which have to be done the following week. During this time everyone drinks a local spirit, which makes them all rather mellow, and at the end of the evening we sing traditional songs and occasionally we dance. It is a very relaxing time and we all look forward to it.'

It was already apparent to me that all the villagers were much more animated than previous evenings so Amazon's explanation of what was to come made sense – they were anticipating a bowl of the local jungle juice followed by a knees-up.

When we had finished the food the women cooks came around the circle to dish out more food from a pot held by one of the men. The food was different – a mixture of maize, herbs and spices, which complemented the previous food. This was followed by various types of fruit cut up into small pieces and sweetened with a type of molasses or honey. Then came the local spirit. I have not the faintest idea what it could have been and when I asked Amazon she shrugged her shoulders and said:

'The men brew this and each group has a different recipe, which we try each week. Some is better than others but they all have the same effect!'

I sipped at my bowl somewhat cautious about its strength and Amazon watched me closely.

'You are right to take it easy with this drink. As you're not used to it it might affect you but it shouldn't be too strong. In a minute the chief will start addressing all the villagers. You will not understand what he is saying and I will tell you afterwards.'

I continued taking small sips at the bowl, which was replenished by a man, whom I took to be one of this week's brewers, from a pot he was proudly carrying around. I smiled at him. 'Very good,' I said and he beamed a smile in response. By now the sun had long since set but the moon was full and casting a clear bright light on the circle and everyone in it. The warm night and the brewed jungle juice produced a very mellow and contented feeling within me and I sat there observing all around me. The villagers were talking in an animated way to their neighbours; some were shouting across the circle to others on the opposite side. Everyone was very cheery and clearly enjoying themselves.

Soon there was a banging on a drum and all conversation ceased. The villagers looked towards the chief on his dais who started talking quietly but in a very clear voice, which could be easily heard by everyone in the circle. He occasionally emphasised a point he was making by the waving of a hand but in the main remained still, his face expressionless but his piercing eyes looking around the circle seemingly at every man, woman and child. Although I could not understand a word he was saying, his voice was compelling and I could not take my eyes off him. Suddenly though I had the strangest feeling. I put my hand on Amazon's arm and lent across to whisper in her ear.

'Something's wrong,' I said, 'something bad is going to happen.'

She looked at me irritated and whispered back. 'What's wrong? What's bad?'

'I don't know,' I replied, 'I have this terrible feeling something is not right. I cannot identify it; I do not know what it is. I just feel all is not well.'

Amazon looked me straight in the eye in a very penetrating way. She took hold of my left forearm and squeezed it. Brother might have the muscles but she certainly was not lacking in strength. The squeeze was vice-like. 'Just sit still and be quiet. Watch the chief and do not take your eyes off him,' she said. Her words were like a command and the look in her eyes gave no doubt that she was to be obeyed.

Whatever it was I was feeling, it could not interrupt the chief's address to the villagers.

I did as I was told and fastened my eyes on the chief who continued talking in the same quiet and clear way. Now I have been blessed with very good peripheral vision and out of the corner of my eye I saw a man come from behind one of the huts and stand about one pace behind the ring of villagers to my right. Those seated in front of him could not see him; those on the opposite side of the ring were so intent on looking at and listening to the chief it seemed to me they had not noticed him. I did not take my eyes off the chief but concentrated on my peripheral vision for it was there I felt the danger was going to come. I tensed my body ready to jump up or roll away as may be necessary. The chief's voice became louder and he raised his right hand high above his head as if emphasising a fundamental and crucial point, then with a loud exclamation brought his hand swiftly down to his lap. At the same time the standing man brought a large club from behind his back and struck the man immediately sitting in front of him a mighty blow to the head. This smote man collapsed forward, face down on the ground. Another man appeared from the huts and together with Club Man they dragged the unconscious, perhaps dead, man away out of sight. A moment later both men returned and sat in the space in the circle where the unconscious man had been.

None of the villagers took any notice. Some turned to look at the man when he had been felled but then looked away, back at the chief. It was as though this was a regular occurrence and invited neither curiosity nor question. I felt Amazon's vice-like grip upon my arm again and took this to be a sign that I should remain still and quiet. I obeyed. The uncomfortable feeling that I had had disappeared and I continued to be mesmerised by the chief's monologue.

When he had finished speaking there was a respectful

silence and gradually conversation started up again. The jungle juice brewer continued his rounds filling up empty or partially empty bowls as though nothing had happened. I was full of curiosity and questions and although the night was still balmy with joyful people around, the edge had gone off it for me and I felt restless. Amazon, feeling my restlessness, took hold of my forearm again, this time in a light and friendly manner, and whispered in my ear.

'What you saw is not usual here. The man in question,' which I took to be the felled one, 'has seriously upset the chief and all the villagers. He had to be punished and everyone accepts this. There is nothing to be concerned about.'

'What did he do?' I asked.

'It is not something that need trouble you at this moment. If it becomes necessary I will tell you.'

'Just a minute,' I replied, 'from what I can tell this man was punished to death. Either that or he has the hardest skull in the world. The blow he received from the club would carve most men in half. I would really like to know how he seriously upset the chief and the villagers for I would hate to inadvertently fall into the same trap.'

'Oh,' she said, 'there is no fear of that. Just relax, drink your drink and watch the singing and dancing, which is going to start in a moment.'

I cannot say what she said put my mind at rest but I understood I could do nothing more and certainly was not going to get any information from Amazon at this time. I could not conceive of how it would become necessary to tell me what the poor man did but I had to accept no information for the moment. I therefore relaxed and took a deep swallow of my drink, feeling the faintly fiery liquid running down my throat and warming my stomach. A few more bowls of this and I wouldn't care too much about whether what I did could seriously upset the chief and the villagers.

I continued watching the villagers and noted that Jungle Juice Man was becoming very selective as to whose bowl he would fill. Those he gauged as becoming a little worse for wear he either passed by or he merely tipped a small slip of liquid into their bowl. I was quite impressed. Whatever happened this was not going to turn into a drunken party; merely a merry gathering. Soon a number of men arose from the circle and gathered drums of various sizes from the shadows and started to beat out a rhythm. Slowly, a chanting-cum-singing emanated from some of the villagers, which spread around the whole circle with everyone joining in. The rhythm increased in intensity and the chanting became slightly frenzied with some women standing up and dancing to the beat. It was not long before other women joined them with the men smiling and watching, clapping in unison with the music. A change of tempo and the men too got up one by one to get into the dance. Only the very old remained seated. The children forming their own group also danced, mimicking their elders.

I looked around to find that both Amazon and Brother had disappeared without my noticing. I could not see them dancing, nor were they sitting anywhere else in the circle so I assumed that dancing was not for them and they had moved back to their hut – wherever that might be. I stayed seated with the rhythm of the beat eating into my body, causing me to sway from side to side in sympathetic motion with the music when Graceful Young Lady with another woman of equal grace came up to me. They both leaned down and each grabbed one of my hands, pulled me to my feet and led me towards a group of dancing men and women, indicating that I should join in. The steps, body movements and gesticulations were completely foreign to me but I tried to mimic those around me, at first promting laughter from the watchers, but then broad smiles of admiration when I began to master the dance and not look like a complete idiot. I cannot say that even after a number of these dances I would ever turn out to be any good but in the end, just before exhaustion hit me, I felt as though I was making a good show of it and I was certainly not attracting unwarranted attention. Everyone treated me as one of them.

I really do not know how long these festivities lasted. When the party broke up and I got back to my hut it felt like the middle of the night and I was dog tired. I took off my clothes to hang them on the pegs of the upright wall structure and noticed that my dirty clothes I had taken off earlier in the afternoon had disappeared. No doubt used as kindling for the fire! No sooner had my head hit the mattress, than I was fast asleep.

Surprisingly, I woke at dawn the next morning and even more surprisingly did not have a hangover or indeed any ill-effect from the jungle juice or my dancing. The latter was very much a bonus point. I was getting a little fed up with my body aching or paining in one way or another. As Amazon had told me the night before that the day after the party work did not commence immediately, I slowly got up, put on my clothes and wandered out to the circle to find a few women who were getting together a cold meal. I went to the well, took a small drink and returned to my hut to pick up my bowl and spoon to have some cold breakfast. I was eating this slowly as others appeared from their huts to also have a bowl of food when Amazon spoke from behind me.

'Today, you will start repairing your own hut. I will take you to your teachers who will inspect your hut and tell you what has to be done. Finish your meal. I will be back in a little while.'

I completed the breakfasting, returned to my hut to wash out my bowl and then went back to the circle to find Amazon standing there waiting for me. She silently led me to the store, which kept the grass and a number of strips of wood used for repairing the structure of huts. My thatching teacher was there sorting through the wood. Stopping when he saw us approach, he looked expectantly at Amazon. She engaged him in a fairly lengthy conversation and he nodded and smiled. She turned to me and said:

'Mugobo here will go with you to your hut and show you what has to be replaced and the best way of repairing it. After that you are on your own. As you are a novice still he thinks you will take at least a week to do the job properly so this is a challenge for you. See if you can do it within a week.'

She smiled and walked away and Mugobo beckoned to me to follow him. This is certainly an improvement, I thought. The first name of a person I had been told. Could it be possible that my dancing style had so impressed that I was now considered one of the village? I doubted it, but certainly something had changed. We got to my hut and Mugobo walked around it casting a practised eye over its condition and then we went inside where he started tapping and shaking the structure. I swear I heard the intake of breath between the teeth so beloved of English tradesmen when they are looking to estimate for a job that is going to turn out far more expensive than anyone could have anticipated.

'Dis piece here,' he said, 'needs completely new,' and, walking around, selected two other vertical wall timbers, 'and dese two as well.' I was flabbergasted. He could speak English.

'You speak to me in English today,' I said, 'why did you not speak to me before?'

'Sabra tole me I could speak to you now.'

I assumed Sabra was Amazon. 'But why now?' I asked, 'do all the other villagers speak English?'

'I don't know why. Perhaps you pass a test. I don't know. Many speak English and maybe they speak to you now. I don't know.'

He continued walking around the inside of my hut and selected a few more pieces of vertical timber, saying, 'Dese you can repair by cutting and putting new piece in here, and here, and here.' He pointed to weak parts of the timbers, which I could see needed repairing. 'De wood in de roof will be all right but you check when you are patching de grass on de roof. I will take you to get a ladder, a knife and materials. Den it is all up to you but you must replace de wood first.'

We went back to the grass and wood store where Mugobo selected a number of pieces of wood, pointed to a ladder propped up against the store roof and gave me a long sharp parang.

'You can cut the wood with dis,' he said, pointing to the parang, 'and dis should be enough wood but you can come back and take more if you like. I will come and see you tomorrow to find out how you are getting on.'

I gathered the wood and took it with the parang back to my hut, going inside and looking at the areas which required replacement. I was uncertain as to how load-bearing each vertical piece of wood was so I decided to put a temporary piece next to the rotten wood, pushing the temporary piece firmly into the ground and lashing its top to the horizontal piece of wood forming the top of the wall and upon which the roof structure lay. I then cut away the rotten wood, cut the new section to size and pushed it firmly into the ground, carefully lashing the top to the horizontal then removing the temporary prop. I looked at my handiwork and gave it a good shake. It seemed secure and I was quite pleased at the result although completely surprised how long such a simple task had taken me.

I followed the same routine, replacing the rotten wood, but spent a good deal of time working out how I could insert a patch into the vertical pieces, which were only partially unserviceable. After putting in the temporary prop, I took out an offending vertical piece and decided the best way forward was a sort of splice-cum-joint, cutting out the old section and inserting a new piece. With just a parang and no saw or other woodworking tools this was a challenge indeed but I managed a rather crude 'V' splice where the new fitted reasonably neatly into the old. I went back to the store to see if I could find some glue but there was nothing even approaching this substance so I took some lengths of grass securing cord and went back to my hut, binding the splice with a tight whipping I had learnt from my small sail-boat experiences. I had no idea whether this was satisfactory but I was sure Mugobo would not be slow in telling me where I had gone wrong.

When I had finished replacing or repairing the vertical wooden struts in the walls I decided to check the horizontal timbers and found that one, which looked perfect on the inside, was virtually rotten; simply the bark of the wood covering a soft mush. I therefore replaced this, taking the same precaution by putting in a temporary piece to hold the vertical struts in place while I carried out the work.

The wood replacing took me all of the first day and most of the second so I had just started replacing and repairing the grass on the roof when Mugobo came to inspect my handiwork, a day late, for which I was rather pleased for I had achieved something. I climbed down from my ladder and went inside the hut with him. He walked around and looked at the timbers I had replaced or repaired.

'How did you repair dese?' he said, pointing to my spliced lashing. I explained and he nodded slowly.

'The trouble was,' I said, 'I could not find any glue. Do you know what I mean by glue?' He nodded. 'So,' I continued, 'I lashed my splices tightly with the whipping. I believe the joint will take vertical forces quite easily but obviously any horizontal forces would likely cause the splice to move.'

'We do have glue,' he said, 'you should have asked me for it but I think your lashing will be all right if the joint you make is good fitting. We will see.'

He gave the repaired sections a particularly firm shake and looked satisfied with the end result.

'So you put a new piece at the top,' he said, pointing to the horizontal strip I had inserted. 'It is good you look at everything and find that piece. I no tell you to see if you find it.' I had the distinct impression he was quietly pleased with my efforts. I'm sure he thought that as I had done a half decent job this reflected on his abilities as a teacher and I had not let him down. He went outside to see the beginnings of my roof grass replacement.

'You've got a lot to do. You think you finish in a week?' He asked.

'I am no expert like you,' I replied, 'I will certainly do my best but my first concern is it is all done properly. If it takes more than a week then I would rather spend longer than have my hut falling down around me.'

He smiled, nodded and walked away.

7

The Ability

My hut repairing continued all week and whilst I was careful to ensure what I had done was as high a quality as I could achieve, my work speeded up and by the end of the week I had nearly finished. It was the middle of the afternoon and I walked around my hut to gauge just how much more I had to do, then walked away towards bushes.

As I was approaching the bushes I saw Brother coming towards me. This was a surprise. To see him actually approaching me rather than appearing, seemingly from nowhere, was quite unusual.

'What are you doing?' he asked, 'I thought you were repairing your hut.'

'I am going for what I believe our American cousins call a comfort break,' I replied, 'even the most skilled craftsmen require these from time to time.'

He scowled at me. I then noticed for the first time that he was carrying a rifle.

'Where are you going with that?' I asked.

He looked at me for what seemed to be a long time and then said, 'You go and have your pee and when you are finished come back here and I will show you.'

I did as I was bid and on returning he and I walked for about three hundred yards or so away from the village to a flat area between two dips in the ground. He stopped and looked ahead. Following his gaze, I could see five pieces of white timber a foot or two apart stuck in the ground. From this distance it appeared that each piece was about two feet high and around four or five inches wide. He raised the rifle up to me and said:

'This is a new Kalashnikov assault rifle. It is the AK–74. You probably know the AK–47, which was the standard assault rifle used by the Russians for many years. This is an improvement and very much up-to-date, being far more accurate than any previous Kalashnikov.' I don't know if I was supposed to be impressed but I composed my face into an interested expression though frankly really couldn't give a damn how new, accurate and all-singing, all-dancing it was. Guns had never been my sort of thing and whilst I had surely heard of the Kalashnikov I couldn't have recognised one to save my life.

'What are you going to do?' I asked.

'Watch,' he said.

Brother laid down on the ground, spreading his legs as if to form a stable platform with the Kalashnikov in front of him and looked at the five white planks of wood. He adjusted the rear sight of the gun, put the gun to his shoulder and carefully pulled the trigger. None of the pieces of wood appeared to have been hit and when the rifle shot died away, Brother readjusted the rear sight and once again raised the gun, looked along it and pulled the trigger. This time the piece of wood to the right visibly moved and was half knocked over. He got up with a smile on his face and said: 'That is what this gun can do. It is very accurate.'

I made impressed type noises and smiled back. He looked at me and handed me the rifle. I held it, not quite knowing what to do or why he had given it to me, and in answer to my puzzled expression he said, 'Now you have a go.'

'No,' I said. 'I have no idea how to shoot a gun. I have

never held one before. I really do not think it is something for me to do. It just isn't my thing.'

A scornful look came over his face. 'Just try it,' he said, 'humour me if you like.'

I wasn't quite sure whether this was a challenge for him to demonstrate his expertise over my ignorance or he really wanted to see if I could handle this machine of destruction. I had no desire at all to show him I couldn't shoot and, in his eyes, show myself up, but he stood there looking, waiting, so I slowly got to the ground, imitating the posture he had adopted and raised the gun to my shoulder, looking down through the rear sight to the forward sight to line it up on one of the pieces of white painted timber. I had seen television pictures of Olympic contestants shooting both hand-guns and rifles with the commentary explaining how it was all done, and I racked my brain to remember what I should do. I took a long time looking through the sights, slowed my breathing and relaxed. I pulled the rifle gently into my shoulder and as I looked at the white piece of timber my whole mind focused upon it and it seemed to grow larger. The television commentators had emphasised that the trigger should be squeezed and not pulled so I very slowly and gently squeezed the trigger, keeping my whole mind and eyes focused upon one of the white pieces of wood.

The kick from the Kalashnikov was less dramatic than I had anticipated and to my amazement I saw that that the piece of wood upon which I had been focusing all my atten-tion had fallen over. I hit it? Impossible, I thought. I looked up at Brother who had a startled expression on his face.

'Beginner's luck,' I said, 'and,' thinking quickly, 'obviously your expert adjustment of the sights gave me an edge.' He looked far from pleased and said, 'Come,' striding down towards the pieces of wood. I scrambled to my feet and awkwardly carrying the rifle followed after him. When we arrived at the area where three pieces of wood were still standing both he and I noted the right-hand piece of wood, at which he had shot, had a nick in it on its left edge causing the wood to move when hit. The target I had aimed at was flat on the ground with a hole dead centre. Now I was amazed.

'Very lucky indeed for a beginner,' Brother said, 'are you sure you have never shot a rifle before?'

'Absolutely,' I said. 'The closest I've been to any firearm before this was passing the security policeman in an airport. I really can't explain it.'

Brother started to walk back to where we had fired the shots and I followed him, still carrying the rifle. Although I did not feel at ease with it, somehow after seeing the results of my efforts it felt more comfortable in my hand. We reached our firing position and he looked at me very carefully and said, 'What I want you to do is to lie down again and shoot at the last three pieces of wood. I know you were lucky first time.'

Whilst initially I had absolutely no desire to continue touching the rifle let alone shoot it, I suddenly felt intrigued as to why I was able to hit a target with my very first shot. I really believed it was very much beginner's luck but by the same token curiosity in me was aroused and so with far less reluctance I lay down once again to sight and shoot at the three remaining pieces of wood.

This time I took even longer preparing. I blanked my mind off everything except a white piece of wood one hundred or so yards away, which I was aiming to hit. I again slowed my breathing and concentrated very hard. The more I concentrated the clearer the target became. When I eventually squeezed the trigger, internally I had no surprise at all to see the target topple over. I moved my sight to the next piece of wood, going through the same exercise and this time the piece seemed even bigger and easier to hit. It too toppled. The third piece became enormous in my eyes.

It was as though there was nothing in the world except this piece of wood, which was going to be hit by my shot. I was totally mesmerised by it. I fired and it fell over. I got up and handed the rifle back to Brother who was totally silent. Whether struck dumb by my demonstration or piqued by my apparent expertise I couldn't tell. We tramped slowly back to the pieces of wood and each one had a hole dead centre. If I was to lay all four pieces of wood, one on top of the other, there would appear a single hole through the whole stack, in precisely the same place.

'I think you can shoot,' said Brother, 'it looks like you're a natural. Let's try some more.'

We did. I shot. They fell. Same result.

It would not be unfair to say that up to now Brother had been somewhat hostile towards me and I was firmly convinced that if he had had his way I would have been shot at the aeroplane. I could tell by his expression that he could hardly believe his eyes. He didn't look hostile any more, simply bemused, tinged with a certain amount of respect. I barely stopped myself from saying, 'Okay, now you have a go,' but felt this was unnecessary and indeed might bring back the hostility.

'I do believe you have a talent,' he said, 'go back to your hut now and continue working. We will talk on this later.'

I handed him the Kalashnikov and walked back to my hut to continue the wall thatching until mealtime. There was a very odd sensation running through me. I can't say I was elated but I certainly felt a sense of achievement, pleasure even. I could not get out of my mind the feeling of the targets getting closer as I concentrated upon them. It was as if I was mesmerised by the targets and consequently my whole being had been taken over by them.

The afternoon shooting excursion had delayed me and there was no way I was going to finish within the allotted week.

So before having my bowl filled with food I searched out Mugobo and said to him, 'You are perfectly correct, I have totally failed you. I have not completed my hut but I should finish tomorrow.'

He looked at me in a satisfied sort of way and said, 'Yes, I had seen you were not going to make it. Never mind, you have done a fairly good job and no one will worry that you have not done it in time. If you finish tomorrow then that is good.' He patted me on the shoulder and walked away.

That evening meal went off without incident. As was usual, I joined another group of villagers to eat and I exchanged pleasantries and names in halting English. I confess, I have never been very good at remembering people's names unless repeated several times and African ones are particularly difficult so now I have no idea who told me what name but they all seemed happy to identify themselves. Whatever I had done, I was now fully accepted as a part of the village.

The following morning I had nearly finished repairing the walls of my hut. I was intending to complete this task and then go over the roof and walls carefully to see if I had missed anything or whether my securing arrangements were in any way inadequate. I was confident my work would not be anything like the high standard of my teacher's but as Mugobo had not made adverse comments last night I believed what I had done was satisfactory. So with the bright sun on my back I was happily stitching together the last few pieces when I was conscious of a presence behind me. I looked around and there was Amazon. Although I knew her name was Sabra, I still thought of her as Amazon and would continue to do so.

'Ah,' I said, 'the ghost arrives to inspect the poor handiwork of the skinny white man.'

'Ghost?'

'Oh yes,' I replied, 'I'm sorry about that but both you and your brother seem to be able to appear and disappear at will without me hearing or seeing your arrival so I'm not sure whether you are human or you are ghostly apparitions with a short time on this world.'

She smiled. 'I am human enough,' she replied, 'but we have learned to walk about quietly for often our lives depend upon it. Speaking of which, do you have some time for me?'

This was a bit of a turnaround. Amazon asking *me* if I had time for *her*. Up to now I had simply done that which she had asked or commanded. There was certainly a change of approach and I could not believe it was just the fact that I was able to repair a hut which had brought about this change.

'Of course I have time for you,' I responded, 'at any time, day or night. I am wholly indebted to you and you do not have to ask.'

She smiled at that. 'Come with me then,' she said and started walking away. I followed her until we came to a small tree casting a little shade. She sat down and patted the ground beside her. 'Sit down,' she said.

We sat there for a while in silence and I had no idea whether she wanted me to say something. Eventually she turned and looked at me full in the face, her eyes soft and penetrating as though she was searching my soul for an answer to a question she didn't even know.

'My brother says that you can shoot. You are a natural. He has never seen anything like it. You may not like my brother very much but he is a very good man, extremely talented, and is one of the best shots I have ever seen and yet he says you are better. Is that true?'

I shrugged. 'I have no idea if I am a good shot or not. I certainly hit the targets yesterday and in all honesty I found it very easy. Whether that was just what you would call a good day or a natural talent I cannot say.'

'Would you mind if we try to do it some more?'

'Not in the least,' I replied, 'I am perfectly happy to have another go. In fact it might be good for me as I might not be able to replicate what I did before and this would show that I was simply a flash in the pan.'

'You have asked me many questions about who we are and where you are; what we are doing and why we are doing it. I think I will be able to answer these questions shortly but I would very much like to see you shooting if you do not mind.'

'I do not mind at all if you watch me. I either succeed or fail; whichever way, you would know about it anyway so why not be a witness,' I replied.

'Okay then,' she said. 'Go back and finish your hut and this afternoon we will have more shooting.'

With that, she stood up, smiled at me and walked away. I too got up, returning to my hut and my repairing, wondering why it was so important for her to know if I could shoot or not. I had no doubt of her brother's expertise and he went up in my estimation several notches in that he had confided to his sister there was someone better than he. It takes a true human being to admit that someone whom you feel is an inferior is in fact, in some respects at least, superior. I had no fear or trepidation about the potential shooting contests that afternoon. Either I could do it or I could not. It didn't matter that much to me even though I came away from the first experience with an amazing feeling of achievement and comfort. I had imagined that people who play with guns were somehow masochistic or even lacking in some way, using the power of a firearm to cover their own faults and inadequacies. Now I was far from certain. What could there possibly be in pulling a trigger that could give a feeling of comfort? Am I going weird? Is the sun affecting me? I mentally shrugged my shoulders and got on with the work.

I had just about finished by the midday meal and would have spent the afternoon double checking my work but I knew I was assigned to other things. After I finished eating I wandered back to my hut to tidy up the tools and very soon Amazon appeared.

'Are you ready?' She asked. I nodded. She turned and walked away to the shooting area where a large circular piece of wood, very similar to an archery target, was set up and some thirty to forty yards in front a table with a number of handguns. Brother was waiting for me and immediately handed me an automatic pistol. 'It's a Glock 17,' he said, 'hit the target.' I pointed the gun towards the target but it did not feel comfortable; too light. I could not hold it steady. Seeing the problem, Brother gave me another. 'A colt M1911 automatic holding seven rounds, heavier and it might suit you.' It did indeed and I had no difficulty emptying the magazine with each bullet very close to the centre of the target. Brother moved me back another thirty yards or so and again I hit the target though this time not all the shots were so close to the centre. Knowing the inaccuracy of a hand-held gun, I was surprised at my performance, which emphasised my natural shooting abilities.

Target practice over, Brother took the gun from me and exchanged knowing looks with Amazon. They said nothing but it appeared to me that those looks spoke volumes although what the volumes contained I had no idea. I had no feeling of trepidation or indeed concern but somehow there was an air of complicity between us though quite where that might lead I did not then have a clue.

'Go back to your repairing,' said Amazon, 'we will see you at mealtime tonight.'

I wandered back to my hut, musing gently over the afternoon's events. Like the rifle shooting, I felt perfectly relaxed with a handgun but had not quite come to terms with my ability, to use both. Though at the aeroplane I had seen that

Amazon and her merry band were well armed, I was surprised at the guns that Brother had produced. I well knew after the fall of the Iron Curtain there was a brisk trade in Russian firearms throughout the world. I vividly remember with some amusement a client sitting across my desk shaking and perspiring heavily with the thought of many years in jail because his ship was found to be carrying illegal arms. He swore to me he was an innocent victim but I did not quite believe him; luckily the authorities did not quite have enough evidence so he got away to fight another day, though, I was sure, considerably chastened.

I also knew that the Chinese were investing large sums of money in Africa in a type of colonisation. Not the old-fashioned style of conquer and rule by the gun but a more subtle approach dictated by foreign currency availability. With this investment and the presence of Chinese experts to assist local workers also came Chinese arms. But Brother had what he claimed to be the latest and most up-to-date Kalashnikov assault rifle. This could not have come from the flow of arms following the fall of the Iron Curtain; nor could it be a Chinese import, for as I understood it, and here I was certainly no expert, the Chinese had developed their own type of automatic assault rifle. So, where then did Brother get his arms?

I finished the renovations to my hut well before evening mealtime and I went off to find Mugobo for the final inspection. He walked around shaking the structure here and there and eventually gave it a good bill of health. He did not actually say what I had done was any good, simply intimated it was sufficiently satisfactory for the moment. I was pleased. With about an hour to go before the evening meal I took the opportunity of having another wash down and hair wash. This time there were no prying eyes.

With bowls and spoon in hand I went to get my food and

saw Brother and Amazon sitting together. She looked up and beckoned me over. I sat down and started eating.

'When we have finished,' she said, 'I would like to speak to you if that is all right.' I nodded with my mouth full. 'Good,' she said and carried on eating.

We ate our food in silence and when it was completed Amazon said, 'Go to your hut, I will join you in a moment,' and moved off with Brother.

I went back to my hut, washed my bowls and spoon and was putting them away when Brother and Amazon appeared. Amazon was carrying two bowls of a drink and Brother a small, low table with what appeared to be an oil lamp on it. They both ducked into my hut, Brother set the table on one side and lit the oil lamp. Amazon put a bowl of offering each side of the lamp and beckoned me to sit down. Brother left.

I picked up one of the bowls and had a sip, discovering it was one of the jungle juice concoctions.

'Are you trying to get me drunk and have your way with me?' I questioned humorously.

She smiled. 'Certainly not,' she said, 'but I wanted to talk to you and I see no reason why we cannot have a relaxed conversation.'

She took a small mouthful from her bowl, set it down and looked me straight in the eye. The light from the oil lamp in my dark hut gave out a yellow glow, and with eyes adjusted, I could see Amazon very clearly, particularly the expression on her beautiful black face.

'As you now know, my name is Sabra. My brother's name is Ajani. You are in Babwemiz, which is a country in fear and poverty as a result of a dictator who calls himself president, Baumge.'

Being an international lawyer I was naturally fairly well up to speed with international events and well knew the fate of Babwemiz as a result of its president dictator. The TV news bulletins often showed the poverty and degradation of the country with western leaders condemning lack of human rights and failure to supply the people with basic necessities. The usual hot air and no action. So I nodded indicating I was not unfamiliar with the problems of the country.

'I am sure you have heard of the poverty and the atrocities that have been committed.' I nodded. 'Reality is that it is not anything like the full truth. There is no such thing in this country as free thought or any opposition to Baumge. There are no opposition political parties as you have in England. No one would dare raise a voice against Baumge. He has driven this country into the ground. We have many minerals here and our agriculture used to be good and prolific, allowing export to neighboring countries. Now, nothing. Most people cannot even feed themselves.' Her eyes left my face and she looked down at the ground in a wistful, almost defeated away. She continued: 'Baumge's power is guaranteed by what he calls his palace guard. This palace guard is in reality an intelligence gathering and spying organisation with a death squad which has no conscience, no feeling, no regrets. The police and army carry out Baumge's wishes because if they do not they know they will be subject to the wrath of the death squad; or rather the palace guard, I should say. Whilst the atrocities committed by the army and police abound and are without mercy it is nothing to that which the palace guard hands out. As you have experienced.' She paused and looked at me.

'You mean Death's Head and his merry men at the aeroplane?' I asked. She nodded and took a deep drink from her bowl. Sighing, she looked back at me.

'Yes indeed,' she said, 'your fellow passengers were subject to the attention of the palace guard and it was only the radio message, which obviously called them elsewhere, that prevented atrocities being committed to the dead bodies. In fact I can assure you that if the palace guard had not been called away they would certainly have found you and probably, as you had escaped their first assault, they would have tortured you just for fun; particularly as you are a white man. You really do not know how fortunate you were.'

'But,' I said, 'you were in the area, close to me, and I have every confidence that you would have intervened to save my life.'

She looked at me straight and seriously. 'Oh no we would not. There is no way we would have tackled the palace guard. There are many reasons for this and perhaps one day someone will explain to you why. I cannot now but I can assure you absolutely you were on your own and we would not have lifted a finger to help no matter what the palace guard did.'

This brought me up sharply. I did indeed appreciate how lucky I was but could not understand why Amazon was so adamant that no one would have intervened to save my life. I could, perhaps, understand that they might not have been close enough to do anything about the other passengers but they were certainly on hand to protect me if they had wished; clearly they had no desire to do so. I really wanted to find out why there was this reluctance but from the expression on Amazon's face I knew this was neither the time nor the place to dig deeper. I too took a deep swallow from my bowl and the alcohol cheered me up. A long silence followed and I was not sure whether Amazon was collecting her thoughts as to what to say next or whether she was letting the reality of the words sink into my brain. Eventually she began speaking again.

'I say there is no opposition to Baumge and the palace guard but in fact that is not quite right. Everyone in this country opposes him in their heart. Even his cronies are so frightened of Baumge and his palace guard that they would welcome any change, for whatever came next could not be half as bad as what we have now. Also, there are members of the government who simply pay Baumge lip service and would, if they could, organise an overthrow but they dare not. They simply keep quiet and out of the lime light, knowing that if they resigned, then they would meet a certain death for Baumge would believe any resignation amounts to revolt. Unfortunately, any gatherings or meetings, even private dinner parties, which the palace guard suspects as being what they refer to as revolutionary, are immediately stamped upon. There are spy networks and intelligence is everywhere. Anyone suspected of being a dissident is beaten, killed or, even worse, thrown into jail and tortured. It is not a matter of lack of free speech; it is no speech at all. The air of fear in the whole country is palpable; you can almost smell it.' She paused again and looked hard at me, obviously weighing up what she should say next, if anything at all. I returned her look and set my face to accommodating, open, and waited.

'You have seen the group from my village, which is armed as soldiers, and acts as soldiers. Apart from Ajani and me, there are eight others; you have seen six. The other two were engaged on something else the day we rescued you. They are all a part of the opposition to our dreadful government. As it is so impossible to organise anything in the towns, this organisation is being done in the villages; the further the village is away from the capital, the easier it is to organise but it is still very difficult and fraught with enormous danger. So dangerous is it that even though I know there are groups like mine in nearby villages, I do not know who is a part of them. We have been forced to adopt a system used by the French resistance during the last world war. Obviously everyone in my village knows who the members of my little resistance group are but no one knows who in the neighbouring village is also a part of the resistance. Just one of our number knows one of the nearby village members and any messages or information is conveyed that way. This means if any of us is captured or tortured, it minimises the risk of discovery.

I was quite impressed at the sophistication of these arrangements but if indeed Death's Head and his merry men were as dedicated and ruthless as Amazon maintained, I cannot say I would hold out too much hope that this structure would actually hold up.

'This sounds extremely organised,' I said, 'but even the most organised of resistance or opposition cells have to be able to get together in order to carry out the necessary tasks and duties to overthrow a government. I hasten to add, I am certainly no expert in this. But from my limited knowledge of history, one has to fight fairly hard to overthrow a government and this you cannot do unless people band together and form a formidable army, so with your current structure I cannot see what chance you possibly have. Also, I would guess there are a number of tribes in this country, and tribal unity is not renowned. How are you going to overcome this?' Amazon lowered her eyes and her beautiful face looked almost defeated. She knew what I had said on both counts was true and I guessed she had been battling with this conundrum for a long time.

'Tribal rivalry is not very high in my country. There are, of course, many tribes but only two of them are what you might call dominant, one of which is ours. The other is not too far away from here but the rivalry is friendly rather than warlike and we are hoping when the time comes we will be able to band together against the oppressive government.'

'What is it then you actually do?' I asked.

She looked at me for a long time, appearing to weigh up whether to tell me any more, but from her expression I guessed that the reason for our discussion was somehow to get me on board, though quite how I could be of help was not immediately apparent.

'We are doing several things. The first is that everyone in

this village is being trained to use firearms in case of need. We are doing this slowly but we hope when the time is right other villages will be similarly trained so that if there is a possibility of changing the government and force has to be used, all the villagers will be able to unite to do this.' She paused, as if gathering strength. 'As I have indicated, the biggest problem is the palace guard, and the fear it has managed to generate is so strong that even the most highly trained and dedicated would be very slow to attack it; certainly at the moment.'

'Is there really no way of removing the palace guard?' I asked.

'The difficulty is not just the fear. Not only is the palace guard the most highly trained group in this country but its control by terror over the police and army could well mean these organisations would fight alongside the palace guard rather than support any uprising. The fact that the opposition cells in the villages are largely secret and the total number is unknown means that although the army and police would welcome shaking off the shackles of Baumge and the palace guard, at the moment it is impossible for them to gauge how many people would support them. I cannot emphasise too strongly the grip of fear the palace guard has over the government, military and police.'

She took a drink from her bowl, set it down on the table and continued.

'The palace guard is about two hundred and fifty in number, of which approximately fifty remain in the capital at all times, basically organising the spying and intelligence, with a few in control of the army there to protect Baumge. The remaining two hundred were originally split into four sections of fifty men each who were allocated separate parts of the country, which they patrolled; they maintained support for the government and encourage, through fear and intimidation, the people to spy on each other. Death's Head, as you call him, keeps two or three of the guard with him most of the time and tours around the countryside to check on what is being done, reporting back to Baumge in the capital.

'As I have already said, all the palace guard is very highly trained and has the finest weapons including rockets, anti-tank and anti-personnel equipment. Therefore, even if we could get fifty or so of our trained resistance to take on one section of the palace guard we would be outgunned and certainly outmanoeuvred. Therefore it has been decided to weaken the numbers of palace guard in any one area so there are occasional hit and run attacks on and general harassment of the palace guard activities, which has meant the fifty-strong in each section have been split into two sections of twenty-five men each to enable them to oversee more of the countryside. This gives us a much better chance when we have become fully trained.'

'How do you harass the palace guard?' I asked.

Amazon smiled. 'This is surprisingly easy. As you know, this country receives much foreign aid including food from humanitarian organisations. The majority of this aid does not reach any of the inhabitants of my country but is siphoned off, stolen, by the palace guard. As the foreign governments and food agencies try and supervise this aid from the capital, it would not be wise of the palace guard to keep their ill-gotten gains there, so every so often they load up lorries and drive them to the countryside to special depots and stores, which are supervised by the palace guard with access denied to everyone else. To be as inconspicuous as possible, the palace guard does not take the lorries out of the capital in convoys but one at a time and each lorry goes to a different location. We, and other groups, get to know when those lorries are on the move and so hijack them. They are driven away from the roads and camouflaged so they cannot be easily found by either a land or air search, the content is offloaded and then some of the lorries are driven back to the road and set on fire. The hijacking group then informs, through our cell structures, others in the area and the villagers collect the goods and distribute them amongst all the other villages.'

'But if you do this regularly, surely the palace guard would protect the lorries with more troops and so prevent the hijack,' I said.

Amazon smiled again. 'The groups are very selective as to where and when they carry out these hijacks. It would indeed be foolish to try and hijack every lorry so attacks are carried out at irregular intervals at different places, which means either the palace guard has to deplete its number by protecting every lorry or simply hope the attacks will be kept to a minimum. What they have done is to provide a single jeep escort of four soldiers, a lorry driver and another soldier in the lorry. This does deter an attack to some extent because the number of places to hide and carry out an ambush is limited.'

'You say not all the lorries are returned to the road and burnt. What happens to the remainder?'

'When all the cargo has been taken out the lorries are inspected to see whether they are worthwhile keeping and if so they are driven to a secure place to be kept for use in the future when there will be a general uprising. There are an amazing number of places where vehicles of this size can be hidden.'

'Do the lorries just carry foodstuffs?' I asked.

'Mostly, yes. However, sometimes the palace guard also transports its own stores and equipment, which includes tents, furniture, clothes, cooking equipment and up-to-date firearms.'

Ah, I thought. That is where the Kalashnikov came from. I didn't think it was prudent to mention this though.

'How long do you think you can carry on doing this before

the palace guard makes a really concerted effort to try and stop the hijacking?' I asked.

'I really do not know,' she replied. 'The palace guard is very arrogant and it might well be that it will divide its number into even smaller units to cover more of the country to interrogate the people to find out what the villagers know about the hijacking. If this is so, then we certainly have a better chance of eliminating these smaller groups. Whatever actually happens, we must continue with our actions as other village groups are doing the same. I am hoping that these successes, although small, will be recognised by the police and military and so convince them that there is a viable support for an overthrow of Baumge. We do have contacts in the capital, even in the government, and the position is being monitored. I do not think it would be wise at this moment to tell you any more.'

Whilst I certainly appreciated being brought up to speed I did not understand why she was telling me all this. I guessed there must be a good reason so I prompted her.

'Why are you telling me all this now?'

She gave me one of her long, intense looks and replied, 'I want you to help us.' Before I could say anything more she continued. 'You have demonstrated a truly remarkable skill with firearms and we could use that skill. When we ambush a lorry with its attendant jeep it is imperative the driver of both is killed quickly to stop them racing away. With your expertise this can be done from a greater distance and so give us more time to finish off the rest.'

My initial reaction was 'no way, José,' but I felt such a response rather indelicate bearing in mind all the kindnesses she and the rest of the village had shown me. Nonetheless I could not see me killing someone at all; let alone for a cause not directly affecting me. Let's be clear here. I am not saying for one moment it would be impossible for me to kill in what is commonly called 'cold blood', just unlikely. Indeed if I had thought about it at all I would rather hope that any killing that I might have to do would be in cold blood for at least this would mean it was planned and executed carefully so I would have a fighting chance of getting away with it. Killing as a result of hot temper or passion on the other hand would surely lead to detection. Nonetheless, killing was not for me so I therefore tried to sweeten the pill.

'I understand very clearly what you are trying to do and have immense sympathy for the reign of terror which grips your country. I also understand negotiated or democratic means of overthrowing the current government is out of the question and that if there is going to be any change it is likely to be violent and, I'm sure, bloody. However, I am not a trained soldier, nor am I a mercenary, and I have been brought up to believe killing in any form is wrong so I could not do as you ask. It is against my nature. The fact I seem to have some talent with firearms does not, I'm afraid, extend to killing other human beings. I am truly sorry. It is just not in me.'

Amazon continued to look at me with no expression at all on her beautiful face. The oil lamp started to flicker, indicating it was running out of oil as it cast an eerie light over her.

'If I was to fuck you, would that change your mind?'

I smiled. 'Let's give it a try and find out.'

'I was thinking more of a commitment first rather than a definite maybe afterwards,' she retorted.

'Very wise. So I take that as a no then,' I said.

She picked up her bowl of jungle juice and slowly drained it then got to her feet, looking down at the flickering flame. As she stood, she said:

'The lamp light is dying and I take it to be an omen that our conversation is over. Ajani said you would refuse. We can't make you help us but in a couple of days we are going out to ambush a truck and you will come with us to see what we do. You can come voluntarily or, if necessary, we will carry you. I think you really ought to see first-hand what we are doing.' I was about to speak but she held up her hand to stop me. 'You may well think that by being with us you will be an "accessory" but the reality is you are already that. Just being in the village and knowing our little military group is more than enough for the palace guard to treat you as a terrorist or a mercenary, whatever you prefer. Coming with us will not change this at all and so you will come.'

I didn't doubt for one moment the palace guard would not take into account any subtleties concerning my position in the village nor indeed how and why I got here. I could see the sense in Amazon's argument and I did owe her an enormous debt so I felt it would be churlish to take a puritan stance and degrading in the extreme to be carried to the scene of the intended ambush so I replied: 'I will certainly go with you. I must though make it clear I will not take part in any of your actions.'

I confess when saying that I wondered what would happen if the tables were turned and the attending palace guard successfully defended the lorry and started killing Amazon's little group. Would I continue with my pacifist approach? Frankly, I did not know but rather feared I would not. I could probably justify it in my mind as self-preservation or self-defence. Rather lame really so I hoped that either the lorry didn't show up or, if it did, everything went according to Amazon's plan.

Amazon ducked out of the entrance of the hut and as she left so the oil lamp finally extinguished, leaving me in the dark. I sat there thinking over our conversation and wondering if I could have done or said anything that could have kept me out of the impending ambush, but concluded

Amazon was a determined women and she had already mapped out in her mind what was going to happen. I finished my bowl of jungle juice, lay down on my bed and drifted off into a slightly troubled sleep.

8

The Attack

I woke up the following morning as usual when the sun rose and went to have my morning meal. As I was finishing, Amazon approached me and said, 'We will be going off tomorrow at first light. You will be ready then.'

I nodded, feeling that there was nothing I could say one way or the other that would change the situation, and I did not want to convey any more reluctance.

Although the thought of what was going to happen the following day dwelt upon my mind, nonetheless the day passed rather enjoyably. The children thought it was time I learnt how to look after and milk goats and I expended much energy chasing around trying to catch one and then, amongst peals of laughter from the children, I vainly attempted milking. I've seen this done many times on television but there was a definite knack. Not only does the teat of the goat's udder have to be massaged gently to squeeze out the milk but the stream directed into the waiting bucket without spilling any. My massaging attempts were pathetic, causing goats to kick me and run away, which meant I had to chase them again to bring them under control to try once more. Eventually I got the hang of it, but I was nothing like as efficient as the youngest child who, with a broad smile across his moonlike face, milked with one hand while waving his other hand in the air to demonstrate how easy it was.

I stayed with a group of children in the evening for our meal as each regaled stories of my efforts during the day to their friends amidst much laughter. I sat there looking contrite and amused, winning many friends.

I was awake the following morning well before dawn and, after eating the morning meal, washed my bowl and spoon outside my hut then walked to the circle to find Amazon and Brother standing talking to several other villagers. Amazon gave me a knapsack and a bundle of clothes.

'The knapsack carries your food, water and a few essential items. Put on these camouflage clothes so that you will blend into the countryside. I don't want you standing out like a sore thumb.'

I returned to my hut, took off my normal clothes and put on the camouflage dress worn by the group. I returned to the circle with the knapsack on my back. The other members of the group had congregated and we moved off towards the hidden cave where each disappeared in turn to come out in camouflage uniform and armed with automatic rifles. As before, when they emerged, two of the group – one whose name I later learnt to be Brumbo – carefully obliterated any sign of tracks or disturbance around and leading to the entrance.

We started walking to the south in the same fashion as before with Amazon leading, me behind her and Brother bringing up the rear; the other eight fanned out on each side at a respectable distance. After we had been walking for about an hour Amazon said to me, 'The palace guard jeep and truck will come from the capital on the main road towards their camp. This road is not tarmac but hardened earth so the vehicles throw up a dust cloud, which makes them easy to see. The road itself is very much exposed until it gets to the hills to the south of us. In the hills there are places we can hide so that the palace guard cannot see us before we attack. The hills are the best and safest place to carry out this operation but we are very careful not to do so on every occasion for this would give the palace guard warning that it could be attacked there and take extra precautions when the lorry goes through the hills. The road's nearest point is about half a day's brisk march from the village but where we are going in the hills will take just over a day and a half. Our information is that the lorry will be setting out from the capital tomorrow mid-morning, which will mean that we must be in place by midday for the lorry should arrive in the hills by mid to late afternoon. To be sure we are not late we will have to increase our pace. I hope you do not become too tired!'

'I will certainly do my best to keep up,' I replied, 'although I am afraid I have still to learn to walk with the same grace as your troop. They seem to glide over the ground. What is the secret?'

'Many years of hunting. I'm afraid you will never be able to master it but I suggest you relax your body as you walk; this means you do not put one foot in front of the other in a determined or forceful way and so your impact on the ground will be less.'

I tried to do as she said but found it very difficult. The pace picked up and I concentrated on looking around at the tundra to take my mind off the way I was walking and thought about having a relaxed, if swift, stroll through the countryside. This seemed to work for I fell into a rhythm and, from the slightly approving glance from Amazon, believed I was not doing too badly at all.

Just before our stop for the midday meal Brumbo, who was out on our right flank, came towards us and motioned us to follow him. There was no urgency or alarm in his demeanour and we dutifully did as we were bid until he stopped and, looking at the ground, pointed towards it. By this time all the group was around us and whatever they saw on the ground meant something to them but nothing to me. I was about to enquire when Brumbo motioned me to silence, pointed off to the right and slowly, with his eyes on the ground, walked in that direction with the rest of us following.

After about five minutes Brumbo motioned us to slow down as we approached a clump of bushes with a couple of trees casting slight shadow over them. Suddenly, I saw four lionesses lying on the ground relaxing under the shade of the trees. We stopped, not twenty-five yards from the lionesses and looked. They returned our gaze, not in a hostile way, but with total indifference. I was enchanted. They lay there virtually motionless with only an occasional flick of a tail or twitch of an ear, eventually turning their heads away from us as if to dismiss our presence as of no importance. After a few minutes one of the lionesses raised her head high and uttered a roar. I am not talking here about the sound heard in the movies or from wildlife programme on the television. This was a roar of such feeling and intensity as to virtually defy description. I have heard nothing even approaching it before, and to emphasise the point, in my London flat I have a very sophisticated sound system, costing far too much money, and the sound of a lion's roar from that, impressive though it is, does not even approach the real thing. This roar was loud, not deafeningly so but with a penetration that seemed to carry it to the four corners of the world. It was effortless yet deep with incredibly melodic reverberations, not at all threatening but simply making her presence known. In the open plains the sound did not echo but gave the impression it lingered before slowly dying away. All other noise around was drowned and even afterwards nothing chirped or squeaked or buzzed as if the beings of Africa were giving silent homage to the mightiness of the roar. I had barely got over the effect of the first roar when the lioness raised her head once again and repeated the exercise for no apparent reason other than to convey that she could. It was electrifying. I cannot say my spine tingled but I felt as if all the hairs on by body were standing up.

Brumbo motioned us to withdraw and slowly we moved back, away from the lionesses to resume our walk. My mind was still reeling from what I had seen and heard and I confess my earlier attempts to emulate the groups' 'walking on air' deserted me. Brumbo came alongside of me.

'She was signalling for her mate,' he said. 'I could not tell how close he might have been, for a male lion will respond when he is ready. He will not be dictated to by a lioness even in the mating season, which we are shortly approaching.'

'Were we in any danger?' I asked.

'No, none at all. If the male lion was really close and he thought we might be interfering with his mates then he would have made a fearful fuss but unless cubs are threatened or the lions are suddenly surprised, it is rare indeed that they pose any threat to humans. There are stories from time to time of a rogue lion snatching babies and young adults but this only occurs most exceptionally if the lion is too ill, injured or old to share the food killed by the females.'

With that, Brumbo went back to his flanking duties.

The stop for the midday meal was briefer than before and we continued walking after sunset before stopping to eat the evening meal and sleeping. As usual during our stops the troop exchanged banter in the local dialect and it seemed to me one or other were chiding companions for not keeping a proper lookout or blundering into a bush or similar. It was all very lighthearted. Brumbo tried to explain to me the signs on the ground and around, which indicated the presence of animals, and though I listened attentively, I confess I did not really understand what he was saying. We were up before sunrise and, after a quick handful of food, again struck out towards the hills to the south. Surprisingly, I felt little strain in my legs when I awoke. Perhaps it was the relaxed approach.

Relaxed walking or not, by the time we started walking up the hillside I could certainly feel my legs beginning to protest. I was conscious of my pace dropping but as it appeared we were ahead of schedule, Amazon brought the pace of the others down to mine and we continued over one hill, the next and down it to a valley where I could see a beaten earth road snaking through.

Amazon took us to a vantage point overlooking the road where there were numerous well spaced rocks large enough to hide the group. After the group had checked around to ensure everything was safe they lay down on one side of the road about twenty yards from it and fifteen to twenty feet above. Each man knew where to go and spaced out some twenty feet from each other except for Amazon, Brother and me. We three settled down side by side behind a series of boulders at the highest point and I could see to my left the valley road went up a fairly steep incline to disappear over the crest of the hill. The jeep and lorry coming from the capital would have to ascend the hill the other side, coming over the crest and drop down the incline into the valley. I could understand why Amazon had chosen this spot. The dust thrown up by the jeep and lorry would be seen before they crested the hill and so the group would be prepared and out of sight. As the convoy was coming down the incline it would be something less than a hundred yards away and so give the sharpshooters plenty of time and a good line of sight to do the necessary to dispense with the drivers of the vehicles. Once the drivers were dead, or wounded, the vehicles would either slew off the road or continue on for a short distance. Either way, the occupants would be at the mercy of the group's automatic rifle fire.

'Do you know if the lorry is going to be accompanied by a jeep and if so how many of the palace guard will be in the convoy?' I asked.

'Our information is that there is a single jeep with four palace guards and, as usual, one palace guard sitting beside the driver of the lorry,' she replied. 'All we have to do now is wait.'

'Would it not be better if one of your men was to go to the crest of the hill for he should be able to see the convoy approaching and give you more time to prepare?'

'No,' She said. 'There is another short valley the other side of that crest and so the amount of time we would gain would be very small. Also, the object is complete surprise and anyone looking over the crest of the hill would likely be spotted by the palace guard who will be scanning the hilltops and every area for the slightest sign of life. It is important that they are in the right place not knowing the attack is going to come. Ajani will shoot the driver of the jeep first and only when that shot is made will the others in the group open fire. No one will shoot until Ajani has fired. That's the way we do it.'

I nodded and settled down to wait. I took a sip of water from the bottle in my knapsack and got myself comfortable. It could be a long afternoon.

Indeed, the afternoon was long. I was beginning to think that my prayers had been answered and the convoy would not appear at all when I spotted a cloud of dust over the crest of the hill. I was amazed how much dust was being thrown up. If it is just two vehicles, I thought, there is no way they could create that much dust. The cloud was enormous and seemed to float up into the sky. As the jeep appeared over the crest I had the most horrible, horrible feeling. It was not fear or apprehension of the action ahead but far deeper and more sinister. Before I could stop myself

I said to Amazon: 'Do not open fire. Do nothing. Let them go through.'

She immediately looked at me in disbelief.

'I'm really serious,' I said, 'something is far from right. It is going to be a big mistake. Please do not fire. Don't do it.'

Amazon looked at me very hard indeed. Amazon's eyes seemed to penetrate into my brain. I met her gaze and repeated: 'Please trust me. I am not being a pacifist Englishman. There is something seriously, seriously wrong.'

Amazon looked away and spoke in a low voice to Brother who brought his rifle down from his shoulder and turned to look at me. His face was a mask of fury; whether it was directed at me for interfering or Amazon for preventing him concentrating upon his shooting I could not tell. Amazon spoke to him again in a very low but commanding voice. He nodded imperceptibly and turned back to look at the approaching convoy.

Confident that no attack was going to take place, I too looked at the approaching jeep, followed by a lorry. It seemed from this distance there was a driver and three palace guards in the jeep and a driver with one palace guard in the covered lorry, as Amazon's information had reported. The dust cloud coming from the back of the lorry was incredible and the back half of the lorry was made almost invisible by this dust. We kept our heads down but our eyes fixed on the convoy. As the jeep passed it was clear that although the driver was real the other three palace guards were not in fact people but dummies strapped to the seats. The lorry passed, enveloping everything in an enormous cloud of dust and I could just see at the rear of the lorry a metal contraption dragging on the earth road. This contraption must have had spikes or similar sticking into the road for it churned up the dust cloud making it impossible to see what was immediately behind the lorry. It seemed, though I was not certain, that the passenger in the lorry was a dummy as well.

The reason for the metal contraption behind the lorry then became apparent. The dust it was throwing up masked an armoured vehicle, which was bringing up the rear of the convoy, about eighty or ninety yards behind. This armoured vehicle had a large gun turret on top. It did not take a leap of imagination to realise that the jeep and lorry was bait for anyone attacking who would be blasted by the big-calibre gun on top of the armoured vehicle. Obviously the palace guard was willing to sacrifice one, or two, drivers to eliminate the ambush party. The convoy drove through the valley and disappeared around the bend in the road. The attacking group sat up and all, to a man, stared at me.

'Why did you stop us?' asked Brother.

I shrugged. 'I just knew something was not right. It was a feeling I had. Maybe the amount of dust was too great for just two vehicles. I don't know. Perhaps we were just lucky.'

Everyone got to their feet and started walking back the way we had come. Whilst the same pattern of deployment was used and the pace rapid, there was a very eerie feeling coming from everyone. It was as though they had lost enthusiasm for everything. Perhaps they did not trust themselves? I did not know. Our meals on the way back to the village were eaten in silence. There was no idle banter. At night we went to sleep and then woke up with no one saying anything. Every time I looked at Brother his eyes were boring into me and indeed the remainder of the group seemed to spend more time looking at me rather than looking at where they were going or for potential danger around us.

9

The Aftermath

We arrived back in the village, first going to the hidden cave where we all took off our combat gear. Surprisingly, my daily clothes were neatly folded up inside the cave so I too changed. On arrival in the village, each of the men disappeared to their respective huts except Amazon and Brother who went to the chief of the village. I hung around not knowing quite what to do. Both Amazon and Brother had a long conversation with the chief who looked his usual grave self, nodding from time to time and then interjecting with what appeared to be questions. Not once did any of them look at me so I felt surplus to requirement and wandered off to my hut.

I sat on my bed in the gloom of the hut thinking about what had happened. When I first came to this village I felt relaxed, if somewhat tired and aching, with everyone being friendly. Since then every villager had helped me in one way or another; even the children had made me feel a part of them all. Now, it seemed to me that things were different. I could not put my finger on it. Maybe it was the looks of the group on our way back from the aborted ambush that changed everything. I suddenly felt an outsider. The more I thought about it, the more uncomfortable I felt and the walls of the hut seemed to be drawing in and around me so I decided to go outside and get some fresh air. I went out of my hut and wandered away from the village for about half an hour, sat underneath the shade of a tree, leaning against its flimsy trunk. The sun was entering the last quarter of the day and losing its fierceness. Being outside with the smell of Africa gently wafting I began to feel less claustrophobic and more relaxed. I closed my eyes and listened to the sounds around me, slowing my breathing and letting my body go completely limp. I began to feel far more normal and wondered whether I was being realistic. It is not as though I had done anything wrong. I could just be imagining it all and at the evening mealtime everyone would be as they were before. I smiled to myself and was about to open my eyes to get up when:

'A picture of harmony,' came a voice from behind me. I turned around and saw Amazon standing quite still not an arms length away. Her posture indicated she had been watching me for some time. I had been listening to the sounds around me but had not heard her approach. There was no doubt at all that both she and Brother did have a ghostlike ability to appear and disappear at will.

'To be truthful,' I said, 'though I was beginning to feel harmonious, before that I was very disturbed indeed.' She looked at me and tipped her head to one side in an enquiring way. 'I felt that after the aborted ambush everyone was against me or perhaps suspected me of something. I was therefore feeling very uncomfortable and not at all happy. Sitting here in the late afternoon sun has improved me and I was hoping that everything could carry on as it had before.'

Amazon moved in front of me and sat down on the ground cross-legged. She put her hands on her lap and looked at me straight in the eyes.

'I don't think things will carry on quite as they have been before. You have saved our lives and although we are grateful we are also afraid.'

'Why are you afraid?' I asked. 'The palace guard had no

idea you were there and I do not believe we were detected when we came back to the village. The only difference is that other tribes who were expecting to have a free handout of food will not get any this week.'

'No,' she said, 'you misinterpret fear. Tell me, and it's quite important, how many times have you had these feelings before, the feelings that made you believe there was danger?' Before I could answer she continued. 'To my certain knowledge you have had at least three such experiences. The first was when you did not approach what would seem to anyone to be a rescue party after the plane had crashed; then, secondly at our weekly festive meeting when one of the villagers was punished; and now at the ambush when none of us, and we are all very experienced, had any apprehension at all that something could possibly be wrong.'

'Quite honestly,' I replied, 'I hadn't thought of it like that. So far as I'm aware I've never had any ability to foretell the future or particular apprehension that events could be wrong. I think it is just coincidence.'

'We really do not believe that,' she said. I raised an eyebrow over the 'we' and she waved her hand. 'I will explain more later. For the moment please think carefully. Has there been any time in your life when you have not done something, or not made a decision for reasons you could not, at that time, explain?'

I thought back but nothing sprang to mind. I closed my eyes and then did remember one very small incident, which might have some bearing. I really did not think it did but by the same token Amazon seemed intent on pursuing the subject so the very least I could do was to give such help as I could.

'There is only one time where such apprehension could possibly have played a part. I was about to sign up to a personal deal that seemed on the face of it, and with the supporting figures, very advantageous; indeed a virtually no-lose situation. I was presented with the final papers on a Friday and went carefully over them during the weekend, and late on the Sunday I felt that this deal was just not for me at all. I therefore did not sign up on the Monday and, as a result, incurred considerable wrath from my fellow would-be partners. In fact it turned out to be a disaster and everyone lost far more money than they first invested. To my certain knowledge one is still paying off his debt to avoid bankruptcy. I don't know if that counts as the sort of feelings you mean.'

She nodded slowly. 'Yes indeed I think it is. Let me explain a little more about the village. As in most villages in my country we are divided into four very loose groups. There are the wise people who make the decisions for the whole village, the hunter warriors, the workers and the thinkers. The wise are normally the elders of the village for with age and experience comes wisdom. The chief, you have seen, is the head of the wise and although it seems he makes the decisions and runs the village, in fact he is just the mouth-piece for the other wise men and women. The hunter warriors are those who prove themselves in their youth able to hunt and are the best at hunting animals and if necessary fighting.' She smiled. 'Ajani and I are hunter warriors, in case you haven't guessed. Then there are the workers. These are the people who do not fall naturally into the other groups but do most of the work around the village. I hasten to add that these groups are very loose and we all help one another so the mere fact someone is wise or a hunter warrior would not stop them carrying out the most menial tasks or assisting any other workers at any time.'

She then took her eyes off me and looked into the far distance as though steeling herself to carry on. After a while she looked back and smiled. 'Now I come to the difficult bit. The thinkers. These are very few in number, sometimes none at all, but often only one or two in any village. If you know your own ancient history then you might recognise what I'm about to say as being what ancient Britain's used to call "dreamers".' I did indeed know what dreamers were. They were usually women who were able to dream the future. I was surprised such an ancient belief still abounded over two thousand years later.

'The thinkers do not necessarily have dreams as to the future. They certainly do not tell fortunes or read omens from leaves or bones. They are simply able to keep an open mind about everything and dispassionately look at all the options, which often lead them to a view that is different from everyone else. They do not have visions, as such, but certainly feelings; feelings very similar to those you have demonstrated. The wise often consult the thinkers and between them decisions are made which are beneficial to the whole village. Occasionally, and I have to say it is very occasional indeed, the thinkers disagree with the wise and if this is so then normally the thinkers' view prevails. The thinkers in all the villages are treated with particular respect because of their gifts although they are not given extra priv-ileges, nor can they shirk any work that has to be done.'

Amazon looked at me to see if I understood. I nodded slowly but didn't know quite how to respond or indeed why she was actually telling me all this.

'I have discussed this very carefully with the chief who has consulted the wise and also the thinker. We have only one thinker in this village – Vana.' I raised an eyebrow as if to indicate 'and who is Vana'? when Amazon continued. 'She is the woman who first helped you at the well and then gave you the bucket and cloth to bathe with.'

Well I'm blessed, I thought, Graceful Young Lady is a thinker. Not at all surprised really. She certainly had an air about her. It didn't take much reflection to realise she was something special.

'I have also talked to Vana to get her advice and she has

persuaded me the way forward. From the outset Vana believed you were a little different – not just a skinny Englishman!' At this Amazon's face broke into a broad grin. 'She said you had talents and was not at all surprised when she found out you were an exceptional shot with both a rifle and a handgun. She believes it would be very beneficial to the village if you and she initially got to know each other better and exchange thoughts and ideas. I have no idea where this is going to lead but Vana has never steered us wrong yet and so I would ask whether you would consider spending time with her.

Well, on any view Graceful Young Lady was a joy to the eye and if indeed she was a thinker I could not see any problem spending time with her, swapping ideas, if that is what was required. Whilst I was fairly confident I would not be classed as a thinker as well, at least the time I spent with Graceful Young Lady would mean I would not be one of the hunter warriors and so have to go out on another killing expedition. Furthermore, as she was very much respected, although I would not wish such respect to be rubbed off on me, nonetheless association with her may well mean the group who seemed so far away from me on the trip back to the village would no longer believe I was a pariah.

'I am more than happy to spend time with Vana if that is what you think is best, if indeed she is willing to waste her time with a skinny Englishman and we are able to communicate meaningfully.'

'Good,' Amazon said. 'Do not worry about communication with Vana. She can speak English far better than I can.' I marvelled at this, indeed believed it was impossible for Amazon's English was really excellent. 'I think it will be best for all of us at this moment and let us see where it takes us. Go on back to your hut. It will not be long before the evening meal.'

With that, she stood up, looked down at me with a smile

and wandered sedately off towards the village. After a few moments I too got up and went back to my hut.

As I walked in I was greeted by a number of oil lamps lit around the edges of the hut, a small low table set to one side upon which there were bowls of food and drink with Vana sitting across the table as if waiting for me. Before I could think of an appropriate comment Vana said:

'Welcome, I hope you had a good conversation with Sabra and that you are in agreement with my suggestion that we get to know each other much better.'

'Thank you for the welcome,' I said, 'I am more than happy to get to know you better. Indeed bearing in mind your position in the village it would be a privilege for me to talk to you. I am far from sure though whether you can get as much pleasure or information from me as I will surely get from you and your company.'

She laughed and her whole face lit up showing a beauty far more delicate than Amazon's but equally compelling.

'I thought that if we were going to get to know each other better it would be best to start off straight away, and rather than eat with everyone else tonight, we can have a private meal. Come and sit down.'

I went to the table and sat down opposite her and she handed me a bowl of food with a spoon. I looked around and saw three buckets, one brimming with water and some rugs or towels against the wall of the hut. Before I could enquire as to the reason, she said, 'Come on, eat up and tell me all about your life.'

I took a mouthful of food and slowly chewed it, looking at her as she too watched me. 'What you do not want to know,' I replied 'is *all* about my life. It is at best boring and often embarrassing. I am happy to give you a synopsis.' She nodded and I gave her a rough breakdown of my youth, schooling, university, career to date and general activities. She was particularly interested in my sailing boat

128

experiences and indicated that she had always envied anyone
who could go out on the sea, far away from land, for that,
she felt, would give the greatest tranquillity of life free from
interruptions and distractions. I didn't think it was an appropriate time to tell her that the sea, although in itself beautiful, could be nasty and vicious and a reefed down sailboat
battling against ten to twelve foot waves cannot be described
as anything like tranquillity. Vana asked questions from
time to time, probing a little deeper, particularly in areas
I was trying to skirt over. It was all done light-heartedly
and in Vana's friendly, almost intimate, way. The meal had
long since finished and the bowls of jungle juice emptied
before I had concluded my little story.

'Now,' I said, 'how about you? Your life history with all
the details.' I smiled and she laughed once again.

'All in good time,' she said. 'We do not wish to rush into
anything. There is much to learn for both of us.'

With that she stood up, picked up the table and moved
it to the side of the hut. She walked across and picked up
one of the towels and laid it on the floor. She then carried
two of the buckets and placed one each end of the towel.

'Come and stand in the middle here,' she said, indicating
the centre of the towel. I frowned, not understanding what
she was intending.

'Didn't Sabra say you must trust me?' My frown deepened. 'Well, she should have. You must trust me. I am going
to trust you. Come and stand here.' She almost commanded
and pointed to the centre of the towel. Like a lamb, I obeyed
and stood in the centre of the towel looking at her. I realised
that she was tall, if not as tall as Amazon, certainly getting
close to six feet. She put her hands each side of my face
and looked deeply into my eyes. I cannot say I felt hypno-
tised but there was a sense of calmness emanating from her,
almost soporific. She let her hands drop slowly down my
neck and across my shoulders, down my arms to the tips of

my fingers and she pulled my hands towards her, looking down at them. She then put my arms down and started unbuttoning my shirt. Before I could protest or take any action she had the shirt off my back and walked behind me.

'You really do not know how to bathe properly, even for an Englishman,' she said.

She walked back in front of me and with a frown on her face, said, 'Will I have to teach you everything? This is going to be really hard work. Just stay where you are and do not move. Do not make life more difficult for me than I can see it already is.'

Before I could take all this in she undid my trousers and pulled them down, tugging my ankles out of the legs of the trousers. I stood there before her completely naked. She looked me up and down.

'Well, I suppose you're not that dirty bearing in mind you've been on a three-day walk. You should though have had a wash down when you returned rather than lazing about under a tree enjoying the good life. Now watch me carefully so you know how to do it properly in future.'

She looked down into the empty bucket and pulled out a flannel cloth with a lump of soap, soaked the cloth in the water and went behind me, gently soaping me down from head to foot. When she had done this she went to the side of the hut to pick up the third bucket, tipped a small amount of water in it, rinsed out the flannel and then wiped me down slowly. The water was cool and relaxing. After my daily trek I felt totally relaxed and I could almost have gone to sleep on my feet. She then turned to my front and with a 'watch carefully' repeated the exercise even more delicately than before. When done, she picked up another towel and gently dried me from head to foot.

'We will not have the hair done tonight, this can wait until tomorrow. Now, you have seen how it should be done, let me see if you have learnt anything.'

She gently pushed me off the towel, stepped in the middle and slipped off her garment, throwing it to one side. I was mesmerised by the gracefulness and beauty of her body and was rooted to the spot.

'This is not a peep show,' she said, 'there's time for all that later. I want to be clean as well. Get on with it.'

As instructed, I picked up a flannel and soap and gently washed her back from head to foot, trying my hardest to be as delicate as she was. To me even my most careful admin-istrations seemed rough and course compared with Vana's delicacy, and when I got to her front she said, 'Don't you miss anything; and I do mean anything!' I did as I was bid and the result was certainly a slightly cleaner Graceful Young Lady. When I had finished towelling her down I helped carry the buckets back to the side of the hut, picked up the towel on the floor and hung it, with the other one, over one of the pegs to dry. She moved close to me once again holding my face between her hands, this time gently caressing my forehead, cheeks and neck with one hand whilst the other held me firm. She pulled my head down and kissed me very lightly. I felt passion flame up inside me. It seemed unseemly but I could not stop myself. I wanted to grab her. But I restrained myself. She pulled back from the kiss and looked deep into my eyes, running a finger across my lips.

'Do not be the frigid Englishman,' she said, 'just relax and go with the flow. There is much we both have to learn.'

With that she kissed me again, this time with more passion, more determination. I responded with equal passion and we came together in a deep embrace, her body pressed hard against mine as if she wished to get inside of me. Her arms gripped my shoulders and pulled me tight. It seemed like a long time, or no time at all, I could not tell what time had elapsed as it seemed suspended, when she pulled gently away from me.

'Oh that is better,' she said. You are indeed human. I do

not have to fear you as an evil spirit.' She giggled and pulled me over towards the mattress where we both lay down in a close embrace. She sensed I wanted to move forward very quickly but she gently restrained me and ran her fingers lightly over my back, shoulders and down my legs as if trying to relax me but in truth it inflamed me even more. I held myself back and let her continue. Her fingers eventually reached my manhood and I thought I was going to explode. Before I could do so, she stopped, took my hand and placed it over her left breast, pressing it hard and kissing me once again. The effect did not calm me but slowed me a little. I too now realised it would be foolish to rush. This was heaven and I might never be here again so I mentally took a grip on my straining and pulsating body, forcing it to relax and enjoy; enjoy it certainly did.

Once I had managed to calm myself we seemed to spend forever exploring each other's bodies. Every touch was electric and sensational. Every kiss harmony and pleasure. Eventually, at just the right moment, she rolled me on my back sat astride me and slowly lowered herself on my engorged manhood. I thought I was going to explode but she kept ice still until I calmed and then slowly, very slowly started to gyrate and rub herself on me. She looked deep into my eyes and I held both her breasts gently, one in each hand, her nipples hard and straining. As she slowly rotated faster so gradually she started moving up and down, moving me towards the end game and eventually, too soon, she reached a pulsating climax, which triggered me to do the same. Spent and drained, she lent forward and laid on me, keeping me inside of her by closing her legs tight. I held her as our breathing slowed to normal. In the warmth of the evening we had both perspired and she felt erotically slippery to my touch.

We stayed like this for quite a long time when eventually I shrivelled and slipped out of her. We laughed and she rolled off me.

'Oh,' she said, 'that's not so good. You cannot stay inside very long.'

'After that,' I said, 'I'm surprised it has not broken off!'

This sent her into a peal of laughter and when it subsided she said:

'I'm only joking. You were not bad at all. In fact I have to say I enjoyed it very much indeed. With a little bit more practice from you I could become the envy of the village.'

'I would like to take from that,' I said, 'that this is not the first and last time.'

She playfully punched me in the arm and laughed even more. 'If you're a good boy, who knows where it might lead. Now I think we ought to have a drink and relax a little, don't you?'

I didn't know about the relax a bit. I was quite frankly whacked out. A day's walk was enough but with these shenanigans as well I was surprised my eyes were still open. She got up, went to the table and picked up the two drinking bowls, handing me one. She then went back behind the table to produce a jug of jungle juice, pouring some into my bowl and hers as well. We both took a deep drink and she laid her bowl down beside me, going to the bucket of water, dipping a flannel into it, and came back to where I was lying.

'Let me cool you down,' she said.

'No,' I said. 'That is not fair, you must be first. I am an Englishman. Ladies are always first!'

She laughed at this and handed me a flannel so I stood up and gently wiped her down and, getting the towel, dried her off. I then did the same to myself, handing over the flannel to her for her to do my back. When finished, she returned the towel to the side of the hut and came to lay down beside me. She propped herself on one elbow, lent forward, kissed me very gently and picked up her bowl.

'I knew you would be a good omen as soon as I saw you.

You are different. Okay, skinny, I grant you. We can work on that. I can feed you up!'

'It's a great advantage of being lithe,' I retorted.

This sent her off into more laughter and I just had to join in.

'Are you going to tell me about your life and the village?' I asked.

'Of course, I will tell you everything, but not now. This is not the right time and anyway I've got other things to do.'

With that, she put her bowl down and moved over to me, pulling me close to and started kissing my eyes, my nose and then my mouth.

'Just a minute,' I said, 'the mind is willing, indeed over willing, but I'm afraid the body is a bit weak.'

She giggled. 'Don't you worry one little bit. It's amazing what I can do. Besides which, that jungle juice, as you call it, is one of my special remedies. You'll see.'

She moved back to me and continued with her kissing and caressing. Indeed it was amazing what she, or maybe the jungle juice, could do. We again very slowly and quietly made passionate love. I can only call it 'love' because that is how it felt. With a smile on my face and my arms around Vana I fell into a deep and totally untroubled sleep.

I awoke the following morning to find Vana had gone and the hut cleared of the tables, bowls, buckets and towels of the previous night. I had not felt her leave me nor heard her moving around and as I dressed quickly I wondered if it was all just a beautiful, beautiful dream.

I went out of my hut with my eating bowl and spoon and walked to the circle where Vana was standing looking towards me. She greeted me with a big smile.

'Please tell me it was not a wonderful dream,' I said.

She laughed. 'Well if it was, we both dreamt of the same!

Come on, let's have something to eat.' With that she took hold of my hand and pulled me towards where the women were dishing out the morning meal. I realised that I was just a little late, but there was still food available. As the food was dished out to me so the women gave me a knowing look and shy smile. Vana had already eaten and so I sat by myself to eat my food. When I'd finished and washed up my bowl and spoon I returned to the circle to seek out Vana who was drawing water from the well.

'Today, we both have jobs to do and I suggest you help me. It is women's work but there is no shame in helping.'

'I will be more than happy to give it a try,' I said, 'but I do not think I will be able to balance a jar of water on my head!'

'No, that is certainly a woman's art and not for a man to even try. We are going to do some gardening in the vegetable patch. You go there and I will take this water back to my hut and get some tools for you.'

I approached the large vegetable patch where a number of women were already working. As I arrived so one young woman looked up, saw me and turned her back to me as she hurried away. I felt this was rather odd but thought no more about it.

The whole day was spent tilling the soil, removing weeds and, under the guidance of the women there, picking some vegetables for the evening meal. Everyone was as friendly as before, if anything more friendly, and there was much laughter and talking. At one stage they all burst into song and I tried to join in but my efforts were so pathetic that they all fell about with laughter and totally destroyed the musical moment. I don't know if the prior evening had anything to do with it but I felt I was walking on air all day. I could not believe that simple, physical tasks could lead to such joy and pleasure. If anyone had asked me at that moment, I would have happily said I could spend my whole life just doing this. Reality, of course, is always different. Fate was not going to allow me to be a farmer.

The evening meal was eaten alongside Vana, Amazon and Brother. They talked generally, in English, about the village and what needed to be done over the following weeks. Then Brother turned to me and said: 'Are you comfortable with Vana?'

I was not quite sure what he meant by 'comfortable'. Whether he was making reference to her as a person or the activities we had engaged in the previous evening I could not tell. Also, I felt it was a little indelicate asking such questions in front of Vana. Nonetheless, I smiled and replied: 'Perfectly.' I turned and looked at Vana. 'She is the most perfect of women, most wise and instructive.' I swear Vana blushed at this though it was impossible to tell from her dark features. Amazon, on the other hand, gave me a very old-fashioned look.

When the meal had finished I returned to my hut and in the gloom felt there was something very different. As my eyes accustomed to the light I saw that my single blanket on top of straw had disappeared and in its place was a fine double grass-filled mattress, which looked plump and inviting. There was also a low table on which sat an unlit oil lamp, two extra bowls and a neat pile of clothing to one side. I went over to examine the clothing when Vana entered the hut.

'What are you doing rooting around in my clothing?' she asked, 'are you kinky?'

'Well I could be, if that's what you wanted,' I replied, 'but I was actually trying to find out what was in the pile and why it was here.'

'Well,' she said, 'it is far too soon for you to come and spoil my hut. It is full of delicate and important things and I do not want you blundering around and breaking anything.

Therefore I decided the best thing for the moment is for me to stay with you in your hut. That is, of course, if you do not mind.'

'Well,' I replied, 'I have to think about it. I am now quite used to my own company and I don't really want strangers blundering around here.'

I'm afraid I could not keep the laughter out of my voice and she approached me, punching me fiercely in the chest.

'You can't tease me,' she said, 'you would beg me to stay here if I asked you.'

'Possibly,' I said, 'but thankfully it seems we are both of like mind at this moment. However,' I continued, 'is it usual for men and women to stay in the same hut if they have not gone through a ceremony of marriage or similar?'

'We are very free here. We do not believe in putting unnecessary constraints upon anyone unless it is for the good of the whole village. It is true, there is a ceremony of marriage or joining before men and women stay in the same hut on a permanent basis but it is not at all unusual for there to be temporary arrangements if it suits the people concerned and does not offend anyone in the village. I have no father, mother or siblings to be offended and it seems to me the whole village is delighted that I'm turning you into a half decent human being. You would never have entertained us with your fine singing if it wasn't for me!'

'If there is a compliment in there somewhere, I'm afraid it passed me by,' I retorted. 'I do not pretend to have an operatic voice but it has a delicacy that obviously you all did not appreciate this afternoon for I felt you were less than charitable to my efforts.'

'Let's be charitable then,' she replied, 'you were bloody awful. If you were a dog I would have had to put you down to relieve you of your obvious misery.'

Recognising a good deal of truth in this, I burst out laughing; she joined in, clinging to me and shaking with mirth. I held her tight and we started slowly kissing. I gently pulled away.

'When are we going to start talking about you?' I asked.

Vana slipped off her dress and said: 'Now if you like. But there again, you may wish to defer it until tomorrow or even the next day.'

I certainly didn't need a second bidding and we sank onto the mattress together in a cocoon of desire.

We spent the next few days mostly in each other's company, working in the village or taking long strolls out into the countryside. Our discussions ranged from everything to nothing and gradually Vana told me her life story. In essence, she was an only child. It was most unusual for village parents to have just one child but for reasons no one could explain her mother stopped conceiving after Vana was born. This lack of other children, far from driving Vana's parents apart, drew them together and they were a very happy family. Her father was a hunter warrior and much revered in the village. He was a very kind and considerate man, being the first to help anyone in trouble or need. When Vana was just twelve years old her father was killed. Apparently a village about five days away was raided by soldiers or mercenaries who took everything of value including all the animals and food, destroying the crops. The villagers were starving. Vana's father went to see if he could help but for reasons no one could understand the soldiers or mercenaries returned and killed her father. Apparently, he put up a fantastic fight, killing six before he himself was mortally wounded. The shock of this sent her mother into spasms of sickness and she eventually died.

At that time missionaries and workers from England were going around the countryside preaching to and helping villagers and, learning of the death of Vana's mother, one persuaded the chief of the village to allow Vana to go to the capital to an English school cum-orphanage. It was at this school she learnt to speak English so well, and to read and write. It seemed her education was fairly wide, for on many of the topics we touched upon she had deep knowledge and understanding.

During the latter part of school life she began to get visions. These were not visions in the accepted sense but more a feeling of what was going to happen and whether something was the right thing to do or not. With these visions came a longing to go back to her village and even though she had every opportunity of a good job in the capital she returned home. She naturally explained to the chief and elders why she wanted to stay in the village rather than have a job in the capital and they realised that she was a thinker.

At that time there was an old woman thinker in the village who took Vana under her wing and taught her the ways of the countryside and how to use and develop her talent. The village soon accepted Vana's ability as a thinker and she was regularly consulted by the wise. When the old woman died Vana slipped easily into her place.

She was very evasive about the subjects upon which the wise asked her opinion. She did not give me any indication of the visions or thoughts that had set her aside as a thinker. It was not as though she was trying to keep secrets, merely a demonstration of her natural and beautiful modesty. As each day passed I wondered more and more why she was bothering to spend time with me. Initially I had assumed it was because Amazon and Brother wanted to use my talents for shooting in the group and that they thought Vana could persuade me. However, she never approached the subject or even mentioned the group and when I tried to probe in this area she merely smiled and waved her hand dismissively as though she was not part of the hunter warrior group and therefore what they did was of no concern to her. I could not believe this was so and eventually one afternoon when we were walking far from the village and she was explaining the various uses to which the villagers could put plants and shrubs scattered around I tackled the subject head-on.

'I really do not want you to take this the wrong way,' I said. 'I am in fact very reluctant to raise the subject at all but I really must. I am not stupid enough to believe I am the catch of the century whereas you undoubtedly are, therefore I have to ask why are you spending so much time with me? Is it because Sabra and Ajani want me to do something for them?'

She looked away from me and was silent for a very long time. I was not quite sure whether I had embarrassed her or whether she knew this question was going to arise but did not want to face it immediately.

'Believe me,' she said, 'I am with you only because I want to be. There is nothing anyone could have said to convince me to do something I did not want to do. You may not be the catch of the century but I was attracted to you from the moment I first saw you. I knew you had a depth and talents that were not immediately obvious.' She smiled and looked me straight in the eyes. 'Besides, I am a thinker and surely a thinker must recognise these things.'

'Thank you for that,' I said. 'But this does not explain why you actually decided to spend your time with me.'

'It is indeed true that Sabra and Ajani approached me and told me about the feelings you had which saved their lives. They were very frightened of you and, perhaps, the power that you held. They asked me to speak to you to find out whether you were human or a spirit.' She looked at me with a very serious face. 'Do not laugh. We are all educated in this village but nonetheless everyone believes there are such things as spirits. There is so much unexplained in life not to have this belief. We live in a harsh countryside with our lives continually governed by the weather and in times of drought or prolonged rains or strong winds or dust storms our whole livelihood could be wiped out.'

She slipped her arm through mine and we continued walking very slowly. Her head was down as if she was thinking about what to say next or rather how to say what was needed to be said.

'Well,' she said, 'I have certainly proved that you are human!' She leaned over and squeezed me gently between the legs, laughing. 'Whether you have the same powers I do, I really cannot tell yet. I don't think it matters. You are who you are and I am who I am. I simply cannot believe you are any threat or danger to the village; in fact everything that has gone on so far since you arrived shows that you are an asset and certainly no liability although your hut-building skills need more than a little attention!'

We walked a little further and she stopped. Turning to me, she said, 'Sabra and Ajani did not ask me to convince you to join their group. They didn't need to for everyone would like you to join. Whether you do so or not is completely your decision. I certainly would not pressure you, nor indeed, now, would anyone else. I can certainly understand your lack of desire to kill another human being even if that human being is evil and has committed many, many crimes and atrocities. I feel the same way. I cannot think of what would be needed for me to take another human life. Remember, my father was killed unnecessarily but I still have no desire for revenge. We though have to be realistic. The government of this country is corrupt and destroying the people. Those who have a greater understanding than I about politics believe the only way to get change is by overthrowing the government and this is bound to be by bloody revolution. I can understand the tactics currently being employed and it seems to be working. The more palace guards killed and the more stolen goods taken from them encourages the people to believe there can be an alternative to Baumge. I

141

have spoken to politicians who slavishly follow Baumge's will not because they want to but because of fear. They make excuses to themselves and certainly, like Hitler's generals, would say they are simply following orders. This is of course pathetic in your eyes but believe me, you really cannot understand the fear which abounds in this country. I know that being a thinker I can, perhaps, perceive more than others but I can tell you with absolute certainty when I'm in the capital, and thankfully that is very infrequently, I, like others – certainly Sabra – can smell, even taste, the fear in the people. So even the smallest victory of the various groups around the countryside brings hope to the people. I have spent days contemplating the problem but I'm afraid I do not have enough power to look into the future to foretell when and how any revolution could take place.'

She turned away from me and started walking slowly again, this time towards the village. I caught up with her and we walked silently side-by-side. There was nothing I could really say. If Vana did not have the power to foretell when any revolution would take place or indeed if it would be successful then my meagre abilities, if in fact I had any, would be useless.

She broke the silence. 'As you know, the adult men and women in the village are being taught by the group to fight. Some are better than others but all want to learn to prepare themselves for the day when they might be needed. I understand this is happening in other villages as well. It is not beyond the bounds of possibility that the palace guard have got to hear of this for their actions on whole villages have recently increased and become more bloody. If I was to advise you at all, and I hasten to say I'm not encouraging you or telling you what to do, I would suggest you consider using your talents to show the villagers how to shoot. Ajani holds classes once or twice a week to explain military tactics and get the villagers to shoot at targets. Since your arrival these classes have not been held for we were all uncertain how things would be with a stranger in the village. Now Ajani wants to start the classes again. It seems the majority of the villagers can't hit anything at all. Therefore with your help they may well improve.'

I thought about this. Nothing I could do or say would prevent the villagers from being trained in warlike activities and I suppose if I could help them to hit a target then at the very least they would not kill each other if they were ever involved in a revolution.

'Yes,' I said. 'I can see the sense in what you are saying. The trouble is I have no idea what I do when I shoot. It just seems to come naturally. However, I will certainly try and help the villagers for I cannot see what harm it could do.'

'I suggest then you speak to Ajani tonight at the evening meal and tell him you will help. This will please him enormously and I am certain he will welcome your assistance. How you might teach is something you have to resolve yourself.'

It seemed as though a weight had been lifted from her shoulders for she straightened up and threw both arms around my neck, giving me a big kiss. 'Now,' she said, 'let's get on with our lives.'

We returned to the village and the afternoon passed slowly away in the quiet and secure harmony I had become used to. At the evening meal I sought out Amazon and Brother and sat down to eat with them. After a respectful interval I turned to Brother.

'I understand you used to hold classes for the villagers to teach them military tactics and how to shoot. I have no knowledge at all of military tactics and so cannot help you but I will try to assist in showing the villagers how I shoot and perhaps this may make them more efficient. Are you content for me to do this?'

Brother replied immediately. 'I would certainly like you to help me where you can. What is it you would like me to do to prepare things for you?'

'Frankly at the moment,' I said, 'I have no idea.' I thought for a while and then continued. 'Whilst I seem to be able to shoot I certainly do not know how any of the guns actually work so, perhaps, we could spend a day with you teaching me how to dismantle and rebuild all the firearms you use and explain to me the various parts and what to do if things go wrong. I understand guns do jam from time to time and so it would be fairly essential for me to understand how this might occur and what to do if it does happen.'

'That is a very good idea,' said Brother. 'We will start tomorrow and I will show you everything I know and then we can discuss how you can help the villagers. They really are quite awful. The thought of taking them into any fight fills me with despair. Even some of the hunter warriors who can throw a spear or shoot an arrow straight cannot seem to master a rifle.'

After the evening meal I returned to my hut to find Vana waiting for me. I reported my brief conversation with Brother and she nodded wisely. 'I think that is very good,' she said, 'if you spend tomorrow with Ajani then between you a way can be found to help the villagers.'

The rest of the evening was spent in the now familiar pattern of gentle love-making before we both drifted off into sleep.

As dawn approached I woke up feeling a new purpose had come into my life. I felt vigorous and keen to start along this new path. I was up and dressed before Vana, which was quite unusual, and together we went out for the morning meal. When it was finished she disappeared off to help the women and I went across to Brother who had a knapsack over his shoulder and he took me to the cache of arms hidden in the cave behind the bushes. On my first and only venture into this cave I had not appreciated how big it was for the only light cast was partial through the gap made in the bushes to allow us to get in and change our clothes. Brother took me inside and lit an oil lamp before pulling the bushes back over the entrance. We walked into the cave for about fifteen or twenty yards and there was a large wooden work bench with tools obviously used to service firearms. He put the lamp down on the bench and lit several others, which gave good light to see. There were a number of racks of rifles, mostly similar to the one that I had shot so I assumed they were Kalashnikovs, a rack of handguns and a few cases of what proved to be hand grenades and ammunition. There was one large case right at the back of the cave, which Brother did not show me so I asked him what was in it.

'It is a hand-held rocket launcher,' he said. 'I know how to use it but it has never been used because we have only three rockets for it. I am trying to get more but unfortunately the palace guard does not seem to transport these very often on its lorries.'

'Do other groups in other villages have similar arms hoards?' I asked.

'They all have guns of one sort or another,' he replied, 'some more than we have, others less. There is one village about four days north of us, which is particularly well stocked. They hijacked a lorry which they thought was carrying food aid but was actually completely full of arms and equipment so they have a very good selection of different guns. They even have night vision goggles. Now, let's start with your education.'

He took a Kalashnikov off one of the racks and slowly stripped it down, pointing out every piece and explaining what it did. He then reassembled it and repeated the exercise.

He gave it to me and after some difficulty I managed to reduce the gun to its component parts and then rebuild it. I can't say I was a natural but it was a simple mechanical exercise, which, after several repeats, I seemed to master. He then went through the various guns, which were there, explaining what they were, their strengths and weaknesses. He showed me how to adjust the sights of the rifles, pointing out each was individual and how an experienced shooter could 'zero' the sights although for general shooting – and by this I took it to mean killing men – the default sight marking and grading as the gun came was good enough.

The biggest problem was the various handguns. It amazed me that automatic pistols all seemed to come apart in different ways and the components were not as similar as those of the rifles.

At noon time he produced some food from his knapsack and we ate. 'How do you think you can teach the villagers to shoot?' he asked.

'I confess I have been thinking about this since Vana raised the subject. I still really do not know but I think if I can explain to them what I see and how I feel it might concentrate their thoughts on the same and so make pulling the trigger a natural extension of the body. Apart from that I will simply have to play it by ear.'

He nodded. 'Well I have tried everything I can think of including suggesting to some of the married men that the target is their mother-in-law!' He laughed. 'Unfortunately we do not have any dragon mother-in-laws here so that did no good at all.'

We spent the remainder of the day going over everything once again with Brother testing me with questions. He explained how ammunition should be kept clean and what causes guns to jam and how to fix it. By the end of the day I felt confident that I knew enough to get me by and prob-ably over the remainder of the week when I was teaching the villagers I would become more proficient in the handling of weapons.

After the morning meal the following day, Brother and I went to the cave to collect four rifles each and he took me back to the target area where there were half a dozen village men.

'One rather important thing I failed to ask you,' I said, 'is whether all the villagers can speak English. Sabra has told me many can but it is difficult enough to teach a subject I know nothing about without having to also learn to speak your language.'

He laughed. 'I can guarantee if you spent weeks trying to learn our language you would not get very far at all. It is not a matter of just vocabulary, tenses, and so on. Much of our language is intonation of the words and the way words are grouped together. It is quite difficult even for us. These men here have been chosen as the first group because their English is good so you should have no difficulties. When we get to the villagers who can't speak English very well then I will translate for you. By that time you should have honed your teaching skills so it will be easier for all of us.'

'Okay,' I said, 'I suggest each one of these men fires individually at that target while I watch. I have to say I do not know what I'm looking for but perhaps something will spring to mind.'

I turned to the six men and greeted all warmly. They seemed pleased to be here and I got the impression that the fact I had somehow predicted problems at the aborted ambush gave me a power I could wave over them to suddenly turn them into crack shots. I did not wish to disabuse them of this and so I took on a confident air.

'It is very difficult to say why any one man can shoot and another man cannot,' I said to them. 'Each person has his own way of doing things and what is good for one may not be good for another. What I'm going to do this morning is to first ask each of you to shoot five shots at the target over there, which is some seventy-five yards away.' They all nodded. The target was about five feet in diameter with a large white circle in the centre of two feet in diameter. Whilst I did not expect too many bull's-eyes, I confidently anticipated most of them should hit the target somewhere.

'I will watch and if we work together you should get better.'

Brother loaded one of the Kalashnikovs with five rounds, adjusted the sights for the target distance and handed it to me. I gave the gun to one of the men and said: 'Lie on the ground and shoot at that target, nice and slowly please. We are not in a hurry. I just want to see what you are doing. It is not a competition. As I said, some of you are going to be better than others and there is absolutely no shame in not being a good shot.'

The man lay on the ground and adopted the standard shooting position. Well at least he remembered something Brother had told them, I thought. He then put the rifle to his shoulder and squinted down the barrel, pulling the trigger. Brother handed me a pair of binoculars from his knapsack and I looked at the target. Pristine.

'And again,' I said. Again he pulled the trigger with the same result. By the time he had exhausted all five shots only one seemed to have clipped the target. I could not detect anything obviously wrong with his prone position or the way he was holding the rifle.

One by one the other men did exactly the same with very much similar results. All the while I was thinking, 'What is it I do which they do not?' I mentally went through the process I adopted when I was shooting but could not isolate anything that I could say or do that could help these men shoot better. The only answer, if indeed there was any answer at all, was to explain to them how I felt when I was shooting.

'That was all very good,' I said 'You have the right position, you are holding the rifle well and you obviously know what to do. There is nothing wrong with your actions. Where I think the problem might well lie is in your mind.' They all looked at me with amazed expressions on their faces.

'But we all want to hit the target,' one of them said.

'It is not a matter of wanting to hit the target,' I replied, 'but drawing the target into you so you cannot miss it.' Six puzzled expressions crossed six bemused faces.

'What I want you to do is to relax your whole body and breathe very slowly. Try now.' They all started taking very deep breaths, holding the breath and letting the breath out again.

'No,' I said, 'that is taking a deep breath. What I want is slow, relaxed breaths. Just pretend for a moment you are about to drop off to sleep and your whole body is relaxed.'

'Shall we lie down then?' said one of the men.

'No, but I think it would be a good idea if we all sat down.' We all sat on the ground cross-legged and I said, 'Put your hands in your laps and just relax your body and breathe steadily and slowly. Do not force it; let it happen.'

I watched and whilst initially they were trying to force the breathing, gradually as each relaxed, their breathing slowed and became more shallow.

'By slowing your breathing you are slowing down your heart rate and so relaxing your body, leaving your mind to do what is necessary to shoot. Now keep your breathing slow but make your breaths deeper, do not rush; steady, steady.'

Each of them gradually mastered this deep yet slow breathing and I continued.

'Keep your breathing steady and imagine the target you are shooting at. As you are breathing in so the target is being brought into your eyes; into your mind; you can see nothing but the centre of the target. As you breathe out, slowly, so your finger will gently squeeze the trigger and the bullet with your breath will hit the target.'

I watched them as they went through this exercise. There was no doubt at all they were certainly trying but whether what I was saying and what they would later do would translate into them being better shots I frankly did not have a clue. All I was doing was trying to put into words what I felt and what I saw when I held the rifle to my shoulder and looked through the sights at the target.

The rest of the morning was spent with each of the men firing five shots individually at the target while I observed through the binoculars. There was no doubt at all a great improvement was shown. By the time two women came to us with jars of food for the midday meal most of the men were hitting the target and some of them the centre white circle. I felt quietly pleased.

'I thought it would be best,' said Brother, 'if we ate here rather than go back to the village.'

The two women handed out bowls of food and we set quietly eating. When everyone had finished I said: 'If you will please go to the target and take some earth and water from your drinking bowls to make up a mud paste then fill in the holes in the target.' Turning to Brother I asked, 'Do you have any paint to whiten the centre circle?'

Brother nodded and leaned under the table, producing a jar of white substance.

The men went to the target and started repairing it. Brother looked at me and said, 'There is a definite improvement. I am really pleased. You have done well. However, I wonder, whether they would be any good under fire.'

'No one can tell,' I replied, 'until they are placed in that position. Indeed I would not know myself if I could still hit anything if someone was shooting at me. So far they appear to have learnt to be able to shoot reasonably straight in a calm atmosphere and so, I suppose, we must test this a little more. Let us put five bullets in each Kalashnikov and let them all shoot together to see whether the noise of a fellow shooter will distract them.'

We loaded up the rifles and the men came back. I gave them each a rifle and said, 'Now you must all lie down and shoot at the target together. By that I do not mean you have to synchronise.' Frowns appeared upon their faces. 'What I want you to do is to shoot independently, each at your own speed, in your own time. Pay no attention to anyone around you. Remember it is just you and the target. Your breathing will bring the target into view and exhaling with squeezing the trigger will speed the bullet to the centre white circle of the target.'

They all lay down and started to shoot. It was clear after a couple of rounds the sounds of those around them shooting was a distraction.

'In your own time,' I shouted. 'Ignore the sounds around you. Ignore the people around you. Just do it slowly and carefully. Remember, hit the target. There is no race on here.'

That seemed to calm them and as I watched through the binoculars so more shots were hitting the target. Obviously, I could not tell which shooter was doing best but the overall impression was that they were not distracted by the noise and activity around them.

When they had finished, Brother gave them five more rounds and they loaded the rifles themselves and went on to do the exercise once again. I turned to Brother.

'How much ammunition do we have? Is there sufficient to play around a little?'

He looked at me strangely. 'We have plenty of ammunition. If we are getting short then I can get some from other villages. Ammunition is of no concern. Do with it what you will.

I picked up one of the Kalashnikovs and loaded the

magazine full. I put it down on the table and when everyone had finished shooting their five rounds we gave them another five rounds and told them to repeat doing what they were doing before but more calmly and steadily. They started shooting. After each had fired two rounds I picked up the Kalashnikov from the table and walked a little way behind them, slipping off the safety catch. I fired a full burst about ten yards in front of them raking the bullets across the ground and keeping my finger on the trigger until the magazine was empty. To a man, they stopped firing and all visibly tensed.

'Wait,' I said. 'Turn around and look at me. They all did as I bid. 'Now,' I said, 'I have asked you to concentrate on you, on yourself, on your own space. Ignore everything and everyone around you. You hear a few bangs and you are startled. If you are thinking only of yourself and your target nothing should distract you. You should hear nothing. Or if you do hear something it must immediately go out of your mind.'

I reloaded the Kalashnikov and went back behind them. 'Carry on shooting,' I said.

They turned around, brought guns back up to their shoulders and started firing. It was absolutely clear every one of them was tense, waiting for me to shoot over their shoulders. I did not shoot.

'Relax!' I screamed. 'Relax. You are waiting for something to happen and it may not happen. It might be worse than you think. Concentrate on you. On the target. You and the target are one; breathe it in.'

They finished off their five shots but I guessed, although I did not observe the target, that the results were not good. Brother and I gave them five more rounds each and told them to continue firing at will. This time they were better and when I loosed off a short burst over their heads there was barely a flinch.

We repeated this exercise until about an hour before sunset. Again there was considerable improvement. The noise of me shooting did not distract any more. The target was being hit more and I sensed that each one of the men felt very confident with what he could do. I then gave each five more rounds and asked them to load of the magazines. They did this and I said, 'Lay the rifles down on the ground where you have been, sit up and listen to me. You have done exceptionally well. I am really, really proud of you. You are shooting as well as any soldier who has been training for months. You have the right attitude and right approach. You have shown me you can ignore distractions. I want you all to run to the centre of the village and then back here five times. I want you to run as quickly as you can and as soon as you have finished your five circuits shoot at the target.' I pointed to one of the men. 'You go first,' I said. He jumped to his feet and started running towards the village. When he had returned on his first circuit I sent the second man off; and when they both returned, the third, and so on.

The first man came back out of breath and panting. I told him to lie down, concentrate and shoot at the target. I watched through binoculars. His first shot could have gone anywhere. It certainly did not hit the target. I said nothing and looked down at him. He realised his beating heart and strained lungs were affecting his ability to relax and breathe steadily. I could see him concentrating hard to resolve this conflict. His last two shots hit the target. The second man returned and he too had difficulty calming himself but eventually mastered it.

When they had all finished they sat on the ground with rifles over their knees looking at me.

'You will have seen that although you were out of breath and with lungs straining and heart pounding you could still use your mind to overcome this and make your breathing steady and slow. All you have to do now is to remember your mind can overcome everything. If you think positively then you can achieve what ever you want to do. I think we've had enough for today so please can you give Ajani the rifles back, pick up the spent cartridges and patch up the target for the next group tomorrow and then you can go and have your evening meal. Thank you very much for helping me. It was a pleasure to be with you today.'

When they had completed these tasks Brother and I carried the rifles back to the cave. He lit oil lamps and we cleaned the rifles, checking them over before putting them back in the racks.

'That was a real success today,' said Brother. 'Do you think that they will be able to do as well if they are under fire?'

'I really do not know,' I replied. 'I have not the foggiest idea as to whether I could shoot at all, let alone straight, if I was being fired at. Only time will tell. At the very least if they have to use the rifles in anger they should not be shooting each other. That is of itself a plus.'

Brother nodded and said, 'Another group tomorrow. I hope we have the same success.

When the rifles were cleaned and put away we trudged back to the village circle to get our evening food. Vana and I sat alone.

'How did it go?' She asked.

'Surprisingly,' I replied, 'rather well. I have no idea if it was my teaching or the fact that they believed I could teach them but by the time we finished they could all hit the target. I was honoured. Some of them were budding reasonable shots.'

She smiled. 'Everyone will be pleased and after your success today they will be queueing up at your door for special lessons. Perhaps you can charge!'

'I confess in all my life I never thought for one moment

I could open up a private enterprise teaching people how to shoot. It is not a bad idea though. I wonder what I could charge? For six lessons a cow perhaps; a goat; even maybe their most eligible daughter!'

Vana lent forward and punched me in the chest. I'm sure it was meant to be a playful punch but her slim, graceful frame carried more weight than I had anticipated and I gasped for breath.

'You have no thoughts along that line at all,' she said. 'Remember you are mine.'

With that we both broke into laughter and went across to Amazon and Brother to discuss the format for the following day.

On the next day we went through exactly the same exercise except that on arrival not only were there six new pupils but also all eight of the mercenary group stood around watching. I was more than a little embarrassed with this audience.

'Why are they here?' I asked Brother.

'They simply want to see your technique,' He replied. 'They are all good shots but everyone can learn something. Just ignore them and carry on.'

This I did and soon forgot the audience, concentrating upon the new faces. This batch, and indeed those who followed, all improved, and I was quite enjoying myself as a teacher.

At the end of the week as we were eating our usual festive meal sitting around the circle waiting to hear from the chief, Brother said, 'Do you think we should carry on next week with a fresh batch of villagers?'

I thought about this for a moment and replied, 'No. I think it might be a good idea if we were to choose the best, say, six shots and spend a couple of days with them trying to hone their skills. It seemed to me that several could turn out to be excellent and this must be an asset to you. After that we can take the worst six and work on them. As you have been watching me for a week and I know you are excellent with both rifle and handgun, we can divide the groups into half for each of us to teach. This will have the added advantage that more will be going on with more distraction so they will have to concentrate even harder to improve.'

'Good,' he said. 'We will do that. We can have a side bet as to whose group will turn out the best.'

'Absolutely not,' I replied. 'Whilst I'm sure you would not pick the best for yourself, nonetheless I believe you are actually better than I am.'

He laughed. It was amazing how Brother had changed, certainly towards me, over the last week or so. I always had the feeling there was some antagonism there and he rarely smiled in my presence. Now, he seemed completely relaxed and more than willing to join in conversations and exchange humorous comments although from time to time I still had the feeling he was looking at me as if he didn't quite trust me.

The following week went according to plan: at the beginning of the week were the best shots; in the second half, the poorest ones. The only difference was that the good shots demanded that I should demonstrate my own skills so they could watch and emulate. I was a little reluctant to do this at first for whilst I had shown a high ability to hit the target where I wanted, I was unsure as to whether I could replicate it. Nonetheless I followed their bidding and found there was no change at all. By simply concentrating on the target it became large in my mind and my eye, and squeezing the trigger sent the bullet to the centre unerringly. The fact I could actually demonstrate and prove that what I was saying would work helped enormously for they all tried much harder. I was beginning to feel very confident that those in the village, if called to arms, would account for themselves extremely well assuming, that is, they did not panic under the pressure of someone else firing at them. It was in this area I could not assist at all for I had never been under gunfire and so did not know whether I could hold my cool and do that which may be necessary. I asked Brother to explain what it was like to be under fire and he did this very carefully but whether it would make any difference at the end of the day only time and experience would tell.

10

The Turning

At the end of this training week, during the festive meal, I was sitting with Amazon, Brother and Vana. We were discussing things generally, with no particular subject, when Amazon said to me:

'In a couple of days we are going to see a white farmer. He is trying to help our organisation but he is in a very difficult position because the government is doing its best to get rid of all the white farmers. I think it would be beneficial to you if you came with us. He can tell you more about what is happening and with your training from Vana to be a real thinker this information could assist us all. Would you come?'

I was not aware Vana was training me for anything. Perhaps her subtleties were such that it passed me by but I was not going to admit to Amazon, or anyone, I was so unaware. I looked at Vana but she did not meet my gaze. She was looking intently at her bowl of food and eating very slowly indeed. This rather surprised me.

'Yes of course,' I said. 'I would be more than happy to come with you if you think it will be helpful. I really do not know what more I can contribute but you have all been so good to me and helped me so I will certainly try and see what I can do.'

I looked back at Vana who was still, eyes down, eating

slowly. I had a feeling she was not happy with either the request or indeed my response.

When we got back to the hut that evening, after some rather violent dancing, I questioned Vana upon why she was not happy with me going to see this white farmer.

'I am not unhappy that you are going,' she said, 'and I am certain everything will be all right as far as you are concerned. You will indeed learn more of my country and our predicament. I know the farmer well and he is a very, very good man. All I would do is to ask you to take very great care. I sense some evil somewhere.'

'So do you feel something is going to happen?' I asked.

'I am sure everything will be all right for you. I have been having a feeling for a good while now that something is going to go wrong in our area. At first I thought it was going to affect our village but now I'm certain it is not that. I cannot put my finger on it even though I have tried to concentrate upon all the things that can go wrong.' She looked at me. 'Indeed,' she continued, 'it might well be just an adverse change in the weather!'

With that her beautiful face broke into a beaming smile and she reached for me holding me close and kissing me gently.

It was the next morning when Brother and Amazon approached me at the morning meal and said:

'We have decided to go off today if that is all right with you.' Before I could reply Amazon continued: 'This is not going to be a military mission, therefore we will wear our ordinary clothes. I will see to it a knapsack is packed for you if you could get yourself ready very shortly.'

'If I am to go as I am,' I said, 'I am ready. I would just like to say goodbye to Vana if that is possible.'

'I am here behind you to say goodbye,' came a voice and I turned around to see Vana standing and smiling at me.

She held me close and wished me well, took my empty eating bowl from my hand and with that turned and went towards the vegetable patch.

The troop going to see the white farmer was just Amazon, Brother and me so, dressed as we were and knapsacks on backs, we set out at a good pace, walking to the south-east. I was told the walk would take just under three days but in fact it took us five. The reason for this was that mid one morning we passed through a village en route about to have a wedding ceremony and they all begged us to stay to participate.

I have to say, the nearly two days I spent in this village were among the most enjoyable of my life. The village itself was about half the size of Amazon's village but the people there were completely different. Amazon's village people were friendly but these were extraordinarily so. The moment we walked into the village all the children came up and ran alongside me, waving, smiling and shouting at this strange Englishman. Some of the younger children went to touch my legs to see if I was real. After I had been introduced to the chief and exchanged pleasantries the children immediately took me off to show me what they were doing. Tending goats, helping with the vegetables, carrying water. No matter what it was, they were keen to show me and all the time were laughing and joking. Those who could speak English a little did not hesitate to use every word they knew and encourage me to speak back to them. In the first evening, I sat on the ground with them, pointing to various items of my clothing, tools around and other things, saying the name in English and getting each one to repeat back to me. This was done with much laughter and when it was time to go to bed each one of the children came and kissed me on the cheek.

The adults were equally friendly and not at all curious about me. After the children had gone to bed the young woman who was to be married the following day put her arm through mine and walked me around the village introducing me to everyone. I was sure that so close to her wedding night she would have had much more important things to do but that did not seem to concern her.

When eventually she let me go I found Amazon and said: 'These people are amazingly friendly. They take everything on trust and seem so happy.'

'You are absolutely right,' said Amazon. 'This is the happiest village in the world. They are born happy, no matter what adversity strikes them they are still happy and joyful. If a storm was to come and blow down their huts they would laugh and then rebuild. Not one of them has an evil thought in their mind or a bad bone in their body. They are quite outstanding and extraordinary and I thought you would like them. It is unfortunate our journey will be delayed an extra day but as there is a wedding ceremony tomorrow afternoon, we could not leave without attending as this would have been bad manners. I hope you do not mind.'

'Weddings are supposed to be happy events,' I replied 'and I cannot wait to see how these people can be more joyful than they are now. I am quite taken aback.'

We all three slept in the same hut that evening, and I took it this hut was set aside for passing guests. The next morning the children at once came and gathered around me to drag me off somewhere but this time the adults intervened. They shooed the children away in a mockingly fierce manner but the smiles on their faces and the joy from the children showed no ill will. The adults took it in turns during the morning to walk me around the village and point out everything to me. It was, as I said, not half the size of Amazon's village but somehow it seemed to take us until the lunchtime meal before we had seen everything. Everyone we came across needed to talk to me in English, or sign language coupled with their own local dialect, which others translated. Everyone that is except for a small band of men who came back into the village late in the morning covered from head to foot in dirt, dust and mud. They simply nodded in my direction in a friendly way and walked on towards their huts. I wondered why they were so dirty, then remembered the ancillary well being dug in my village so assumed they were doing the same in this village. By the time of the midday meal, I was quite glad to sit down in some quiet as my sides were aching with laughter.

'After we have eaten,' said Amazon, 'we should wash and get ready for the wedding ceremony this afternoon. There will be water in the hut so you and Ajani can go first and I will follow later.'

We did as we were bid and, when washed, Ajani and I returned to watch the preparations for the evening meal and the wedding ceremony. It seemed all the women were helping in the cooking on the fire in the centre of the circle or dashing off to the intended bride's hut to help out there. Where the bridegroom was, I simply did not know. I'm sure I was introduced to him but I could not remember who it was.

By the middle of the afternoon the villagers started to congregate in the centre of the village. Then with drums and flute-like instruments a number of men came into the circle, settled themselves on one side to make sure they were comfortable and spent a little time banging or blowing their instruments as if to tune them. Some other men came with a large arch about eight feet in diameter covered with grasses, flowers and coloured twigs. They dug the arch in the ground, checked it was secure and went to fetch a small dais upon which they put a chair, setting both up by the arch. When everyone had gathered in the centre of the village there was a slow banging on one of the drums and a man wearing a loincloth, with feathers on his head and his body painted with designs of squares and circles, walked from his hut to the centre of the village to stand under the arch. Then a couple of men, walking to the beat of the drum, came in and stood to the right and one side of the groom. These men were also in loincloths with less elaborate headgear and only a small part of their bodies covered with paint designs. The drumbeat stopped. There was an air of expectancy. Then quietly, with no sound at all, the bride with two young girls in attendance walked slowly into the centre of the village. She was dressed in a grass skirt down to her knees, bare breasted and wearing an elaborate headgear with flowers and grasses intertwined. She too had some body painting and a large necklace made of bones and stones, which sparkled in the sunlight. Her attendants were similarly garbed though less elaborately. Obviously she cut a pretty sight for there was an intake of breath from all of the women present. The bride stood under the arch next to the groom with her attendants behind her and to her left.

Then the drum started a slow beat again. The person who was going to officiate the ceremony, surprisingly to me not the chief of the village, walked in. He was wearing a long multicoloured robe along with a simple headdress containing sparkling stones. He climbed upon the low dais and sat down. The drum beat increased in intensity then was joined by another drum, then another, coming to a crescendo before all felt completely silent. The official stood up and started speaking to the bride and groom as well as to all of the villagers present. I turned to Amazon to get an explanation of what he was saying but she was transfixed so I did not wish to disturb her concentration. After a while there was a big cheer from everyone in the village so I assumed the ceremony was nearing its conclusion. The official got down from his dais, walked behind the two and they turned around. The official took a bowl from the men on the groom's side and offered it first to the bride who took a shallow drink; then to the groom who did the same; then the official took a drink and, with some words, handed the bowl back to the groom's men. He took a second bowl from the girls with the bride. Bride and groom held out their hands, close together and palms up. The official poured the contents over both palms, uttering words, and when the bowl was empty, the whole village made a single clap in unison.

The official turned around and started walking around the circle of villagers followed by the bride and groom, hand-in-hand, and behind them the four attendants. When they all returned to the arch the official bowed and walked away and the bride and groom separated; one went around the circle clockwise, the other anticlockwise, smiling and waving at all the villagers who were laughing and stretching out to clasp their hands or touch their bodies. After the circuit was complete all the men from the village went to the groom and started talking to him and slapping him on the back.

'You must go up and congratulate the bridegroom,' said Amazon. 'If you do not do so it will seem as though you are not wishing them luck.'

I walked towards the groom, looking for Brother, and found that he was already with the other men in the village, slapping the groom on the back in a congratulatory way. The groom was laughing and beaming with happiness though from time to time a playful slap on the back pushed him forward and I wondered whether by the end of all this congratulation he would be battered and bruised. I followed the lead of the other villagers and too slapped the groom on the back although being careful not to put too much force in it.

After a while the men walked away and the women came up to congratulate the bride. There were no slaps on the back here. It was simply hugging, kissing and much talking.

When all this was over everyone started milling about, talking to each other while some of the women went to the fire and arranged the pots of food, which had been warming in the embers at the edge. The fire burned up and the food reheated. When it was ready the women put the food into eating bowls and started handing the bowls out to all the villagers who moved away to sit in a circle around the fire, the bride and groom sitting to the right of the chief. Men too were involved for they poured bowls of drink, which were handed around to everyone. When a food bowl was empty it was refilled with another course until all the food had gone. Then the drums started their hypnotic beat, later joined by the flute-like instruments. With the bride and groom leading, slowly everyone got up to dance. The children joined in, laughing and moving their bodies in harmony to the beat of the music.

After a while I joined in the dancing but my total inability to follow all the dancing movements sent those around me into hysterical laughter; one or two, either overcome with my antics or suffering from the jungle juice, which had been distributed, fell to the ground, rolling about in mirth. Not wishing to interfere with the dancing activities, I withdrew to a safe distance from the dancing and sat on the edge of the circle watching the merriment.

As dusk fell and the night darkened so the dancing became more intense. The bride and groom were in the thick of it and although both had lost their headdresses the bride's necklace sparkled and flashed from time to time as the light from the fire fell upon it.

Late in the evening Amazon came up to me.

'The music and dancing will go on for a long time and I think we should go to bed as we have an early start tomorrow.' I nodded, got to my feet and walked towards the hut where Brother was already preparing to sleep. Although the reverberations of the music and laughter of the dancers could be heard clearly in the hut, I drifted off to sleep very quickly.

We three were up at sunrise the next morning and went to the circle to find only a few people there. Obviously the revelry of the previous night had caused some oversleeping this morning. There were some pots of cold food close to the now dead fire and we each took a little, with Amazon wrapping some up in large green leaves and putting the packages into our knapsacks. We started to make our way out of the village but suddenly villagers appeared to bid us farewell with much hugging, kissing and laughing, and we had to force ourselves away otherwise we would have been there all morning just saying goodbye. I was quite amazed at such friendliness and joy and as we were walking I was smiling to myself. Amazon turned around and looked at me.

'I see you enjoyed your stay in the village,' she said, 'you still have a smile on your face.'

'I honestly cannot believe it,' I replied, 'as you said, they are truly the happiest people in the world.'

Brother picked up the pace as we strode purposefully towards our destination and I concentrated upon my relaxed walking style. We stopped only briefly at noon for the food Amazon had packed earlier and then continued to walk south-east. By late afternoon we struck a dirt road and went along it, passing the occasional cultivated patch, or rather, neglected cultivated areas, until we came to a large well-kept bungalow with an open veranda all around. I saw a number of farm workers milling about some detached farm buildings but was surprised I did not see any fields of crops growing or animals grazing. As we approached the bungalow a tall white man came out onto the veranda and raised his hand in greeting. We were obviously expected.

I was introduced to Johann Baz who was friendly and

jolly. He had the obvious signs of an African farmer with a very dark tan on his face but halfway up his forehead a distinct line, with less of a tan above, showing he wore a hat when out in the field. He had large calloused hands, strong but also delicate.

'Do come in,' he said. Turning to me: 'I have heard so much about you, not least how lucky you are still to be alive after the plane crash.'

We went into the cooler air of the living room of his bungalow where a fan in the centre of the ceiling turned slowly, giving the air movement in the whole room, which was very pleasant. He pointed to easy chairs and waved at us all, saying, 'Sit down,' and went out of the room to shout to someone. Into the room came an old African man who smiled at us all.

'This is my farm manager, Johnny,' said Johann. 'Johnny is not his real name but everyone calls him that. I rely on him for everything; he is not only my right hand but also my eyes and ears as well. He has been with the family for more years than even he can count. In fact he is one of the family.'

Johnny beamed and sat down in one of the chairs as an elderly, stout woman came in carrying a tray with five glasses full of what appeared to be fruit cordial. Johann handed out the glasses and said:

'Although it is nearly sundowner time, I guess you would prefer to have a cool soft drink before you wash ready for the evening meal. This is a special concoction of mine, it is lime-based, which, thankfully, we can still grow.' When he said that, his face darkened and he frowned. 'Never mind,' he continued, brightening up, 'we can talk all about that later. Tell me how was your trip here?'

He looked at me when he said this and so I related the steady passage from the village to the farm, explaining our delay, the happiness in the village we stayed at and the marriage ceremony. Johann chuckled at this indicating he was aware the ceremony was going on and anticipated we would be delayed a day or two. He also agreed with me that it was the happiest village in the world and although he had not been there for some years he had fond memories of it.

After we finished our drink Johann showed us to our rooms in the bungalow where water, soap and towels awaited so we could freshen up. When I had washed I returned to the sitting room to find Johnny standing, waiting.

'I thought you would be the first,' he said, 'you English like to do things quickly. We are more relaxed.' With that he gave a deep chuckle and beckoned me outside to the veranda where a table was set for an evening meal. He waved me to one of the chairs. He sat opposite and asked me to tell him about the plane crash. I was a little reluctant to say too much but it was clear he was aware of the involvement of the palace guards and so I told it, as it was, blow by blow. He was truly interested in my account particularly of the missile coming towards the plane. He asked me several questions about this and I answered with as much detail as I could.

'I think you must have a gift.' He looked down into his lap and then back up at me, continuing, 'our old hunters used to say when they were in danger time stood still so they could take the right evasive action. You seem to have a similar gift.'

I thought the whole plane incident was so bizarre that I was simply mesmerised by the rocket and, whilst in my mind it seemed time had stood still, I certainly could not have taken any evasive action. Johnny said nothing about my ability to shoot and so I assumed he did not know or, perhaps, he was being a little delicate.

After a while Johann joined us at the table and we made polite conversation until Ajani and Sabra appeared and also sat down.

'Now,' said Johann, 'a gin and tonic is a must. I know Sabra and Ajani like gin and tonics and you, being an Englishman, must also like them.'

As he said this the elderly, buxom woman appeared with a tray upon which rested five glasses, a bottle of gin, several uncut limes, ice and bottles of tonic. Johann busied himself cutting the limes and making gin and tonics, one for each of us. We sat there savouring this nectar and Johann said:

'This is a good time of day and it used to be the most wonderful time particularly if I had been away working in the fields for several days or had had a hard day's work around the farm. Just sitting here on the veranda with a gin and tonic in hand and the sun setting gave me a feeling of deep contentment and satisfaction. Alas it is not the same today as it used to be.'

Johann and Johnny exchanged glances.

'Unfortunately, things are not the best here now,' said Johnny. 'I sometimes think we had more than our fair share of love and enjoyment and those times will never come back again. I have been on this farm ever since I was born, and worked, played and loved every moment of it. I have been involved in everything on this farm and each day has been a joy. But for the first time, now I am beginning to fear. This is my country and we have wonderful people here who are willing to work, willing to share and liberal in their views. Until this terrible, terrible government we did not have discrimination at all. Even in the colonial days out here in the countryside everyone had to get on together and work together to survive and build farms so there was never any distinction as to whether you were white or black. Everyone joined in. Now this government is turning everyone against everyone; not just black against white but also black against black. It is all done in the name of wiping colonialism from the face of the country and it is simply awful. I do not know what is going to happen to us all. How we can continue to survive.'

169

He looked down into his lap and I swear he had tears in his eyes. Johann's face was still and expressionless. It did not show fear but it certainly did not show optimism. His body language was not of someone who was being defeated but of one who simply could not understand why things were happening the way they were.

'Sabra and Ajani have brought you here so that I can explain what is happening to my country. It is quite honestly depressing and I would also say frustrating but that would not explain it sufficiently. However, for the moment we have a meal to eat and I'm not going to ruin good food by being a miserable old white farmer. So let's finish our gin and tonic, eat and enjoy some fine wine. I still have a few bottles left; not many, but certainly a celebration tonight I think is in order because I am amongst friends.'

We had an excellent meal, more the western than I had been used to in the villages, with the main course being a very large and very tender steak. The wine too was good but bearing in mind Johann's indication that he had but a few bottles left, I drank rather sparingly. Whilst Amazon and Brother seemed to be able to drink local jungle juice without any effect at all, after just two glasses of wine they looked decidedly changed. When we had finished and coffee was served Johann put on a serious face.

'I know you are aware of the political situation in my country,' he said, 'and what I would like to do is to explain it all from my perspective.' He took a sip of his coffee and frowned as if concentrating upon how to continue. 'My grandfather, with the help of everyone around here, made this farm, which was taken over by my father, and I carried on from him. The land around is good and although water is, as everywhere, in short supply, we had good and careful irrigation systems, which meant we could grow crops, vegetables and fruit, with sufficient grass here and in the uplands in summer to keep good herds of cattle. Quite frankly, we made a very good living. Both my grandfather and my father were sensible men and made sure all the workers on this farm were fed and housed properly and at one time we had a school for all the children. In his latter years my grandfather brought in a teacher from England for the school and my father continued with this, employing English women from time to time.' He smiled. 'These women were good teachers and in fact I actually married one.' His face darkened again. 'Unfortunately the trouble is so bad now, I sent her back to England with my children because I fear for their lives.'

There was a long silence while we finished our coffee.

'You must know the policy of this government is to remove all the white farmers and replace them with black. Now whilst this is my heritage and I love it dearly, it would be foolish of me to say that I had an absolute right and my family should stay here forever. The world changes and we must change with it. However, the problem is quite simply that the government is not replacing the white farmers with black farmers but with government ministers' cronies. These men have not the faintest idea how to farm and everything is going to rack and ruin. They do not even have the sense to continue employing the farm manager on the jumped up pretext that the farm manager was too close to the white colonial and therefore must be unreliable. I have so far managed to escape this takeover, first because my farm is quite a way from the capital, but second, I believe, because many of the children brought up on this farm and educated by my grandfather and my father moved to the capital and some are in government so for the moment I'm being spared. This will not continue for ever. In fact I will probably go bankrupt before I am replaced.

'As I said, this farm was very prosperous and we all had a very good life. Now there is no money and no market. The fruit and vegetables we grew in abundance and exported

171

are no longer grown simply because there is no export market. If a lorry is loaded up with vegetables and sent to the border it is stopped every few miles and "fined" if we are lucky; more likely both lorry and content confiscated. Now we don't even have the fuel to send a lorry anywhere. You probably did not see any farm animals as you walked into the farm lands. This is because the few that I have left have been sent high up into the hills to avoid being stolen by the palace guard or their cronies. You have just eaten one of the herd!' He smiled. 'The meat is not as good as it used to be because we cannot tend the animals as well as we could but it is still not bad.

'Our workers, my people, are being harassed and encouraged to leave the farm. I'm getting to the stage where I have no money to pay them but luckily we can still grow enough and slaughter an animal or two to keep everyone fed. This, you may have thought, would be appreciated by my people but even our most loyal workers whose fathers and grandfathers have worked on the farm and have all been educated on the farm are having their minds poisoned. Now there is no sunny face or jaunty walk around the farm. People shuffle about with heads down and frowns on their faces. This is not how it should be. The really, really sad part is that although things are diabolically bad on my farm in just about every respect, this is probably one of the best farms in the whole countryside. Everywhere people are starving and to survive they have resorted to snaring and killing animals on farms, private game ranches and conservancies. Poaching is rampant with impala, warthog, kudu and wildebeest being killed simply to feed the people. This is not to mention the cross-boarder trophy hunters who are able to sneak in and out of the country with no organisation here geared up to stop them.

'The tragedy of it all is if I was allowed to grow what we used to grow and transport what we used to transport then I could alleviate a vast amount of this hunger but this does not appear to be in the interests of the government. Those in power are deranged. I really cannot understand what they're trying to achieve; the country is on its knees and we will soon disintegrate. Our money is worthless and inflation has long since passed double figures.'

Johann looked at Sabra and Ajani who nodded in agreement. 'The villages to the north of here are very lucky because they are just too far away for the palace guard to take too much notice so they can grow crops and raise animals and most can feed themselves but they cannot trade in the capital as much as they used to. You have been told about the palace guard?' I nodded. 'No matter what you've been told, it is not the half of it.'

Another long silence followed and I felt there was nothing I could say. There were no questions I could ask as the desolation of the man in front of me was so obvious. He had referred to 'my country' and 'my people,' showing his oneness and dedication to everything and everyone around. For the first time in my life I felt at a complete loss. I had so often had clients with desperate tales to tell; insurmountable problems to overcome; woes beyond measure. All of these had an answer somewhere. It was just a matter of examining, isolating, identifying and acting. Now, I felt, there was nothing, absolutely nothing I could do to lift the ominous cloud enveloping this man, indeed enveloping the whole country. I really wondered why Amazon and Brother had brought me here. I did not want to be depressed and the problem was just out of my league. It is not as though I was a man of importance in England who could return and somehow force change in this beautiful country, which was being ravaged by stupidity. Even if I were to apply my shooting ability, and nothing Johann had said changed my mind on this, it would simply be a prick in the side of the oppressive organisational machine and would achieve very little, if anything at all. The evening which had been so beautiful, with good food and wine, excellent company, and the warmth of the evening sun, suddenly became alien and nasty. It was not as though Johann had spoken with great passion, simply that he had spoken at all, and had showed such under-standing, compassion and sympathy for his country and its people.

Johann looked up and snapped out of his reverie. Smiling, he turned to Amazon and Brother and asked, 'Do you two want a night cap or would you rather go to bed?'

'I think we would both prefer to go to bed,' said Brother. 'I'm sure you have things to say to Nigel that can be better said if we are not around.'

Amazon nodded and they both got up, bid us good night and disappeared into the bungalow. Johnny remained. Johann also got up and walked to a table at the end of the veranda, which held several bottles.

'Would you prefer to continue drinking gin and tonic or would you like a Scotch? I have to say whilst I am more of a gin and tonic man I do find when I'm really fed up late in the evening a good Scotch whisky helps me and I have a couple of really good bottles here.'

'Scotch will be fine for me,' I said, 'I would like a little water in it if I may.'

'Nothing for me, thank you,' said Johnny.

Johann nodded, poured two very generous portions in enormous cut-glass tumblers and brought them across to the table with a jug of water.

'Put in as much as you like. I find other people either pour in too much or too little water.'

I did as I was bid and we both took a sip of an excellent malt whisky. I was not really a whisky drinker but there were occasions when it went down well and suddenly this was one of those occasions. The dark cloud that had been pushing down on me lifted and I looked at Johann.

'What is it you really want to tell me?' I asked. 'Sabra and Ajani have brought me all the way here for a good reason. I'm sure you know about my apparent shooting skills and my refusal to become involved with killing people.' He nodded and looked me straight in the eye. 'Therefore, merely putting personal detail on what I know already is not going to change my mind although I hasten to add to hear from you what is happening on a first-hand basis really does affect me enormously and, if I may be honest, what you have said has destroyed the ambience of the whole evening.'

'I know,' said Johann. 'This is why I wanted us to eat first as the meal was good. I really enjoyed it and I believe everyone else did. But I was asked by Sabra and Ajani to tell it like it is and that I have done. They have been great friends and allies over the years and I value that friendship enormously so even though I was reluctant to ruin our evening I would rather do that than upset those two. They are particularly wonderful people – brave beyond measure – and would do anything to help anyone no matter who that person might be.' I thought on this for a moment. I fully agreed that Amazon fulfilled that category but my recollection of Brother when I was at the aeroplane was slightly different. Maybe, though, 'anyone' meant anyone in this country, not some foreigner who had dropped in uninvited.

'I think the reason you are here is for me to explain a little more about the palace guard. It is difficult to put into words and I'm sure, as an Englishman, if you were told by a black African about spirits, witches, wizards, and so as. you would dismiss it all as old superstition. You may be right but there again you could be horribly wrong. I am frightened, man. Really frightened. There is an evil here, which is beyond reason or explanation. I come from a long line of intrepid explorers and fighters so when I tell you I'm frightened I hope you will not think I am a wimp. I will try and explain.'

He took a deep drink of his whisky and put the glass down on the table. Pressing his hands together in a prayer-like manner, he lowered his lips on his fingertips and thought for a while.

'You have been told about the structure of the palace guard and you have heard they commit atrocities and are evil. I can confirm, without any doubt whatsoever, they hold this country in the palm of their hand. They have injected such fear everywhere that the mere mention of the palace guard will make people scuttle into their homes and huts. Their appearance in any village strikes terror. There is hardly any man, woman or child in the whole country who would actively oppose them. Therefore what Sabra and Ajani are doing, with similar groups in other villages around, is of the highest and most extraordinary bravery. I am not part of it; oh yes, I sympathise and try my hardest to help in every way I can but I do not think I would have the bravery these groups have.'

He finished his drink, stood up and beckoned me to finish mine, taking both glasses back to the small table at the other end of the veranda and replenished them with the fine malt whisky. When he returned, had added a little water to his glass, he leaned back in his chair and smiled at me.

'What I'm about to tell you now, you will probably not believe but I urge you to. As I have said, I am descended from a great line of intrepid explorers and fighters so I'm not someone who would be easily afraid. But I am scared deeply, for I speak from some first-hand experience. The nub of the fear is Zaban. You know him as Death's Head. He is the man you saw at the plane in charge of killing the passengers. Zaban has, so far as anyone is aware, no other name and he appeared one day, no one knows from where. Baumge had been in government and in power about three years and was developing his own oppression through the formation of the palace guard. There was a certain amount of resistance from the army against not only the formation of what was, in effect, an elite, politically driven force, but also a consolidation of absolute power. One small army group in particular, to the south of the country, was thought to be planning an overthrow or at least strong opposition. One day Zaban, with a dozen men, appeared from nowhere, dressed in a ragbag of clothing and, without warning or compassion, shot every single person in this group and then mutilated them by cutting off their testicles and stuffing the testicles in the mouths of the corpses. They left the bodies where they were and drove to the capital in vehicles they took from this group. Zaban somehow got an immediate audience with Baumge and, I'm sure, told him the potential resistance was over. Since that time Zaban has been in charge of the palace guard and his cronies are now commanders of the units.'

I looked across at Johnny who was gently nodding with a completely expressionless face. I was not sure why Johnny was still with us but I guessed he was there to confirm what Johann had to say. Again, a long silence ensued before Johann continued.

'Zaban very quickly developed the palace guard into the unit it now is. As I'm sure has been explained to you, the guard was initially split into five units of about fifty men each but recently the four units in the countryside have been further split in half to allow greater control over the small villages. I believe the occasional attacks by Sabra and Ajani, together with other groups, have been a contributor to this split up. Zaban himself spends time with each group and travels around with two or three of the palace guard in a high-powered jeep. Occasionally, he travels by himself. As you have seen, he is a man of striking appearance and seems to have no muscle on his skeleton at all; what we would call a skin and bone. By nicknaming him Death's Head, you would have noticed his face is more like a skull with skin attached but what you did not see was his eyes. They are the palest, palest blue you can ever imagine. Pale blue in a black skeletal face. And those eyes have no expression whatsoever. There is no hatred, fear, contempt, passion, understanding or acknowledgement in those eyes; they are totally dead. Dead but boring. When Zaban looks at you his eyes bore into yours, into your skull; into your soul; into the depths of your being. Once he has locked gaze with you he seems to enter your body.'

At this point Johnny interjected. 'It is true,' he said.

'You may wonder why I know this to be so,' said Johann. 'Before Baumge had strangled the life out of this country he invited various foreign dignitaries and local farmers to a banquet in the capital to explain how this country was going to develop under his enlightened leadership. Zaban had recently been appointed in charge of the palace guard and he was at this banquet. I was introduced to Zaban, quite why, I did not know, and I tried to make light and polite conversation. He answered in monosyllables and just looked at me. The evening was warm and, as you can imagine, a banquet with wines and good food meant we were all rather hot but I can tell you when Zaban looked at me I turned icy, icy cold. I felt as though his eyes drew out of me all of my thoughts and history to be stored away in his own mind for future reference. I knew from that moment he was evil and my overwhelming feeling was of gratitude when someone interrupted our rather one-sided conversation to take him away somewhere else. I could not get warm for the whole of that night and was unable to shake out of my mind the hypnotic gaze that seemed to tear me apart. Even now, I occasionally wake in the night to feel his eyes boring into me.'

Johnny continued nodding. 'Luckily,' Johnny said, 'I have not had the misfortune to receive the deep look from Zaban but I've been close to him and I can confirm his eyes are truly frightening and with the rest of his appearance it is no wonder he can so easily terrorise everyone he meets.'

'I fully accept what you say, 'I replied, 'but even the most formidable person is only a man and, even if daemonic, can be brought down as any man can. I have been fortunate, or perhaps unfortunate in some cases, to meet many successful people: captains of industry, if you will. Some of these have charm and charisma, others are simply single-minded with compelling ambition sweeping everything and everyone to one side. No matter how successful they might be or how frightening they appear they are all still human.'

'Ah,' said Johann, 'you have neatly come to the bit where I am afraid we must disagree. As I have indicated, I would not expect you to believe in or understand spirits, wizards and similar, and five years ago nor would I. Remember, I have grown up in this country and even the most educated have respect for the spirits even if they acknowledge that there is probably no such thing. That was before Zaban. Quite early on in his reign of terror there were a number of people in my country who realised if Zaban continued in his post things would get worse and so there were plots to get rid of him. As I said, he travels around in his jeep with two or three palace guard and on one occasion a dissident group ambushed his jeep. There were about twenty of them, all with high-powered automatic rifles and they emptied magazine after magazine into the jeep as it approached, killing everyone and riddling the jeep so full of bullets it was totally useless. When all the shooting had finished this group of men walked to the jeep to see their handiwork and as they came close so Zaban stood up from all this mayhem and simply looked at them. He was unarmed. He said nothing. He just stood and stared at each man. They all turned and ran away. It is said there is no way a human being could possibly have survived the onslaught. Too many bullets were fired and later inspection of the jeep and the three guards showed total destruction. The bodies of the palace guards were so riddled with bullets as to be almost unrecognisable as humans and the fact the rifles used were high powered meant that the bullets went through body, metal, steel and so it would not have been possible for Zaban to have hidden behind anything or just been "lucky". As you probably know, although film and television thrillers show people sheltering behind an open car door with bullets flying, in fact even a modern automatic handgun bullet will easily pass through a car door and I can assure you the trajectory of a high-powered round from an AK–47 would hardly be interrupted.'

Johnny was nodding enthusiastically at this stage. 'This is not just a story,' he said, 'it has come from reliable sources and I have actually spoken to one of the men in the ambush. He was a man petrified. He just confirmed what Johann has been saying but would not elaborate any more for he was frightened out of his mind. At any moment he was expecting the spirit of Zaban to attack him. I know I am a black man and I freely admit I do believe in spirits, both good and evil. So you might think this belief has coloured my judgement but I can assure you it has not. I have never seen anything like such fear before in my life. Naturally, witch doctors and spirit healers were summoned but no one could do anything. Every man in the attacking group either died within a year or went out of their mind.'

There was a long silence and whilst I did not in any way doubt the word of both Johann and Johnny, nonetheless I was unable to accept that if indeed the attack had been as efficient as suggested, Zaban could have survived. Events later related are, in my personal experience, often embellished and rarely accurate, so it might well have been the shooting of this group was not quite as sharp as they would, later, lead everyone to believe.

'I can see from your face,' said Johann, 'you are sceptical.

There is more. You will have undoubtedly heard of the Valkyrie plot against Hitler during the last war and that he was saved from a bomb by a heavy oak table.' I nodded. 'Well the same thing happened to Zaban but on this occasion there was no heavy table at all. The bomb was taken into a meeting he was having with several of his aides by a woman who was serving them drink and food. She was a close relative of one of the attacking group who had since become insane and she felt very deeply that Zaban was an evil spirit to be eradicated. She said, and of course we do not know if this actually happened, she was going to stand next to Zaban and detonate the bomb so he could not survive. The bomb certainly went off and everyone in the room was killed except for Zaban. The windows of the room and doors were blown out; the whole room was wrecked and hardly a recognisable piece of body was left except Zaban who simply walked from the room, his tattered uniform splattered with dirt, dust, debris and other people's blood. There is no account of him being injured in any way at all.'

Johnny continued the tale. 'The fact that Zaban appeared from nowhere, that no matter how hard we have all tried we can find no trace of him in this country before his sudden appearance, that those questioned in surrounding countries have never heard of him either, together with these verified stories of his survival and his strange appearance and haunting eyes makes everyone believe he is an evil spirit risen from the dead and totally untouchable; indestructible.'

I tried my hardest not to look disbelieving but I'm afraid I have always dealt with the practicalities of life and although I have been fascinated by the tricks and antics of magicians I did not for one moment believe in magic for a logical explanation could always be found. I did not know quite how to reply but thought honesty must prevail.

'I respect everything you both have said, particularly as I know you are very level-headed people. I can quite readily believe that Zaban may well have the fabled nine lives of a cat but I'm afraid I find it difficult to leap from good fortune and luck to a spirit rising from the dead.'

Johann laughed although it did not contain too much humour. 'I am not in the slightest surprised at your reaction. I too cannot fully believe in the evil spirit rising from the dead but Zaban can undoubtedly exude power and control and has demonstrated complete evil with not the slightest regard for humanity, so it is not surprising he is feared, and even if he does not have the power attributed to him, everyone in this country thinks he has and that of itself is a danger. You are a foreigner here and would certainly not be welcomed by the government, therefore I have to warn you, trust no one, not even me. I'm sure Sabra and Ajani are treating you as one of the village, one of the family even, and they would not willingly do anything to bring harm upon you but neither of them has actually met Zaban and so they do not understand the evil power he could have over them. The bottom line is if this man finds out about you he will hunt you down and no one will stand in his way for more than five minutes. If he can frighten me with just one look then what he may do to others just does not bear thinking about.'

With that Johann got up and walked to the table at the end of the veranda, picked up the whisky bottle, another glass and returned, passing the empty glass to Johnny and putting the bottle on the table.

'You have one for the road, Johnny,' he said. Looking at me, 'And please help yourself. I am going to have one more before I go to bed.'

He put a generous portion of whisky in his glass, added a little water and passed the bottle to Johnny who did the same. I was happy to sit with my glass still a quarter full.

'I am sure,' said Johann, 'you expected me to try and convince you to join the resistance group against this government and Zaban in particular but I have no intention of doing that at all. A man is who he is not by his talents but by his choices and if you have chosen the way you have, we all respect it. If I was to advise you at all, it would be to leave this country as soon as possible but I apprehend your current circumstances,' and with that he gave a sly and a knowing smile, 'incline you to remain here. I urge you, though, do not outlive your welcome. While you are in danger you can bring greater danger to those around you and I care very much about Sabra, Ajani and their people.'

He smiled and this time it was the warm 'old Johann' smile full of friendliness and hospitality. He drained his glass, saying, 'It's time for my bed and I suggest you do not linger here too long for knowing Sabra and Ajani they may well be up at first light to take you trekking back to the village, and believe me you would not wish to walk in this heat with a hangover!'

He left us and after some small talk with Johnny I got up to go to bed as well.

'Nigel,' said Johnny, 'I understand you cannot believe everything we have told you but please remember it and take care. Every story has a grain of truth. Good night; sleep well.'

I left the veranda and walked to my room, slowly undressing and getting into bed. The events of the day and the whisky made me suddenly feel tired but I could not drop off to sleep immediately. Everything Johann and Johnny told me was going around in my mind and although I really believed that there was a logical explanation to Zaban's cheating death, nonetheless I had a horrible feeling that there was more to it. Eventually I drifted off.

The following morning I awoke well after dawn and, having washed, walked into the sitting room to see a low table set for breakfast for one person. As I looked around so the buxom old woman walked in carrying a tray, which she placed on the low table.

'I do not believe you are a breakfast person,' she said, 'so I have not cooked anything for you but have here some freshly made bread, coffee and that orange jam you English like so much.'

She bustled out and left me to it. I was quietly amused than no one who was not British could understand our liking for marmalade first thing in the morning but I didn't have the heart to tell her it was normally spread on toast, not fresh bread. Nonetheless, I tucked in and found coffee, fresh bread and the orange jam most enjoyable. When finished, I wandered out onto the veranda to see Johnny at the door of one of the farm buildings. He waved to me to join him so I went across.

'Ah,' he said, 'at last. Do not worry, we all overslept a little this morning. Sabra and Ajani have gone for a walk to see one of the elders of our commune who has some information for them. They should be back at lunchtime. In the meantime you can help me with the horses.'

He went into the farm building and there were four beautiful horses being rubbed down with straw by presumably the grooms. They all greeted me warmly but there was no joy in the voice and the body language was of acceptance rather than any pleasure in their surroundings.

'Do you ride?' asked Johnny.

'Extremely badly,' I replied.

Johnny grunted and took me around each horse showing me the finer points from time to time and joking with the grooms to indicate that a certain part of one horse, or another, had not received the attention it should. It was clear Johnny loved the horses and I was surprised a farm that I was told was so bereft of produce still maintained horses. Johnny explained.

'Even when we had all the petrol we needed both Johann and I preferred to use horses when we could. It is a fine way of seeing the farm for at the pace of a horse without the noise of the engine nothing is missed. We both love riding and at one stage Johann's father developed a string of polo ponies but, alas, all that is gone. These horses are taken out for a few days each week to the foothills to graze but we have to be so careful because they will be stolen. Now with a lack of petrol the horses are even more important but, of course, there is so little cultivated land left to supervise. I suppose if we were realistic we could get rid of two of them, perhaps all of them, but I'm afraid Johann is very sentimental and I think it would break my heart if all the horses went.'

When the horses had been groomed to Johnny's satisfaction, and he had head patted and talked to each one, we left the barn and walked towards the house. Surprisingly Johnny linked his arm into mine and in a conspiratorial way said, 'Last night was good. I enjoyed it and your company. I know you find it difficult to believe everything we told you but all I would ask is for you to keep an open mind. I am not a thinker as you are,' I was surprised at this but said nothing, 'but I do have a feeling you're going to be good for us.' We carried on walking slowly in silence with Johnny's head down as he gazed at the earth. He drew me to a halt, turned and looked at me straight in the eyes. 'You must be careful, very careful. Whatever decisions you make, remember they will affect all around you.'

With that he laughed, let go my arm and walked to the balcony where Buxom Lady was standing with two large glasses of a fruit juice drink on a tray.

'You talked last night about powers,' I said to Johnny, 'and I have to say the fact that food or drink appears precisely the right time when one is thinking about it might just convince me there is something to this supernatural bit.' We both laughed, took a glass of fruit juice and sat on the veranda looking out over the farm.

It was not long before Amazon and Brother appeared with Johann.

'We hope we have not kept you waiting,' said Johann, 'but we went to see a very old lady here on a farm who had something she wanted to tell Sabra. I do not know what it was but I'm sure it was worthwhile. In a moment we will have a bite to eat and then you will be off back to your village.'

As he spoke so Buxom Lady appeared to lay the table for what turned out to be a light, very enjoyable lunch, and when we had finished Johann bid us farewell as he went to saddle up one of the horses to ride out into the farmland. Buxom Lady appeared with our knapsacks and, after thanks all around, we started back on the dirt road towards the village.

We stopped somewhat earlier than usual for the evening meal for, as Amazon explained, we were too far from the happy village to make it before sunset so it was best if we waited until the following morning. She said that she had assumed I would enjoy spending another half day there and we all agreed it would certainly lighten our spirits. When I asked what the old woman had to tell, Amazon was particularly evasive, indicating, not too convincingly, that it was something of a family matter. We settled down and went quietly to sleep with the sounds of Africa around us.

The next morning we were up with the sun, ate a handful of food and struck off towards the joyful village. I did not know if it was anticipation of the joy and laughter that was ahead or my practised expertise at last bearing fruit but I seemed to glide over the ground somewhat better and easier than I had before. I certainly felt I was walking more on air rather than thumping into the soil.

As the village came into view we smiled to each other but the smiles soon turned to frowns as we could not see anyone moving around. No cattle or goats were about and the village had an air of everyone still asleep. Unusual, indeed almost impossible at this time of day. The closer we got my apprehension increased. I felt a cold knot in my stomach, knowing with absolute certainty something was very wrong indeed. None of us spoke but our footsteps became heavier and our pace slowed as though we were putting off actually arriving. I wish I had never arrived.

I do not have the skill or the words to convey the horror which greeted us. I can only record the facts. Every man, woman and child was dead. All adults had been shot or hacked to death, the women – young and old – obviously raped for they lay on the ground with legs wide open and clothing torn or cut off. Children had been battered to death, their skulls split open with blood and brains scattered across the brown earth. Not a living soul remained. We walked around the village in total silence, checking every hut for the sign of some life but there was nothing. A village once full of happiness was now a mortuary. The smell of death was everywhere and flies were beginning to attack the bodies. I suppose I should say I was sickened but I was not. At that moment I felt nothing at all. I was totally numb and could not believe that such wonderful people had died at all let alone been massacred; wiped out. I really did not know what to do next. The bodies should have been given a decent burial but there were just too many of them for the three of us to deal with. I was looking around, desolate, my mind grasping for a solution, some action, anything that could be of some constructive use. I saw Amazon beckoning me to join her. I crossed to the edge of the village and she pointed to the ground where I could clearly see the indented tyre marks of vehicles, which I had to assume in this terrain were jeeps. The only people who used jeeps were, of course, the palace guard.

This hard fact snapped me out of my reverie. 'Why would anyone wipe out this village?' I asked Amazon. 'They were not only the most joyful people in the world but no threat at all to the government, far less the palace guard, for they did not participate in any of the revolutionary activities or entertain any political thoughts. Their whole life was being happy and helping other people. I can't understand it.' I think at that stage I was very, very close to tears.

'The palace guard from time to time makes examples of certain villages but this is the first time to my knowledge it has wiped out a complete village. Why it chose this one, your guess is as good as mine. Vana said before we left that there was evil somewhere in this trip but I could not possibly anticipate or understand why anyone could do this; not to these people.' I got the impression, how or why I could not say, she was not telling me everything.

I looked around and saw Brother was a distance away from us, walking slowly, looking at the ground. He stopped, concentrated and then turned around and waved to us to join him. When we reached him he pointed to the ground and I could see tyre marks of heavier vehicles, which may well have been lorries. 'Look over here,' said Brother. We followed him and saw the ground had been churned up by the hoof prints of animals, cattle and goats, which had been herded into the lorries and taken away. 'And over there,' said Brother, 'go and see; I cannot again.'

We walked in the direction he was pointing and there on the ground was a body of a child who had probably been defending his herd. He had been knocked over by a great force and the tyre marks of a lorry went across the lower half of his body, crushing it into the earth. I could picture his heroic, but in the end pathetic, gesture and the sadness I felt welled up inside of me burning like a quiet anger. Before I could say anything Amazon patted me on the arm and led me back to where Brother was standing.

'We can do nothing here,' said Amazon. By the time we send sufficient people to bury these poor villagers the animals will have got them so they are best left alone; let the wild take care of them. Perhaps it is best that they do not have a grave for it will be a monument of depravity and sadness. Come, let's move on.'

11

The Decision

We turned our back on the village and started walking away. We walked slowly and did not speak, just putting one foot in front of the other, heads down. The alertness that both Amazon and Brother, together with the other members of their group, had previously demonstrated was now gone. It was almost as if they didn't care what happened to them. My helplessness remained and the burning anger subsided to be replaced by an absolute and driving desire to somehow avenge this terrible atrocity. I didn't want revenge but felt the need to redress the terrible imbalance of the cruel and haughty obliterating the happy and meek. At noon we stopped for food but none of us felt hungry so we just sat there looking at the ground.

'How far away is the encampment of the palace guard?' I asked.

Brother waved his hand vaguely in a south-westerly direction. 'About two days over there,' he said.

Without thinking, I replied, 'Take me there.' Both Amazon and Brother looked hard at me.

'Why?' they both said, almost in unison.

'For the moment I am not sure except that I want to see it. Will you take me there?' They both continued to look at me but said nothing. 'Look,' I continued, 'all we are doing is just seeing the encampment. Apart from a few days, we lose nothing by going there.' They still said nothing. 'Humour me,' I said.

Brother gave a huge sigh and shook his head. 'There is nothing to see there except a few buildings so I don't see the point but if you want to go then I can see nothing wrong with taking you there. We can move quickly on the first day but will have to be very careful the second day to make sure we are not seen by anyone. I have been there several times before and there is a low hill fairly close by where we can observe what is going on, if that is what you want.'

'I have no idea what I do want except to see the encampment. I think it is important.' They both looked at me again, Amazon shrugged her shoulders and got to her feet. Brother and I followed and we started out towards the palace guard encampment.

My request, no matter how bizarre it may have seemed to both Amazon and Brother, gave them a purpose, for they started walking briskly with the old alertness returning. When we stopped for the evening meal there was very little talk but neither Brother nor Amazon looked quite so dejected as they had when we left the terrible scenes in the joyful village. I expected to be haunted in my dreams that evening but I was not. Whilst I remembered, indeed could never forget, what I had seen, it was as though my mind banished the horror pictures to a corner of my brain to remain unvisited unless I deliberately chose to do so.

By the afternoon of the second day the walking pace had dropped considerably with Amazon and Brother fanning out to each side to check every bush, tuft and hump to be sure there was nothing or no one lurking there to alert of our approach to the encampment. We came upon a small hill, climbed halfway up and Brother carefully guided us around the side to a place where we could lie to look down upon the camp, which was about a quarter of a mile away.

'Just stay still and wait for a while,' Brother said, 'I'm sure we are undetected but if someone has seen movement they will be concentrating on looking at this area so if we are completely still for a while they will lose interest.'

After, I would guess, half an hour or so, Brother opened his knapsack and handed me a pair of binoculars. 'The sun is to your right and slightly behind you so there should be no reflection from these but move them about carefully.'

I sat myself in a comfortable position with the binoculars to my eyes and looked down on the camp and the palace guard. The compound was about two hundred yards by two hundred yards in size, surrounded by a wire fence, which looked about eight or ten feet tall. Coils of barbed wire were lazily draped over the top of the fence. In the centre was a two-storey building, with a flat roof, which seemed to me to have been made from concrete. The outside was unpainted and I could not detect any lines that denoting breeze-block or similar building material. It stood like a big square grey slab and in the side facing me was one window on the ground floor to the left of the front door – I assumed it was the front door as it faced the entrance to the compound – and one window on the upper floor slightly to the right of the front door. I couldn't see the other faces of the building. Immediately in front of us there was a break in the wire fence with two large metal and wire gates, which had been propped open with, to the right on the outside, a small wooden guard hut. I could not detect any movement inside this guard hut. About fifty yards each side of the gate were two long wooden structures with numerous windows and pitched wooden roofs. Looking carefully, I could see that the one to the right of the gate was occupied as several men in military type garb were walking around, out into the compound and across to the central building. It seemed as though this hut was a dormitory and I calculated that it was certainly large enough to take twenty-five beds and with the other hut of the same size, this confirmed the accommodation for fifty palace guard, which could be assigned to our area.

On the opposite side of the compound, behind the central concrete structure, was another large, square wooden building without windows but also with a pitched wooden roof. At one end it appeared (I could not see clearly from my vantage point) that there were two large double doors so I assumed this was the store room where the palace guard secreted goods pilfered from humanitarian organisations. Each side of this building lorries and jeeps were parked and close by was a structure comprising half a dozen uprights and a grass roof containing what looked like work benches and bits of machinery – the workshop. To the left of the concrete building was the wooden cookhouse. This had three walls with small windows, the fourth wall being open to the elements, and I could see pots, pans and stoves, which were being lackadaisically tended by the male cooks.

I continued scanning the compound, watching for every movement. Not too much was happening and there was certainly no sign of the cattle or goats taken from the joyful village. This did not though dissuade me from my belief that the culprits were sitting, lying and walking before me. Brother tapped me on the shoulder and whispered in my ear: 'We must go.'

'Is it possible for us to stay here until just before sunset?' I whispered back, 'I would really like to see as much as possible.' Brother nodded and settled down to wait while I continued scanning the compound.

Over the next couple of hours I did not see too much of great interest although I got the strong impression that those there were lazy and probably slovenly. They may well have been highly trained so far as fighting was concerned

193

but as a military, or at least quas-military establishment there was little sign of order and discipline and certainly none of spit and polish. As dusk was about to gather, Brother tapped me on the shoulder and nodded in the direction we must going so I handed back the binoculars and we slithered away from our vantage point around the back of the hill where we made a speedy yet careful descent. Even after darkness fell we continued walking for while to put a little more distance between us and the palace guard encampment. Eventually we stopped for the night and all ate, if not heartily, at least with some enthusiasm. I questioned Brother about his knowledge of the compound but he could add very little to what I had seen. He confirmed that certainly in the last few months there had been no more than twenty-five palace guard stationed there any one time. He also agreed that the big hut with the double doors and without windows was the likely place where the palace guard stored their ill-gotten gains. Regarding the centre concrete building, Brother said that this was the office of the commander-in-chief of this unit and he understood there were two or three bedrooms upstairs, one for the commander-in-chief and one for Death's Head when he was in attendance. The rest of the bottom floor was taken up with interrogation rooms and cells.

We all seemed to sleep well that night and continued at a good pace back towards our village. The second night, after we had eaten, Brother turned to me and said: I think you are planning something. What is it?'

I returned his gaze. 'I am not actually planning anything at the moment, just thinking about options. I have something in mind but it is too early to explain.'

Brother grunted and turned away to settle himself down to sleep.

When we arrived at our village I accompanied Amazon

and Brother to the chief, where, as usual, they reported what we had done and what was seen. The chief's face was, as ever, impassive and he asked a few questions but otherwise took the terrible news without emotion. When the audience was over we returned to our respective huts.

'I don't like what you're thinking,' said Vana as I entered the hut.

'Oh just wonderful,' I said, 'not "how are you" or "did everything go well" but "I don't like what you're thinking". Not a greeting I was expecting.'

She put a finger on my lips. 'I'm sorry. I already know what happened because someone from another village came here yesterday and told us of the massacre. But I still do not like what you're thinking.'

'How do you know what I'm thinking?' I asked. 'And if you heard of the massacre did you not think that we might have been caught up in it?'

Vana smiled. 'I knew you were all right because the man who came to us yesterday was a tracker and he had looked around the area of the massacre and identified two clumping great footprints walking away and this could only have been you.' So much for my walking on air then, I thought. 'As to your thinking, I do not know what it is, I just know I don't like it. You're hatching up something aren't you?'

'I'm not actually hatching anything,' I replied, 'I am certainly mulling various options over and I cannot see what there is for you not to like. I've made no decisions.'

She grunted and looked at me, unconvinced. 'I have to go to help prepare the food for tonight,' she said, 'it's my turn so I must leave you now.' She kissed me briefly and hugged me sufficiently for me to understand that she was glad to see me back and then disappeared. I washed the dust of the trail from my body and then walked around the village awaiting evening meal readiness. My mind was picking

over various possibilities and ideas that were forming themselves into a detailed plan. There were a lot of rough edges
still but I could work on it.

12

The Middle

The last dribbles of light from the setting sun seeped through my cell window and fell upon the pad full of my writing. I was still sitting on the wafer thin mattress with my back against the cell wall and my knees up, upon which the pad rested to allow me to write my tale. There was insufficient light for me to continue so I put the pad on the floor of my cell with the pencil on top and I slowly got to my feet to stretch my body, relieving the cramps that had begun to take hold but which I had barely noticed in my writing intensity.

The cell door opened and a guard walked in with a metal plate of food. He put the food on the floor, turned around and walked out, slamming the cell door behind him. I don't know if it was the fact that I was writing something, which my interrogator hoped to be a confession, that had prompted a dietary change but my meals since I had started writing were almost edible and certainly contained more goodness and protein than I had been offered before. No knife, fork or spoon of course so I sat down and slowly ate with my fingers.

I pondered over what I had written and considered what I would write tomorrow. It had all been surprisingly easy. I was used to writing factual reports and legal opinions and so I suppose relating what had happened since I had left

England was not very different even if I had to be careful to disguise people and places so far as I could. Everything was fresh in my mind although I had lost all track of days and weeks. I tried to work out how long I had been in this country but failed. Life in the village was so peaceful and orderly, days merged into weeks, making time unimportant. It was only the celebratory meal followed by the dancing that marked a week's end and try as I might I could not count up how many of those I had enjoyed.

Knowing my interrogator would be back in five days, I had taken the precaution of scratching a mark on the cell wall with the edge of my dinner plate as each day passed. I thought about how much I had written and the number of days I had left and wondered if I would complete my tale in time. I was certainly writing at a great pace though I strongly suspected what I was putting on paper was no masterpiece.

Not for the first time, as darkness fell, I questioned whether my efforts were going to gain me anything. Would what I'd written be sufficient to sate the political appetite of my interrogator? Even if it did; even if I had done enough; even if I could demonstrate a willingness to cooperate I feared it would not save my life. Executions at this prison were far too frequent to anticipate any cognisance of human rights. And these people were just the military. They were not the palace guard who handed out death without thought, let alone compassion. If I did not satisfy my interrogator then perhaps he would turn me over to the palace guard and, on reflection, death would be better than that.

I had no answers to this and my nature was that I didn't worry about something I could not fix so I lay down on my mattress, closed my eyes and drifted off into a dreamless sleep, ready to write the next day's chapter of events when the sun was high enough to give me light.

13

The First Phase

Amazon, Brother, Vana and I ate the evening meal together, mostly in silence. The usual babble of voices around the camp-fire seemed subdued that evening. The news of the massacre, although now well over a day old, still had an effect on everyone in the village. At the end of the meal I turned to Brother.

'You said the village to the north had a lot of munitions and equipment hidden away.' He nodded to me. 'You also said a part of that equipment was night vision goggles.' Brother nodded again. 'Do you know if they have silencers for automatic pistols?'

Brother looked at me hard. 'I do not know for sure but I would be surprised if they didn't. Why do you ask?'

'Is it possible for you to get me the night glasses and two automatic pistols with silencers? Ideally automatic pistols with more than the seven rounds capacity the Colt has and also some spare ammunition?'

'Yes it is certainly possible,' he replied, 'but you must tell me why you want them.'

'I am thinking of some action but at the moment the plan is not fully formed and it would be pointless telling you something still somewhat embryonic. The village with the munitions is, as I remember, some four days north of here and so it will be eight days before we know whether they have silencers for automatic pistols and by that time I will have the plan worked out completely so we can discuss it. I am assuming there is no radio contact with this village for I have seen no radios here.'

'You are right. There is no radio contact,' Brother said, 'the palace guard monitors any radio traffic and so it would be foolish to attempt to use radios at all so we use runners for communication. If this village has the silencers, which I am fairly sure it will, they will be back here with you in three days.'

'But I thought you said the village was four days away.'

'In fact it is somewhat less than four days when walking normally but we have runners and I can send a runner to the village with the request and they will send a runner back with the equipment so we will have it here in three days; probably less than that.'

'Three days will be good,' I said 'in fact much better than having to wait eight days.'

Brother frowned. 'I know you. That plan of yours is already formulated. You don't need another ten days thinking about it or even three do you?' He looked across at Amazon for moral support and she nodded in agreement. 'I am not going to send a runner for anything until you tell me what the plan is.'

I realised that I was somewhat cornered and I could understand Brother's approach. What I was going to do could certainly affect the village and, I assumed, any plan would have to be approved by the elders so I may as well come clean now.

'My observation of the palace guard camp is that security is poor and the men there are lazy with an arrogance that no one can possibly touch them as they are who they are. This being the case I am certain that at night they do not post extra guards or take any particular precautions, therefore I plan to go into the compound at night and shoot every man there.'

I looked at the three faces around me; they carried no expression at all.

'I knew I didn't like what you're thinking,' said Vana, 'how can you possibly kill twenty-five or so all by yourself?'

I smiled at her. 'I calculate it will be considerably easier than you may think. As you have seen, the moon is waning so in five or six days time the nights should be moonless, or at least fairly moonless. With night goggles I can see clearly and anyone without night goggles will not be able to see me too well, if at all. If my calculations are correct, I can walk up to the guard hut and shoot the guard with a silenced automatic pistol and then go into the sleeping hut and shoot the remainder, one by one. I appreciate even a silenced pistol will make some noise but if I move carefully and fairly swiftly it should be all over before anyone can be aroused.'

I looked at the three faces and watched my words sink in.

'It is a big gamble,' said Brother.

'No,' I replied, 'it's not a gamble at all. There is a calculated risk element I grant you but I will be alone and if something goes wrong then it is just me and no local villagers to become involved. That said though, I would appreciate it if you could take me there because there is no way I could get to the palace guard camp without getting hopelessly lost.'

'We will all go, that is all of the group,' said Brother and before I could protest he put his hand up to stop me. 'If you are going into the lion's den with more than a fair chance that you will be caught then sooner or later you will tell them about our village and they will come here to seek retribution. Therefore if our group is there then we can make sure you do not live to give the palace guard information.'

'Good,' I replied. 'I rather hoped you would say that because I agree with you completely. Also, it helps with the second part of the plan.'

'There is more?' Said Vana. 'Don't you think the idea of killing twenty-five people is enough!'

201

'On the assumption I am successful then Death's Head and the remainder of his merry men are not going to be happy bunnies. They will, quite obviously, seek retaliation and retribution somewhere so what we must do is to deflect that away from our village. What I would like someone here to do, if it is possible, is to go to the capital in a day or two and spread a rumour that a dissident group in the capital has been formed and is going to take some action against the palace guard in the capital. If the palace guard's intelligence is as good as you say it is, it will not be long before they hear this rumour and if, after I have done the killing, we oil the wheels, so to speak, by driving the jeeps and lorries towards the capital and abandoning them at some point along the way then this will give weight to the rumour that the attackers came from the capital itself. The fact that the attack did not take place in the capital will probably be regarded as disinformation.'

'I like it,' said Amazon, 'you have thought things through. I think if the worst comes to the worst and you do not succeed in killing everyone in the camp then we could certainly finish them off and drive the lorries towards the capital to be abandoned. It is a bold plan, far bolder than we would have ever attempted so I think it will work.'

'So then,' I said, 'the first thing we must do is find out whether the silencers are available. If not the whole plan will have to be revamped. Also, do you know anyone who would go to the capital and spread the rumour?'

'Me,' said Vana.

'No,' I exclaimed, 'I don't want you to go.'

'I am the most logical person to do this. Being a woman will help and in fact I go to the capital more regularly than anyone else to see my former teachers and my friends so it would not be unusual for me to be there. No one will question me and if they did they would accept my explanation. Anyone else in the village, apart probably from Sabra, could be suspect. Also, I know the right people to talk to who would spread the rumour to make sure it got to the right ears at the right time. Just talking to anyone in the street would not necessarily mean that the rumour would even start let alone get around in time. No, I am the ideal person.'

Both Amazon and Brother nodded in agreement. I was clearly outvoted.

'I will send a runner,' said Brother, getting to his feet and walking across the village centre. The other two were silent while he was gone and when he returned he said, 'A runner will be gone in less than thirty minutes.'

'Do you have to put my plan to the elders?' I asked.

'No,' said Amazon, 'anything of a military nature, the decision is taken by us. The elders know we would not put the village in danger if it can possibly be avoided. We only tell the chief what has happened, when it has happened. It is better that way for, I suppose I can say, security reasons. Your plan will be known to just the four of us. We will not tell the group until we are en route to the palace guard encampment. I suggest we all mull this plan over to see if we can find any faults or any improvements and we can discuss it again when the runner gets back.'

With that we drifted off back to our huts.

'What are you going to do for the next three days?' asked Vana.

'I need some hard physical work so I will join the men digging the new well. I have found if a plan is made or problem solved it is often best to do something to take one's mind off it completely as that leaves room for new ideas or additional problems to spring up.' Vana nodded wisely.

'And by the way,' she said, 'I reckon that plan was formed fully in your mind when you were looking at the encampment. Wasn't it?' I smiled and half nodded. She grunted and pulled me down onto the bed.

*

The next two days were spent helping with the well digging. It was indeed very strenuous and arduous. I was fairly well whacked out by the midday meal and really had to drive myself in the afternoon to pull my weight. This physical work had the desired effect for it did rid my mind off the plan, so when, in the evenings, I rehearsed what I was going to do, it was fresh and I could consider all the various options. In the end I felt it was best to keep it simple: in, shoot and out. Easily said.

During the midday meal of the third day a runner appeared carrying what looked to be a fairly heavy knapsack. He came and spoke to Brother, giving him the knapsack and then walked away. I confess I was staggered. It had taken him less than a day and a half to run a distance that would take a normal person nearly four days to walk and yet he did not even look out of breath. These guys could teach the Greek messengers of antiquity a thing or two!

'Everything you want is here. What are you going to do now?' asked Brother.

'I will take the pistols, silencers and ammunition to the practice area so I can shoot them both this afternoon. I have to get used to the feel of the pistols and also I suspect the silencers will have some effect on the handling and accuracy. On the assumption everything is all right and you all still believe the plan is viable, do you think we could start off tomorrow morning for I believe by the time we get to the encampment that will give us the best moonless night.'

'Yes,' replied Brother, 'we will be ready for tomorrow and in the meantime Vana should make her way to the capital.' He paused and looked at Amazon and Vana. 'Whilst I am sure we are all rather apprehensive about your plan, I do not think we can improve upon it and we all agree something has to be done so why not your plan?'

It all being decided, I bade Vana a very fond and some-what prolonged farewell and walked to the practice area with the knapsack.

I spent the whole of the afternoon practising shooting the automatic pistols with and without the silencers. I did not feel particularly comfortable with them for they were very light in the hand although, surprisingly, each held twenty rounds in the magazine. They were both Belgian FN 5–7 automatics without safety catches. That rather surprised me. It was good that I did practise. The handling and charac-teristics were different with and without the silencers and it took me a while to become reasonably comfortable with them. I anticipated my shooting would be very short range but nonetheless I had to practice for greater distance just in case. I rather hoped that I would not have to shoot further than twenty or so yards because I could not get the same feel with these two guns as I could with the far heavier Colt.

At the evening meal Amazon, Brother and I discussed the plan again; looking at it to try and find a serious flaw. We came up with many maybes and ponderables but nothing better. It was decided that the whole group would be fully armed with AK–47s, including me, and once I had entered the compound the group would get as close as possible to the gate without attracting the attention of any casual observer and wait for me to do the deed. They would remain where they were unless they heard shooting from a non-silenced gun, which would indicate that I had been detected. If that happened they would burst in to finish the job I had started. If all went well I would appear at the gate for them to enter and drive away the jeeps and trucks. Simple. I just needed a rather large slice of luck.

When I got back to the hut I tested the night goggles. They were fairly easy to use and gave a strange, eerie image of everything, which took a little while to get used to. I briefly went outside with them on and was pleased to find at fifty yards images were clear and even at one hundred yards there was sufficient detail to make out what I was looking at. Very satisfactory.

It was really quite odd sleeping in my hut that night by myself. It took me quite a while to get to sleep but when I did, it was dreamless.

The next morning the group and I left the village with knapsacks containing food the women had prepared for us. First we went the cave where we all changed into combat gear and took up our weapons and ammunition. We struck out at the usual steady pace towards the palace guard's encampment, and mindful of Vana's 'heavy booted' comment, I tried even harder to walk lightly and effortlessly. Whilst I seemed to succeed in my mind, I had no idea whether in fact I achieved anything at all.

With the usual stops for meals and overnight sleep we arrived well before dusk at the hill where I had previously observed the encampment. We sheltered under bushes to wait and I took the opportunity of rubbing burnt bark on my face and hands so that my whiteness, rather now deep sunned bronze, did not stand out at night. When the sun was safely down we carefully made our way around the base of the hill and very slowly crawled towards the entrance of the compound, keeping well apart. The noise of movement in the camp diminished and, putting on my night goggles, I could make out people walking back to the sleeping hut. The last to enter were the cooks. I could not see into the guard hut at the gate so did not know whether there was a sentry on duty though assumed someone would be there.

I read somewhere that the first two hours of sleep are the deepest so as I judged everyone was in the hut by about ten o'clock, I waited until just before midnight then tapped Brother on the shoulder to indicate I was going in.

Even though the sky was moonless, the stars gave light

so I carefully crawled to the back of the sentry hut, all the time scanning through my night goggles to see if anyone was moving about in the camp. When I got to the hut I waited and double-checked everything around me. It was silent with no movement. I looked back to where Brother and the group were lying and was pleasantly surprised to see, even through the night goggles, that they had pressed themselves to the ground behind bushes where they were difficult to see. I stood up, pulling a pistol from my belt, slowly and carefully walked to the front of the hut to see a soldier guard dozing on a hard wooden seat. I shot him between his closed eyes. In the stillness of the night the silenced pistol was a little louder than I had anticipated, which gave me some concern, but by now I was committed. More noise was caused by the soldier who fell off his chair when shot, propelling it to bang heavily on the side of the hut. Luckily, no one was listening.

On the basis that someone sneaking around would arouse curiosity, I walked slowly and steadily through the gates as if I had no care in the world. My Kalashnikov was slung over my shoulder in the small of my back in such a way that I could easily put it to my front to fire; my right hand, holding the silenced pistol, was down by my side. The other silenced pistol was tucked in my belt. When I got to the sleeping hut I found the door open and I quietly walked up the steps hoping the boards would not creak. I was in luck. No sound at all. The hut was just one big room with beds down each side. All the beds bar one (I assumed this was the guard's bed) had a sleeping figure. Sounds of heavy breathing and occasional snoring mixed with the overpowering smell of unwashed bodies greeted me.

I moved out of the doorway so that I was not silhouetted should anyone awake and look, and stood with my back to the wall, calculating the next move. I eased the second pistol out of my belt with my left hand in case of need. I was not too good a shot with my left hand but if things went wrong here, it would be all close range stuff and I should be able to hit what I aimed at. After taking a psychological deep breath – not a physical one because the smell was over-powering, I pointed a revolver at the head of the first sleeper and at about one foot away from his forehead squeezed the trigger. It had the desired effect but no one stirred. I quietly walked to the next bed and then the next and then the next, just pulling the trigger, gently sending bullets into the head of each bed occupant. I felt nothing and quickly developed a steady rhythm, going up one side of the hut squeezing the trigger and then, after changing the pistol from my left hand into my right for maximum magazine fullness went down the other side doing the same. Before I knew it, I had finished. Every one of them was dead. Not a peep. Not a protest. I certainly felt no remorse.

I walked out of the hut and across to the concrete building in the centre of the compound. Here the door was closed and when I opened it there was a squeal from un-oiled hinges. I paused but the noise did not seem to rouse anyone. To the right there was a corridor that seemed to run down to inter-view rooms or cells, as Brother had related, and I ignored these for the moment. To the left was a large empty office and ahead of me stairs to the upper floor. The stairs were concrete so no fear of squeaking floorboards when I walked up. At the top of the stairs were doors to three rooms. I opened the first door; the room was empty. I went to the second door and this room too proved to be unoccupied. In the third room was a big fat sleeping figure breathing surprisingly easily until that is I snuffed him out with a bullet between the eyes.

I returned to the compound and briefly went around the cooking area to make sure that no keen cook was sleeping there; then checked the jeeps, lorries and repair workshop. No one. I then went to the compound gate and beckoned Brother and the group to come in.

'I believe everyone is dead,' I said to Brother when he arrived, 'but take no chances. I may have missed someone somewhere so please tell your group to keep their eyes about them. I am going back to the centre block to check out the interview rooms and cells.'

'Okay,' said Brother, 'we will go around to the lorries and jeeps and also see what they have in their big store room. If there is something of use we will load up lorries.'

'But keep it quiet, if you can,' I replied.

I went back into the centre block, down the corridor looking into a room which contained a single table and a couple of chairs. The three cells had iron doors, which were unlocked, with no one in them. I confirmed to myself that this building was indeed made of concrete. Even the internal walls were concrete. The builder really wanted this to last for ever. I went back upstairs to double-check the bedrooms but there was nothing in them of any use or to indicate which one Death's Head would occupy when he was here. I confess I was a little disappointed Death's Head was not in the compound but in reality I knew it was an unlikely chance he might be around. There was a ladder propped up at the end of the corridor against a trapdoor leading to the flat roof. I climbed out and onto the roof to look around the compound. Through the night goggles I could clearly see Brother and his group loading up one of the lorries with foodstuffs and, if my eyes did not deceive me, some of the rockets he dearly wanted for his rocket launcher. I smiled. I anticipated when we walked back to the village we were all going to be loaded down with a couple of heavy rockets each.

I clambered down from the roof and out into the compound, going around to where Brother and the group were loading up a lorry.

'We decided to load one lorry with foodstuffs and some ammunition,' he looked a little sheepish when referring to ammunition, 'and this can be driven off to our usual place where other villages will unload and distribute the content. We found cans of spare petrol at the back of the store hut and we are putting these into the jeeps and other lorries so that when they are abandoned we can disable them and then set fire to them. Do you agree?'

'Absolutely,' I said, 'but I suggest you do not leave the rockets in the back of the food lorry but distribute them amongst the men to bring back to the village.' He laughed and slapped me on the back. 'Those night vision goggles must be very good!' he retorted.

Following my advice, he took the rockets out of the food lorry and put them on another one and when the food lorry was loaded it drove off and the rest of us got into a jeep or a lorry and drove out of the camp down the dirt road towards the capital. Brother was leading as I knew he would find the best place to abandon the vehicles. After about an hour of driving Brother pulled off the road into a slight depression in the tundra. We followed him and got out of our vehicles.

'I think this will be a good place to leave this lot,' he said, waving his arms towards the vehicles. 'Jumba is the magic mechanic here so get on with rendering those engines useless.' Jumba laughed and moved away to the lorries. He opened the bonnets and tinkered with something or other inside. As he finished with each lorry, and then each jeep, the remainder of the group soaked the vehicles in petrol after removing the rockets from one of the lorries. When all was done we moved off to a safe distance and Brother threw a lighted stick in the middle of the vehicles. The petrol took light immediately and the lorries were enveloped in gratifying flames.

The rockets were distributed with each of us having two strapped to the top of our knapsacks. The rockets were no light weight and I suspected my 'walking on air' gait would be unattainable with this load.

'Now,' said Brother, 'we must walk to the road towards the capital and then on the edge of the road, occasionally straying off it to leave tracks. After about a mile the road becomes mostly tarmac where tracks will not show up, so we can turn around and walk back, this time in the centre of the road where any of our footprints,' he did me the favour of not looking particularly at me when he said this, 'can be covered up. This should confirm to the investigating palace guard that the people who did the dirty deed came from the capital.'

We struck off towards the capital and when the road became more tarmac than dirt, turned around and walked back, single file, in the middle of the road. The last member of our crocodile carefully and expertly swept behind us with some twigs, obliterating any footprints.

Upon arriving in the village after depositing the rockets, arms and combat gear in the cave, Brother and I went to report to the chief. Again the chief's face was impassive but his eyes never left mine. Whether he was looking at me in approval or disapproval I simply could not tell. When the interview was over he nodded to both of us and we returned to our huts.

Over the next two days I spent the mornings with the well-digging team lifting buckets of earth out of the deep hole and depositing the contents in the designated pile. In the afternoons I coached some of the girls to improve their shooting. I have to say that the women of this tribe were far more receptive than the men. Not that they were particularly better shots but I only had to tell them something once and they remembered. There was much laughter and cheering when they hit the target. It all felt more like a party game than serious instruction.

It was during this period that I made a surprising discovery. After a shooting training session one afternoon I returned, alone, to the cave to clean the rifles. Brother normally accompanied and helped me with the task but on this day I had not seen him at all. When I had finished I sat on the work bench for a few moments for no reason other than to kill time before the evening meal. As I sat there, thinking about nothing in particular, I looked down at the rock and partly dusty floor and saw a curved scuff mark running from a corner of one of the rifle racks. It took me a while to realise its significance. It was as though that rifle rack was hinged on one side and opened towards me. The weight of the rifles in the rack had slackened the hinges causing the bottom of the rack to scuff on the floor as it was moved. I looked at the other racks but there was no similar scuff mark. Odd, I thought. Why have one that moved? I reasoned the rack must be hiding something so I got off the bench and pulled at the side of the rack above the scuff mark but nothing. I then pushed the rack. There was a small amount of movement. Clearly, if this rack opened like a door, there must be a catch somewhere. I inspected the side; nothing. Then, inside, after removing rifles close to the end – here I found a cleverly concealed lever, which would not have been spotted unless the looker was intent on finding something. I pulled the lever, at the same time pulled the end of the rack towards me and it swung open, scraping slightly on the cave floor, revealing an entrance to another cave. I picked up the oil lamp and entered this hidden cave, which was about six feet high – I had to stoop slightly to walk around – and about twelve feet by twelve feet in size. Stacked from floor to almost ceiling were wooden boxes. Closer inspection revealed guns of various sorts, and ammunition. Enough for a small army. Four of the boxes were square and open. I lifted the lids and saw two contained military combat-type clothing; one was full of an assortment of boots of various sizes (so that's where my footwear came from); and one, curiously, was full of small, soft canvas bags. These bags were about the same size as used by banks for silver or copper coin but with a draw-string closing. I puzzled for a long time but could not work out what these bags could possibly be used for here in a village in the middle of an African country. I would have to ask when the time was right, though I felt my poking around in an obviously secret area could raise some resentment so I would have to be careful.

I came out of the small cave, closed the rifle rack door, making sure it was secured properly on its latch, replaced the rifles and ran my foot over the floor to make the scuff mark less obvious. Very strange. Brother had previously told me other villages had arms caches – and one of the villages far more guns, ammunition and peripheral military ware than here – which, together with the amount of guns and ammunition in this cave, struck me as much more than could possibly have come from the occasional raid upon palace guard lorries. I could not think of any reason why the palace guard would have transported so much armament around the countryside. Mystery indeed but no opportunity arose for me to bring up the subject and I soon forgot about it.

Mid-morning of the third day Vana arrived and came straight to me at the well digging.

'How did you get on?' I asked.

'Let us go back to the hut so I can wash the dust of the road from me and I will tell you.'

I made my excuses to the well-digging team who immediately understood and had broad smiles on their faces when we walked towards the hut!

In the hut I got the wash water for her and she stripped off, washing herself down slowly as I sat and watched. When she finished, she put on a clean robe and sat beside me in silence.

'Well?' I said.

She laughed. 'It went incredibly well. I was very lucky.

When I got to the capital I went to my friend's house and quite unexpectedly my former teacher was there having tea. He is a very nice man and an excellent teacher but has two faults. The first is he thinks he knows everything; and the second is he is the biggest gossip on this continent. It took me no time at all to bring up the subject of dissidents in the capital and as he believes he knows everything he responded that he was aware of a group acting somewhere and it was easy for me to make him think he knew they were planning an attack in the capital. My former teacher is very well connected and I was certain when he left us he would be gossiping to all his friends about the impending dissident attack.'

She paused with a smile on her face and looked at me. 'I went around to see all my friends, as usual, and after your attack I was invited to an evening cocktail party. Quite coincidentally a member of the Cabinet was there and he was spitting fire. To anyone who wanted to listen he regaled the story of the massacre of the palace guards and how his intelligence service had confirmed the attackers came from the capital. He went on to say that every source they had in the capital was being tapped and arrests would be imminent. I was obviously delighted that the suspicion was directed towards the capital rather than towards one of the villages but was somewhat concerned that innocent people would be arrested and tortured. However, my later discreet enquiries revealed that the intelligence network turned up nothing in the capital and the palace guard was furious that its spying services were not working properly.'

'But surely they would arrest someone, just for effect,' I said.

'Yes, I would have thought so too. However, I strongly suspect, and I have no real evidence of this, that our sympathisers in the government deflected enquiries because at the moment there is a Pan-African conference taking place and

the last thing Baumge wants is for the leaders of other countries to believe the palace guard would act without firm
evidence. I would hope by the time the conference is over,
at the end of next week, things will have calmed down a bit
and the intelligence arm of the palace guard realises that it
cannot trace or identify any dissidents in the capital. This
of course is true for no one dares band together in the capital
for they would be detected immediately.'

'Is there a chance that they may suspect one of the outlying
villages?' I asked.

'No, I do not think so. They are really convinced it is
someone from the capital and as their own investigators and
trackers have advised of this by reading the tracks leading
to the capital, there would be too much loss of face to now
say the attackers came from outside.'

'So then,' I replied, 'we seem to be lucky and will probably get away with it.'

'Yes. There is one more thing as well. The successful attack
on the palace guard was obviously a topic of conversation
everywhere. Whilst everyone had to be careful what they
said, it was absolutely clear to me the fact the palace guard
has proved to be vulnerable has given everyone hope. The
air of absolute doom seems to have been lifted, for the
moment at least.'

There was a long pause as Vana looked at the ground
before turning to me and saying: 'How about you? How do
you feel? Do you have remorse?'

I replied immediately. 'I feel absolutely nothing at all. I
certainly have no remorse or regrets. What had to be done
is done. It might well be, though I believe it unlikely, those
who died did not carry out the massacre of the village, but
whilst they may not be guilty, all are responsible.'

'Come,' said Vana, 'we must find Sabra and Ajani to
report to them on my trip to the capital. They will be anxious
to know, as indeed will the elders.

We left the hut and sought out Amazon and Brother and together with them went to the chief's hut. This time he was not sitting outside so, after calling out, we entered. I was very impressed with the furnishings. The chief's hut was twice as big as mine, containing a large double bed, a chair and various rugs scattered on the bare earth with one or two hangings on the walls. The whole effect was simplicity but homeliness.

The chief was sitting on the floor as we entered but he got up and moved to his chair. He motioned us to sit on the floor, which we did and Vana quietly and firmly retold what she had already told me. She spoke in clear English, which the chief understood. When she had finished he asked questions, very much along the same lines I had asked, and appeared to be satisfied. For the first time, his expressionless face changed into a broad smile as he looked at me and said:

'To be truthful, young man, when I was told what you had done I was not happy. I cannot deny those horrible men deserve their fate but I worried mightily that the palace guard would seek retribution everywhere. It does seem probable from what Vana said that this is not going to happen and now I am happy. I, like you, do not believe in taking human life for we should all live happily and peacefully side-by-side. However, those men who you killed were evil and if you can live with what you have done, I certainly can. Well done but please take care. Think carefully about what you want to do next.'

'It is not for me to say what should be done next,' I replied to the chief, 'though I believe it is in all of our interests if we do nothing at all for several weeks, if not a month or so. Let the dust settle and consider carefully what might or could be done after that.'

The chief nodded and spoke to Amazon and Brother in the local dialect. From their reply it seemed to me they very much agreed that now was the time to let things lie.

216

We left the chief's hut and started walking across the village centre. Amazon linked her arm in mind and said in a conspiratorial way: 'What do you really think we should be doing next? Should we lie low or continue with the initiative to make things as difficult as possible for the palace guard?'

I stopped walking and all three of them crowded around me waiting for my reply.

'First of all I must emphasise that nothing is my decision. You guys are in charge here. Okay, I fully accept I steamrollered you into the action against the palace guard but that was exceptional. We were all emotional after seeing what they did to that lovely village and I suppose we were also a little numb. That in fact was a weakness and we should guard against it.' At this point Vana nodded slowly. 'Let me set out what we know now,' I continued. 'There is quiet but undemonstrated support for a government overthrow in the capital and this must be nurtured. Also, there is what I will call mercenary groups in the outlying villages who are trained or being trained in military matters; this should continue. We have depleted a fairly sizeable chunk of the palace guard, which has two immediate effects. First, it gives the people some heart that resistance can be worthwhile. Second, and this is more important so far as we're concerned, the palace guard will be ever vigilant now so there is no way we could repeat such an exercise.'

There were nods all around as they waited for me to continue.

'The essentials are making sure that people are encouraged to believe resistance against the government will be successful coupled with not one of them being hurt. In a nutshell, what do we consider can be done without us being caught and when should this be done?'

'That is politician's speak,' said Brother who looked irritated, 'what we want is a viable strategy. You are the thinker.

217

You should be able to work out a plan for us to evaluate. You should know these things.'

Vana immediately jumped to my defence. 'That is grossly unfair. He is not one of us. Nigel has done more than any of us in a very short space of time but that does not mean he is burdened with the responsibility of making plans and decisions for us. That is our job. If he can help, wonderful. You should not expect so much.'

'Thank you,' I responded. 'There is sense in everything you all say but surely we must all pull together here. If I was to make any suggestions at all it would be that another attack takes place within the next two weeks, three at the most. This will be long enough for the government and palace guard to relax a little bit and soon enough to nurture the belief of the general population that the initial strike was not simply a one-off. But the place of any attack has to be selected very carefully. I would still not advocate a full frontal attack upon the palace guard if they are as efficiently trained in fighting as Ajani has said, so we must be sneaky. We need on the ground information. Is there a place we can select to, say, ambush half a dozen or so palace guards somewhere that is a long way from any village that might suffer retribution?'

Brother responded. 'There are, of course, large tracts of land in our country where there are no villages but the palace guard would have no need to be in such areas unless of course they were enticed there in some way. It might be possible that as this section of the palace guard has been wiped out there will be a reshuffling of men because there is no way they can recruit twenty-five good and loyal assassins immediately. I will send runners out to all the villages to enquire as to palace guard movements. I think that will be the best step. Once we know what is happening then we can think again as to what to do.'

'I know I have no need to say this,' I said, 'but please be

very careful indeed that the runners do not draw attention to the fact someone is interested in palace guard movements and more particularly do not draw attention to this village.' All three nodded in unison. 'One other thing that might be a shortcut for us is to find out from the capital what the palace guard intends to do. That is, not only its redeployment plans but also if it is looking to carry out retribution on any village or purge any area.'

'I think it would be a grave mistake if Vana went back to the capital straight away as this would certainly arouse suspicion,' said Amazon. 'I have not been there for quite a while now so I think I should go. I expect security will be very high and the palace guard a little jumpy but I can handle myself in those situations. The other advantage I have over Vana is that I know who in high places, so to speak, can be relied upon to pass us good information without arousing suspicion.' She looked up at the sun. 'It's too late for me to start out now but I will go first thing tomorrow morning. I will take two or three other women with me with some produce, rugs and baskets to sell, which is what I usually do, so if anyone enquires, I am just following my normal pattern.'

With that, we went back to our respective huts. On entering, Vana put some water in two drinking bowls, handed me one and sat cross-legged on the floor. I sat in front of her and took a drink from the bowl, not realising until then how thirsty I was.

'I have come to know you very well,' said Vana, 'you are not a freedom fighter, nor do I believe you want to be. Yet you seem content, determined almost, to help the fighters in their cause. I am a little worried because I do not think it is you; it is not right for you. Will you consider what I'm saying?'

Whilst I didn't need to, I thought for a while. 'You are perfectly correct, this really is not in my nature, nor is it my fight although I owe you all so much. As I indicated earlier the attack on the palace guard compound was what I believe is called a knee jerk reaction. I do not think it was a mistake but the decision to do so was taken in a mistaken way. If there are to be any further actions they must be cool and calculated, not tinged with any emotion. I certainly believe if our actions have given hope to the people then those people should not be disappointed, but there again, is it my fight?'

There was a long silence while we drank our drink with neither of us really wanting to take this conversation further but both knowing it had to go on. Eventually I broke the silence.

'I really need your support and assistance. I do not want to instigate any action that could possibly be harmful to this village. I have been very lucky so far in what I have done and it strikes me that both Sabra and Ajani are inclined to follow what I might suggest. This really would be a big mistake because, as has been said, I am not one of you; I do not know the country; I do not know the people. My gut instinct is that another attack of some sort, assuming it to be successful, would be good because it would not only give heart to the people but also confusion to the enemy. Whether that is followed up by more it is far too early to say. The wheels have been put in motion to get information and I suggest we wait to see what comes back before making any firm decisions at all. Will you help me get it right?'

Vana smiled. 'I will always help in every way I can. Whether that help means we get it right or get it wrong is in the lap of the gods, not my gift.'

'Looking back over everything I have seen and heard it strikes me the nub of the problem is Death's Head, Zaban. If he could be eliminated then whilst that would not be the solution, it would go an awful long way towards a solution.'

Vana grunted.

There was nothing more that to be said and so we busied ourselves around the hut until the evening mealtime.

14

The Second Phase

Something over a week passed before information concerning the palace guards started filtering back to us. Much was no use at all and some struck me as rather fanciful. After another four days Amazon returned looking just a little smug. As ever, her first call was to the chief where a long conversation ensued and although I was hanging around in the area, expecting Amazon to call us all together, she did not do so instead when walking away from the chief, she said, 'I will see you at the meal tonight.' Tantalising!

Well before the evening meal I was ready to go out with my bowl but Vana held me back. 'Do not appear too eager,' she said, 'let her wait a bit.'

I do not know whether this was a power-play or just Vana being mysterious but I did as I was bid.

We were one of the last to get our food and went to sit with Amazon and Brother, neither of whom showed any emotion at the fact we were delayed. They had nearly finished eating and when their bowls were empty they sat patiently waiting for us to eat. Vana was being even more irritating by eating very slowly. I can't say I matched her speed but I certainly did not bolt my food. Eventually all bowls were empty.

'Ajani has filled me in on the information you have so far obtained from the other villages,' said Amazon, 'and some of it fits in well with what I have learned. There is to be a reorganisation of the palace guard to cover the gap left by those who were killed. Zaban wanted this done immediately but, surprisingly, was prevented by ministers from starting anything at all until the end of the Pan-African conference. Even after that there was some squabbling about what should be done, which, before now, would have been impossible to imagine actually happening. The wiping out of twenty-five palace guard really has had an effect on some of the government ministers who were up to now simply sheep following their leader and frightened to death of Zaban. Now they seem to have found their voice. Admittedly, that voice is not too loud but it has been enough to throw Zaban's plans somewhat into disarray.'

She paused for us to consider what she had said. I fully expected our little escapade to have repercussions but I did not anticipate a partial catharsis. I did not know whether to be pleased or worried.

'Essentially men from the current palace guard will be replacing the unit that has been wiped out. This would have meant taking three men from each of the surviving countryside units and one from the capital, giving a strength of twenty-two men in each of the countryside units. That was Zaban's initial plan together with a fierce recruitment and training drive to bring the strength of the palace guard back up to a total of two hundred and fifty. The combined voice of the dissident ministers was to the effect that taking three men from each unit would not give a cohesive force that could do any good unless it went through rigorous training and familiarisation. This could not be done because Zaban was going to recruit and train others so the unit that was wiped out is going to be replaced by ten men from each of the two units in the south – who have worked together before – and twenty men from the capital will go out and join the depleted units in the south. This move really pleases everyone

223

in the capital for it means there are less spies and palace guard strutting around the streets to intimidate. Zaban is not happy but for the moment he has no choice though undoubtedly he will reaffirm his grip on the government in a very short space of time.'

Again another pause to let that sink in. In fact one of the reports we had from a village close to the capital was that palace guards from the capital were being sent out into the countryside to strengthen units but we thought this was somewhat unlikely. Obviously not. Another report that came in only late last night suggested a unit to the south was gearing up for some action but now, on reflection, this could just have been getting ready to move out ten of their men to our area. Things were fitting in.

'So then,' said Brother, 'how can we take advantage of all this?'

He looked at me long and hard as indeed did Vana. I returned his gaze and smiled.

'Well,' I said, 'do you think this can give us any opportunities? If so how do you think we can take advantage?'

Brother was obviously not too enamoured with me throwing the ball back to his court but was not without guile for he replied:

'There will be three units of palace guard travelling around. Two of ten men each from different camps coming to our area and twenty from the capital going to southern units. This, it strikes me, gives an opportunity to single out one of the units coming to us and ambush it. The trouble is, of course, timing.' Turning to Amazon: 'Do you know when all this is going to happen?'

'Unfortunately not,' replied Amazon. 'Even with our excellent runners I think it will be very difficult to find out when the two lots of ten men will be setting out from the south in sufficient time to do anything positive. I am bearing in mind what Nigel said, and I do agree with him that any attack should be well away from us and other villages. Those leaving the capital would be easier because there is a reasonable chance we can find out in time when they are leaving but the problem is there will be twenty of them and only eleven of us.'

I noted that Amazon included me in the fighting force. A long silence followed with each thinking their own thoughts.

'What do you think we should do, Nigel?' said Vana, looking at me with a steady eye and a half smile on her face. I took this as an approval for me to make a suggestion. I smiled at her in grateful thanks.

'Looking at it from the palace guard point of view, as commander I would assume that twenty men coming from the capital would be safe not only because of their number and consequent firepower but also they would be particularly vigilant. However, it might be the weakest link.'

There was much frowning around me and I realised that their thoughts were concentrated upon the two units of ten and not those coming from the capital.

'The units in the countryside have been exercising their horrible skills on villagers and, as we have seen, whole villages for a goodly while now. They are used to driving through the countryside and have doubtless formed a method of ensuring their safety – something along the lines that you do when you travel through the countryside but adapted to vehicles. If they haven't done this already, they will certainly be doing so now because of the loss of one of their units would put them on their guard. Therefore although they will be fewer in number I strongly suspect they will be more difficult to attack successfully. On top of this is the fact that it will be difficult for us to find out when they are on the move so we can have sufficient time to do anything. Those from the capital, on the other hand, have been enjoying the fruits of civilised living and I am sure a lazy life for a long time, and skills will not be honed either in fighting or indeed observation. Therefore, although they are more in number, I would anticipate they would be less of a threat if attacked. Unless they have a particularly strong and forceful commander with some experience there may be a good deal of confusion when they come under fire.'

This produced different reactions from each of them. Amazon raised an eyebrow; Brother looked a little confused; and Vana was giving a sly and contented smile as if to say 'crafty sod'.

'We do have to plan this carefully and not get carried away,' I continued. 'If we're going to do anything I would strongly suggest we do not rush but by the same token do not waste any time. The first and most obvious thing is to find out when the palace guard from the capital is going to move, assuming, that is, they have not gone already.'

'Come on,' said Amazon, 'let's be real. We are not talking Desert Storm here. These clowns would take a week to find their tooth brushes, assuming, that is, they had any. No, I can assure you they have not left yet so I can send a runner to someone who will find out quicker than anyone what is happening so we should get the information in good time.'

I was pleased at this so said, 'Secondly, and this I believe is in fact the most important, is there an area between the capital and the southern units where an attack can be made without obvious retribution on surrounding villages?'

'Oh yes,' said Brother. 'The southern units are very far to the south and there is a small wasteland, almost desert, which the palace guard from the capital will have to cross. The downside is that it offers absolutely no cover at all for an ambush but it is ideal for making sure an attack is not attributable to any village.'

'I take it this area has a delineated road. If not tarmac then certainly one that the palace guard will use?' I asked.

'Indeed yes,' said Brother, 'the advantage of that area is no vehicle would stray off the road for the terrain can be very soft in places, bogging down a lorry very easily, and even a jeep would have difficulty.'

'Right then,' I said, 'let's get the information from the capital, prepare to move at a moment's notice and then we can decide whether or not to carry out an attack.'

'You're taking charge again,' said Vana.

'Yes, you're absolutely right. I am really sorry. I get carried away with my own enthusiasm sometimes.' I smiled at them all. 'Please ignore what I said, what do you think?'

'I am sure we all agree with what you have said,' said Amazon. 'First, information from the capital, then we can discuss the plan – I am assuming you already have a plan fully formulated in your mind!' I half nodded and we broke up with Brother moving away towards the area where the runners seemed to congregate, and I saw him bringing a man back to Amazon who was giving him specific and detailed instructions.

When we got back to our hut, Vana said, 'When do you think you will be telling them your plan? I suggest you do not leave it too late because whilst it may be a good plan in your mind you must remember they are experts in this area and could see an obvious flaw that might pass you by.' I thought for a moment and realised Vana was talking a good deal of sense but I was a little concerned over security, and telling everyone the detail of the plan too early could lead to a leak, implausible as this might be. The whole thing was audacious and much could go wrong so I felt it prudent to give minimum information. However, it was not wise to tell Vana of my concerns.

'You are right up to a point. My idea is fairly straight-forward although my primary concern is actually getting away from the ambush if it is not totally successful. Ajani said the ground was open and afforded no cover, which would, quite obviously, mean if we were retreating under heavy fire we would suffer casualties. That has to be addressed now but I will keep the whole detail of the plan under wraps because until we get to the ambush point I will not really know how it is all going to pan out.' Vana gave me a look that showed she did not quite believe all I said. 'I will rethink my ideas overnight and speak to Sabra and Ajani tomorrow to make them fully aware of my concerns.'

'Well for my part,' said Vana, 'you won't be getting too much time tonight to think,' and with that she threw herself at me, taking us both to the ground on top of the mattress and she started to nibble my ear and kiss me as she slowly undressed me.

Contrary to Vana's prognostication I did indeed think over the plan quite a lot that night. Whilst I could quite easily have gone to sleep after our lovemaking I lay with my eyes closed, turning over the ideas to see whether there was a fault somewhere. There was no doubt about it, escaping if the plan did not go well troubled me the most. Unsurprisingly, my failure to go to sleep immediately did not escape Vana, for after an hour or so of my lying there, immobile, thinking, she put her arm around me and said, 'Enough thinking. Sleep and let your dreams find faults and errors; even perhaps a different plan.' She kissed me on the cheek and I drifted off to sleep.

The following morning at mealtime I sought out Amazon and Brother, indicating I wanted to speak to them after the meal, and it was clear from the expression on their faces they were very pleased at this, for whilst they obviously accepted my ability to formulate plans, nonetheless I was still really an unknown entity. Vana was right, I might have the ideas but I certainly did not have the experience or the knowledge to ensure I would be successful, but I really believed it was not a good idea to tell them everything now.

When we finished eating, Amazon and Brother took me

out of the village to sit under a tree. I was quite surprised to see Vana already there. I raised an eyebrow and she gave me a look as if to say, 'It's no good being a thinker if you can't think of the obvious.'

When we were settled I started. 'As Vana pointed out to me last night, I do not have the experience you do and also I am very unfamiliar with the terrain where the attack is likely to take place so I will very much need your input and advice before we actually attack, for at that time, when I have seen the ground over which we have to operate, the plan I have in mind will be formulated fully.' Vana gave me one of her disbelieving looks but Amazon and Brother seemed to accept what I said at face value. 'There is, though, one thing we have to settle now.' All eyes were upon me.

I paused for a moment to gather my thoughts. I was uncertain how to approach what was going to be a very delicate topic. I looked at them, and began.

'So far all your actions have been successful but we have to face the grim reality that this time we may not succeed fully or even at all.' I paused to let this sink in. Their eyes did not leave my face. 'You say the ground will be open with little or no cover, therefore if the palace guard is able to survive our first onslaught then it will be fighting back and we will be completely exposed. The guards, on the other hand, will have some cover from the vehicles, and whilst I appreciate high velocity bullets will penetrate the metal of a truck or a jeep, nonetheless if they are hiding behind the vehicles we will not have clean shots at them, whereas as we are in the open they will have clean shots at us. So we have to plan a retreat and I have no idea how this can be achieved if the ground is as open as you say.' I paused again and looked at Brother and Amazon in an enquiring way, suggesting I was more than open to ideas.

'In any retreat,' Brother said, 'the reality is someone has to cover the retreating forces and that person or those persons are likely to be sacrificed. We have to accept this and, as I am the leader,' this produced a scowl and disapproving noise from Amazon, 'I will be the one to give covering fire to allow a retreat. Until we actually see the ground where the ambush is taking place I don't think we can take it any further.'

I was not at all surprised that Brother was holding himself out as, in effect, a sacrificial lamb and I was very pleased indeed that he realised so quickly the potential pitfalls of the attack we were planning to make. Amazon, too, was attune to the possible problems and, although obviously unhappy that Brother would be left behind if things went wrong, she could not immediately come up with a better idea.

'Yes,' I said, 'you are right and I cannot think of a better man to give covering fire. As you say, we cannot go into any more detail at this moment but we can give us all an edge.' This produced sharp glances from everyone. 'You have that lovely rocket launcher and enough rockets now to be able to use it. If we take the launcher and, say, four rockets, then these can be used in the attack, but more particularly for our current problem, if there has to be a retreat then explosions from rockets going off around the palace guard will certainly keep their heads down and more than likely give you time to escape as well.' This cheered everyone up considerably and, whilst in theory it could well work, I had no experience at all in rocket launchers so had not the faintest idea how quickly one could load and fire or even how accurate it could be. Brother, though, seemed to have no such misgivings.

'How do you actually plan to attack?' asked Amazon. I was hoping she would not be quite so direct. I smiled and gave an 'I am still considering' type expression before answering.

'It really very much depends upon the ground where we

choose to attack. I have various alternatives but until we get there and I get your views it really would be counterproductive to go into what I think we should consider.' I could see that no one was totally convinced by what I said so I thought they should be deflected. 'As I understand it, it will take us about five days careful walking to get to the place where you think it will be best for an attack.' Nods all around. 'And on the assumption that the palace guard will not waste time once it leaves the capital, it will take them half a day or so to get to the same place.' Everyone agreed. 'Therefore, we have to be in place early and ensure the runners know where we are to give us as much warning as possible as to when the convoy will likely arrive. Do you agree?'

'Yes,' said Brother, 'we have to be in place in good time and at the moment we have no idea when the palace guard might be leaving the capital. It therefore seems to me we ought to move out today otherwise we may well be too late.'

'If our runner has managed to contact the person I know in the capital,' said Amazon, 'then we will certainly get a very good indication of when the palace guard is likely to move, but although I anticipate this will not be for many days yet, I could be wrong, so I believe you are right to get there early.'

'Okay,' I said. 'Let us prepare to move out after the midday meal.' Eyebrows were raised at this point, no doubt wondering why I was willing to sacrifice the best part of half a day. 'We have some things to do before we go. First, we must be fully armed with your rocket launcher and four rockets. Second, we must each have a shovel or similar tool as well as a parang or similar to cut things.' Puzzled expressions. 'And also each man must have twenty or better twenty-five of the laths used as cross members under the grass for hut-building, plus binding thongs.' Puzzled expressions deepened so I hurried on. 'Food obviously for two weeks and, very importantly, as much water as we can carry unless you know

231

of an unattended water-hole before we reach the desert.'

'There is one water-hole en route,' said Brother, 'which should give us refills at this time of year but, just in case, we will carry extra water bottles. I will go and get the guns and ammunition ready and, of course, my rocket launcher,' turning to Amazon, 'can you warn the group we will be moving out early this afternoon and make sure they each have a digging tool? They always carry a parang. Vana, I would appreciate it if you could organise the food and water. This leaves you, Nigel.' He looked at me in a mischievous way. 'As you are the hut-building expert amongst us I will leave it to you to get the laths and binding material ready in time though I have no idea why we should be burdened with these loads unless of course you want to give us a lesson in hut-building!'

I did not rise to the bait so we all got up to carry out our various tasks. I went to the covered area, which stored the hut-building materials, and spent a good deal of time convincing Mugobo I needed the laths and bindings, but in the end he helped me gather up bundles and tie them together, although he was clearly very unhappy that his store was being so heavily depleted. I told Mugobo the group were going to carry one bundle each and he devised an ingenious carrying strap, which allowed the bundles to be slung over a shoulder without interfering with the knapsack on anyone's back. When all this was done it was nearly time for the midday meal so I returned to my hut to collect my bowl and wandered out to where the food was being prepared to find Brother, Amazon and Vana there already talking amongst themselves.

Seeing me, Brother said, 'We were just discussing how best to get the runners to find us to give updated information on the palace guard moving out of the capital. We have decided it would be wasteful of time to have the runner come back to the village and then another runner to catch us up so if we walk at double pace to get to the watering-hole we should be there in well less than three days and can hide ourselves to await the runner from the capital with updated information. Unless we are incredibly unlucky we will have at least four days notice of the palace guard moving out and even if it is only two days, that will be enough time for us. I will send a runner to the capital now to tell our runner there to bring his news to the watering-hole. A second runner in the capital is a good backup in case things change.' It seemed like an excellent idea to me so I nodded approvingly.

After we had eaten, I said goodbye to Vana who handed me a heavy knapsack full of food and water bottles and went to the hut material store to pick up my bundle of laths alongside which was a makeshift wooden spade, which I took as well. Quite who put it there I had no idea. I left the village and walked towards the cave entrance, which was already open, and the group were changing into their camouflage uniforms, checking firearms and ammunition, with Brother bustling around handing out four rockets, which were strapped to knapsacks. Bearing in mind the weight of my own knapsack, the wooden shovel and the laths coupled with the Kalashnikov and ammunition, I was very glad he did not select me as one of the rocket carriers. I felt it was going to be difficult enough to walk at normal pace and if we were marching double time, as Brother had indicated, I wondered whether I could stay the pace.

Once we were all ready, the cave was closed and, with our tracks around it covered, we started out. Brother set a good but steady pace, which was not too fast for me although my 'walking on air' technique went with the wind as I had to concentrate on putting one foot in front of the other. As before, the group sent out flankers, each side and a little ahead of Brother, Amazon and me, to keep a watchful eye on the surrounding countryside. I soon got into the rhythm of the walk and by nightfall I was ready to stop, though quite surprised I did not feel exhausted. I was very happy to take the weight of the knapsack and bundle off my shoulders and, after I had stretched to relieve my muscles, I realised my right shoulder was smarting. I unbuttoned my shirt and saw the ingenious harness fashioned by Mugobo had rubbed the skin raw. Amazon noticed and handed me a thick cloth.

'Put this under your shirt tomorrow. It will protect you,' she said. I was very grateful and replied, 'Do you always carry a piece of spare cloth with you?'

'No. As soon as I saw the way we were going to carry those bundles I knew the cord was going to cut into my shoulder so I put a piece of cloth there as did most of the other is in the group. I noticed you did not so I brought a piece, knowing you would have soreness there. I'm surprised you lasted until now.'

'Thank you very much for your forethought and concern. I suppose I didn't realise my skin was being rubbed raw because of the agony of the rest of my body trying to keep up with your fast pace.'

'We were simply strolling along today. If the runners give us news that the palace guard is leaving the capital early, we will have to walk much faster. Do you think you will be able to keep up?'

I stifled a groan and replied, 'I can but do my best.'

We ate our evening meal with the usual banter between the group and I was somewhat heartened to see that those who did not have the foresight to put a piece of cloth under the Mugobo harness also had sore shoulders but, being warrior fighters, they shrugged it off as merely a little discomfort and no particular problem. Their colleagues ceremonially toure their piece of cloth in half and handed half to the slightly suffering, and whilst at first this gesture was waved away as unnecessary, by the time the meal had finished and we prepared for sleep, with the group scattering in the usual way, I noticed the proffered halves of cloth had disappeared.

I needed no rocking to get to sleep and awoke with the sun rising, feeling refreshed if a little stiff. A quick morning meal and then we set off once more. Brother set a slightly faster pace in the morning but, after the midday meal, slowed it a little as the flankers of the group spread out more to check the surrounding areas and the way ahead. It was clear Brother was concerned that we did not blunder into danger but was conscious we had to make good time. I managed to keep up with the pace and was very grateful I was not one of the flankers who were in fact covering almost twice as much ground as I was as they moved in and out, side to side, to check around. Even with Amazon's piece of cloth firmly in place I felt the soreness in my shoulder though I was very grateful indeed that the harness was not pressing on completely unprotected skin.

We arrived at the watering-hole as the sun was setting on the third day. There was plenty of vegetation around the watering-hole and we ate our evening meal well away from it and moved even further away to hide under bushes to sleep. Amazon explained it would be unwise to sleep close to the watering-hole because at sunset and during the night animals would come to drink and if they were startled by sleeping humans they could attack. Also, we wanted to keep out of sight of any travellers who would naturally make straight for the watering-hole.

The following morning I went with Amazon to the watering-hole to check the amount of water there while the others fanned out into the countryside to see if there were any travellers or other signs of human life. The watering-hole proved to be what I can only describe as a large puddle about fifteen feet in diameter, though I had no idea how deep it was. I suspected not very. The surrounding earth was pitted with animal tracks but with my ignorance I could not tell what sort of animals had come during the night to drink, though I was fairly certain there was no mark big enough to be an elephant! The water itself was certainly not bright and sparkling. Indeed it looked incredibly uninviting. I gazed at it with some dismay.

'It does not look brilliant,' said Amazon, 'but if you are dying of thirst it will be like nectar. We will drink the water we have in our water bottles now and fill up before we move off. With a bit of luck we will not need to touch this water but it is essential we have it just in case.'

I spent most of the day wandering aimlessly around the watering-hole with nothing to do at all. Amazon and Brother appeared to join the rest of the group checking the surrounding countryside and I ate a lonely, sparing, midday meal. In the middle of the afternoon the group started appearing one by one from various directions. Although I was waiting for them and looking out for them, I was surprised at the way they could move and remain largely unseen. The vegetation around the watering-hole was fairly thick for about one hundred yards or so but after that it was the usual beaten earth, struggling grasses with the odd bush here and there and an occasional insipid looking tree. Somehow the group could use this apparent lack of cover to remain invisible. When we were all gathered together Brother checked the water bottles and, not for the first time, I was surprised to see how little they had all drunk. I thought I was being particularly sparing in my sips of water but compared with the others it seemed I was profligate. This worried me a little, not least because I would be carrying more of the uninviting water from the watering hole and so be drinking it fairly soon.

After discussions in the local dialect Brother confirmed to me there was no one in the area at all and so we were safe for the moment. Before sunset four of the group would scatter wide to keep a lookout and they would be relieved during the night by others. I volunteered my services, which were politely declined. I was not sure if they were trying to protect and look after the skinny Englishman or simply had no faith at all in my ability as a lookout. If the latter, I was fairly sure they were on strong ground.

'We have to wait for the runner to update us as to the palace guard movements so we could be here for several days,' said Amazon, 'however, if we have to move off quickly there may be no time for you to explain your plan or indeed develop it too much when we arrive at the ambush spot. Therefore I think tomorrow you should tell us all what you have in mind. We will then all be prepared.'

'Yes,' I said, 'you are absolutely right. In any event I would like all of your input before the plan is completely finalised because there may be a big flaw in it that I have not spotted. Also, as you say, if we arrive at the ambush point with little time to spare then it would be best that each one of us knows what our duties and tasks are.'

After eating the following morning, the lookouts came to the water-hole and we all sat in the shade of the big bushes. They looked expectantly at me and I was suddenly very worried that I was not going to wave the magic wand but set out a rather uncomfortable plan, which had absolutely no guarantee of success. My mouth was a little dry and I would have loved to have taken a sip of water but I resisted. No other option but to launch into the plan.

As there was no natural cover in the area for the ambush, on each side of the road we would dig individual shallow trenches to lie in. The laths would be made into a frame and long grass woven into the frames to form a cover for the trenches, on top of which the surrounding soil would be scattered to disguise each trench. As on all the group's previous expeditions, the signal to open fire on the palace guard would be Brother firing first, though this time with the rocket launcher aimed at a lorry. Possible retreat under fire had to be considered and after much discussion it was agreed Brother should remain in his trench shooting rockets as the explosions ought to give the necessary cover for the rest of us to get away. To maximise upon the speed of rocket firing Brother's trench would be dug big enough for two and one of the group would lie with him, helping in the reloading.

All that was left was the distance we would be from the road; too far away and our accuracy would be compromised; too close and we would be exposed if things went wrong. Brother was confident that at one hundred yards he could hit the lorry though others in the group wanted to be closer. In the end we compromised at fifty yards.

'I think it is the best we can do,' said Brother, 'and I am all for it. Let us just sit here for a few minutes thinking about it and see if we come up with any better suggestions or modifications.' There was agreement all around and everyone sat looking at the ground, obviously thinking about what I had said. After a few moments one of the group leapt silently to his feet and put his hand up towards all of us, gesturing silence. He slipped quietly and swiftly into the undergrowth. The other members of the group reached for their rifles and quietly melted away, leaving Amazon, Brother and me. Brother motioned me to lie on the ground and he and Amazon moved slowly and quietly away. 'What the hell'! I thought as I lay there with my face pressed into the dust, 'what are they doing now?' The answer to this unspoken question came swiftly, for a man, surrounded by the group, appeared as if from nowhere. Sharp ears these guys! The man was obviously the runner from the capital who was completely different from the other runners I had seen. They had covered miles at high speed and arrived looking refreshed whereas this man looked close to death and was wheezing;

barely able to draw enough air into his lungs to live, let alone run. He had obviously run at breakneck speed, which, even to my untrained mind, did not augur well.

The runner tried to speak but was unable to do so. Brother motioned him to silence and said, 'Wait a few moments, it is better you give us the whole message properly in a few minutes time rather than kill yourself now without passing the message at all.' The runner looked grateful and stood with his hands by his sides, eyes closed, drawing deep breaths into his lungs. After a very short while his breathing changed from death rattle to normal panting and he began to speak, slowly, in English.

'The palace guard plans to leave the capital tomorrow.' He paused. There were groans all around.

'There is absolutely no way we can get to the ambush point by tomorrow,' said Brother, looking defeated.

The runner waved his hand, both acknowledging and dismissing this comment. He concentrated and continued talking. 'I know this to be so and I am afraid I have taken a big chance.' He paused again for breath. 'I have spoken to a minister who is loyal and sympathetic and asked him if there is any way he could delay the palace guard leaving. I had to indicate to him an ambush was being planned.'

At this Brother exploded. 'You did what! This must jeopardise any potential attack.' The runner again waved his hand.

'I know it is a great chance but I do not think so.'

'Which minister did you speak to?' asked Amazon. The runner gave a name, which meant nothing to me, and I certainly do not remember it. 'That is not so bad at all,' said Amazon, 'this man is extremely discreet and I am absolutely certain he would do nothing to put any of us at risk because he is very sympathetic to us.' Brother grunted in a way that neither agreed nor disagreed with what Amazon said.

'The minister,' continued the runner, 'said he was going to get one of his aides to suggest that as the palace guard was leaving the capital it should be given a farewell party. Because of lack of time it would be impossible to organise such a party tonight so at the earliest it would be tomorrow night. The minister was confident the palace guard would agree to this for everyone likes a party and even if Zaban disagrees, as he is bound to do, he will not make too much of a fuss for if he does it will be bad for morale and show he does not care about his men. He probably doesn't care, but at the moment he is not in a position to ride roughshod over everyone. It is therefore very likely the palace guard will set out from the capital the day after tomorrow and if they are encouraged to be enthusiastic at the party it is expected that most will have sore heads the following day so they will not be starting out from the capital at first light.' The runner leant forward and put his hands on his knees, breathing deeply. Some colour was coming back into his face though his lungs were still heaving. 'There is one more thing, the twenty palace guard will be in two lorries. There will be no escort. That is the best that can be done and I hope I have not displeased you too much.'

'No,' said Brother, 'I was far too hasty. You have done extremely well and I think we are all particularly pleased to know there will be no escort to the lorries. However, the time we have is very short and we have to start out immediately, travel at a very high pace and continue well into the night.' Looking at me, Do you think you can keep up?'

'As ever,' I replied, 'I will do my best. The one thing that concerns me is that we have to collect some grasses before we arrive so that these can be woven into the frames we are going to make. Is there somewhere suitable en route?'

'Unfortunately, the ideal place I had in mind would deviate us from the most direct route so we will have to compromise with some much poorer grasses. With our time constraint we have no choice. Right, let's get organised. Everyone take their water bottles out and put them on the ground, then check arms and ammunition and everything else and be ready to move in fifteen minutes at the most.'

We all took out our water bottles and set them on the ground. Three of the group picked up the bottles and topped up part-filled bottles from other part-filled bottles and distributed the full bottles evenly between us, taking the empty and partially empty bottles to the water-hole to fill up. These were also divided equally between us. I felt this distribution was very unfair because I had drunk far more of the clean clear village water than anyone else and I started to protest but one of the group smiled and said, 'We are all in this together; every man is equal.' I was grateful.

By this time the runner had sat down under the tree and was starting to look more like a human being. His breathing was slowing and he waved away any offer of water or food, indicating we should not waste our time with him. Leaving him where he was, we set out south towards the intended ambush point. Brother set a fierce pace and whilst the usual formation of flankers each side was maintained they did not stray as far as they normally did. It was a compromise between speed and safety where speed was the dominant factor. Surprisingly, I did keep up. It was a good deal of mind over potential exhaustion and the very short stop at noon for a quick bite to eat was just enough to give me added strength. By the time the sun had set, and we were still walking at the same pace, I was ready to give in but luckily the cooling air somewhat invigorated me and I managed to keep going. I assumed it was something after midnight before we eventually stopped.

'Tonight no guard or lookout,' said Brother, 'we all need our rest so I suggest we eat a little and then go to sleep. I want to be up before the sun.'

I slumped to the ground ready to forego any food simply

241

to close my eyes to gain the unconsciousness of sleep that would numb the exhaustion, but Amazon indicated I should eat something, which, reflecting now, was very good advice indeed although at the time I could barely force the food down my throat.

True to his word, Brother got us all up before the sun and, after a quick handful of food, we set off once again. I struggled into my knapsack and lath harness and a couple of the group offered to carry them for me but, with grateful thanks, I declined. I thought I might have to reverse his decision later in the day but at least I must show willing and do my best. The midday meal stop was slightly longer than the previous day and just before sunset we arrived in a bushy and fairly grassy area where Brother stopped us for the night.

'We are doing well,' he said, 'if we collect as much long grass as we can find here now, before the sun goes down, and start before sun-up tomorrow then we should get into position well before noon.' Everyone went off to collect as much long and tough grass as possible while the light still held, and I felt the resultant pile should be sufficient to do the job, if only barely. The grasses were bundled up and strapped on the top of our knapsacks ready for the next morning.

Once again, Brother was able to awake before sunrise and we set off in the gloom towards our destination. Bearing in mind Brother had said the area we were aiming for was desolate and semi-desert I was a little sceptical that we could arrive in such a place before noon for where we had slept was full of vegetation. However, Africa continued to surprise me for by the time the sun had fully risen we were walking on dry, hard ground with not a tree, bush or any real vegetation in sight. As the morning wore on so the terrain became even more desolate, strewn with plenty of stones and small rocks but nothing sufficiently large to hide behind.

After a couple of hours we hit the road, walked along it to a spot where Brother judged would be the best place for an ambush, and each of us started digging our trenches in the knowledge that providing the convoy had not already passed we would have plenty of notice of its arrival from the dust cloud thrown up. Luckily, the trenches did not have to be too deep because digging when armed with just the wooden spades and tools we had brought was difficult in ground which was at first soft and yielding, then became full of small rocks. When sufficient earth and rocks had been excavated it was time to build the frames out of the laths and weave in the grass to make a cover over which earth could be scattered to camouflage us. Suddenly, I became very sought after. My hut-building skills, derided by my teachers, were far greater than anyone in the group, and there was much fumbling with the frame-making so I gave assistance. In fact, I made mine very quickly and finished up making a good part of everyone else's. They all smiled grateful thanks and, whilst I was expecting a sarcastic comment from Brother, none came.

With no sign of the approaching convoy, Brother selected one of the group and showed him how to load the rocket launcher, and between them they practised dummy firing and reloading. It was then decided we should get into our trenches, pull the framework over us and let the expert track coverers scatter the earth and generally disguise our presence.

Vana's comment about my lack of knowledge and experience proved to be rather valid because once I was lying in my trench, gun ready to shoot, I realised my vantage point may well have been good to shoot at vehicles on the road but was so low it was impossible to see more than two hundred yards or so along the road. I should have realised this fairly self-evident point and I was about to struggle out of my trench to get a reasonable view in the distance when I saw one of the track coverers standing outside his trench looking towards the direction from where the convoy would come. I chided myself for not thinking of this but was glad of the group's experience, which covered my ineptitude.

Glancing up at the sky, I noticed the sun was close to its zenith and if the convoy had started out shortly after sunrise it should be with us fairly soon. However, time passed and nothing appeared. The sun was beating down through the camouflage cover and I was drenched in sweat. I took cautious sips from my water bottle. Whilst initially I was very pleased the convoy did not appear immediately, so allowing my body to gradually recover from the strenuous walking, which would mean that my aim would not be affected by fatigue, the furnace-like heat in the trench was becoming unbearable and I was concerned I might pass out. As I was beginning to feel more and more light-headed, so there was a shout from the watcher who scrambled into his trench, carefully pulling the cover over the top. I took it the convoy had been sighted and immediately all thought of discomfort left me to be replaced by excitement, tinged with apprehension.

The dust cloud from the two lorries became visible and as the convoy came closer so each lorry became clear, emerging from the heat haze. I trained my sights on the second lorry, focusing where the driver would be, and as his form took shape through the dusty windscreen I flicked off the safety catch to be ready. I squeezed the trigger at the same time I saw the smoke from Brother's rocket coming out of the trench to my left and slightly in front of me. I had no idea whether my bullet hit the target. Brother's rocket slammed into the first lorry, which exploded with a great flash, hurling the lorry, in pieces, in the air and off the road. The second lorry was completely obliterated by this flash and either I killed the driver with my bullet or he panicked, but whichever way, this lorry also veered off the road and ran into what little remained of the first lorry. There was a stream of automatic fire from all of the group and I too emptied my Kalashnikov into the back of the still intact lorry, but before I could insert a new magazine Brother sent off another rocket, which hit the second lorry square on, enveloping it in flame and mayhem, sending bits of everything high into the air to fall around us. I don't know if there is a competition for fast rocket firing but if there is, my money is on Brother.

After the second explosion, all of us stopped firing and there was a silence. The pieces of lorry stopped falling from the sky and the dust settled. I was, for the moment, rooted to the spot. Where there had been two lorries, there were now none. I am not talking here about severely damaged vehicles but a sight of devastation I could hardly believe. If I hadn't known there were two lorries it would have taken me a long time to work out what the mess used to be. I continued to lay there, not believing my eyes.

The rest of the group were quickly on their feet, running to the mess to seek out any palace guard still living. I slowly got out of my trench and walked to the road. At first I thought the two lorries had been empty because I could see no sign of human remains at all. It was not until one of the group about thirty or so yards away called me and pointed out bits of body that I realised we had indeed done what we set out to do. I wandered around finding pieces of former humans scattered everywhere and so mutilated that but for the fact I knew it was human remains I could not otherwise have identified the bits as such. By the look on everyone's faces they were as shocked as I was at the complete and utter devastation.

We congregated back on the road but there was no jubilation. The scene was just too shocking for that. I noticed a couple of the group had blood seeping through the back of their camouflage overalls, indicating that parts of the lorries had fallen through the makeshift trench cover and hit them. Others tended the wounds, which appeared to be slight.

After a while Brother said, 'There is nothing more we can do, let's go.'

'No,' I responded. 'If we leave things as they are then even the dumbest palace guard investigator will see there has been an ambush. I have been told that Zaban has created an air of mystery so let us try and fight fire with fire.' Every one looked blank. 'I am certainly not an expert but I would venture to suggest that if these lorries had been destroyed by land mines there would be enormous craters in the road.' Nods from the more experienced fighters. 'On the assumption the palace guard does not have experienced forensic experts looking at the scene,' this produced giggles of laughter, 'it is not immediately apparent what caused this devastation. Any bullets we fired will be scattered around after the explosions and the strewn lorry parts and bodies, whilst suggesting an explosion, do not point to any particular way the explosion could have occurred.' Frowns replaced giggles. 'So then,' I continued, 'if we fill in our trenches, disguise the fact they had been dug at all, remove our covers and also cover up our tracks as we leave it is unlikely anyone looking at the scene will be able to detect any human presence.'

There was a long pause while everyone considered this. 'And so what?' asked Brother.

'Well, what is to stop us spreading a rumour that the spirits are unhappy with the palace guard and have sent down thunderbolts to destroy the evil.'

Much laughing. 'It'll never work,' said Amazon.

'No, it might not but there is always someone who will believe. Once a rumour starts it is very difficult to disprove and what are we going to lose?'

'You're right,' said Amazon, 'we have all the time in the world so why not just clear up here and try and leave no sign of our presence; at the very least that will sow some seeds of doubt.'

'Okay,' said Brother. 'You,' pointing to the expert track coverers, 'go around where we have all been trampling and remove any tracks you can find. The rest of us will fill in the trenches and then we can disguise the fact anything has been dug at all.'

Everyone went off to their allotted tasks and, when finished, congregated back on the road, each holding the screens we had built out of laths and grasses. We waited while the track coverers checked the former trenches and performed magic over the ground, eliminating any sign of human presence. When they returned we started walking back up the road, each carrying our screens as our tracks were wiped away behind us.

15

The Lull

Our return to the village was at a steady pace. On the first night we dismantled our frames and bundled the laths with the grasses to continue carrying them until the second night when we made a discreet fire, burning all the evidence.

By this second night everyone had regained their composure and even my body had recovered from the earlier forced march. After we had eaten, I said to Brother, 'What sort of rockets did you fire?'

Brother looked a little sheepish and evasive but broke into a broad grin and replied: 'Well, whilst you were concerned at my ability to hit anything at a hundred yards, that did not trouble me at all. These rockets are truly excellent and accurate and at two hundred yards I would not have failed. What worried me was the fact that they are anti-tank rockets, which means, although they would have surely hit the lorries, they might have passed straight through without exploding.' Noting the shock on my face, he smiled even more. 'I didn't want to worry you, besides that you were being pessimistic enough for ten men and if you had realised this you might have called the whole thing off.'

I refrained from saying anything but secretly had to agree that had I known the rockets could have passed straight through the lorries I would have been seriously concerned.

'Therefore,' said Brother, 'I had to make sure that I hit

a really solid part of the lorry so I aimed for the engine and I could see, as I was certainly looking for this, the first rocket hit the first lorry engine and the explosion ripped through from front to back. The second rocket I was not so sure where it hit but it did the trick.'

I grunted. 'Good shooting anyway,' I said, 'and fast as well.'

'Yes, it was certainly helpful having someone in my trench to get the rocket ready. That was a very good idea of yours. How do you feel now?'

'To be frank, a little numb. It all went off much easier than I expected but I still cannot get out of my mind the effect of the rockets. We achieved what we set out to do and I suppose now our concern must be what retaliation Zaban will take. When do you think he will know his men have been annihilated and when will it be possible to start spreading the rumour of the spirits not liking the palace guard?'

'I don't know how good the radio contact is between the units in the south and the capital but let us assume it is good, which will mean the southern units will know the two lorries were scheduled to leave the capital yesterday morning and so they would have been expecting them at the first southern unit by late last night. There are always delays and quite often breakdowns so the fact the lorries did not arrive as anticipated would be no great concern. I know all palace guard jeeps have good radio communication and we must assume the lorries had radio communication as well so, looking at things from your pessimistic view of life, we have to assume that no radio messages from the lorries and their lack of appearance last night would mean the palace guard, Zaban, would suspect something had gone wrong by the very latest first thing this morning. So it seems to me, by midday today he will know of the loss of his twenty men. If our efforts at disguising our presence have worked then there will be much mystery so I would expect Zaban will not immediately broadcast to everyone the disaster. As to the rumour-spreading part, I have discussed this with Sabra and we have agreed that tomorrow she will go off to a village close to the capital, change into more suitable clothing and go and see her contacts to start spreading the rumour. She is probably the best one to do this as there has to be a certain amount of subtlety as well as speaking to the right people. She should be in the capital in two days, three at the most.'

There was nothing more I could say or add so we settled down and went to sleep. Sure enough, halfway through the following morning, Amazon handed her weapons to Brother and went off on her own. I was a little concerned that someone in combat gear would stand out and if she came across any palace guard she would have no chance. Brother though dismissed my worries out of hand, intimating that under normal circumstances it would be unlikely any palace guard would be around the area she was going to, and following the loss of the two lorries, their attention would be directed more to the south.

After we got back to our village, depositing our weapons and combat gear in the cave, I went with Brother to the chief where Brother reported, this time in English. For the second time the chief smiled.

'I am pleased of your success and even more pleased none of my people have been lost or seriously injured. I am particularly happy about your idea of the rumour that the spirits sent down a lightning bolt. I really do not believe it is going to work but it will certainly make everyone think and upset the palace guard no end.' He chuckled to himself.

I went back to my hut, meeting Vana on the way, and told her blow-by-blow about our expedition as we entered the hut. She sat quietly listening without interruption; her body language indicated interest, tinged with concern. I knew she was worried about retaliation but when I got to the bit about the rumour-spreading she rolled about in laughter.

'Oh I do like that,' she said. 'I think it might work better than anyone here thinks. You are perfectly right, Zaban has been capitalising upon the fact everyone believes he is raised from the dead and possessed of spirits, and if people have such a mindset then they will be more than open to bolts from the blue by dissatisfied spirits. Zaban can hardly go around saying there is no such thing as spirits, and if he cannot find any hard evidence of human intervention then there will always be doubt, and in this case doubt is a good thing.'

Well over a week passed before Amazon returned, and during that time I worked in the village as was required. The new well was taking shape rapidly and every indication was that it would yield good clean water. After Amazon had reported to the chief, we convened outside the village under the same tree where we had sat before. Amazon was looking pleased with herself and could barely keep a smile from her face. When we were all settled she started to tell us her news.

'I got to the capital easily without any trouble at all. When I arrived there seemed to be less palace guard activity and I was not challenged once. I went to my usual haunts and wandered around talking to people, none of whom had heard anything about the twenty palace guard who had been destroyed. I could not believe Zaban was unaware of the fate of his men so he was obviously keeping things quiet for the moment. I felt I was in a bit of a dilemma. If the news of the massacre was being kept under wraps then I couldn't start a rumour that the deaths were caused by dissatisfied spirits so I had to find a way to get both pieces of information circulating. There are several old women in the capital who are believed to be in touch with the spirits and who are consulted on a regular basis to divine whether a marriage or a birth or some event in people's lives will be good, and one of those women is known to us and in fact Vana has spent many hours with her after Vana realised she had the potential to be a thinker. This old woman is very wise, crafty as well, for she has great ability to get information from you without imparting anything herself and yet you go away believing she has told you everything. I decided to go and speak to her. I made it plain that this was not a consultation, simply old friends meeting, but she is sufficiently wise to the world to know there is no such thing. She did not say so openly of course but we both knew I was there for a reason and a part of the reason was to get her help.'

Amazon paused to look into the distance as if recalling her conversation with this wise old woman. Vana was quietly smiling to herself, her face showing approval that this particular wise old woman had been visited, and I made a mental note to ask Vana more about her experiences and knowledge of this woman.

'We talked as usual about everything and nothing, with the old woman carefully conducting the conversation around to the reason why I was there. I knew what she was doing and I made sure my body language showed her I was not being fooled by her subtleties. This pleased her enormously for there is nothing she likes better than a challenge, particularly against someone who believes they can outmanoeuvre her. I knew I could not do this but we spent the best part of an afternoon jousting around the subject without actually mentioning the palace guard.'

Amazon paused again but this time to stare at the ground with a frown on her face.

'Now I have every respect for this woman and she features very highly on our list of the trustworthy, discreet and well-informed. I also know, as we all know, she did not become the revered wise old lady without being able to read people and signs to find out the real reason for any visit or conversation. However, I was totally taken aback when quite out of the blue she said to me, "So what happened to the palace guard?"'

Amazon looked at all of us in turn to emphasise that the question was totally unpredicted.

'I do not think for one moment that my face remained impassive when she asked this question, for it was such a shock. I did though frown and tried to look a little bemused, asking her why she said this. She did not reply immediately but cocked her head to one side with a knowing smile and then told me that the spirits had been speaking to her of a potential disaster, which was to do with the palace guard, and as there had been no news in the capital of the deployment of some of the palace guard units in the south to replenish the twenty-five who had been previously killed, so it seemed to her that some ill had befallen those who had left the capital to replenish the southern units. I asked her why she thought I might have any information on this and she replied to the effect that she well knew of our operations and that my visit to the capital twice within one month could hardly be a coincidence, so it was likely I was there for a good reason and what better reason than to find out what Zaban and the government was saying about the palace guard who had left the capital. If this were so, and here are her eyes penetrated into my brain, then it was likely I had something to do with it and so my visit to her was not coincidental, though she said she welcomed seeing me, but to impart some information or knowledge rather than seeking advice and guidance. All this of course was so true but I was not going to admit anything even though I trusted her completely. I therefore said, "If indeed your spirits are correct in that some ill has befallen the palace guard on its way to the southern units then do you not think it is likely the spirits had a hand in it? We must both agree the palace guard has been, and is still, acting in a way that must displease the spirits as much as it displeases and frightens people, so would it not be reasonable to expect that the spirits' patience has been exhausted and it is they who have taken action against the palace guard en route to the southern units? If this were not so then why would the spirits talk to you about this? It is not as though members of the palace guard not in the capital would or could have any effect upon the people here in the capital. It seems to me there is a deeper meaning in what the spirits told you and they will, perhaps, explain more in due time."'

Amazon smiled broadly at this point.

'The wise old woman thought deeply for quite a long time and told me it was certainly true the spirits had not completed their message to her and she could not understand why. Perhaps it was, she said, the spirits were sending me to her to fill in the gaps. She did not, though, become wise without being sensible and have knowledge of the way the world worked so she suggested that unless the palace guard on its way to the southern units disappeared completely, there would be some trace of what happened and an investigation would likely show what had happened to them. I replied that this might well be so but it did not detract from the basic premise that the spirits could well have motivated and controlled anyone involved, but more particularly, if there was no sign of human intervention, this must undoubtedly mean the spirits were acting by themselves, and if so, no clearer sign could be given of their displeasure of the palace guards. This caused the wise old woman to think even deeper and even longer with her eyes closed, almost as though she was communing with the spirits there and then. She eventually opened her eyes and looked straight at me, saying, "If indeed the palace guard going to the southern units has been destroyed and if indeed there is no sign of human intervention the only conclusion we can draw is that the spirits acted against them. How do you think they did this?" I looked around her room as if seeking inspiration and suggested that perhaps the convoy had strayed off the road, become stuck in the sand and they all perished from the heat or even they might have been struck by a thunderbolt. The wise old woman nodded sagely, knowing, as indeed did I, that even if the convoy had become stuck in the sand the likelihood of everyone dying was extremely remote. We carried on talking generally about things for a little longer and I left her knowing that she had fully understood our message.'

'That is really good,' said Vana, 'this wise old woman has many contacts and is often consulted by members of the government, so if she wishes, I'm sure she can plant the idea that the spirits destroyed the palace guard. Knowing her as I do, I am certain she would do this.'

'Absolutely right,' said Amazon. 'It was but two days later when I was visiting a minor government official when he confided in me that information from the very centre of government was being suppressed as the palace guard going to the southern units had been destroyed by a thunderbolt sent by the spirits. I could hardly keep the smile off my face and suggested that without an official government statement, this could not be true, but clearly he believed it and so the rumour had already started. By the time I left the capital it was rife. Zaban did his best to bluster that all units were being deployed as planned but there was no official statement from the government denying the loss of the men who had left the capital so the idea of the vengeance of the spirits is being firmly entrenched in the whole populace. It could not be better. Finally, as I was leaving the capital, the wise old woman's maid chased after me with a message that a senior minister had sought consultation and had been advised of the power of the spirits. This message meant nothing to the maid but confirmed to me the rumour had been planted in the centre of government.'

'That is quite brilliant,' said Brother. 'What we must decide now is how we can capitalise on this. What can we do?'

He looked at me when he said this. I had no plan, or any idea of a plan simply because I was not given a situation that required a solution. I realised some time ago I was not particularly an original thinker but was extremely good at finding a solution when presented with a problem. Here there was no problem except, of course, for the remaining number of palace guards scattered around the countryside and Zaban himself. I absolutely had no quick fix for this. So then I resorted to my standby. No information, no matter how trivial, is wasted, so better to get more than is necessary rather than risk having less than is required.

'Thanks to Sabra, we know the people in the capital believe the palace guard is offending the spirits and I would suspect that this weakens the palace guard and gives people hope. What we do not know is how the villages in the countryside are taking this. I know your plan is for an uprising but I do not know whether any action would achieve a change of government and I rather suspect that even if the dissidents in all the villages banded together, it would not produce a sufficient cohesive force to overcome what is left of the palace guard and indeed the military loyal to Baumge. Therefore we must have more information. Can the villages be made ready to move? Would they be willing to serve a single leader? If so who would that be? I have particular concern over your tribal rivals. They have to be freely and firmly on board otherwise the whole thing is lost before it starts. Then there is the military. Will it remain loyal to the government? If not how many and under what circumstances would join any revolution? There are far too many questions completely unanswered. We are really full of ignorance, not knowledge, and we must get this knowledge. I think now would be a good time to start sounding out those in the military and perhaps in the government who would be supportive of a revolution and at the same time find out how all the villagers in the countryside feel. If the majority are still frightened by the palace guard and the government, any attempt at an overthrow would be doomed from the beginning. Revolutionaries must have confidence and absolute dedication. First, though, is your tribal rival. It is hopeless trying to win the military over unless we are united in the countryside.'

This produced a long silence while all three of them thought, and a short discussion ensued, concluding that this information was indeed necessary so various villagers would be sent out to the surrounding countryside to establish how other villages felt and whether there was any general support for an uprising. I had no practical knowledge of such things but was aware from television documentaries and the like that revolutions tended to require a charismatic leader and so far as I was aware there was no such person in this country. True, both Brother and Amazon were leaders and I am sure would command the respect of villagers but I was far from certain, from what I had seen so far, whether either could, or indeed would, take up the mantle, so I pressed home the point that it was time an opposition to the government was formed, either officially, and accepted by Baumge – which would be highly unlikely – or alternatively as an unofficial political party with a known and visible leader. At this both Brother and Amazon looked at each other and I wondered whether they believed either of them would be the leader but I did not enquire further. This was very much a decision for them. We left the shade of the tree, each of us having our own thoughts.

Later in the day, when I came across Amazon, she told me that Brother was going to the rival tribe himself to sound out what they felt and attempt to get agreement on a leader. My strong impression was that Brother intended to set himself up as the leader if this was at all possible.

I discussed all this at great length with Vana who was not at all surprised Brother was taking the initiative and likely putting himself forward as the leader of any opposition. She said that although Amazon was in fact in charge, Brother was just as much a leader but was quite happy to take a back seat as and when it became necessary. He was more inclined to play the long game and go along with decisions with which, perhaps, he did not agree, providing he was not deflected from his eventual goal. He was a very determined man and the reality was that this country was not ready for a woman leader, so if one was to come from this village, it had to be Brother. All we could now do was wait to see what news came back from the other villages, particularly the village of the rival tribe.

16

The Rivalry

Several weeks passed during which time I settled easily and happily into the village routine. I occasionally held shooting lessons when prevailed upon to do so and it was pleasing to see the enthusiasm of everyone, women included. One day I held a competition. The group were banned from entering on the grounds, I told them, they were much too good and would be bound to win. Whilst there was protest, I got the distinct impression they were not actually displeased for it would have been extremely embarrassing if any non-hunter warrior beat them. In fact one of the women nearly won and from the accuracy of the two finalists I reckoned our group would have been hard pushed to compete.

After the contest, following much back slapping and cheering for the winner, I returned to the cave and cleaned the rifles, putting them back on the racks. When I had finished, I picked up the Colt, loaded it with seven bullets and, wrapping it in a piece of cloth, hid it under my shirt to return to my hut. I then hid it in the wall of the hut between layers of grasses. I did this automatically, without thought, with no particular plan or intention in mind. It just seemed like the right thing to do.

From time to time visitors arrived with news from surrounding villages and the capital, the most important of which was that Zaban was moving heaven and earth to reinforce the palace guard, giving recruits a short training in the capital before sending them out to units for further and complete training. Apparently, at first there was more than a little reluctance for anyone to join the palace guard because of the belief that the spirits were displeased, but such reluctance was being overcome by Zaban's energy. The camp we had annihilated had been cleaned up and was now occupied by twenty or so palace guard taken from other units with new, raw recruits. Although not surprising, it was a pity that Zaban was regaining his iron-like grip and control so quickly but the upside was the palace guard was more intent on reorganising and training itself than causing terror and havoc in the countryside.

The calm and serenity of the village was wiping from my mind all thoughts of violence and combat and I was feeling very contented even though a realisation was creeping up on me that I really should not be there and, more specifically, be involved in what might very well be a revolution in the fairly near future. Whilst I appeared to have an aptitude to fight and, sadly, kill other human beings I really did not feel comfortable with it and as each day passed my hope that I would no longer be involved grew stronger. I said nothing to Vana about this but occasionally I saw her looking at me in a strange way. I should not, of course, have been surprised she had an inkling of my thoughts for not only was she a thinker but also we were very close and seemed to be drawing even closer.

Eventually Brother came back late one afternoon and, after the evening meal, we convened under the conference tree while he related what he had found out in the rival, if I could call it that, village. Apparently everyone there was extremely buoyant. The weakening of the palace guard had given them extra hope and energy and they couldn't wait for an uprising, pledging their full support and the support of all the minor tribes who looked up to them.

Very encouraging but I rather felt Brother was not coming clean.

'What of the all important leadership?' I asked.

Brother looked at me hard. 'That is no problem. I have the chief's full assurance that as our tribe has contributed the most so far then the leader of the uprising should come from our tribe or someone in the government in the capital.'

This pleased me though I did not actually feel comfortable with what Brother had said. It was, perhaps, his body language rather than his words. I didn't think it appropriate to probe further and it was agreed that tomorrow or the next day Brother should go to the capital to sound out his friends, see whether it would be possible to set up an official opposition party and, most importantly, get firm agreement as to who the leader of the revolution should be. Nothing more to be said or done, we went off to our huts to bed.

I awoke in the middle of the night completely alert. I did not move but lay listening with my eyes wide open.

'So you're awake too,' said Vana very quietly in my ear.

I barely nodded. There was something wrong. I could not tell what it was. I could hear nothing. I very quietly and carefully moved off the mattress, slipped on my trousers and went to the area of the hut wall where I had hidden the Colt behind a layer of grasses. I carefully removed the package, unwrapped the gun and crept stealthily out of the hut door, around the back, keeping low and close to the shadow cast by the hut. There was a small amount of light from the moon though the sky was clear and the stars sparkled down allowing reasonably good visibility. I did not know where I was going but I continued creeping away from the rings of huts, and when I was clear of them I turned to my right, circling towards where Brother's hut was. I had no idea why I was going in this direction; my feet automatically sent me there slowly and carefully.

As I was approaching the area of Brother's hut I was conscious of movement ahead of me. I stopped and stared hard, gradually making out six or so heavily armed, stealthily moving shadows. In the night light I could just make out human forms, one behind the other about ten yards apart, carrying rifles. They could not have been any of our group for if they were, there would be no need for the stealth movement. It seemed to me they were making for Brother's hut but were a little uncertain as to which one it was. I had to raise the alarm but were I to shout, my presence would be immediately detected and if, as I suspected, they were up to no good I would be the recipient of a large number of bullets from automatic or semi-automatic weapons. The Colt held only seven bullets and, whilst I knew I was a good shot, in the semi-darkness there was no way I could effectively dispose of these men before they fired back. Also, there may well have been others who I could not see.

I reasoned that whoever these men were, they were not palace guard for palace guard would not be creeping around. Their *modus operandi* was to appear in jeeps, bull-headed, as it were. Bearing in mind the comments and Brother's body language concerning the other major tribe, I suspected it was this tribe that was trying to capture or eliminate Brother following his approach to them about being the leader of a future uprising. I had to do something so assuming they were concentrating upon that which lay ahead I took the chance they would not be giving too much attention to something behind them. I moved as swiftly and quietly as I could towards the man closest to me. I was within a pace of him before he realised something was wrong and turned, looking over his shoulder. I shot him in the chest, hoping the noise of the Colt would arouse sleeping figures in the huts, and threw myself at him so we fell to the ground together. We landed in a patch of low bushes, which, although not shielding us from the other potential attackers, made it difficult for them to see if more than their comrade was lying there. His rifle, an early Kalashnikov, had fallen from his hands but its strap was still around his shoulder so I yanked it off and then patted him down, looking for spare magazines of ammunition. None. I didn't have time to curse his stupidity or arrogance in setting out without spare ammunition for by this time his comrades were down on their knees, rifles to their shoulders, scanning the area where I was lying. I brought up the Kalashnikov and let off a short burst, hitting the two nearest, but although I could have swung the gun and hit one or two more, I was fearful bullets would speed through or pass them into huts and injure or kill someone from my village.

The burst of gunfire was enough to make the survivors dive to the ground and I rolled madly away out of the clump of bushes, across a flat area and into another clump of bushes. I had seen this done many times in films and on television without our hero being hit and, sure enough, it worked, for although the survivors blasted off in my direction, nothing came close to me. What to do next? I was unsure but confident the village would now be fully awake, although none would be armed and there would be insufficient time for anyone to get to the cave and return before I was picked off. I didn't know how many bullets were left the magazine so I switched the gun to single fire. I could not afford to waste any ammunition.

So far I had been lucky but that luck was beginning to run out. A burst of gun fire thudded into the ground very close to me. Worrying, but more worrying was the fact that it came from a different direction than the men I had seen before. They had backup. Firstly, I daren't return fire because I could not see a target to hit; secondly, I knew I was short of ammunition; and thirdly, making any movement would undoubtedly have given away my position. I was not covered by the bushes but in this light there were a sufficient number of them to make it difficult to see where I was. I lay there looking around the best I could without moving my head too much, hoping my white, actually now brown, sunburned body, would not stand out. One of the men I had previously seen rose slowly to his knees to get a better look at the surrounding area. I could have taken him down without any effort at all but that would have identified my position to his backup. A second man joined him, and then a third, all three gradually rising to their feet. As soon as they were upright they would see me so my hand was forced. Three steady but swift shots eliminated them from the game but produced a hail of gunfire from the backup. The bullets hit the ground around me closer than before. Either they were lousy shots or their position was such they could not actually see me. Whatever, this was heartening, but unless I could find a way to make them retreat it was only a matter of time before mine was up. I silently cursed the lack of spare ammunition on the first man I had killed, for a prolonged raking burst from a full magazine would have been sufficient to keep the backups' heads down and for me to get away to somewhere a little less exposed. I had no choice but to stay where I was, hoping that I would see them before they saw me.

The village by now was fully awake. I could hear shouts and sounds of people milling around but this was of little comfort for I knew they were unarmed and would not be foolish enough to approach an area where bullets were flying. Then the unexpected. From way off to my right a burst of automatic fire. A full Kalashnikov magazine no less. None of the bullets came anywhere near me so either the backup was shooting at someone else or someone was shooting at them. Before I could toss the mental coin to choose which it might be another full magazine from the same area. This had to be friendly fire so I got to my feet and sprinted to the largest tree I could see, flopping down behind it. No one shot at me. Heartened, I peered around the trunk of the tree, looking for movement, and about one hundred yards away I saw a figure retreating slowly away from the village. Even in this light, an easy shot. I may not have killed him but he sure went down. I gradually stood up, keeping behind and close to the trunk of the tree, scanning the area, but there was no more movement. Sounds were still coming from the village but they were subdued and I remained where I was, watching and listening.

'I think you have got them all,' a voice said from behind me. I jumped. Turning around, Amazon was standing naked, almost alongside me. How the devil could she possibly have got that close to me without me hearing. She must be a spirit, a spirit who slept with no clothes on. I pretended not to look but had to admire. Very nice indeed.

'I don't know how many there were,' I replied. 'I cannot see any movement and they are certainly not shooting any more. Who else was firing at them?'

'Ajani. Ever since he came back he has had a gun in his hut.' This confirmed to me my initial thought that things had not gone as well in the rival tribe's village as he would have us believe.

At that point Brother appeared off to my right, walking slowly with a Kalashnikov slung nonchalantly across his naked body. Someone else who sleeps with no clothes. I walked towards him, looking carefully from side to side to see if there were any survivors. There was no movement and other villagers appeared, mostly naked, walking around the area and finding dead bodies. There were the six I initially saw plus four others dealt with by Brother and the last one I had hit. The dead bodies were dragged to a flat piece of ground where Brother inspected them. The chief arrived in a loincloth and spoke to Brother. When they had finished talking, the chief returned to his hut, leaving the aftermath for us to deal with. The villagers quickly stripped the bodies of guns, effects and clothing and the bodies were carried to be buried far away from the village.

'I take it they were the rival tribe who did not take kindly to your suggestion you might be the best person to lead a revolt,' I said to Brother.

'You're right. However, the problem is solved because one of the men you killed would have been my rival.'

'But how do you know his death will mean that the rest of the tribe will follow you and not seek revenge?' I asked.

'I do not for sure but we must address this tomorrow. Nothing more can be done now. I'm going back to bed.'

With that, he turned on his heel and walked to his hut. Amazon followed and I was left standing by myself. I did not feel too much like sleep but I went back to my hut to find it was empty. I wrapped the Colt in the piece of cloth and put it back in its hiding place in the wall of the hut. I went to the wash water and, dampening a cloth, briefly wiped the dust and dirt from my body. Vana came in, carrying two bowls.

'I thought you might like this' she said.

She handed me a bowl of jungle juice and its gentle fieriness slipped down my throat relaxing my body. I sat on the bed with Vana alongside me as we slowly sipped at the bowls.

'Were you awake before me?' I asked.

'Possibly, just. I think we both woke up at virtually the same time. We both had a premonition.'

I continued sipping the bowl, considering this. Why did I wake up? I could not have heard a strange sound for those guys were moving silently. Equally to the point, why had I brought the Colt back to the hut? I shook my head.

'Don't try and understand it. It is as it is and you are what you are. Just be grateful, as all the village is.'

When the jungle juice was finished we both lay down and eventually I drifted off into a restless sleep.

*

The next morning, after mealtime, Brother, Amazon, Vana and I went to the conference tree. No one suggested we should go there; we just drifted there automatically and sat down in the usual places.

'We have to thank you again,' said Brother, 'whilst an attack was not wholly unexpected, without your intervention I would certainly have been caught off my guard.'

'There was a good deal of luck in it,' I replied, 'but in any event Vana was awake and alive to the danger so you would have been all right. What now concerns me is that if the leader of the other tribe is now dead at our hands this may lead to tribal warfare. I am certainly no expert in these things but if there is tribal rivalry anyway, killing eleven of their men is not going to go down well.'

Brother smiled. 'Actually, it is not half as bad as you might believe. Their hunter-warrior leader was very belligerent and resented our recent successes even though he has had a few successes himself. He was an excellent hunter-warrior but somewhat short on diplomacy and tact and was not wholly popular even with his own tribe. I have to build bridges but I do not think it is going to be too difficult because although there is definitely rivalry between our two tribes, it is not a violent rivalry. All I have to do is ensure that if we can band together under my leadership then when the revolution is successful the politicians in the capital also include people from our rival tribe in the government as well. This will certainly happen anyway. There is also one further point to be borne in mind. No matter how fierce tribal rivalry might be, it is not acted out by sneaking up in the night to assassinate. When his village learns what has happened then they will be acutely embarrassed and will expect us to demand compensation. Obviously I will hint that massive compensation is due but I will diplomatically decline it on the basis we are all one people striving to overcome an oppressive government. This will put them in our debt and will ensure loyalty until the revolution job is done.' Brother chuckled to himself. 'In fact, it's worked out rather well and somewhat better than I could possibly have anticipated.'

'We must not be too complacent,' said Vana. 'I could tell from what the chief was saying last night he could see the advantage we can get but we must approach it carefully because nothing is worse than gaining a resentful following for that will surely breakdown sooner or later.'

Brother was obviously a little put out that his diplomatic skills were being, if not questioned, then certainly probed, but the good sense in what Vana said was obvious so he let it pass by.

'I will go now to this village and tell the chief what has happened and seek his help and guidance as to how we can make amends between us so the revolution cause is not jeopardised. After that, I will go to the capital to see our friends there to sound out how they are feeling and if they can help us.'

There was nothing more to say so we got up and wandered back to our respective huts.

17

The Rescue

Life continued in the village while we waited for Brother to return. Once again I slipped into the calm and serenity of the people, being quite content to let each day pass happily by.

It was just before dawn one morning when all calmness and serenity was completely shattered. Vana and I were on the verge of waking up when Amazon burst into our hut and pulled us from our bed. Amazon was shaking and almost incoherent.

'They've got Ajani,' she said.

'Who? What?' I said, trying to banish the last remnants of sleep from my brain.

'The palace guard. They have captured Ajani. They have taken him to the camp where we killed all those guards. They will torture him before they kill him and even Ajani will not be able to hold out and resist their torture for ever and this will mean they will know we are the group that has attacked the palace guard and so this village will be anni-hilated.'

Amazon who, up to now, had shown determination and leadership looked crumpled and totally incapable of doing anything positive so wracked was she by this devastating news. As Vana began to try and comfort her, Amazon's whole body started shaking. There was no doubt Brother being taken by the palace guard was a problem; a big problem. But there again I am good at problems. Before I knew I was actually saying anything I reacted and took command.

'Right,' I said, 'we have no time at all to lose. Sabra, I want you to immediately find a runner and send him to the nearest village with one of the captured palace guard lorries and have it driven to the main road leading to the palace guard camp. Vana, tell the group to immediately go to the cave, change and pick up their arms with plenty of ammunition. We have no time for food or to collect food but if we can get some water to the cave for us to take before we set off that will be good.'

Amazon looked at me and although she did not snap out of her grief she stopped shaking and started to regain control of herself.

'Come on,' I said to her, 'we cannot hang around. As soon as you can, send the runner off and join me in the cave to get everything ready. I will go there immediately. But first tell me how long will it take for a runner to reach the nearest village with a palace guard lorry and then the palace guard lorry to get to the main road in a position where we can intercept it?'

She visibly took a hold of herself and said, 'If we can convince the village with the lorry not waste any time and we double march towards the road then we should meet up within half a day, hopefully by noon.' She straightened up and began to look determined. 'I will tell the runner it is an emergency and speed is the most important.'

'Excellent,' I replied, 'let's get moving then. See you in the cave.'

With that I set off at brisk pace towards the cave and when I got there I pulled the bushes back, without any ceremony at all, went in and started changing into my camouflage overalls, picked up my Kalashnikov, an automatic pistol with silencer and then assembled ammunition for the group as they arrived. The news of Brother's capture had already spread throughout the village and the group knew we were going to take action though, of course, quite what action they were unaware. Before, when we had set out on our excursions, the group were all very much laid back and relaxed but this time there was no banter but a steely determination in each one of them. Their love of Brother was evident and I could see that they were more than prepared to lay down their lives to save him, if save him was at all possible. Just the right attitude we needed.

'As soon as we are ready,' I said, 'we will double march to the nearest point on the main road leading to the palace guard camp. I believe it is highly unlikely, almost impossible, Ajani would have told them anything about our activities or the village so I do not anticipate meeting any palace guard on our way to the road.' In fact I did not believe that Brother would not succumb to torture at all for we didn't know how long the palace guard had been holding him, nor indeed the diabolical nature of torture they might have used. However, my affirming a belief in his strength to resist questioning pleased the group and chased away, if it did not completely banish, their own fears, and to build on this I continued, 'We must take an extra Kalashnikov for Ajani when he is free.' This positive approach produced a few steely smiles and one of the group immediately plucked a gun off the rack, checked it and slung it over his shoulder with his own Kalashnikov.

'Our efforts will be on speed, deploying only the most minimal of scouts and lookouts. I would expect the palace guard at the camp to be concentrating on questioning Ajani rather than be in the countryside, particularly, as we all know, because there are a number of new recruits there who are unlikely to be fully trained yet. When we get to the road I hope we will meet an ex-palace guard lorry from the nearest

271

village, which is being driven to join up with us, and we will use this lorry to get to the camp quicker. I will explain what we will do as soon as we get to the road.'

Fully dressed and equipped with knapsacks on back, the group left the cave and, even though we were in a great hurry, the track smotherers briefly covered up all signs of us outside of the cave and made sure the bushes were properly replaced.

We set off towards the road at double speed and, whilst my weeks in the camp had not been strenuous, nonetheless I not only kept up the pace but felt keen and fit. As Amazon predicted we reached the road by noon but there was no sign of a lorry so we started walking at normal pace along the road towards the palace guard camp and I explained the plan.

'Any full-frontal attack on the palace guard camp will likely fail not least because I am assuming Ajani is being held in the reinforced concrete block in the centre of the camp, which could hold out from any attack for a long time. Also, if the palace guard believes it is going to be beaten then it will almost certainly kill Ajani and that is what we are trying to avoid.' I felt it was not prudent to suggest that Brother's death, before he divulged any important information, would have solved the problem! 'On the assumption the lorry gets here in time, I would like one of you to take over driving of the lorry to the camp. I will sit in the front with the driver and the rest of you will be in the back. We will drive up to the camp gates, which I hope will be open as usual, I will shoot any guard who is there,' pointing to my silenced automatic pistol, 'and we will drive straight up to the centre concrete building, quickly disembark and go inside. If we drive the lorry steadily but determinedly, anyone in the camp will just think it is one of their lorries coming from the capital, or somewhere else, and take little or no notice of us. Providing we move swiftly and silently

272

we ought to be able to get into the centre block without too much trouble. After that we simply have to play it by ear.'

I motioned them all to stop and pulled them to the side of the road to a dusty spot. I lent down and drew a plan of the block, showing the various rooms and corridors.

'As you all know, I've been in this block before and had a good look around so I can tell you, as we go in through the front door on the left-hand side is a large office, which occupies the whole of the left side of the building with a window looking out towards the camp entrance and the two accommodation huts, and another window opposite in the rear wall looking over the store shed. On the right-hand side of the entrance door is the corridor leading down to an interrogation room and three cells. There are no windows looking towards the compound gate but the interrogation room and each cell has a barred window facing the store shed. There are stairs opposite the front door leading to the first floor which contains three bedrooms. One bedroom at the front of the building has two windows: one overlooks the compound entrance and accommodation blocks, and the other, the workshops at the side; another bedroom at the back is directly opposite the store shed, also with a second window overlooking the workshops; the third bedroom, over the office, has a window facing towards the cookhouse. None of the windows have glass in them and I cannot remember whether they are fitted with shutters. They are essentially a hole in the wall. Five of you,' I pointed out the five which included Amazon, 'will go down the corridor, kill anyone you see and release Ajani from the cell. Three,' I pointed to three of them, 'will go up the stairs to the bedrooms and do the necessary there. We two,' smiling at the remaining unselected of the group, 'will go into the office. Any questions?'

'What if we are detected before we get to the block?' asked one of the men.

'Unless we are exceptionally unlucky, I do not think it will make too much difference. It is highly unlikely the palace guard in the camp will be walking around fully armed so we should be able to get into the block before any really determined attack and once we are inside, we will have a place to defend. Obviously any gunfire or commotion before we get into the block will alert those inside but I'm afraid that is a chance we just have to take.'

'And how do you plan we should leave?' asked another.

'I have no such plan I'm afraid. Once we attack the men in the block, the rest of the palace guard in the camp will be alerted and we must expect retaliation. Until we secure the block and see exactly what sort of firepower is directed against us there is no way to make a plan of escape. Once we have freed Ajani we can take stock of the situation and we will be one man more; a formidable fighting force!' I smiled confidently at them all and whatever fears or concerns they may have had were pushed firmly into the back of the mind as they concentrated upon the job in hand. The reality was that although I was fairly confident a direct approach would achieve complete surprise and with a modicum of luck we would not have too much difficulty securing the block, if the palace guard in the camp organised quickly they could quite easily surround the concrete block and keep us in there indefinitely, certainly until reinforcements arrived. It would have been nice to have another group from another village join us for they could have stayed outside the camp and then attack the palace guard from the rear as they formed up to assault the centre block. Unfortunately there was no time to do this and, whilst I considered splitting our group into two, I was not sufficiently confident of their discipline without radio communication between us. I would like to have had Amazon remain outside the camp with four or five men to organise a rear attack on the palace guard as she would certainly have had the discipline, kept the men under control and responded at the right time on a prearranged signal but I knew there was no way she would agree to this. She wanted to free her brother and would not trust anyone else with this task.

With no more questions and everyone mulling over the plan, we moved away from my rough drawing and we walked on for another mile or so before there was a shout from our rear lookout. Turning around,I saw dust being thrown up from a lorry driving at great speed towards us. Even though I assumed this was the ex-palace guard lorry from the nearby village, nonetheless I directed the group to hide just in case it was a real palace guard lorry. I did not have to fear for as it came closer Amazon recognised the driver. She walked out to the side of the road to wave and the lorry came to a sliding dust cloud halt ready to pick us up. I had antici-pated that the lorry driver would leave us and walk back to his village but Amazon told me he was one of the best fighters of his village and he wanted to join us. An extra man would be more than useful. I agreed, helped everyone into the back of the covered lorry, closed the tailgate, got into the cab next to the driver, noting his knapsack and Kalashnikov jammed between the seats, and we moved off at brisk pace towards the palace guard camp. During the journey I explained my plan to the lorry driver who was very relaxed about the non-exit strategy and appeared to be delighted at joining our group and being launched into action. I hoped he was not going to be disappointed.

I am no expert in identifying military vehicles and I guessed the lorry I was sitting in was of American design. To say it was basic would be an understatement. The springs and suspension were either non-existent or had long since passed their useful life for every bump in the road jolted through me. The seat in the cab may well have had springs and padding when the lorry was new but they were no longer functioning and the base of my spine felt as though it was sitting directly on the lorry floor. I felt sorry for those in the back who had little or nothing to hold on to. The inside of this lorry had the bare essentials. A speedometer whose needle bounced erratically across the dial, an engine temperature gauge, which had long since given up the ghost, and a fuel gauge, which showed full but may well have been stuck. The bare metal dashboard appeared to have been bashed into shape rather than moulded or pressed and the holes in the bare steel floor for the accelerator, clutch, brake, gear lever and handbrake were grossly oversized, allowing dust thrown up from the road to percolate through in a steady stream to be blown around by the hot air coming through the open windows of the doors. Indeed, I was not sure whether in fact the doors actually had windows for I could not detect any handles for winding and the doors were so encrusted with hardened baked dust and dirt it was impossible to see if they contained glass. The whole thing was a wreck but the engine sounded relatively smooth if amazingly loud, requiring any conversation to be at shouting level.

As the palace guard camp came into view I told the lorry driver to slow down to the usual driving pace, drive up to the guard on the gate and stop as would happen if this was a normal palace guard lorry. Obviously, my non-black face would be a problem so I ducked down under the dashboard to be out of sight and pulled the silenced FN 57 pistol from my waistband ready to use. So that I could be prepared, I asked the driver to give me a running commentary as to what was happening and what he was doing. Luckily, as we slowed down so the hammering of the engine note diminished and he did not have to shout.

Out of the side of his mouth I heard from the driver. 'Camp gates open. Slowing down for the sentry box. One palace guard looking out. Only one man there. A number of palace guard in the compound walking around, none appear to have guns. I am stopping.'

As the lorry came to a gentle halt, the driver leant out of his window to speak to the sentry and in so doing blocked the guard's view into the cab. The driver slowly leant forward, giving me a big gap between the top of the window and his back to see and shoot the guard. This I did with the guard falling backwards into the hut. This seemed to create less noise than the last time I did it but there again I suppose the sound of the far from quiet idling truck engine would mask any disturbance. The driver and I looked around the camp but no one was taking any notice of us at all so he engaged gear and drove slowly and steadily through the open gate to the centre block, adroitly turning the lorry around and quickly backing it towards the door of the block, stopping about two yards from it. As the lorry was stopping, I leapt out and went to the back of the lorry, releasing the tailboard. Briefly looking around, I saw several palace guard in the compound but none of them was taking the slightest notice of the lorry so, quietly and quickly, with the group forming behind me, I walked the very short distance to the door of the centre block, calmly and steadily opened it and went in. It squealed, as before. Inside was peace and quiet. Our approach was undetected and we could carry out our tasks. I turned left into the office while I heard those behind me deploying down the corridor towards the cells and in the direction of the stairs. I heard from the squeal of the hinges the last one in close the front door behind him.

Sitting and writing at a desk in the office was Death's Head, Zaban. He looked up as I entered and, whilst he realised a white man in combat gear holding a pistol in his hand was not one of his men, no surprise registered on his face at all. I pointed the pistol at him and he slowly put down his pen, stood up and, with his hands at his sides, looked calm and collected and just stared at me. Everyone was right. His eyes had a penetrating stare, which went right into me, seeming to sear my brain. Two pale, almost pastel, blue eyes with no expression focused on my very being. It was completely mesmerising; but there again I'm good at 'mesmerising' and a third eye appeared in the centre of his forehead as the back of his brain exploded outwards from the high velocity bullet of my pistol. He fell backwards, crumpling to the floor. I walked around the desk to look at a very dead Death's Head. He may have been able to survive a hail of gunshots and bombs but the blood and gore of his brains splattered on the wall and floor was a testament to the fact he was not immortal. If a spirit raised from the dead, he had returned from whence he came. Although I was conscious I should be joining and helping the rest of the group, I stood there for a moment looking down at what used to be the scourge of the country. The new recruit lorry driver and the man from our unit who were supporting me stood quite still just inside the doorway and also looked towards the crumpled body, rooted to the spot. He was no less skeletal or frightening dead than alive and the pale eyes, which were still open and staring, below the greying, close-cropped hair, did not seem to have lost their power and it took a conscious effort for me to tear my eyes from him. No wonder, alive, he frightened so many so easily.

I turned, which broke the trance of my two backup men, to walk out of the office. I was met by Amazon, half carrying, half dragging Brother down the corridor. He looked in awful shape. His face was so battered I could hardly recognise him and those strong, firm limbs could barely move. I dragged a chair from behind the desk and my two backup men helped Amazon sit Brother down.

'Give him some water, any food you may find, and tend to his wounds the best you can while I check everyone else,' I said and went out into the corridor, with my two backup following me, to meet the rest of the group.

'There was a big fat man with no clothes on up there heaving up and down on a woman,' said one. 'I assumed he was not the camp priest so I shot him and unfortunately the woman was killed as well. There was also a naked man in another bedroom having his cock sucked by a young girl. They are both dead.' He did not show any remorse. 'The other room was empty and from my examination of Fat Man's clothes he seemed to be the replacement commander here.'

There were two guards in the interrogation room who had been dispatched speedily, and apart from them, Zaban and the four upstairs, the building had no one else in it. We had achieved our objective rather quicker than I had anticipated and without loss of life on our side. The question now was how to get out. Telling everyone to keep down and keep quiet, I went upstairs to one of the bedrooms and cautiously looked out of the window. My shot to dispatch Zaban was silent but short bursts of fire from the Kalashnikovs of the group required to obliterate the others had not gone unnoticed for out in the camp there was much scurrying around as palace guard were picking up rifles and looking towards the central block. Whilst they may well have been used to screams and shouts coming from this block, clearly gunfire was an unusual phenomena. I went to the other bedrooms whose windows overlooked different parts of the compound and confirmed that whoever was in charge was organising the palace guard before advancing on the block to find out what the problem was. I guessed that if the person in charge had but a modicum of common sense he would realise a lorry parked in front of the entrance to the block was unusual and so would assume the worst and be cautious. I was not wrong. I quickly considered whether we could all sprint to the lorry and drive out the way we came but this was a non-starter. Leaving aside the fact that Brother's condition at the moment, even if he was carried, would slow us down, any embarkation into the lorry would leave us completely exposed to gunfire and the chances of the driver being hit as we drove out were very high. The one thing in our favour was that the only cover in the camp was behind the wooden sleeping quarters, lorry repair area, sheds and cookhouse. This would mean that if we applied concentrated automatic fire the bullets would go through the timber and hit anyone foolish enough to be standing up. If the person in charge of the palace guard had any sense he would make sure they were all lying on the ground before they did anything. As I watched, I saw this was what was happening.

I went back downstairs to the group who were sitting on the floor below the window level of the office.

'It seems as though the person in charge out there is not completely stupid and he is organising the palace guard quite efficiently. They are now armed, seem to be lying down behind the buildings and surrounding us. I would shortly expect a challenge from him to see if everything here was well. I'm sure they are used to hearing strange noises coming from this block but not, I suspect, Kalashnikov fire.'

No sooner than I had finished speaking than the challenge came over a loud hailer. That they had a loud hailer at all surprised me but the fact that the palace guard could get hold of one and use it so quickly was more than a little worrying. Whoever was in charge certainly was no fool. We did not answer the challenge and there was a short burst of automatic fire from one section of the palace guard.

'This building is made of concrete, not cinder blocks,' I said to the group, 'and this is very helpful to us as it is unlikely their fire will penetrate the concrete. We must under no circumstances get close to windows and, on the basis they will shortly be firing through the windows, be cautious of ricochets in the room. For the moment I want no one to return fire or be seen at the windows. The longer we can remain quiet and unobserved, the more concerned the palace guard are going to be. Once they open fire in earnest they would expect return fire but if we don't give them a fight yet it will unnerve them. I want our best shot,' I looked around and Amazon pointed to one of the men, 'to go up onto the roof. There is a ladder on the first floor against a trapdoor, giving access to the roof. Stay very low indeed so you will not be seen. There is a very shallow parapet up there, about a foot high, which should shield you a bit. Carefully and very cautiously try and identify the person in charge out there and shoot him if you can. Shoot no one else at the moment and do not fire unless you are absolutely certain you are going to kill him with your first shot. Better not to shoot at all then miss. Understand?' He nodded and moved slowly and silently up the stairs towards the roof ladder.

'Now the rest of you deploy in all the rooms, keeping well away from the windows. If you can find any furniture, heavy desks, cupboards or wardrobes, drag them opposite the window, close to the back wall but far enough away from the wall for you to lie behind. This furniture will help in protecting from ricochets.'

One of the group handed Brother a Kalashnikov before he went upstairs to one of the bedrooms. Brother's battered face looked grateful and he tried to struggle to his feet.

'Please stay where you are,' I said, 'at the moment you're not strong enough to go leaping around so just sit there and gather your strength. We will need you before long and I know you're not going to let us down so please take it easy for the moment. There is nothing anyone can do except wait and see how things develop. Just keep that chair away from the window.'

'You may be right about the concrete walls saving us from their rifle fire,' said Amazon, but what if they have a rocket launcher or similar?'

'Well we know from the equipment we stole from them last time we were here, they certainly have the rockets and no doubt a rocket launcher as well. However, the commander out there must know Zaban and their senior commander are in the building with us, and whilst they may believe Zaban could survive a rocket attack, as he has survived attacks before, they know their commander would not, so I suspect they will be very slow in deploying such a weapon. If I am wrong, then plan B.'

Amazon raised an eyebrow at this – I hardly had even a plan A, let alone a plan B – so I just shrugged my shoulders and smiled.

Another address came from the loud hailer to the effect that if, whoever we were, did not surrender immediately they would open fire and, as we continued to be silent, it was followed by a prolonged burst of automatic fire with, I would guess, every palace guard emptying at least two, possibly three, magazines at the block. As predicted, none penetrated the walls but there were plenty of bullets coming through the windows and burying themselves into the opposite wall. Ricochets were few. Rather pleasing. There followed a silence and no retaliation from us. I went up to the bedroom immediately above the front door of the block overlooking the spot where I had last seen the commander. The members of the group there had pulled a wardrobe to the centre of the room opposite the window and were crouching behind it. The wardrobe was rather liberally ventilated at the top with bullet holes. I slid behind the wardrobe with them and took stock. We were well into the afternoon and the sun was behind the block, casting its ever-lengthening shadow towards where I had last seen the commander, close to the two accommodation huts. This meant the bedroom window was fully in shadow and made it impossible for anyone outside to see anyone inside unless that person was close to the window. Gratifying as this was, this was the direction in which we had to escape, assuming we could escape at all. I slowly stood up behind the wardrobe and looked out of the window. I could see the gates of the camp, still fully open, and a short section of each of the two sleeping quarter huts. Certainly on this side of the building an efficient attack would be difficult because there was just not enough cover for the palace guard. Lying down behind the sleeping quarter huts was all very well but this did not give them a good line of sight to shoot at the block. One man each side of the sleeping quarter huts was the best they could do and I noticed movement inside the huts, which indicated there were men there to shoot out of the windows. Not so smart then! I saw no sign of the commander.

I told the group in the bedroom to keep down and I went to the other bedrooms to see as much outside as was possible. The bedroom with a window facing the sun was the most difficult for it was not at all in shade and movement inside could be spotted from the outside. Again there was a wardrobe dragged to the most advantageous place and I peeped around each side to try and gauge the position of the palace guard there. This window overlooked the barn-type hut where the palace guard's ill-gotten gains were stored. I could not remember if it had an upper floor, for if it did, then, although the palace guard would not be protected by the wooden walls, they could have a much better line of sight through the cracks in the timbers and could make a hole to shoot through with some accuracy. I pointed this out to the group in this bedroom and told them to be especially careful. Checking the other bedrooms, I could detect palace guard movement around the other buildings but they were keeping low and mostly lying on the ground preparing to shoot.

I went down to the office where Brother remained seated in the chair well away from the window. I have to say he did not particularly look any better although he was gathering inner strength to do his bit when it was necessary. Amazon was on the floor beside him talking gently in the local dialect and I assume what she was saying was words of comfort and support. She looked at me enquiringly.

'We are completely surrounded by, I would have to guess, at the most twenty-five palace guards although probably just twenty. If we were to make a run for the lorry I do not believe there is any way we could get out without suffering severe casualties. In fact if they were to hit the driver then they would likely massacre us all. We have to stay where we are for the moment at least.'

They both took this very stoically and the fact they were together again gave them inner strength to accept the not too heartening position.

'Do you see any weakness at all we can exploit?' asked Brother between bruised and battered lips.

'Not at the moment,' I replied, 'but there is time yet. The sun is going down and the lower it gets, it will be in the eyes of the palace guard, protecting the exit gate. This will be quite helpful to us once we have moved out of the shadow cast by this central building. Before then, though, we have to inflict some damage on them and devise a way of keeping them down while we escape. The obvious way is to use the lorry as this will be the fastest way to get away but if the commander outside had any brain's at all he would realise this and shoot at the lorry now to immobilise it. We therefore cannot bank on having transport.'

'Can we create a diversion?' lisped Brother.

'Possibly, but the reality is we only have one way out, through the main gate. Even if we had some bolt cutters to get through the fence, the distance between the centre block and the wire fence, plus the time needed to cut a hole big enough to allow us through, would mean a high number of casualties before we could possibly get away. I would appreciate it if when you feel a little stronger in a few moments you could go upstairs and shield yourself behind the wardrobes and furniture in the bedrooms and look outside to see if you have any ideas or can spot anything I have missed.'

284

I did not have too much hope that Brother would come up with an original idea; that is not to denigrate his ability but merely reflected the position we were in. Allowing him to do something would make him feel useful and gave me a little more time to think. My knack for instant solutions had evaporated but I did have a germ of an incredibly risky idea.

I went back upstairs, up the ladder to the roof, and crawled on my belly towards the sharpshooter lying there.

'The commander?' I asked.

'He is behind the sleeping hut on the right-hand side, keeping well out of sight for the moment. When he shouts at us through his loudhailer he sticks his head around the hut but there is not enough of his body showing for me to get a good clean shot. I am certain though no one has yet spotted me. Do we have a plan of action?'

I realised that to admit I had no solution to this problem was not going to be good for morale so I patted him on the shoulder and smiled. 'There are a couple of things bubbling up but we have to swing the advantage a little more to our side. I would expect some more gunfire from the palace guard fairly shortly and again we will not return this fire. The longer the palace guard, have to wait before we show any sign of retaliation will not only mean they will be uncertain as to the number of men we have here but also they will get a little complacent. At the moment most are lying on the ground, hiding behind the huts and buildings but there are some in the sleeping hut and I would expect a number inside the other buildings, though I have not seen any. As far as you are concerned it will be a great help to me if you do not shoot at all until you have the commander in your sights. Ignore what we are doing completely. Just, please, concentrate on the commander. I think that if we can eliminate him this is going to help us enormously as he obviously is good at his job and I suspect his second-in-command, if he has one, will not be so brilliant.'

Faced with such an important task, he nodded grimly and resettled himself to keep watch for his target. I wriggled my way back to the trapdoor, down the ladder and back to the office.

'Our sharpshooter on the roof is going to try and pick off the commander. So far that guy has been very cagey but I would hope if we can continue to remain silent and out of sight he may get a little bolder and show himself sufficiently to get a clean shot at him. If the commander can be eliminated this will help us.'

I was about to continue but the palace guard opened fire again with a prolonged barrage of automatic rounds slamming into the walls of the building and through the windows. We all hunkered down to be out of the way of any ricochets. It stopped as suddenly as it began.

'If I was commander out there, I would be thinking that perhaps there is no one in this building at all or possibly people injured by the first barrage. They have had three goes at us so far with no shots in reply and I'm sure they have not been trained for such a scenario. Being, basically, soldiers, they will want some action and I would expect under the next barrage they will be sending a number of men forward to try and get in here. The most obvious entry is through the front door but I reckon the commander will be craftier. He knows the sun is at the back of the building overlooking the storage barn and I believe he would have put men on the top floor, if there is one, or at least high on the rafters to peer through the cracks in the walls into the bedroom window on that side of our building. If they see any movement then they will get a clear shot, which will likely be successful. So at the moment at least we can't return fire from this bedroom window. Here on the ground floor, the only windows facing towards the barn store are the back one of this office, the interrogation room and the three cells. I expect another barrage very soon with a few men, three or four, perhaps, coming from the storage barn under cover of the firing to get to the rear lower floor windows and lob in a few grenades. If they are really good then these men will not come from directly in front of the windows but diagonally from one side, so restricting detection. The cells are easily dealt with for we can just shut the iron doors and let the explosions occur. Even if the cell doors are damaged, it is unlikely they will be blown off their hinges. As the interrogation room is in the centre of the building, directly below the bedroom window, I would not expect an immediate attack on this window but only after the grenades go through into the cells. The covering fire will have to be high at this stage otherwise they will be hitting their own men. I suggest, and I welcome your views, we have two men in the corridor outside of the interrogation room and as soon as they hear the explosions in the cells, they rush to the window of the interrogation room, lean out, pick off the palace guard and immediately drop back in under the window before the support fire can pick them off. The palace guard under the window will be concentrating upon getting their grenades ready and will not expect someone to lean out and shoot them.'

Both Amazon and Brother agreed and together honed the details of our makeshift strategy which included Amazon taking care of any approach to the office rear window.

This done, I went up onto the roof to clarify our position with the sharpshooter.

When I got back to the ground floor I singled out our new recruit – the driver – and asked him if there was any way he could assess whether the lorry was damaged in such a way whereby it couldn't be used and if it was not, would it be possible for him to somehow get in the cab to start it up without being detected. He looked very keen, if a little blank, and said he would see what he could do.

Everyone was ready for the next onslaught and before

long it started: prolonged automatic fire from the palace guard. There was nothing I could do except remain sitting in the corridor and wait. Sure enough there were explosions in the cells, which, because of the big steel doors, were rather muffled on our side, but I anticipated sounded a little more dramatic outside. How Amazon was getting on I had no idea but following the cell explosions the designated men leaped through the door of the interrogation room towards the window and I swiftly crawled to the door to see two of my gallant little group leaning out the window and giving someone or other a full blast of their Kalashnikovs. They dropped back inside to the ground, crawled around the walls and out through the door with big broad smiles on their faces. The barrage from the palace guard continued and both men looked at me and put their thumbs up. That made me smile. At last something positive to cheer us all up.

When the firing stopped I realised that the front wooden door had virtually disappeared. Prolonged high velocity round exposure was too much for the old wood and it had pretty well disintegrated. This caused a bit of a problem because going from the passageway leading to the cells into the office was past this door and the stairs were immediately opposite the door so any movement in this direction could be spotted: luckily the lorry parked directly in front did shield the doorway to some extent and did not give any of the palace guard an easy shot. On the basis that human nature, tinged with a bit of discipline, would mean that once they were told to stop firing, the palace guard would not be squinting down their barrels anticipating a sharp shot through the door, I leaped across the open space into the office.

Amazon was sitting on the floor, leaning against the wall with blood running down her left cheek. As soon as she saw me she waved away my concern and broke into a smile.

'I was a bit unlucky,' she said, 'a bullet chipped some concrete off the wall and it hit me in the face. It's only a minor scratch. I got my men though, there were two of them.'

I crawled across to her and had a look at the scratch on her face to see it was a somewhat deeper cut than she would have me believe. I crawled back to where my knapsack had been discarded in the corner of the room, opened it up, got out a basic first aid kit and went back to Amazon, cleaning the gash to apply a field dressing.

'For a man who purports not to have any powers, it is amazing you were able to foretell what the palace guard would do,' said Amazon as I was putting on the field dressing.

I grunted. 'I think you will live,' I said, 'well done with the shooting. That was fantastic. The guys in the interrogation room got their men as well but as yet I don't know how many. The downside is the front door is virtually gone so we have to move across the opening fairly quickly to get back in the corridor for an update.'

We crawled to the office door together, got into a crouching position and sprinted across the doorway into the cell corridor, once again sinking to the floor.

'Update, Sabra has taken out two. You guys?'

'Two between us,' they replied. 'I'm afraid we probably used more bullets than Sabra to do the same job.' We all laughed.

Just at that moment we were joined by the sharpshooter from the roof.

'You are absolutely right,' he said, 'the commander did show himself after the explosions and I hit him. I am not absolutely certain I killed him but it was an upper body shot, which knocked him backwards and he was immediately pulled behind the sleeping huts by one of the guards before I could put in a second shot. I am fairly certain his injury will be bad and we will be very unlucky indeed if he takes any more part in the proceedings.'

I slapped him on the back. 'Absolutely fantastic,' I said,

'if that guy is dead or at least badly injured then we have a much better chance because although the palace guard will have someone to take over, I will be surprised if he is as sharp as the one you have just shot.'

I thought for a moment and said, 'There are four men down for certain, possibly five counting the commander, and they know we are able to shoot back and do so effectively. Even if the deputy now taking over is as thick as two pieces of wood he will know he faces a fight and I suspect he will try and tie us down overnight until reinforcements arrive tomorrow. I am sure they have been in radio contact with the capital reporting the potential incident in here and now they have confirmation of a fighting force. The commander may have been reluctant to let the capital know he could not cope but a deputy commander would not feel so constrained. Speaking of radio, I'm surprised there isn't one in this building. Has anyone seen a radio?'

There was a mass shaking of heads. It was the new recruit driver's turn now. He tapped me on the arm and said: 'I cannot tell from here whether the lorry is damaged in the engine. We can all see holes in the canvas canopy at the back and I suppose it is likely bullets have been fired into the cab but whether the engine itself still works I really cannot tell from here. Now we have no front door, it would be possible for me to crawl out, under the lorry and have a look to see whether oil or water is pouring out as that would be a sure sign of bad damage.' I frowned, thinking that whilst he should quite easily get from the door to the back of the lorry, crawling underneath it he would be seen. He anticipated what I was about to say. 'The underside of the lorry will be cold now and I can lift myself up and along the drive shaft until I get to the gearbox and then hold onto the gearbox with my arms and my feet around the drive shaft. This will keep me off the ground and I shouldn't be seen.'

'Okay,' I said, 'do it when you can. Do not take any risks.' He moved to the door and wriggled his way out of sight while we sat there waiting. I dearly wanted to go up into the bedrooms to get a report from the men there as well as look out into the camp to see for myself what was happening. However, I dared not go anywhere near the doorway at this moment as it might have attracted the attention of the palace guards who could well spot as driver hanging from under- side the lorry. An age seemed to pass before he returned.

'That was easy, wasn't it?' he said. 'There is no oil or water coming from the engine itself and, feeling around, I could not find any damage at all. It looks ready to go if we are.'

'How good are you with engines?' I asked.

'An expert, as good as your Jumba and I know this lorry very well as I have been keeping it running.'

'Do you think it is possible to start the engine from under- neath, where you just were, and get the lorry moving towards the compound gates without actually getting in the cab?'

'Oh yes,' he said. 'Quite easy really'. He explained the procedure.

'How long do you think it would take?' I asked.

'Difficult to say,' he replied, 'if I didn't have to hang upside down, only a few minutes, but working from underneath, trying to cling on will be a problem.' He thought for a moment. 'If we take one strap off a couple of knapsacks, I can sling these around my back and secure them to a bracket in the engine bay which will hold my upper body and give me free use of my arms and that should speed things up considerably. The problem is can we find any wire stiff enough to pull down the clutch and accelerator through the holes in the cab floor?'

'No idea,' I said, 'you go off and have a look while I go upstairs to see how the guys up there are getting on.'

I returned to one of the bedrooms to find two of our

group lying on the floor behind wardrobes and cupboards. I joined them on the floor. The furniture was peppered with bullet holes but no one had sustained injury. I told them the front door had disintegrated from the intense firing and asked them to make their way down the stairs, to the corridor, one at a time, carefully so they would not be detected from outside. But first they should tell the others in the other bedrooms to do the same. As I was lying there I was conscious of a pile of clothing about a foot or so away from me. Clothes, I assumed, from the man who had been shot in this bedroom, but they were not army-coloured but light grey; a suit? I leant forward and pulled the clothes towards me, confirming an Armani jacket and trousers. Rather up-market for a palace guard off-duty wear. I rolled over to where the two dead bodies were covered by a blanket, raised the blanket and saw a young black girl's body and that of a middle-aged white man. From what was left of him he appeared well groomed. Before I could wonder any more our driver crawled in with a beaming smile on his face.

'I have found the wire. Mattress springs will be just the job.'

'Great.' I told him to get on with them and, when he was ready, to come down to the corridor to join us. I returned to the corridor and waited for everyone to arrive. The last was the driver brandishing two wire hooks, which had been bent at the other end to form a rough and ready handle.

'On the assumption the commander out there is dead or seriously injured I would expect his deputy will be considering a full-frontal attack but if he has the slightest sense at all he will not do so. He knows concentrated firepower will not go through the concrete walls of the building and he must realise we are all keeping well away from the windows. The only way in is through the front door or the lower ground-floor windows, which he knows we can defend. Even if they concentrate all their fire power on these openings to keep us away, as soon as any of his men try and get in they will be silhouetted and easy targets for us. Remember, he has no idea how many are in this building and he has seen sufficient from us to know we are not amateurs. Consequently, I anticipate he will try and hold us down here until reinforcements come from the capital. By the way, has anyone found a radio in here?' They all shook their heads and I was somewhat curious as to why the central office did not have radio communication with patrol jeeps and the capital. Very odd, but there it was.

'So the long and short of it is we have to get out of here before reinforcements arrive. I think we all agree, to make a run for the lorry will be a disaster and if we break out straight for the main gates it will be a bit like *Butch Cassidy and the Sundance Kid.*' This resulted in bewildered looks on everyone's faces. I smiled. 'A more than an amusing cowboy film where our two anti-heroes are trapped in a building by many soldiers and, realising their fate, run out to fight it out in the open with the obvious result of a very swift, bullet-riddled death. I would like to avoid that.' Nods all round.

'I estimate it will be sunset in a little over an hour and this will mean before then anyone looking towards this building from the gate or from the sleeping huts will be looking into the sun and the front of this building will last a long shadow. With a bit of luck, we can create a diversion because our good man here,' I patted the driver on the shoulder, 'is going to crawl under his lorry, start it up from underneath, release the clutch and let it drive itself, with no one in it, towards the main gate. Anyway, hopefully the up shot is that the palace guard believes we all somehow got on board without them noticing and we are making a run for it. All being well, they will concentrate their thoughts, eyes and firepower on the moving empty lorry.'

I looked around and saw that they were all hanging on my every word. Slightly worrying for I was new to this sort of thing and was, truth be known, winging it! I explained what the rest of us would do to capitalise on the diversion, how at the right moment we must maintain maximum firepower and how, as forward and rearguard groups, we would cover each other as we made our escape. At least that was the theory.

I looked at Brother. 'You will be up to it?'

'Absolutely right,' he said, 'I will be like a gazelle, you just watch me.'

I did not doubt his spirit or his endeavour but I had some fear that his gazelle quality would not be dissimilar to my walking on air ability.

'There is just one small thing,' said our friendly lorry driver, 'I cannot clamber under the lorry and do the necessary if I'm carrying a Kalashnikov and ammunition.'

'No problem,' I replied, 'I will carry your gun, knapsack and ammunition out to you and you can take them over when you get up to sprint to our first position. Finally,' I continued 'everyone take their knapsacks with them and check around to make sure you leave nothing behind to identify us. I am assuming the palace guard will not have DNA capabilities from the expended bullet casings scattered about.'

Amazon raised an eyebrow and gave me one of her old-fashioned looks.

'All prepared then?' I looked around at each one of them. They all looked keen and ready to go. 'Okay. I want to do all this while the sun is still up so let's get a move on. Everyone to their places quickly and quietly. If you see any movement from the palace guard give a shout but do not move from your place.'

Our friendly lorry driver wriggled out the front door with his improvised harness and two pieces of wire towards the lorry as others silently crept upstairs to take their positions ready to fire out of the windows at the huts as soon as the lorry started moving. I shrugged on my knapsack, checked the Kalashnikov and slid two extra magazines in my breast pockets for easy access. I put the lorry driver's gun and knapsack containing extra magazines close to my left hand ready to grab as I ran out the front door. We waited.

There was no sound of anything from the palace guard. No more loud hailer, and the lack of warning from anyone in the bedrooms indicated the palace guards were remaining where they were.

It seemed like for ever. Time ticked slowly by during which I said to Amazon and Brother through the office door, 'One of the dead men upstairs was white.'

There was a long silence before Amazon replied. 'Not surprised. The palace guard gets friendly with the western aid workers and if the dead guy was of any importance then Zaban would not have hesitated in ensuring he was offered every hospitality, and what better than a nice young black girl in an out-of-the-way place where no one would say anything.'

Logical, I thought.

I was beginning to doubt that our lorry driver friend could actually do what he so confidently said could be done, but suddenly there was a whirring of a starter motor, and the engine of the truck fired up, clattering to full revolutions. The noise from the engine was almost deafening even inside the building where we were and it could not have escaped the attention of the watching palace guard. I wanted to peep around the door frame to see what was happening but restrained myself because I did not want to attract attention away from the lorry. When the clattering engine had reached fever pitch it dipped and then started to grow again, which I took to be our lorry driver friend letting out the clutch to get the lorry moving forward. Indeed it must have been for there was a staccato fire from the palace guard, shortly followed by prolonged bursts of our group. I picked up the lorry driver's gun, spare ammunition and knapsack, beckoned to my two companions and sprinted out of the front door, keeping low. I was expecting to see the driver lying on the ground a few paces from the front door but in fact he was some twenty yards away. He scrambled to his feet as we approached him: I passed him the Kalashnikov, ammunition and knapsack as we ran the fifty yards to our first position to fall to the ground ready to fire upon the buildings in and behind which the palace guard was hiding. During this short run I was not conscious of being fired upon by the palace guard. None of us was hit and, so far as I could see, no bullets were striking the ground around us. I mentally congratulated the group still in the block for maintaining a high rate of fire to keep the palace guard pinned down. As predicted, the lorry had veered off to the left smashing into the sleeping quarter block there and eventually stalling the engine as it was forced to a halt.

When we were in position we opened fire, raking all the wooden buildings we could see to allow the second group to come out of the centre block. We could not see the store shed, which was immediately behind the centre block, which meant of course they could not see us nor shoot at us. A couple of the palace guard there obviously realised this for they appeared at a crouching run towards the workshop sheds to get into the action. A big mistake. They were like sitting ducks and crumpled in a heap as our bullets hit them.

Not for the first time I was amazed how quickly a Kalashnikov could eat up and spit out bullets when set to automatic fire. I had emptied two magazines and was just fitting the third before the second group appeared at the doorway, running towards us. I paid no attention to them but concentrated upon the buildings around the block to see if I could detect any movement from the palace guard. There was none and the second group ran past us to take up its position at the compound gate. My scepticism of Brother's ability was badly misplaced for he went past me like the wind. How much it was hurting him I could but guess but he certainly did not let us down.

When the second group opened fire we, in the first group, retreated past them, scrabbling in our knapsacks for more magazines to replenish those now empty. We flopped down well outside the gate and started firing at the only buildings we could now see – the two accommodation blocks. The second group joined us and we slowly crawled backwards, firing the occasional burst to keep the palace guard occupied until we reached a dip in the ground affording cover. I called a halt to the firing and looked back at the palace guard camp. Nothing was stirring. I did not suppose for one moment we had dispatched everyone there. Almost certainly most in the store shed had survived but I rather hoped there was sufficient injury and mayhem to keep them occupied. I directed our second group to retreat further while I remained with the first group to watch to give covering fire if necessary. Amazon, Brother and the rest moved off swiftly, keeping low as we in the first group scanned the camp for activity. By now the sun was setting and the shadows in the camp made it difficult to detect any movement but very shortly the darkness would give us the envelope to get away completely.

Although I did not see anyone in the camp, when the second group was far enough away we gave the camp a final one magazine burst to show we were still around and then we sprinted towards the second group which had by this time reached the outcrop of rocks close to the foot of the hill. In the final light of the day it was time to take stock.

'Anybody injured?' I asked.

There was some murmuring and grunting, the upshot of which was that a couple had received minor flesh wounds that were quickly tended. We had quite amazingly got away without losing anyone or suffering a bad injury.

297

'That is brilliant. Well done everyone. We will wait here for half an hour or so and then when the sun is fully down we will move off.'

'But what about you?' said the lorry driver. I looked puzzled. 'Have you seen your arm?' he asked.

I looked at my arm but could see nothing, then I was conscious of a fairly steady drip of blood from the fingers of my left hand. I had felt the stickiness earlier but put it down to tension-induced perspiration. I looked at the back of my left arm and in the dimming light could see a long red mark from shoulder to elbow. Amazon came across and looked at it.

'Very impressive,' she said. 'It seems you have picked up the best trophy wound amongst us. That's pretty deep and ought to have a few stitches but in this light that would be difficult. A temporary repair is needed.'

She took out a knife and cut open the sleeve of my camouflage overalls to expose the wound, which must have been caused by a ricocheting piece of metal for it was indeed fairly deep with nice clean edges. The blood was flowing freely from it and dripping to the ground. Amazon poured some powder she had got from her knapsack into the wound and squeezed it tight. I have no idea what that powder was but I can record if one is looking for means of torture, pouring this powder into an open wound would be fairly high on the list. It was all I could do to stop screaming. Amazon looked at me as though I was a wimp so I tried to set my face into a 'that does smart a bit' expression while she applied a field dressing tightly enough to contain and then stem the bleeding.

'That will do for you. What next?' she said.

I was quite surprised that she still regarded me as the leader of this expedition for we were now back in territory familiar to her and everyone else and fairly alien to me. I mentally shrugged.

'Give it another half an hour or so to get darker and then we will move off back to the village. On the basis that sooner or later the palace guard will try and track us, I suggest we start out in another direction and at daylight you can advise when it would be best to change tack towards the village. In the meantime, I could kill for a bacon sandwich. Does anyone have any food?' There was much shaking of heads all around. We had a few more days then without any food unless of course our intrepid hunters here could show me how to live off the land.

Brother moved and sat next to me. Even in the semi-darkness he looked quite awful. His eyes had puffed up even more and he peered at me through slits.

'What do you think? Will they follow us?' he asked.

I considered a moment and replied. 'I think we were very lucky indeed. I do not believe they will follow us from the camp. I think I was right in saying our lack of return fire initially made them complacent and far more of them were in the wooden buildings than there should have been. Your combined fire raking those buildings when we sprinted out the front door probably caused a high level of injury so I strongly suspect at this moment they are more concerned with tending their own wounds than chasing us. On the basis they radioed for reinforcements I would expect those reinforcements will try to chase us. What we don't know is when the reinforcements are likely to arrive so I believe our chosen course from here should be away from the road and over ground that allowing us to move fairly quickly in darkness.'

'I agree,' said Brother. 'It would be nice to know when, indeed if at all, they radioed for reinforcements. Like you, I was amazed there was no radio in the centre block. The office was their hub of operations and it would be usual to have the radio there. If there had been a radio then we would have known precisely what they were doing and this could have inhibited their decision-making.'

We all got up and in single file walked around the base of the hill and then, adopting the usual pattern of flanking lookouts we set off at a steady pace away from the camp. We walked all through the night and, although I occasionally tripped on an unseen small rock or tuft of vegetation, Brother, walking ahead of me, with all his injuries, just plodded on steadily without a break in his stride. I had to admire the inner strength which kept him going.

18

The Aftermath

At daybreak we were in an area of heavy vegetation with bushes and trees all around. I called a halt and we sat under a tree so I could consult with the group.

'From here on in it is up to you,' I said to Brother. 'You know the territory like the back of your hand and can pick off the best route to the village and the way of avoiding anyone following us.'

Brother looked grateful that I had chosen him as a leader rather than deferring to Amazon because of Brother's still poor physical shape, and he visibly grew stronger as he took charge.

'We must now start taking extra precautions with our movements and be particularly careful that we are not taken by surprise by a helicopter.' At this I raised my eyebrows and looked surprised. I thought he had said some time ago that the palace guard helicopters were fairly unserviceable and were simply kept for show. In answer to my surprise he continued. 'It is possible that the palace guard may have one serviceable helicopter or they may even commandeer one from the army. When the reinforcements get to the camp and see what we have done there they will probably realise there is insufficient time to track us and catch up with us and so they may well call upon a helicopter. This means during daylight hours we have to keep to terrain that will give us cover from the air and so we will walk on now until midday then rest for a few hours to get some sleep, which I'm sure you will need.' He looked at us all in a patriarchal way but I guessed he was more in need of rest than any of us. So far as I was concerned, I was still firing on adrenaline. 'When darkness falls we will resume our walking again.'

With that, he stood up and talked to several of the men in local dialect and they fanned out as everyone else got to their feet and we started walking in the direction indicated by Brother.

Just before midday one of the flanking lookouts sprinted to us, grunting something at Brother who waved everyone to take cover. Kalashnikov at the ready, I knelt behind a bush, looking around to see what had attracted the attention of the lookout. It was quite a while before two lookouts appeared flanking four women carrying bags on their backs. One of the women was Vana. I stood up, amazed, and walked over to her.

'Do you think I would let you starve?' she said with a knowing smile on her face.

The four women put down their bags, opened them up and started to distribute food. Welcome and needed though this was, I was impressed at the professionalism of the group for four of them ignored the offering and left us to go out and continue scanning the surrounding area for possible hostility. I gratefully accepted the food and sat down to eat. When Vana had distributed the food she came and sat beside me.

'How did you know where to find us?' I asked, 'and even more to the point how did you know we had escaped?'

'I never doubted you would be successful and I had a very strong feeling you would get away from the camp. All I had to do then was to consult with some trackers in the village as to what route you would likely take and they advised me that you would not come directly back to the village but lead any followers astray. I thought about it for a while and decided you would take a course away from the main road and I judged the point at which you would likely change direction towards the village so we four set out towards where I thought you would be going.' I was impressed and about to say so when she said, 'Not really difficult when you think about it.' I was still impressed.

I munched quietly on the food, which was not a bacon sandwich but really tasty and thoroughly enjoyable. I took a sip of water from my water bottle and lay back contented.

'Didn't you take a chance at being picked up by the palace guard?'

'Not really,' she replied, 'if you were keeping those in this area occupied at their camp then it was unlikely there would be any palace guard around and even if there was then we had a cover story that we were taking food to a nearby village suffering particular hardship. The palace guard may not have liked it but they would have understood.'

My mind dwelt upon what the palace guard could have done to them if in fact they had been detected and my thoughts obviously transferred to the expression on my face for she patted me on the arm and said, 'You worry too much. We would have been all right.' I rather doubted it.

Four of the group, having eaten, got to their feet and went to relieve the four who were keeping watch. They came and tucked heartily into the offerings given by the women. When everyone had finished and the food remnants had been packed away in the women's bags Brother said, 'We will stick to our plan and stay here under cover for the rest of the day and then set out after sunset. In this vegetation our pace will be slow at night but after a couple of hours we will come to an open plain where we can pick up pace. No helicopter will be flying at night so whilst we must remain vigilant we need not worry about eyes in the sky."

As the sun was setting so we had a little more to eat and then set off in the usual formation with the four women sandwiched between Brother and me with Amazon bringing up the rear. Our pace was somewhat quicker than I anticipated, largely because of Brother's skill at finding good ground to walk on in the vegetation, and when we hit the plain we fairly galloped along until sunrise, pausing only briefly during the night for a short rest and sip of water. At sunrise the plain had turned to tundra with bushes and a few trees, which we all huddled beneath to gratefully eat a meal before taking a well-earned rest, guarded, as ever, by the vigilant lookouts. I drifted off into a half sleep with the sun first warming my body and then beginning to bake me. By midday we were up and walking again but our friend the lorry driver did not join us. With fond farewells he went off towards his own village.

Towards mid-afternoon one of the group called out and pointed to the sky in the distance. Looking carefully, I could just make out a black dot, which was not a bird, so no doubt a helicopter. It was a long way away and we had plenty of time to take cover and wait. The helicopter was flying low, did not appear to me to be carrying out any particular search pattern but was aimlessly flying in our general direction. We kept perfectly still as it passed close enough for me to see it was painted a light blue, with no markings, and could carry four, perhaps six, people. I could just make out two people looking out of windows on its right side. It flew past and carried on into the distance, eventually disappearing. We lay there for a goodly while after it was out of sight just in case it retraced its flight path, during which time I mused that whilst Brother had said palace guard helicopters were fairly unserviceable, the one that had just passed looked in very good condition. I assumed it was a palace guard helicopter rather than one from the army as any military helicopter would be painted in the usual camouflage colours. What did strike me was that either the flying pattern of the helicopter did not indicate a determined effort to find us or those on board were very inexperienced in searching. No matter, it was to our advantage.

Eventually we continued our trek back to the village with the lookouts keeping very beady eyes on the sky just in case the helicopter reappeared. It did not.

We got back to the village, stowed all our military gear in the cave and, as usual, reported to the chief. He again listened without expression and when Brother had finished explaining everything to him the chief looked at me.

'You really are a surprise aren't you?' I took this to be a rhetorical question and said nothing. 'We are all very grateful to you. Although we were confident Ajani would not tell the palace guard of our village there was always a chance someone would recognise him so you have saved the whole village.'

I did not wish to pour cold water on the chief's pleasure and when we left him I called Amazon, Brother and Vana to one side.

'We have been very lucky so far but I do not think we should assume this is the end of it. The chief is right, someone may well have recognised you and more to the point is how and why you were captured. You have been to the capital many times and did not attract attention before so why now?'

Brother looked at me and said, 'Yes, we must consider all this. Come, let us go to our usual tree outside the village and sit down.' He smiled. 'Now we are home I have to admit I am absolutely exhausted and don't think I could stand for one moment longer.'

'I'm sorry,' I said, 'I'm being very selfish. Why don't you go back to your hut and rest because we can talk about this tomorrow.'

'No, certainly not,' said Brother. It is something to be discussed and considered now.'

Vana walked away from us towards her own hut as we three slowly went to our conference tree and sat down under the shade. Vana shortly joined us with four bowls and a pitcher of what turned out to be somewhat diluted but exceptionally refreshing jungle juice, which visibly perked up Brother and made me feel pretty good as well. We just sat for a while letting the jungle juice fire the body and allow the aches and pains of our adventure to dull. While we had been walking back to the village my injured arm had not troubled me too much. It had hurt but I had had more to think about than a bit of pain. Now I was back in the village the arm was throbbing fairly mightily and I surreptitiously felt it to see if there was any swelling or, what would be more concerning, any heat coming from it denoting the start of blood poisoning. It felt okay, if tender to the touch, and I noted Vana frowning at me with some concern. I shook my head to indicate there was no problem.

'I must tell you what I've been doing these past weeks, while you have been holidaying here in the village.' Brother looked around with a smile on his face; that is, as much of a smile as a battered face could show. It must have hurt him to even try. 'I first went to a couple of villages to sound out how they were feeling at the moment and the overwhelming response was that the palace guard had been shown to be vulnerable, and whilst there was still fear, it was no longer ingrained in the villagers but simply something to be taken into consideration. Their mercenary groups were still being trained and that training was spreading to other people in the villages well. They were very receptive to someone bringing all the villages together for an uprising against

Baumge but obviously needed to be convinced when the time to do that was right.'

Brother paused and took a long drink from his bowl. 'When I got to the capital I went and saw my friends, particularly those in government, to see what their opinion was. Being at the hub, as it were, they were much more up to speed with what the palace guard was doing and the palace guard's reaction to the recent successful attacks on it. Essentially, although Zaban was enthusiastically shrugging off the attacks, admitting nothing and madly recruiting, there was a great uncertainty in the palace guard, and this rubbed off on those in government who suddenly did not feel quite so confident that their position was protected. This was giving encouragement to those who would oppose the government, if it were possible, and even the people in the streets were walking about with more certainty. For the first time in years I felt the capital was not being submerged under a dark cloud.'

'That is encouraging, indeed wonderful,' said Amazon. 'At last we are getting somewhere. For so long I feared that whatever we did was geting us nowhere but now it is all worthwhile.' Not having experienced the oppression everyone in this country had been under, I was not so certain but kept quiet.

'As to the important point over whether there was going to be a formal opposition and if so who would lead, that was much more difficult. Naturally, every politician wanted to be in charge but on reflection they realised if they were seen to be leading a revolution their families would be immediately wiped out and this rather cooled their enthusiasm. I suppose the really good thing was that there was talk of an opposition, which would have been unthinkable, impossible, a few months ago. I managed to get together a number of the more influential politicians who were keen to have Baumge replaced and would support an uprising if it was likely to succeed. That, of course, was the key, success. Talk is cheap but to get these people active one has to have what, on the face of it, appears to be a sure-fire plan, and at the moment we don't have one of those. I won't bore you with the topics of conversation or some of the outlandish ideas that were postulated but in the end it boiled down to the following. The politicians would subtly plant an idea into the minds of the civil servants and general political hangers-on that it would be internationally helpful to the country if it appeared we had an opposition party. There is much international criticism at the moment over human rights and the totalitarian regime, whereby foreign aid is being restricted, but if the government could demonstrate an active opposition party, even if it was only paying lip service to opposition, it would be good for the rest of the world to see.'

There was much grunting from Amazon at this stage as if to indicate 'opposition, fat chance'.

Undaunted, Brother continued. 'I actually think this ploy might well work. Several times the Pan-African conference, which has recently finished, brought up the lack of opposition in this country although I have to say many of those heads of government attending didn't have too much of an opposition in their countries! If we can get an opposition party going then we will have a political leader in the capital, which would be the focal point for the foreign media. Everyone agreed that leader should not be in charge of the physical revolution of the people and I was not surprised that to a man they agreed I should organise and lead the military action that would have to be taken. It was obviously left up to me to get all the villages to agree to this and so there is still a lot of work ahead.'

Again another pause while Brother took a drink from his bowl and looked around at us.

'What, as we know, is lacking is a revolutionary military force in the capital. Up to now the palace guard secret service has had a stranglehold on the populace and it was simply impossible to even contemplate setting up a clandestine organisation. Quite frankly, I did not believe the, then, recent events would change this but the politicians I spoke to were very keen for me to get something moving in the capital and so, against my better judgement, I was persuaded to meet someone who was more vociferous than most against the government and whom, the politicians felt, could bring together a fighting force in the capital. The idea was that this man would recruit prospective fighters who would come out to the villages to be trained and then go back, armed, ready for the uprising. A grand plan, which *should* happen if we are to be successful, but I felt we were running before we could walk. However, as I said, I was persuaded to meet this man and discuss ways of recruiting, training and soon. I was fairly sure this was my downfall.

'I was given directions as to where to find him but when we met in an inconspicuous and neutral place I did not really warm to him at all. I can't put my finger on it. He was affable enough, determined, outspoken and certainly enthusiastic but there was just something in his demeanour I felt was not right. At the time I put it down to the fact that he had to be so careful in the capital not to be caught or branded as someone preaching against the government, but on reflection, if, as I had been told, he was vociferous in his criticisms it was an enormous wonder he had not been arrested. I now believe, although I might be wrong, he was actually a palace guard plant preaching against the government to attract others who the palace guard would arrest.'

We all considered this and certainly Amazon and Vana felt Brother's assessment was more than likely correct.

'The fact I did not feel comfortable with this man meant that I told him very little. We talked about setting up a military opposition in the capital, how it could be done and that it was possible to send recruits out into the countryside to be trained. I was particularly vague about where these recruits could go and tried to give the impression that I only knew about these things possibly happening rather than being an active participant. I don't know how convincing I was and when I left him it was on the basis that he would do the recruiting while I went to find someone who knew more about armed resistance in the countryside to bring them both together. I said I would return to the capital in a month to see how he was getting on though I was determined before then to make more enquiries as to who this man was and how reliable he could be. I should have made enquiries before I met him. That was a big mistake.

'Luckily, I left the capital on the day I met him and did not go back to see any of my friends. I made my way towards another village, which I knew was sympathetic to our cause. I thought I was keeping a good lookout but, obviously, being alone it is difficult to be thorough, and when I was eating my evening meal I heard the sound of jeeps. I did the best I could to hide but the palace guard was upon me in no time at all and I was captured. I was surprised they did not take me back to the capital but went to the camp we have just left. Thinking about it, I suppose there were not enough trained palace guard in the capital to organise a manhunt so those at the camp were sent out to do it. They interrogated me in the usual fashion and I managed to hold out and say nothing, although I have to say I was alarmed when they told me Zaban was coming to the camp specifically to talk to me.'

At this point his injured face broke into a smile.

'Zaban arrived the very morning you attacked. He came to see me and gave me a kick or two but spent most of the time just looking at me, trying to frighten me, which was not difficult, and telling me what ill was going to befall me if I did not tell him who my co-conspirators were, how many people were planning revolution and what politicians were actively seeking to overthrow the government. He left me to dwell upon it and then you arrived so you know the rest.'

'Is there any chance this person you met in the capital can find out who you are?' I asked.

'I would imagine it would not be too difficult if he put his mind to it,' said Brother. 'He must know that I had some support in the capital from politicians, and although my friends there are incredibly discreet, it would not be impossible to imagine that in casual conversation they might mention I had visited them and the village I came from.' Seeing the concern on my face, Brother shook his head. 'With a little bit of luck, and we don't need too much of that, the problem is being solved. On the way back from the camp I was speaking to the man from the other village, the lorry driver, and told him the name of the person who I felt had betrayed us, me in particular, and our friend the lorry driver went off to the capital to sort it out.'

I frowned as if not understanding what he meant by 'sort it out'. Brother continued.

'Sabra told you our friendly lorry driver was a good fighter but she did not tell you everything. He is far more than that. He is the best man I know to blend in anywhere and get information and he has been used before as an assassin. He is really very good with a knife. When he left us, he did not go towards his village but back to the capital and I would be surprised indeed if he hasn't already identified and dispatched the informer.'

I thought about this and wondered how our friendly lorry driver could get into the capital dressed in combat gear with a knapsack and Kalashnikov over his shoulder. As if to read my mind, as she probably could anyway, Vana said, 'I think you will find that he took off his clothes and hid them with his equipment and walked into the capital in just a loin-cloth. A virtually naked man would raise no suspicion at all and he would soon get the clothes he needed to do the job in hand. If anyone could silence our informer before harm was done he is the man.'

We all thought our separate thoughts for a while and I was turning over in my mind the various possibilities and potential problems. Eventually I said, 'It would be wise for us to assume our lorry driver friend was not successful or has been successful but after the informer had identified Ajani. We must also consider whether any of the palace guard who captured you knew who you were or even that the local dialect you spoke could identify the village or area you come from. I assume that your interrogation was not in English.'

Brother looked at me and nodded slowly. 'You're right, we did not talk in English but I would be surprised indeed if any of the interrogators were alive to nuances in dialect difference. I knew none of them and I am certain they did not know me so whilst we must not totally dismiss the idea that the palace guard could identify me, I really and strongly believe it is highly unlikely. You do though have a point that the informer may have been able to identify me, or least the area I came from, before he met his end.'

Brother obviously had absolute faith in our lorry driver friend for nothing seemed to shake him from the idea that the informer would die; more likely was already dead.

'But even if our worst fears are correct we do have an advantage,' said Vana. 'Zaban is dead and without any doubt at all he is the major driving force behind the palace guard so whoever is in charge now will have his work cut out re-forming a cohesive force, and it will be quite a while before anyone will follow up any information given by the informer. What we do know as a matter of logical thinking,' and at this point Vana looked at me as though I was deficient and had missed the most obvious point, 'even if the informer had identified Ajani or the area he comes from, he did not pass this information before Zaban left the capital because

Zaban would not have wasted his time interrogating, he would have set out with his men to this village to capture everyone in the full knowledge that although Ajani might well be able to resist questioning, many of the people in this village would not. No, I agree with Ajani. I think we are safe but we must not be complacent.'

Again there was a long silence while we all contemplated what had been said. Perhaps Vana was right, I was a natural pessimist. I was happy to accept our friendly lorry driver would do his bit but, bearing in mind the potential for the informer to have passed on valuable information to the palace guard and the fact that Brother had been sprung from capture, I felt the new commander of the palace guard, who would no doubt be ruthless – it was in the job description – would likely move heaven and earth to try and find out who Brother was and where he came from. It would not take a leap of imagination from anyone, let alone a commander of the palace guard, to realise the recent attacks, which had been so successful on the palace guard, were likely carried out by a single group rather than different groups. It was all far too coincidental, and then, of course, there was the likely pressure from those in government who, according to Ajani, were feeling a little unnerved before Zaban was killed and now must be building up a fair old lather. I could not but imagine sooner or later, and I feared sooner, there was going to be retribution somewhere. I was considering whether to bring my fears to their attention when Brother said:

'Tell me Nigel, what do you really think?'

Some years ago I realised that when a client has wined, dined and entertained me for the evening and over a very expensive brandy asks, 'Mr Turner, what do you really think of my case?' the last thing he wants to hear is what I really think of his case. I rather felt that this was not the time to tell Brother what I really thought.

'As we all agreed, we must remain cautious,' I said, 'as ever, knowledge is king and so we should get information from the capital and all villages to see what the reaction is from the palace guard, the attitude and demeanour of the government and also the thoughts and feelings of the people. I suggest we send people from the village to a few other villages and also the capital to try and get this information but it is absolutely essential whoever goes should not draw attention to themselves. I don't know how this can be done or indeed who in the village is capable to do this.' I looked around at them in an enquiring way.

'I can organise that,' said Vana. 'So far as other villages are concerned we trade between us by barter and it happens that no one from this village has done it for several months so it would be quite natural for a few groups to go around other villages, trading goods. I believe the capital is going to be far more difficult and normally I would suggest either Sabra or I went there but we have both been recently and to go again would certainly draw unwelcome attention. What we need is someone who can blend in and yet get information.' She looked at me and smiled. 'You're already on my wavelength. Our friendly lorry driver is the man. I think he will probably take longer than either Sabra or I to get information but what we can be certain of is that whatever he comes back with will be accurate. But everyone agreed?'

Brother and Amazon agreed enthusiastically and I slowly nodded. I was glad Vana felt she could not go back to the capital and I had to defer to her knowledge of our friendly lorry driver's abilities.

'Good,' said Brother, 'I don't think we can take it any further and, for my part, I am absolutely washed out. I really do need some rest. The energy I managed to summon up to leave the camp has gone and if I don't leave you now I do not think I will be able to get back to my hut.'

For my part, I was still amazed that Brother had lasted so long.

We got up, Brother very slowly and rather unsteadily, and went back to our respective huts.

When Vana and I reached our hut she said to me, 'You go on in and take your clothes off.'

I raised a provocative eyebrow and inclined my head to one side in an expectant sort of way. She punched me fiercely on my arm, luckily not my injured arm, then said: 'You have a one track mind. Not that. Your arm needs tending and you stink!'

I adopted a pose of disappointment and hurt, then went into the hut to do as I was bid. The moment I got inside the inner strength, no doubt adrenaline driven, fell from me in an instant. I felt drained and empty. I could quite easily have curled up on the mattress there and then and fallen asleep. Slowly, I took my clothes off and the throbbing of my arm seemed to have intensified. My shoulder was stiff and I could hardly move my arm at all, so getting my shirt off was a long process. Obviously the adrenaline was still active when I had changed out of combats into everyday gear in the cave for I had no trouble undressing and dressing then. I had only just completed taking my shirt off when Vana returned carrying a basket slung over her shoulder, full of what looked like medicines, and carrying a bowl of steaming-hot water.

'Sit down on the mattress and don't fall asleep yet,' she said. Obviously my exhausted state was plain to see and I felt rather humble to be in such a pitiful way.

'Well don't feel bad about it,' she said, 'it's a mental thing. Now you are safe at home your mind has let go and this often translates into a physical exhaustion. I've seen it before and it is not at all unusual. You are just a man after all and a white man at that!'

I did not have the energy to react to her jibe and slowly

sat on the mattress while she busied herself with things in the basket and the bowl of hot water.

'I am going to take the field dressing off your arm and it is going to be a little painful. These field dressings are good and fairly new, which means the impregnated chemical pad will not stick too much to the congealed blood and tear the wound open when I take it off but there is bound to be some discomfort.'

She held my elbow firmly in her left hand and pulled away the field dressing from my arm. It hurt. I kept my face impassive and I was rather pleased I did not even flinch. I don't think she needed to be impressed but it made me feel good.

'Sabra was right, it is a deep gash but it looks clean and not infected at all. Our magic powder works well.' I raised an enquiring eyebrow at that. She continued, 'Whilst we have lots of modern antiseptics, mostly stolen from the palace guard lorries, we have our own herb and mineral powder, which has proved to be exceptionally good on open wounds and has the additional benefit of numbing the pain after a while. The only downside is that applying the powder is often more painful than receiving the wound, but that soon goes.'

'I have to confess,' I said, 'I was a little surprised at the agony. Do I take it I may have to have another dose of this magic powder?'

Vana chuckled. 'No, it has done its job.' She washed my arm and the gash with hot water, clearing away the dried blood, then applied what I took to be an antiseptic, for it stung, before inspecting the gash closely.

'I really think it ought to be stitched up. I could bandage it closed but in a day or so moving your arm may mean the wound will break open and expose you to infection.'

With that she rummaged in her medicine basket, produced a needle and twine and started stitching my arm. As the gash was at the back of my arm I could not see precisely what she was doing but, from the number of times she cut the twine with a knife, I estimated she put in more than six stitches. Her administrations were a little painful but her touch was gentle and caring. When she had finished, she again bathed the area with antiseptic and gently put a pad over the stitched-up cut and bandaged my arm expertly. After that she made me stand up and washed me down, getting rid of the dust, grime and sweat of the last few days.

'Clean and repaired, you're now ready for anything but I suggest you get some sleep. I have to organise people in the village to go out and trade with other villages and also get a message to our friendly lorry driver. It will take me a little time to do all this so you can rest knowing I will not interrupt you.'

In fact she did interrupt my sleep to give me some food from the evening meal. She made me eat it, sitting on the mattress, and also drink a small bowl of jungle juice. When I'd finished she told me to lie down and go back to sleep. Normally, when I am awake I am fully alert and cannot possibly go back to sleep but on this occasion no sooner was my head down and my eyes closed than I drifted off into a deep slumber until sunrise the following morning. I would have expected that after what I had just gone through my sleep would be troubled by a churning mind but it was not. If I dreamt at all, I could not remember it on awakening and when the sun rose so did I feeling incredibly refreshed, though my left arm was stiff with a dull, persistent ache.

The following weeks passed uneventfully, with me, as before, helping out with various tasks. Vana regularly attended my arm, which was healing quickly and cleanly, leaving behind a rather vivid and impressive scar. Brother too healed. Every day he looked better and stronger and he busied himself in the cave, cleaning and overhauling the munitions. There was no training of villagers in the art of shooting though.

Whilst I say the weeks were uneventful, in fact I detected a subtle change in all the villagers. I cannot say for certain but I was under the very strong impression everyone had a pack of essentials ready to grab if the village had to be abandoned. Although Amazon and Brother had given off an air of confidence that we were all safe, the people, probably guided by the chief, were being cautious and ready to flee if this proved necessary. As ever, they all treated me well and the fact I had been instrumental in the release of Brother from the dreaded palace guard enhanced my status, for at first, when my arm was still stiff and difficult to use, I was fussed over by the women and any job requiring the use of both my arms was immediately taken over by one of the men.

Also during this period I went to Brother's hut to see how he was healing and to ask him something. I forget now what that something was. As I approached his hut so I saw a young woman go in so I waited some distance away. I positioned myself to see the hut entrance but not to be noticed immediately by the young woman when she came out. I was sure it was all very innocent but in case it was not then best to be circumspect. I waited a very long time but she did not reappear so I gave up and walked away. I didn't think too much of it at the time though had a nagging feeling I had seen the young woman somewhere before and I was sure every time I had come across her in the village, she had been walking away from me.

As the weeks drifted by, so the hidden and unspoken tension of the village eased, though there was still an awareness. Eventually, we started getting some news from around us.

First to return was one of the band of women and men who had gone to a village to barter and trade. They reported that the attack on the palace guard camp was well known and very popular. No one knew Zaban had been killed. It seemed as though this information was being suppressed. There was no sign of retribution from the palace guard or any indication the villages were expecting any harm to befall them or anyone else. Some days later another band of traders returned and said very much the same.

The last to come to the village was our friendly lorry driver. I was in the centre of the village at the time talking to one of the women, preparing for the evening meal, and he just appeared. I always felt that Amazon and Brother had ghostlike qualities appearing and disappearing at will, but this man was the master. I would have sworn there was no one around me except the woman cooking and suddenly he was at my side. He smiled and slapped me on the back in a friendly and affable way, asking if the 'wounded soldier' was now better, and I told him I was fully fit and raring to go. This produced a deep chuckle. I did not question him at all for I felt I would be told in good time the news he had, so as he wandered across towards Amazon's hut I continued the conversation with the cook.

That evening, Brother, Amazon, Vana, our friendly lorry driver and I sat together eating and talking generally about things. Nothing was mentioned about any news he might have from the capital and I was beginning to feel a little irritated. I was sure something was going on and equally sure it was not bad; just that I was being excluded. I hid my irritation and swapped friendly banter until it was time to go to bed after Brother said we would meet the following morning to discuss all the news.

Back in the hut I expressed my feelings to Vana who shrugged it all off, saying I was imagining things, but she could not look me straight in the eye, which only confirmed something was afoot. I did not sleep well that night, trying to work out what it was I was missing or what was being kept from me.

After the morning meal, we congregated under the conference tree. Brother opened proceedings by repeating what we had heard from the villagers about the villages around, and then gave the floor, as it were, to our friendly lorry driver. Without further prompting, he launched into his news.

'First and foremost, no one is talking about Zaban being dead. My cousin is a fairly senior civil servant and when I mentioned the fact that Zaban had not been seen recently he merely said that was the way Zaban was: sometimes here, sometimes there, with no one knowing what he was actually doing; and that he would turn up when he turned up and not before. It seemed to me that whilst very senior members of the government close to Baumge must know that Zaban was dead, they were keeping it very quiet.

'Second, we were somewhat more successful in our operation than it appeared. All but two of the palace guard in the camp were either killed or injured, and most of them fairly badly injured. This the government could not keep from the people and everyone was talking about it. There was, quietly, euphoria amongst the people with a strong rumour of a fighting force in the countryside opposed to the palace guard. This rumour worried me at first but it seems our friends in government have deflected it away from being potential resistance to the government towards just being a reaction against an intolerant and vicious palace guard.

'Surprisingly, this seems to be accepted by members of the Cabinet, and if everything I heard was correct then Baumge was warming very much to having a token opposition political party to demonstrate to the western world that he was not overseeing a totalitarian regime.'

I was very pleased to hear all this but wanted to have more information as to what the palace guard was doing so I asked him if he had any information on this.

'The palace guard is still recruiting and training but there is little hostile activity in the capital and from what I could hear from people coming from surrounding villages, none in the countryside. It seems as though the palace guard has either realised it should stop massacring or Baumge has told it to hold off while things settle down. I strongly suspect the latter. I was able to speak to Ajani's friend in government who will be forming and leading the opposition party, on the assumption Baumge eventually agrees, and he was very optimistic that things were going to improve in the short term even though he knew, as indeed do all of us, once Baumge gets some stabilisation the horrors will return. Ajani's friend in government emphasised we must not slacken our resolve to build up a strong fighting force and he is looking to Ajani to lead this force against Baumge in the near future.'

Brother looked pleased, smiled and said, 'I appreciate his confidence but think he is a little optimistic if he believes anything is going to happen in the near future. As it appears the government is a little unstable at the moment and the people are becoming confident, now should be the time to make a big move but the reality is we are not sufficiently prepared and what we must do is to get the military on our side before any concerted action is taken. As I said before, the military will not actively join us but we must ensure it will not defend Baumge and that means I have to get the military leaders' assurances that they will do nothing and not interfere until Baumge is deposed, and for the moment the military leaders would not give any assurances to me though once the opposition party is formed that will allow

321

the opposition party to sound out the military and bring it on our side.'

'So then,' I said, 'there is much work to be done in the countryside and in the capital and, whilst it cannot be rushed, we have to waste as little time as possible to be ready before the palace guard has the opportunity, under its new commander, to reaffirm its vice like grip on the country.'

There were agreeing nods all around but no one met my eye.

'Now I say "we" but obviously there is more to tell and I suspect it concerns me.'

If they had been standing, there would have been an embarrassed shuffling of feet. Body language showed uncomfortable, uncertain and difficult things were about to be said. It was Amazon who broke the silence.

'You are, as ever, right. None of us can thank you enough for what you have done here but I'm afraid it is the end. Our friends in government have made it very plain it is simply unacceptable to have any revolt or revolution that would feature or include a white man. It has not escaped the attention of the government that there is a white man in the countryside and the common belief is he is a mercenary sent by foreign powers to overthrow the government. People in the capital are also suggesting a white man is orchestrating the attacks on the palace guard and before long your presence will be widely known throughout the whole country. You have to leave us and go back home. When you are gone we can spread some rumour that a friendly spirit who appeared white has been guiding us and that should satisfy everyone but if you were to stay and be found then we would lose support. Whilst before Baumge both white and black worked together with little of the colonial animosity plaguing other countries, on almost a daily basis Baumge is blaming the white colonial past for the trouble we are in and drumming up hatred that the white man is trying to overthrow the government and rule once more. Most of the people do not believe this but there is always an ingrained doubt and your presence amongst us is going to harm rather than help our cause.'

I kept a stony face, realising what she said was absolutely right. Quite frankly, I didn't think my run of luck could continue much longer and although I had been amazingly and blissfully happy in the village, deep down I knew I could not stay here forever.

'I know it is a blow to you,' said Brother, 'and I would certainly have liked to have had you by my side to help us in our cause. But we have talked about it and agree if the people are not one hundred per cent behind us we are going to fail. Any revolution is risky and we simply cannot take the chance that your presence will be freely accepted. I am deeply sorry. It seems after all you have done we are rejecting you. We are not. We all love you dearly.'

It was pointless me trying to change their minds and, truth tell, I did not really want to. It was their country, their fight and their problem and, whilst I had unwittingly become embroiled in it all, and in so doing found an inner being in me I had not realised was there, I was not awfully comfortable with that inner being, so they were all right: it was time to go. Also, I got the distinct impression Brother was glad I was going. Why this was so I could not comprehend. I was certainly no threat to him or his authority.

'Please do not worry at all. I do not think for one moment you are rejecting me. You have become more than family to me. I fully understand your position and I absolutely agree a puny Englishman is the last thing you want hanging around your necks. Perception is everything and if the people perceive I have been sent by, or a part of, a foreign regime to overthrow your government then this is going to be very bad for you. I'm sorry I did not think of this before. The obvious often passes one by.'

323

I smiled and held my arms out as though it was my fault this very important issue had not been addressed before and all of them, visibly relieved, smiled back and the tension disappeared.

'So then, if you would book me on the next flight out, I'll be away,' I said, 'but I guess it's not going to be that easy.'

'Indeed not,' said Brother, 'we have to make arrangements and it is likely to take a week or so, if you can bear to stay with us that long.'

'Not nearly long enough, so far as I'm concerned,' I replied, 'but I understand you will want me away as quickly as possible so I will wait to hear from you as to what is to be done next.'

With that we all got up and walked away. Vana and I went back into our hut.

'So, I have to go then. Would you come with me?' I asked.

She moved towards me and put her head on my shoulder.

'It is not that simple,' she said, 'I am needed here and I do not know if I could live in your country. Perhaps you can come back here after the revolution.'

I realised it was completely unfair to press her on this. This was her home and we were not living in a stable society where rational decisions could be made at the drop of a hat. Much could happen to both of us. The revolution might never happen or if it did it might not be successful. If the palace guard regained its grip on the country fast enough it might well be that Vana, together with others in this village, would become some of the many victims. I must face up to reality: I was yesterday's news. I was saddened but not sad. Nothing is forever and although I had done things I could not possibly have envisaged six months ago and even now did not feel fully comfortable with, I had enjoyed some wonderful times and had learnt so much about people that I had to be thankful. We sank on the mattress and as the heat of the day intensified just lay there close together but not speaking. There was nothing to be said.

19

The Leaving

It was something over a week before Amazon, Brother, Vana and I reconvened under the conference tree.

'We have made arrangements for your departure,' said Amazon, 'you cannot hope to walk through the capital without being stopped by a palace guard or even a policeman so you will have to have some papers. Luckily, we know a man in the capital who can arrange such things and tomorrow we will take you to him so he can give you a passport and papers showing why you are in our country. When you have these papers we will take you to the British Embassy where you should gain access without any trouble, and there you can tell the ambassador who you really are and he will make arrangements for you to return home.'

'That all sounds very easy. Is it going to be?' I asked.

'The biggest problem will be to get you to our man in the capital to pick up the papers. White and foreign faces are not unusual in the centre and business district of the capital but not so in the suburbs, but we have thought of a way that, though not without danger, should be fairly straight-forward. Can you be ready tomorrow?'

'Of course, tomorrow it is,' I replied.

I spent the rest of the day going around the village helping here and there and not actually saying goodbye to anyone but everyone knowing I was going. The evening meal was somewhat sombre and in our hut at night our lovemaking poignant.

The following morning we all ate together. I got up when we had finished, ready to walk to the capital. Vana gave me a knapsack with the usual food and water. It seemed a little bulkier than usual and, when questioned, Vana said it contained things I would need later. I did not investigate.

As I was leaving the village so everyone there, children included, stood in the centre circle to see me off. They did not wave or make a sound but their presence brought tears to my eyes. Just one word, and I would not have gone. I have never felt such powerful, silent emotion before. It made me appreciate how wonderful these people were. So resourceful, so understanding and so loyal.

Amazon and Brother realised the difficulties of that moment for they quietly bustled me out of the village and we started off on our long walk to the capital.

Brother adjusted our pace whereby we got to the capital as dusk was falling. Amazon explained to me at that time the people were eating their evening meal or going to see friends so there would be less vigilance on the streets. We were all dressed in native clothing and I kept my face down so that I would not be immediately recognised as a white man. We made our way through twisted backstreets to a ramshackle brick-built building, which had shutters at the windows, through which seeped a yellow light from inside. Without knocking, we entered, and in the living room met a middle-aged man dressed in T-shirt and shorts sitting on an upright chair behind a small scarred table covered with various bits of paper.

'So this is the white spirit is it?' he asked. He looked at me quizzically, moving his head from side to side, examining me up and down. 'Yes, I think we can do something with that.'

He picked up a British passport from the table and gave

it to me, saying, 'This is your new identity. You are a foreign aid worker in the capital sent to check on the proper distribution of the foods and medicines being donated.'

I looked at the passport and saw it had no photograph. I raised an eyebrow.

'Yes, I will need two photographs. One for the passport and the other for the World Health Organisation identification card. Letters of introduction,' he waved his hand vaguely at the table, 'will be given to you as well but they do not need any alteration.'

With that, he sat me down in a chair against a wall with a white cloth hanging on it, pulled a battered camera out of a drawer in a cabinet and took several photographs of me.

'Unfortunately, I have not entered the digital age so I'm afraid these photographs have to be processed. There is food in the other room for you all and I suggest you eat and then go upstairs to bed while I do what is necessary down here. Everything will be ready by the morning.

We went into the back room and ate the food, which had been prepared for us. It was palatable and acceptable but not nearly as tasty as the food I had come to relish in our village.

'So what will actually happen tomorrow morning?' I asked.

'When we get up, you will dress in the clothes Vana put in your pack,' said Amazon, 'and with the papers, which will be ready by then, we will take you to the British Embassy. The roads surrounding and leading to all the embassies are patrolled by army, police and palace guard so we must not be seen together. I will walk first with you at least fifty yards behind me and Ajani will be behind you. You probably will not see him but he will be there. I will be carrying a basket and when you see me stop and put the basket on the ground to attend to my headdress that will be the signal for you to go off on your own. I will be stopping opposite a road on my right hand side, which will lead towards the boulevard with the British Embassy. If you're accosted by any police or guards simply look happy and give them your papers, explaining that you are taking a morning walk before the sun gets up and it's too hot. They will understand that. You should have no trouble at all. When you get to the British Embassy just tell the guard you are there to make an appointment for your boss to visit the ambassador.'

I digested this and ran my pessimistic mind over all the things that could go wrong. If the papers were half decent then I could not see any particular problem. Once inside the British Embassy I should easily convince them who I really was. A simple phone call to my secretary in London would do that, for unless she had undergone a serious personality change in the last few months, they would be under no illusion as to my identity. Catherine was, to put it mildly direct and persuasive!

The following morning I put on the clothes Vana had packed for me. My grey trousers and pink shirt, which I had been wearing on the plane and which had gone through much trial and tribulation on the walk from the plane to the village, had been washed, repaired, ironed and pressed, and they looked almost new. My city shoes had been cleaned with the scuff marks largely polished out. These clothes would certainly fool any police or palace guard into thinking I had recently arrived from England.

Armed with a full set of convincing looking papers, we left the forger's house and I let Amazon walk ahead for fifty or so yards, then followed her towards the British Embassy. I did not look behind me to see where Brother was. We walked steadily through the streets, passing shops and a couple of decrepit looking general stores, with no one taking any notice of me. As we were passing a big derelict site, which once contained a building but now was part rubble and part still-standing everything went black. I remember being lifted off my feet but then nothing until waking on a hard-packed mud floor, face down with a boot none too-gently kicking me into consciousness. I looked up and saw the first sight of a man in ill fitting military garb who was to become my jailer and torturer.

20

The Ending

I had written it all; well, most of it anyway. I eased my back
away from the cell wall and stretched my legs forward, which
allowed the last pad containing my scribbled story to slide
onto what was an excuse for a mattress, joining the other
filled-up pads of paper. I guessed from the amount of light
coming in through the bars of the cell window it was
approaching noon on the fifth day following my interrogator's
departure. I had completed my 'confession,' though looking
down at the pencilled scribblings, I did wonder if my interrogator would be able to decipher my scrawl. I didn't think
my writing was too bad, but according to Catherine, coping
with my writing and working for me was nothing short of
an earthly preparation for her beatification. I was surprised
I had written so much so quickly and how, once I had started,
everything seemed to flow.

My concentration in writing over the last few days had
blocked out all the usual sounds of a busy, inhabited jail,
but now that I'd finished, I was once again alive to my
surroundings and conscious of my very precarious existence.
I was mulling over the chances of my interrogator being
true to his word and deporting me from his country rather
than just having me shot when I became aware of gunfire.
I initially took little notice. Probably another execution. But
then I realised this was not the sharp crack of rifle fire but

a sound that had become so familiar to me. A Kalashnikov. My mind suddenly focused. I was trying to work out what would cause anyone in this prison to fire a Kalashnikov when my cell door burst open. Brother was standing in the doorway, a Kalashnikov slung over his shoulder and a big smile on his face.

'Still lazing about when others are working?' he said. 'come on, out you come. You've had a long enough vacation.'

I was stunned, couldn't speak, and initially couldn't move. I had virtually been sitting in the same position for some five days, still carrying the hurt and bruises from soldier beatings, and so could not move with any ease or speed, but Brother beckoned me impatiently and I scrambled to my feet, picking up all the pads of paper upon which my story had been written, and unsteadily followed him out of the cell down the corridor into an interrogation room.

Sitting in the room behind the table was my interrogator and behind him was one of our group, holding a Kalashnikov close to the back of his head. Amazon was standing to one side, leaning against a wall with her Kalashnikov draped loosely across her body. Brother pulled my Colt automatic from his waistband and gave it to me.

'He is all yours,' said Brother. 'Shoot him if you like.'

The group member moved to one side out of the line of fire and my interrogator looked at me impassively. I could not judge whether he accepted his fate or simply could not care one way or the other.

'No,' I said. 'I have no desire to add to the bloodletting. Let him live.' I handed the Colt back to Brother.

Brother laughed. 'Oh that's good,' he said, 'we wouldn't like him dead either because he's one of us.'

Before I could take this in fully or say anything, my interrogator gave me a beaming smile, saying, 'Yes, we are all friends here. We were at university together.'

'What!' I exclaimed.

'Okay, I exaggerate. It was one of your wonderful English polytechnics, not an actual university. I did tell you how much I admired your English educational system because it brings together different peoples who are learning and studying different subjects, and it is amazing how common bonds, sympathies and understandings can be found and nurtured, leading to friendships. Even in those days we disliked the way Baumge was governing our country so we discussed and planned setting up an opposition party but by the time we returned to our country, Baumge had a stranglehold on the government and there was no possibility of forming an opposition political party. When Zaban arrived our fate was pretty much sealed so we had to move to plan B; not, that at the time we were studying together we *had* a plan B, but one just has to evolve and you have been a very helpful part of it.'

'Come on,' said Brother, 'we cannot dally here any longer. Tie him up and let's go.'

The member of the group standing to one side of my interrogator pulled a roll of duct tape from his knapsack and efficiently taped my interrogator to his chair, finally placing a piece over his mouth.

'Surely leaving him behind like this with me gone will arouse suspicion.'

'Don't worry, it's all worked out,' said Amazon, 'we will explain it all to you later. We have no time now. Go down the corridor to the front door where outside there will be a lorry with its engine running. Get into the back as quickly as you can and try not to be seen. We will follow you shortly.'

With my writing pads trapped firmly under my arm – I did not wish to leave any potentially incriminating evidence behind – I ran, rather, hobbled at a fast pace, down the corridor, opened the door and saw the lorry. Sitting in the driver's seat was our friendly warrior driver who waved and smiled at me. I scrambled into the back of the lorry, over the tailgate, and lay prone on the floor so as not to be seen. Very shortly afterwards Amazon, Brother and three of our group joined me, and the lorry drove steadily but swiftly off.

'We are going back to the forger's house so when the lorry stops, get out and go in. We will get rid of the lorry and join you later,' said Brother.

After what appeared to be a very short time the lorry came quietly to a standstill and Brother clapped me on the shoulder, indicating I should get out. I scrambled over the tailgate and walked quickly towards the front door of the forger's house. As I was about to go in I was aware of a young man and elderly woman off to my right in heated conversation with the woman pulling at a bag over the man's shoulder. I looked at them briefly and realised whatever they were arguing over was not only none of my business but not particularly threatening, just a small dispute of some sort, so I went in through the front door which was, as before, unlocked. As I closed the door behind me I realised I had seen a similar scenario before, at the airport in Louta, and also that the woman at the Loutan airport had been in our village; she was the one who seemed to be walking away from me whenever I approached.

My mind was churning as I went into the front room where I had first met the forger. Sitting in two chairs were Vana and Robyn Odubby. I did a double take.

'Wonderful places, English polytechnics,' said Robyn, laughing so loudly that I was fearful people outside in the street could hear him. Vana smiled and shrugged her shoulders.

'You were at the same polytechnic?' I asked. He continued laughing and nodded. 'Why are you here? This is not your country.'

'Quite coincidentally I am here for a lawyer's conference,' said Robyn, 'naturally I wanted to meet my old friends from the polytechnic and they told me of your fate. I really thought you were dead when the plane disappeared and did not appreciate, when we met, that you would turn into a warrior hero. Or should I say a white spirit.' This sent him off into another loud peal of laughter as he rocked on his chair in mirth. I did not focus at the time on him referring to the plane having disappeared, not crashed, and I shook my head in disbelief. Does everybody know everybody on this continent? I asked myself. Before I could enquire more, Amazon and Brother came in, having changed out of their combat gear into national dress.

'Now I have seen everyone safe and sound,' said Robyn, 'I must go back to my conference. I will be in the country for the rest of the week so if you have any problems with the British Embassy, get word to me so I can help out.'

'Don't tell me you have a relation working at the British Embassy,' I said.

This sent him into further laughter. 'No, not this time, but I do know someone there who owes me a favour. I don't want to call on this favour unless I have to but obviously if you are having difficulties I will have no hesitation. I'm staying at the Intercontinental Hotel in the centre of the city if you want me. Good luck.'

And with that he picked up a briefcase, waved to me and walked out of the room chuckling to himself. A really jolly man.

'Sabra and I have to check something out,' said Brother, 'and when we get back we will explain everything to you.' They both left.

I turned to Vana ready to ask questions. There was much to ask. Much I did not understand and the effect of seeing the man and woman outside, tussling for a bag, was still churning around in my mind. However, Vana, anticipating, waved me to silence, saying, 'Later. First take your clothes off.'

I raised an eyebrow, cocked my head to one side with a leery smile on my face.

'Not now. Later if you're a good boy. I want your clothes to have them washed and pressed again. You cannot go out on the streets with crumpled and dirty clothing. It will draw attention to you and you will certainly not be able to get into the British Embassy looking as though you have been rolling around on the floor for the best part of a fortnight. Here, put these on.'

She handed me a casual shirt and trousers as I obediently stripped naked and gave her my clothes, putting on the substitute shirt and trousers. She looked down at my scruffy, scuffed shoes and I took them off as well. She waved me to a chair and I sat down, bare-footed, while she left the room with my clothes and shoes. She was gone a long time but I was quite happy to sit in a decent chair in freedom. The shutters were still up at the window so I could not see out but this did not concern me at all. The fact I was alive and free was contentment enough.

When Vana returned we went to the back room where food was set out on the table and we began to eat in silence. I continued thinking about the woman at the Louta airport as fuzzy pieces of a puzzle slowly started to fit together. Before we had finished eating and I could marshal my thoughts, Brother and Amazon arrived and they too started to eat. When we had all finished I could not restrain my curiosity any longer.

'So tell me, what happened?'

'Starting at the beginning,' said Brother, 'I was following you on the way to the British Embassy when there was a big explosion and I saw you being blown up into the air. As the dust was settling so I was going to run towards where I last saw you but there was an immediate burst of gunfire. I had no idea where it was coming from or who it was aimed at so I fell to the ground and wriggled away as quickly as I could. My intention was to take stock of the situation before trying to find you. However, before I could do anything, half a dozen soldiers appeared, shooting at anything that moved; I believe the only thing they hit was the rather mangy dog. It was clear they were going to search the area to find out who set off the explosion and I didn't think it was a good idea to hang around so I moved rapidly away. Sabra heard the explosion and when she looked around and saw the soldiers emerging from the dust so she too quietly and quickly disappeared. We both thought you were probably dead.'

'But what was the explosion?' I asked, 'as I understand it there is no revolutionary group here in the capital. The soldiers who captured me maintained it was a bomb aimed at them.'

Brother smiled. 'I have to say it perplexed us for a while but, having made a few enquiries, we believe we have got to the bottom of it. You were passing a semi-demolished building when the explosion occurred. About six months ago it was decided to get rid of that building and put up a new hotel managed and owned by one of Baumge's cronies. As usual, anything done by that mob is inefficient. Instead of sending in bulldozers to knock down the building they decided to employ a local demolition team, surprise, surprise, owned by another Baumge crony, who set so-called controlled demolition charges to bring the building down and not scatter it over the whole area. Not all the charges went off and the building was left semi-standing in a very precarious state. The owner of the site was absolutely furious and immediately sacked the demolition team, intending to get in real experts sort out the problem. Piecing things together, it seems as you were passing, a part of the building fell on one of the demolition charges and hit the detonator so causing the explosion that knocked you out. It was fairly obvious the soldiers who captured you didn't have the wit to work this out and believed they were being attacked, and as you were the only one in the area you turned out to be the fall guy.'

'So when did you find out I wasn't dead?'

'It was quite amazing really. We obviously searched the area later but could not find a body and made enquiries but no one knew where you were. Although the soldiers were the obvious choice for knowledge about what had happened to your body they kept absolutely quiet and no word of your capture leaked out. Most unusual. I don't know if, now the palace guard has been weakened with the death of Zaban, the soldiers are feeling more powerful or if they believed they could get some advantage from your capture but the fact was none of them leaked the information that you were in jail. However, their commander was not the sharpest knife in the drawer, for having taken your papers and your watch from you, he decided to make a few US dollars by selling them, and the most obvious candidate to purchase them was our forger friend. When presented with his own handiwork our forger friend was more than a little taken aback and suspicious so he questioned the commander very carefully on the basis it would not be right to purchase illegal papers so wanted proof that they were genuine. The commander quite readily told him what had happened, that the items had come from you and you were alive in prison currently being interrogated. Our forger friend accepted the story and made the purchase.'

'Incidentally,' said Amazon, 'you owe our forger friend a hundred dollars for those papers, US that is.' I patted my pockets as if searching for money. 'You can post it to him later,' said Amazon with a smile on her face.

'Now, the first problem,' continued Brother, 'was that you were being interrogated by the soldiers in the prison and although they were rather unusually keeping it all quiet, sooner or later the palace guard would find out and whilst we had every confidence you would say nothing to the soldiers – once the palace guard started on you then even

338

the strongest man would spill the beans sooner or later. So you had to be got out, besides which, we all owe you a big favour because you rescued me from captivity.'

I rather hoped the second emotion was the driving force behind Brother's actions though I strongly suspected the prospect of me talking and identifying people was far more motivating.

'The second problem was time. It would take time for our forger friend to get a message to me that you were alive in jail and for us to organise an escape. Time was therefore not on our side. So our forger friend got in touch with your "interrogator" for a bit of advice. As luck would have it your interrogator had recently been promoted in the government and so he went to his senior minister and told him of your capture, saying that the rumoured "white spirit" might infact be a white man and it would give the government big kudos if you confessed to being a terrorist. On the other hand, if it was found you had nothing to do with any of the attacks on the palace guard then it could all be kept quiet and no one would be embarrassed. The senior minister agreed with this so your interrogator turned up at the prison informing the commander that this was a top-secret situation where no one should say anything and he would take over the questioning. Realising it would look suspicious to those in the jail if he continued questioning you for a long period while we prepared to get you out, he made up the story of needing to go and inspect other facilities for five days on the excuse that if you were given writing materials you might reflect on the position and write down your confession by the time he got back.'

Brother looked at me hard and then towards the table upon which sat my writing pads. 'He did not expect you to write a book and I'm a bit surprised myself. I'm fairly certain though that whatever you have written has kept our names out of it and you made directions to the various villages very vague?'

'Indeed I have,' I replied: 'Whilst I recorded the factual events accurately I did my best to make identification of individuals as difficult as possible though, to be perfectly truthful, even though we walked around the countryside quite a lot, I would have great difficulty finding your village even if I really wanted to. The countryside is still very much a mystery to me.'

Brother grunted. 'Well that's it. You know the rest. We got a lorry, drove into the capital, up to the prison and took you out. It was all surprisingly easy. Since Zaban's death it seems as though the security forces are not patrolling the streets for the moment and the soldiers are, as ever, not awfully vigilant.'

'Well that's not really the end of it,' I responded. 'Your polytechnic friend, my interrogator, has to explain my disappearance without losing face. The fact that fully armed men turned up at the jail and sprung me would indicate, even to the most stupid, that I could be of some importance; certainly involved in terrorist activities in some way, and that would destroy the "white spirit" rumour as well as severely affecting your polytechnic friend's reputation and chances of advancement in the government.'

'Ah yes, we thought of that. Your interrogator's story will be that after questioning you deeply he came to the conclusion you were not a terrorist but simply an annoying, rather naive aid worker who was in the wrong place at the wrong time, and to ensure you didn't cause trouble about leaving live detonation charges to go off and being interrogated in prison he ordered the commander of the prison to have you shot. The fact you are not there now will not raise any suspicion because you're dead and buried. Also, foreign aid workers are always getting lost or disappearing for weeks on end so the fact no one is making a fuss about a missing aid worker will not be unusual.'

'Just a minute,' I said. 'Is it likely the commander will

back up the story? If he is not that bright I would have thought not. Also there is the guard who took me out of the interrogation room back to my cell and saw your polytechnic friend give me pads of paper and pencils to write my confession. He is unlikely to keep quiet for very long.'

'True,' said Brother. 'Unfortunately when we broke into the prison everyone surrendered immediately except two who happened to be the prison commander and that guard. We were obliged to kill them.'

'An amazing coincidence,' I said with much disbelief in my voice. Brother ignored my sarcasm.

'While you were chatting amiably with our friend, all the soldiers were being tied up and the other prisoners in the jail were being set free so the story will be that one of them was a member of a revolutionary band who had important information so his friends attacked the jail and got him out. No one will be able to check the story and it certainly sounds feasible. We made sure all the soldiers in the jail saw us befriending one of the other prisoners.'

I thought about it for a while and realised that with a small modicum of luck we would probably get away with it. I had one more question.

'Odubby, what part does he play in all this?'

Amazon and Brother looked at each other before Brother carefully replied, 'Let us just say some of our training is not in this country.'

I grunted. The less I knew about that, the better.

We continued talking for a while and I found out that Amazon and Brother had been back to the jail to find the soldiers had been released by one of their member who happened to be out of the jail at the time of attack and that the general talk did not include anything about a white man. Very pleasing. Soon Brother indicated it was time to go to bed. Taking my writing pads with me, I went to one of the bedrooms upstairs with Vana, and in the candlelight she examined my battered and bruised body, which was healing fairly rapidly but had taken on some really nice colours. It looked very impressive and I milked it for all I could get. Vana pretended to be sympathetic and impressed with my manly ability to take beatings so easily but in the end we couldn't keep it up and fell about laughing.

When the laughter subsided, Vana looked at me seriously and said, 'You have worked it out, haven't you?'

I gave her a puzzled look. 'Worked what out?' I asked.

'Nigel, you cannot fool me. Tell me what you have been thinking ever since you came into this house.'

I was very reluctant to say anything but by the same token needed to put my thoughts in order to see if the conclusion I had reached was in fact real or just a product of coincidence.

'Well sequentially,' I said, 'it is as follows. A man and woman at the Louta airport; a rocket attack on a plane; a man clubbed to death in your village; a woman in the village who always seemed to be hurrying away from me whenever I approached; soft canvas bags in a hidden room with far more guns and ammunition than could have come from palace guard lorry raids,' at that point Vana looked shocked so I paused.

'I didn't know you had found the room in the cave,' she said.

'There was no opportunity for me to ask about it so I simply forgot. To continue, there was the digging of our village well, which seemed to give credence to the mud splattered men in the joyful and friendly village who were said to be digging a similar well; sparkling in the wedding clothes; a white man in an Armani suit – and that should have been the real give-away, but I was somewhat more occupied at the time; knowledge of a forger when it seems to me highly unlikely a revolutionary group would need a forger; a high number of runners between villages; a blue helicopter; and

Odubby being here with a briefcase. All that has been turning around in my mind since I got here.'

'And the conclusion you have drawn?' Vana asked.

Up to that point I had not really drawn any conclusion. I had been mulling over the facts to see how they fitted together but suddenly it all became glaringly obvious.

'The sparkling from the headdresses and wedding necklace of the bride in the joyful village was not a result, as I thought, of glass beads but diamonds; I do not know whether they were cut or uncut diamonds as I have no experience in this area. Those diamonds came from an illicit diamond mine being worked by the mud-splattered men in the village. Once mined, the diamonds were probably sent to our village by runners, put into the soft canvas bags (perhaps graded first) and sent out of the country to be sold on the black market. The young woman I saw at the Louta airport was probably one of the couriers and our forger friend would be needed to give her, and others, papers to travel freely. I am assuming Odubby's briefcase did not contain just conference papers.'

Vana's face did not change. She sat on the bed looking at me and patiently waiting for me to continue.

'I guess the man in our village clubbed to death the first night I was there was siphoning off a little profit for himself. I should have twigged earlier that foreign aid workers were unlikely to wear Armani suits so the white man in the palace guard camp was an employee of the International Diamond Group who control the worldwide sale and distribution of diamonds. The fact we didn't find a radio in the office of that camp probably meant it was situated in the barn or store, which I never entered, in a control room or similar set-up to orchestrate the search for illicit diamond mining. The blue helicopter was certainly not military and unlikely to be owned by the palace guard so the property of the International Diamond Group who would have been keen to find those who had killed their man and who were making great inroads into the body set up to protect legal diamond mining and detect those who were otherwise engaged in putting illegal diamonds onto the world market. As to the aeroplane I was on being shot down, I have to stab in the dark. I would guess that the palace guard made a complete mess of identifying the plane on which a courier or two were returning to the country. In short, the palace guard is not the power in the oppressive Baumge regime but protectors of lucrative diamond exports and I suspect the sudden appearance of the skeletal Death's Head Zaban, with the penetrating pale eyes, was because he was an import, so to speak, of the International Diamond Group.'

Vana still said nothing though her face spoke volumes. She was sad and depressed I had come to this realisation, which was so obviously true.

'And I suppose,' I continued, 'the fact that Ajani kept trying to weigh me up when he thought I was not looking at him showed he had deep concerns that I might stumble on the truth and so you were "asked" to get somewhat closer to me to find out what I really knew.'

Vana smiled a very bitter smile. 'I was right. You really are very clever indeed. I told Ajani he should stop looking at you like that as it was bound to arouse your suspicion. But you are not completely right. The palace guard is indeed Baumge's private army formed well before the International Diamond Group became involved and it does keep a tight grip on everyone through fear and loathing. We were unfortunately rather too successful in our mining operation and it came under the scrutiny of the International Diamond Group, which was able to identify the source of the diamonds as being this country, rather than anywhere else in the world. Consequently, they put pressure on Baumge, whose private wealth depends upon legal diamond sales, and as the only cohesive force to try and find out where illicit diamond mines were located – there is more than one – was the palace guard, it was the natural choice for the International Diamond Group. The diamonds we mined and sold were not for personal gain but to finance the revolution. You are absolutely right, the amount of munitions we have scattered throughout the country is far, far greater than could have just been stolen from the palace guard. In fact, they are sometimes air dropped to us and it might be that the palace guard mistook the airliner for one of those air drops. Where you are really so very wrong indeed is the part I played in this. I really did want to get to know you better.' At this point she held up her hand to stop me speaking. 'Everything I have told you before is perfectly true. I was attracted to you the moment I first saw you and I knew you had something special to give to us so I actually volunteered to get, what you call, closer to you although both Ajani and Sabra took this to mean that I would steer you away from any thoughts of our illegal operations.'

We were both quiet, thinking our own thoughts. Mine rather morbid, so I kept them to myself for the moment.

'I am very sorry that we have deceived you. It was not my choice. The elders thought it would be dangerous if you got to know the truth because, being a lawyer, you would not condone illegal activity and if it got out to the rest of the world we were funding a revolution by illegal means, any opposition party would be automatically discredited. The reality though is that we are still honestly trying to help our people shake off the shackles of an oppressive regime and you must admit there is nothing wrong with that although I fully understand you might not be too enthusiastic about the bloody revolution. Nothing has really changed, has it?' She smiled a disarming smile tinged with a little sadness.

'Well unfortunately,' I said, 'everything has changed. Looking at things logically, with blood on my hands Ajani was quite happy to let me return to England knowing that I would unlikely say anything about the activities you have

345

all been engaged in against the palace guard, for to do so would implicate me and even if a revolution was swift and successful, nonetheless international conscience is such these days that the possibility of a war crimes trial or similar would not be out of the question. In essence, I was no threat. Now, though, as you have said yourself, I know about the illicit diamond smuggling and if this is made known then any opposition party, the revolution itself, would be discredited in the eyes of the world. The International Diamond Group is incredibly powerful throughout the world and it would not be slow in drumming up support to ostracise all of you. I assume you have not been sufficiently forward thinking as to get the International Diamond Group on your side, or at the very least assure them if any revolution is successful, their position in this country will not be affected in the slightest.'

Vana shook her head, confirming what I said.

'Therefore, Ajani cannot risk me returning to England. I very much doubt he will take my word that I will say nothing. In his eyes, at least, his whole future lies in the palm of my hand. So as, quite understandably, the revolution should not include an Englishman, I cannot stay here; and the risk is great if I leave. I have to die.'

Vana smiled a lopsided smile and looked down. 'I am right. You are very clever indeed. I do not know the answer. Now that you know everything, I cannot keep quiet and not tell Ajani or Sabra. It would be disloyal of me to keep quiet even though in speaking I know I'm being disloyal to you and I would have done anything to avoid this.' A tear appeared in the corner of her eye and very, very slowly rolled down her cheek. If she was acting, she was really good at it. I would like to believe she was not. 'All I can say,' she continued, 'is that I will try and persuade Ajani to let you go back to England. I believe you will say nothing. Sabra, I'm sure, will also believe this. Sadly Ajani is very sensitive about things and he is not one to take risks so I cannot guarantee anything. I will say nothing until the morning. At least we will have tonight together.'

What with one thing and the other – not too much of the other but that which there was, was very enjoyable – I slept poorly that night. Well used to solving the problems of others though I was, I had never before been presented with something so close to me and upon which my very existence depended. I tried to comfort myself with something one of my clients once said to me: 'It is not a problem but a challenge,' but, however categorised, the absolute fact was that Ajani would feel threatened and I knew from observing him over the last few months he would not tolerate this. The only thing going for me was a strong feeling he would do nothing while we were in this house as it would be in front of and upset Vana. It was said that my feelings were real and meant something, so I comforted myself that at least I would leave the house unharmed, and after that I would have to play it as, or hopefully before, it happened.

The next morning we were up bright and early. Vana left me while I was dressing, and afterwards I joined Brother and Amazon with Vana in the back room eating a small meal. As far as I could tell there was no one else in the house other than the four of us, and food seemed to appear at the right time as if by magic. There was nothing in the demeanour of any of them to suggest Vana had already told them I knew their secret, but I knew it would be foolish to assume the issue had not been discussed already.

'I want us to leave here in half an hour at the latest,' said Brother. 'We will follow the same pattern as last time. Once you strike off down the road towards the embassy, you're on your own though I will try and stay behind you for as long as possible. We have to leave this house fairly quickly because a new family is going to move in.' He saw my questioning glance and continued. 'This is no longer a safe house so just in case anyone has seen us come and go, if we put a new family in here with no connection with us or knowledge about us, any enquiry will lead to a dead end. By the way, you will need these.' Brother fished into his pocket and produced my papers and my watch. 'By rights I should demand the hundred dollars before giving them to you but I trust you.'

He was certainly keeping up the front and giving no indication he had changed his mind about me reaching the embassy and going back to England though I was highly comforted we would be leaving the house shortly. When we finished eating, Vana gave me my clothes, washed and reasonably well ironed, with shoes looking considerably less scuffed than when I took them off. I quickly dressed and we were ready.

'Your writings,' said Vana, 'I'll take them back to the village where they will be safe and perhaps when the time is right, we can get them published.' I looked sceptical. 'That is if, after I have read them, I think they are any good!' I smiled in the confident expectation that my five days hard work would be consigned to one of the end-of-week fires.

With nothing more to be said, I bade Vana farewell once again and, with Amazon in the lead, me fifty yards behind her and Brother somewhere behind me, we were off. We passed the same demolition site once again, which looked far more demolished, though not all of the building had yet collapsed. I confess I walked past it rather warily.

I followed Amazon steadily and easily. None of us were stopped by the police, soldiers or palace guard. Local inhabitants passed me with barely a glance. They seemed to be quite used to seeing foreigners walking around the city and so I was nothing particularly unusual. The embassy being situated in the smarter part of the capital meant we had to walk into a main street past some large department stores,

general stores, I looked at the map and identified the biggest and longest road. Pointing to it I said:

'Have you been to department stores in this road?'

'Ah, I passed stores but did not go in. I was there only a few minutes ago but now lost.'

'When you left this road which way did you turn; to left or to right?'

'Ah, I go right,' he said, waving his left hand. 'No, no. I mean left. I go left. I pass a store with a big motorcycle in the window. An American Harley-Davidson motorcycle, then I turn left.'

A result. This was the store I had dashed into to lose Brother. If he had turned left at the next road this was the same road I had come out on through the side entrance, and so with a little bit of imagination and mental coin spinning I worked out of the rough area we were both currently in and said, 'I am fairly sure we are here,' jabbing my finger on the map covering a rather large area, 'and if we walk back this way,' waving my hand in the direction I believed the major road lay, 'we will find the road with the big stores, and then we will know how you can get back to your embassy.'

'Ah, good,' he said, 'very good, very good, you come with me?'

'Yes of course. Let's go.'

We walked steadily in the direction where I thought the major road was and, guided by the increasing number of people walking in the same direction, we found the road with all the stores, and once there it was fairly easy to orien myself on the map and so work out precisely which direction to go to reach the embassies. I pointed this direction out to my Chinese friend and, after thanking me profusely, he and his map disappeared into the distance.

I had a day to kill and no money in my pocket. This meant I couldn't find an isolated bar or restaurant and sit there so I slowly walked in the general direction of the embassies but deviated towards an area shown on the map as green, indicating there might be a park or similar. I was not disappointed. A park indeed it was; rather a park it used to be. Years of neglect had meant the grass was brown and long, bushes long since untended, spreading out over the ground with pathetic trees forming a faint canopy of shade. I wandered around outside the park looking carefully at the people. They were few in number and were certainly not enjoying the amenity; simply using it as somewhere to walk through. I too started walking slowly through the park. Unobserved and close to a big patch of tangled undergrowth and sprawling bushes, I wriggled my way through and sat down to hide for the rest of the day.

It was still mid-morning. I had a long time to plan what to do next and that time was not a friend but an enemy. When I formulated what I could do I then had time to pick it over and find faults. Every plan had too many faults and in the end I had nothing. Back to basics. Brother would be waiting for me and, from the Chinese man's map, I had noted there were half a dozen or so streets leading into the main boulevard where the embassies were located. Brother could not cover them all so he would have to position himself close to the British Embassy, which would mean the chances of me evading him were slim. I would therefore have to neutralise him or put him out of action in some way. I had no illusions that a face-to-face with Brother would be a disaster. He was a big, strong, athletic man and even if I was fighting for my life, I would have no chance against him. Furthermore, he would likely be armed with a handgun and would not hesitate to use it. There was no way around it: I would have to somehow sneak up on Brother and take him by surprise. Much easier said than done, particularly as I had no real idea of the layout of the area so there was no way around it, I would have to go to the embassy boulevard to reconnoitre without being seen.

I wriggled my way out of the bushes and walked slowly towards the area I believed the embassies to be. There was a steady if not heavy traffic of vehicles and people and I tried to blend myself into the background, which was not so difficult for as I approached the boulevard the number of foreign faces increased. I kept a good look out for places where someone could loiter unobserved but the road down which I was walking towards the embassy boulevard seemed residential with high walls and tall barred gates offering no cover at all for a lurking Brother. This road happened to be a good choice for it brought me out right in the middle of the boulevard and opposite a small grassy area with a couple of trees where a number of people, whom I took to be embassy staff, were sitting, eating a lunchtime sandwich or similar and talking. I joined them and leaned against a tree, arousing no curiosity. I realised I could not stay there very long for being so exposed would leave me open to being seen by Brother, though I was comforted that the number of people around would likely mean Brother would not take the chance to shoot me immediately. I looked up and down the boulevard at the various embassies and was thankful that national pride meant they were all flying flags and so it was not too difficult to pick out the Union Jack occasionally fluttering over the British Embassy. The embassy was about two hundred yards away on the left-hand side of the boulevard. I then concentrated upon looking for somewhere close to the embassy, where Brother could hide and observe. With guards on all the embassy gates, a few local soldiers or police strolling about, and the occasional local army jeep or lorry parked on the boulevard, no one could loiter for very long without arousing suspicion and I was beginning to feel that perhaps Brother would not be able to hide himself away but he was resourceful and I knew he must be somewhere. The obvious would be for him to disguise himself as a road cleaner, maintenance man or similar but there was no one even remotely like that in the area. I was beginning to feel that I was getting nowhere and I knew I could not remain leaning against a tree for very much longer. A group of Scandinavians who had been sitting on a rudimentary bench talking and eating suddenly got up, crossed the boulevard to the right-hand side and started walking down the road. No doubt going back to work. I joined them, staying sufficiently close to look as though I was a part of the group but not so close that they would question my presence. We walked about fifty yards towards the British Embassy and, reaching the junction of a street leading off the boulevard, I felt I could not continue much further without risk so I turned slowly into the street to walk away. As I did so, I looked long and hard at the British Embassy on the opposite side of the boulevard, still some distance away, and saw what I could not see from my first vantage point, an area of greenery like a very small park or a large garden with tended bushes and flowers in the middle of which was a large monument. I knew where Brother was. Assuming that all the embassies would have surveillance cameras as well as guards it would not have been easy for Brother to get to this area unobserved but once there his natural bush skills would mean that he could hide himself away in the undergrowth and remain motionless for hours on end.

Amazon had said that Brother was a very good shot but, knowing he would only have a handgun and also knowing the limited range of such a weapon, Brother would have had to have stationed himself in a position where, first, he could get a view up and down the boulevard to try to see me before I arrived at the embassy, and, secondly, from which he could quickly get close to the embassy gates if I arrived there without him seeing me approaching. This would narrow the area I would have to scan to try and identify where he was lying.

I had to find somewhere where I could assess in what

part of this area Brother could be hiding so I walked briskly down the side turning, turned to my left and walked down to the next road, which I gauged was just past the British Embassy. I turned into this road and walked towards the boulevard steadily but not too quickly. It was still lunchtime and there were various people moving around from the embassies as well as locals going about their business. This provided me a little cover and I did not stand out. As I was getting to the end of the road I slowed my pace even more, looking carefully into the boulevard towards the direction of the British Embassy. I immediately noticed the road I was on formed a crossroads with the boulevard and it continued the other side. That could be useful. I crossed over to the other side of the road so I could get a better field of view, and just before I reached the boulevard I was able to see the green area and monument where I believed Brother was hiding. I stopped, leant against the wall trying to strike a pose that suggested I was killing time before returning to my work, and studied the area as carefully and as closely as I was able. The green area with the monument was about twenty-five to thirty yards from the crossroads and, although it first appeared to be well-endowed with bushes, in fact most were well-tended and close-cropped, which would give Brother no cover at all. There was just one large patch of tall bushes surrounding a tree, which looked promising. The more I looked at this point, the more I realised that if Brother was there, this was the place he would be because it gave a good view of the boulevard towards the British Embassy but a somewhat restricted one towards where I was standing. I slowly moved back into the street away from the crossroads to restrict the chances of my being observed. So I knew where he likely was, now how could I turn this to my advantage?

I turned around and walked away, taking a circuitous route back to the park where I had initially hidden, once again going into the undergrowth and lying down under the bushes. My plan was simple. Brother's view of the boulevard away from the embassy was restricted so if I went down the street opposite to the street I had stood in to observe, I would be out of sight, and if I kept close to the walls of the building in the boulevard immediately before the grassy area there was a very good chance he would not see me approaching. I reasoned that if Brother had been there for most of the day without food and water his alertness would be slightly blunted and he would expect that once dusk had fallen and the embassies closed I would not attempt to get into the British Embassy. The question was whether at that time he would leave his post and return later in the night. I felt he would not be willing to take the chance so I would deploy my early morning theory – that is people are at their lowest ebb in the early hours of the morning – hoping that Brother, if not asleep, would certainly be 'resting his eyes'.

All well and good, but I had already reasoned a one-on-one with Brother would be suicidal, so I had to get an edge. I looked around me and saw some large stones and rocks within easy reach so picked up one a little larger than my fist and weighed it in my hand. It would certainly make a good club if I could get close enough to surprise Brother. Not particularly comforting, but it was the best I could do for the moment. I would have to see how things were when I got there.

With nothing more to do I made myself comfortable and drifted off into a light sleep. I remained where I was until getting on for midnight when I slowly moved out of the bushes, stretched my body and started to walk slowly and carefully towards the boulevard. There were a few people about and no one took any notice of me whatsoever. Obviously, in the embassy area white strangers were not an unusual phenomenon and I suppose it would not be beyond the bounds of possibility that embassy staff went out in the evenings to walk to a restaurant or bar. Not that I had seen any bars or restaurants I would have touched with a barge-pole, but what did I know? I did not immediately go to the crossroads junction from where I planned to approach Brother, but to the top of the boulevard, well away from the British Embassy. I wanted to get a good view down the boulevard to see if there were any people about. The boulevard was not illuminated with any street lights but there was sufficient light from the moon to see clearly down the boulevard, so I stood in deep shadow, watching.

There were a few people going into embassies but surprisingly no sign of any police or soldiers. I had assumed one or other of them would be patrolling this area day and night but obviously not. Or was there? About two streets down the boulevard on the opposite side of the road I thought I detected the bonnet of a jeep. At first I was not sure but the harder I looked, the more convinced I became, so it could well be that police or soldiers were sitting in this jeep. I decided to take a closer look.

I crossed the boulevard and walked slowly down to the first turning on the left-hand side, walked up the road, then to my right and down the road where I judged the jeep to be parked. As I turned into the road I could see the jeep at the junction with just one man sitting in it. Grasping the rock in my right hand, I walked steadily down towards the jeep as though I was returning to one of the embassies expecting the jeep occupant to turn around and look at me. He did not. As I got closer it seemed to me he was asleep. I slowed my stride and adopted my 'walking on air' gait, approaching him directly from the rear, all the while looking around to see if he had any companions. I could observe none. When I got to the jeep I used my rock to effectively put him into an unconscious sleep and he fell across from the driving seat to the passenger seat. I looked around to see if I had attracted attention but there was no one in sight.

I looked into the jeep and saw the soldier had a rifle lying on the floor. If needs be I could use this but it was hardly an inconspicuous object to be carrying around. I lifted him up from the passenger seat, and on his right hip was a holster containing a military revolver. This was more like it. I removed the revolver and shoved into my trouser pocket where it protruded somewhat, but covering it with my arm, I turned around and walked back up the street, abandoning my rock and turning left to go back to my original vantage point in the deep shadow. If the soldier had any companions, before long they would return and discover him, and I wanted to see what they would do.

I remained in the deep shadow for about an hour. There was no sign of any other soldiers or that the one I had attended to had recovered consciousness. I could wait no longer. I left my vantage point and walked off the boulevard down the street to get to the road leading back to the boulevard about twenty-five or so yards away from the grassy area. By this time, there was no one about but I did not attract any attention as I walked steadily and confidently. Reaching the junction of the road with the boulevard, I flattened myself against the wall of a building and very, very slowly walked towards the grassy area with the soldier's revolver in my right hand, held down by my side, ready for the slightest provocation. I reached the grassy area and stepped cautiously over a low bush onto the grass. Looking at the clump of bushes where I believed Brother was hiding, I reasoned that I would be out of his vision, which I suppose was confirmed by the fact that I was standing on the grass and had not been shot. If Brother was any good at all with a handgun, he could not have missed me.

I had arrived safely but, being on grass and surrounded by vegetation of one sort or another, I was very much in Brother's territory, and even if he was half asleep, his well-tuned ear would surely detect me before I could possibly find him. I slowly and extremely quietly sank to my knees and then onto my stomach. The moon was giving a fairly clear light to see and throwing up deep shadows. I slowly, very slowly, wriggled into a shadow and then followed this shadow towards the clump of bushes where I believed Brother was hiding. Having worked out where he would be looking and so how he would be lying, I moved to come up behind him. Remaining prone on the ground and close to the clump of bushes I said in a very clear voice, 'Ajani, move a muscle and you are dead.' I raised the soldier's revolver slightly above my head and slowly, as noisily as I could, pulled back the hammer to cock it. Brother, with his experience of firearms, would surely recognise the sound of a cocked pistol.

'I suggest you stand up slowly, very slowly, with your hands above your head. I can see you and if you make the slightest wrong move I will shoot. I know you intend to kill me so I will not take any chance whatsoever.'

For a while there was no movement in the bushes at all. I pressed my body closer to the ground, hoping that if Brother was silently moving out of his cover he would not see me and, even if he did, would not have a good line to shoot at me. Then there was a faint rustling and Brother stood up slowly with his hands above his head. He was half facing towards me and looking around to see if he could see where I was standing. I was rather pleased he had not anticipated I would be lying on the ground.

'Walk over towards the monument and, to coin a phrase of our American cousins, "assume the position". I want you with both hands on the monument where I can see them, your body well away from it and your legs spread apart. Believe me, I will shoot you if necessary and you know how good I am with a gun.'

I did wonder whether this soldier's revolver would have been any good at all but there again Brother did know I could shoot and didn't know what sort of gun I had in my hand. He did as he was told and walked to the monument, putting both hands against it and spreading his legs in the position. I got up and walked towards him. He did not move. When I got there I kept as far away from him as possible, just leaning forward sufficiently to run my hands down his body to find a rather wicked looking knife tucked into his waistband, but no gun.

'Where is the gun?'

'Back in the bushes. I left it there.'

I had no reason not to believe him so I told him to move around the monument into the shadow and sit down cross-legged with both hands in front of him. This he did and I too sat on the ground away from him but in the shadow. Anyone walking down the boulevard should not be able to see us.

'Vana obviously, and quite rightly, told you I had worked out the diamond scam and, bearing in mind what we have all been through over the last few months, I confess I am very disappointed you did not have more faith in me and resorted to a very primitive reaction. If you are to be a leader at all, assuming you live that long,' I wanted to make sure Brother realised I was in a mood to kill him if necessary, 'you must learn to trust people.'

Although all the cards were stacked against him, Brother did not look defeated but sat there weighing up the options. This was a good sign. If he was to be a leader of men then he would have to try and turn every situation to his advantage. I said nothing more and waited.

'The thing is,' he said, 'we really do not know anything about you, and the revolution is so important to all the people in my country I really felt I could not take the chance. Whilst I hoped you would not knowingly say anything to harm us, something could slip out and, as it is the International Diamond Group we have upset so much, retribution on us would be swift. In my position would you have taken the chance?'

I did not answer. The truth was I could not really put myself in his position but the ruthlessness I had developed over the last few months, completely against what I thought was my nature, worried me to the extent whereby I might well have done what he had tried to do.

'So what are you going to do now?' he asked. 'Do you really have the guts to kill me?'

I smiled a lopsided and, what I hoped to be, an evil smile.

'No problem at all. If it is going to be you or me then I am afraid you are on the shortlist all by yourself.'

I let that sink in for a while and continued. 'Two things are required here. The first is you want to keep me quiet and the second is I want to leave your country. I agree with you, there is absolutely no guarantee at all I will not say anything. I have no intention to do so but there again, as you pointed out, I could inadvertently say the wrong thing at the wrong time. The bottom line is, short of me shooting myself, you have to accept this as a calculated risk.'

I could see Brother's mind racing and tussling. Whilst his eyes never left mine, they took on a blank look as he was calculating the various options. I really wished Amazon had been here with us for I'm sure she could have helped him make up his mind in my favour.

'Even if I say I will trust you and do nothing, how can you believe me?' I liked that. The fact he had brought up in this difficult question showed his mind was going towards the right answer. If he had immediately said he was wrong and should not have tried to kill me that would've been far too glib and worrying. I let a little more time pass by before I said anything.

'As is so often said, trust is a two-way street. So far I have not let you down and I really do believe we can both accept I will not willingly or knowingly betray you. What is concerning you is the likelihood of the International Diamond Group somehow finding out about your involvement but you overestimate the realities of life. I do not move in the same circles as the International Diamond Group and it would be incredibly unlucky indeed if I happened to say something unintentionally in the hearing of someone who would pass this information to the International Diamond Group. It is not impossible, of course, but highly improbable. On the other side of the coin, I have to trust you. If you wished to you could quite easily get information about my activities in your country to someone important – you admit to knowing politicians and government ministers – and the international situation is such that these days Amnesty International or some other such organisation would be baying for my blood, and if nothing else my career would be finished and there's a high possibility I would end up in jail.' I did not mention that if this happened then I could also blow the whistle on him but stayed silent and let it sink in.

After a while I continued.

'There is one more thing you have overlooked. The International Diamond Group is concerned to protect its monopoly and profits. If you were to get a message to them that should there be a revolution they would have free and unfettered access to the diamonds in this country, they would be delighted. No doubt at the moment they are paying heavy bribes to mine diamonds and the prospect of shaking off this shackle would be appealing.'

This clearly had an effect. On the one hand, he saw the wisdom in what I had said, and on the other, was kicking himself that he had not thought of it.

'You're right. I think I have been too hasty and we should have discussed it at the forger's house. Vana was very unhappy about what I was going to do and at one point I thought Sabra was going to kill me.' He smiled. 'Perhaps the women have more sense than we do!'

Frankly, I was still uncertain as to whether or not he would be true to his word and let me go to the embassy, but short of killing him I did not have much choice. I could have tied him up and left him hidden in the bushes but there again eventually he would have been discovered and would have a very awkward time of it indeed. I also very much had in the back of my mind the fact that not too far up the road was a soldier who would shortly be waking up with a serious headache and I reckoned he would not be keeping his own counsel. So sooner or later, and I guessed not too much later, there would likely be a flood of military in the area. Decision time.

I looked at the revolver in my hand and threw it casually into his lap, shrugging my shoulders. I got to my feet, turned my back on him and walked towards the bushes where he had been hiding. Kicking around, I soon found his automatic pistol, which I picked up and tucked into the waistband of my trousers. I walked back to Brother. The revolver was still lying in his lap.

'You took a chance,' he said.

'Trust is trust,' I replied. In fact I was lying. What I had discovered after I took the pistol off the soldier and was back in my secluded spot was that it had no bullets in it. Not too bright of me not to have checked it before. Furthermore, although I turned my back on Brother I had surreptitiously slid his wicked knife into my right hand ready to use it if he had tried to shoot me and, finding the gun empty, attacked me. One-to-one I would have no chance; knife to one, I fancied my chances.

I lent down and picked up the revolver, saying, 'I think we should get out of here. The owner of this revolver is likely to wake up soon and the area could be flooded with military types.'

Brother got up and together we walked into the boulevard up to the nearest side street and away from potential discovery and danger.

We were both a little dishevelled and, for my part at least, hungry, so, after a short discussion, Brother took me to a safe house, which was surprisingly close, where we could spend the rest of the night. We both ate some cold meats, an odd-tasting goat's cheese with bread and generally talked about the hope for this country in the future. As dawn broke I had a quick wash, brushed down my clothing and generally tidied myself up ready to go to the embassy. Whilst I was confident I had convinced Brother to let me go unharmed I did not feel it too disloyal to have an insurance policy. So while I was getting myself ready to go I surreptitiously removed the bullets from his automatic before leaving both guns on the table. I kept the knife as insurance over insurance, as it were.

When we thought the time was right I left the safe house and made my way to the boulevard and the British Embassy, carefully disposing of the bullets as I walked. Somewhat more soldiers than yesterday were standing around in the boulevard with jeeps and army lorries parked, indicating that last night's adventure with the rock had not gone unnoticed. I strode slowly but determinedly along the road, passing various embassies as I went towards the one displaying the Union Jack. No one stopped me and none of the soldiers in the street seemed to have any curiosity as to why I was there. Quite who they were looking for I did not know. Perhaps they thought it was a local who had attacked the soldier. As I passed the green area with the monument I casually threw Brother's knife into the bushes.

When I got to the main gate of the embassy there was a guard sitting in a guard box controlling the opening and closing of the large metal gate. I put on my friendliest of smiles and wandered up to the guard.

'Hi,' I said, 'can you let me in? I've been sent by my boss to make an appointment for him to see the ambassador.' I nonchalantly handed him my papers as though I had no care in the world. He looked at them.

'Why come here and not telephone?' he said.

I raised an eyebrow. 'Telephone?' He looked at me and smiled.

'Yes, I guess it's quicker to come here than try get through on the telephone these days but where is your vehicle? White men don't walk about here, they all drive, even the shortest distances.'

That was probably true and something we had over-looked. I had to improvise.

'Tell me about it, the story of my life. I don't have a motor vehicle because I'm too junior so I have to take one of the pool cars when I need one and this morning two of us were fighting over the one working car.' I shrugged to indicate the lamentable mechanical expertise available to us to keep our vehicles on the road. 'And this battleaxe of a woman told me a gentleman would not think twice about letting a lady have the one and only car as she got into it and drove off. I didn't even have time to tell her that if she was really a lady we wouldn't have had the discussion to begin with. So I had the pleasure of a delightful stroll here with one consolation that it is still early in the day and the sun is not too strong. I'm rather hoping the air-conditioning works inside.'

He grunted to indicate that he was not at all concerned about the air-conditioning inside the embassy and looked at my papers once again before handing them back to me and pressing a button allowing the gate to slide open. I walked slowly in and up to the front door, which had a large brightly polished brass bell-push, which I ignored, and turned the handle of the door, which opened freely and easily. I stepped inside into a large reception area with doors leading off, closing the door behind me, and walked up to a young woman sitting behind a computer screen at a desk. She frowned.

'Can I help you?'

'I really hope you can,' I said, 'it is quite difficult but I would very much like to see the ambassador or at least, in the first instance, a member of his staff, as it is quite important.'

She smiled in a disarming sort of way. 'It is always quite important,' she said. 'If you want to see someone I'm afraid you have to make an appointment and come back in a few days. We are really very, very busy here.'

'Well that is a difficulty. I'm unable to come back in a few days. Indeed I would rather not leave at all. You see, I am sort of seeking political asylum, except I'm British and I don't need asylum but I feel I need protection.'

'I'm sorry, I really do not understand. You have to explain a lot more.'

I realised it was pointless trying to bully her so I thought my best way forward was to come clean, or relatively clean at least.

'You will probably remember there was a plane crash some months ago.' She almost nodded. 'Well I am a survivor of that plane crash and I have been wandering around the countryside ever since trying to get to the capital and the embassy. It's taken me a long time, but here I am.' I smiled and raised my arms to show that I was at her mercy. She did not look convinced but by the same token she realised if she turned me away she could be making a mistake. She looked at me long and hard and slowly picked up a telephone and dialled a number. When her call was answered she asked the person at the other end to come out to the desk, and shortly afterwards a young man, who looked barely out of school and certainly out of character in his very smart pinstriped business suit, white shirt and old school tie, arrived. The receptionist relayed the information I had given to her and the child looked at me very long and very hard. He turned around and beckoned to a security guard I had not noticed and, with a short 'Come with me,' he turned on his heel and I followed him, with the security guard close behind me, into a room off the reception area.

'Sit down and tell me your story,' He said, pointing to one of a number of comfortable looking chairs around a large conference table. I sat down. He went around the table and sat opposite with the security guard close to my right shoulder. I took a deep breath and smiled.

'I am a lawyer on this continent on business. I was on a passenger plane going from Louta to Wandaro and I remember the pilot telling the passengers over the intercom he had trouble with an engine and was going to land. We all fastened our seat-belts and adopted the emergency landing position and that's the last I can remember. The plane obviously crashed, which was confirmed to me by one of the local people I met later, but there again you must know this from the other survivors.' He said nothing and kept looking at me. I paused while appearing to gather my thoughts. 'My next memory was being half awake in a native hut with an old woman bathing my forehead and trying to make me eat some horrible food. I was immediately sick and I think I passed out again. The next few days or weeks, I really cannot remember, I spent half awake and half unconscious either lying in the hut or under a tree. This old woman told me they were laying me out in the sun to get the sun's life back in me. Look,' I said, unbuttoning a small part of my shirt, 'I am nice and brown from all that sunbathing.' I closed my shirt quickly so he could not see the marks and bruises inflicted by the soldiers at the jail.

Still the child said nothing. This time I waited. Eventually he gave in.

'If what you say is correct, how is it no one from the village came to the capital, to this embassy, to let us know?'

I shrugged. 'I have not the foggiest idea. They may not have known I was English. Okay, we spoke a little in English but there again that is the universal language these days. They didn't question me at all. Or if they did I certainly can't remember it. I'm afraid I was in no fit state to do or remember anything. Eventually, I got better. I started walking about and gaining strength and one day a couple of the men took me for a long walk to another village where I stayed and rested for a while, then two more men took me to another village where the same thing happened. Eventually I was brought to the capital here, shown the way to the embassy, and here I am.'

'You don't look as though you have been ill and unconscious for a long time,' the child said. And what the hell would you know about it, I thought to myself.

'I haven't seen myself for a very long time. There are no mirrors in the villages so I really cannot comment. If I give you my name, address – you know my occupation – you can check the airline records to see if I was indeed on the plane and also you can telephone my office in England. I will give you the number, and they will confirm who I am.'

He got up from the table and walked to a nearby sideboard upon which rested a number of writing pads and pencils. He picked up one of each and slipped them across the table to me.

'Name, address, date of birth and anything else you think will be of assistance.' I duly complied with his request. He picked up the pad and walked out of the room, leaving the security guard standing behind me. I suggested to the security guard he ought to sit down and take it easy but he shook his head and remained standing close to me. I waited and waited. At one stage I indicated to the security guard that a glass of water from an inviting looking pitcher on the sideboard would be quite nice, and he grudgingly allowed me to walk to it, fill a glass, sit back down again and drink the water.

Eventually the child came back and beckoned me to follow

him. We went out of the conference room across the reception area and up an imposing flight of stairs to the first floor. We walked down a heavily carpeted corridor to a door at the end. The child knocked and walked in. I followed.

'The ambassador,' the child said and left.

Sitting behind a very large desk was a man who appeared to be in his early forties, well-dressed and extremely slick looking. I was quite surprised. I expected the British ambassador to be an older man with more of a careworn expression from years of experience and political frustration. This man carried none of those signs and I felt to be appointed as an ambassador so young meant he was likely to be a very smart cookie indeed. I was not wrong.

'Ah,' he said, getting up from his desk and walking around to shake my hand, 'please sit down.'

He indicated a chair close to his desk and I sat while he returned to his own chair. As I was sitting, I noticed in one corner of his large room there were two leather settees at a low coffee table and yet he chose to speak to me across his desk. Not a good sign. Interviewing across a desk denotes psychological authority whereas sitting in comfortable settees indicates friendliness. I needed to be careful.

The ambassador looked at some notes in front of him. 'Why don't you tell me your story from the beginning,' he said.

'I'm afraid I have no story to tell you. All I can do is relate the facts.'

His face remained totally impassive with the faintest hint of a potential smile giving encouragement to talk freely to a sympathetic ear. His body language was neutral and attentive, exuding confidence and authority. I was beginning to see why he had been appointed Ambassador so young. He had, though, a fatal flaw. Whilst his face and body language were all under his absolute control, his eyes were not. Those eyes immediately registered displeasure that I had blunted his opening implication that I was going to be a storyteller. I smiled disarmingly, took a deep breath, and started to tell my tale. I told him why I went to Louta and what I did there, and that I had been engaged to go on to another case so took an aeroplane for Wandaro. I then repeated what I had told the child, embellishing a little here and there as I pretended to remember a few more incidental facts. When I'd finished he was silent and impassive but his eyes told me he was not believing one word of it. I waited.

'The difficulty I have,' he said, 'is that in this country we have had no reports of a plane crash.'

I was not totally surprised at this for if, as I suspected, the palace guard had shot down the plane – they certainly massacred all the passengers – it was not something that would have been broadcast generally. So I smiled.

'I have given your colleague details of the date I left Louta, the airline, and flight number so I'm sure you will have checked to confirm there was such a flight and I'm equally sure it will not be difficult to ascertain the plane never arrived at its destination.' His face remained expressionless but his eyes flickered acknowledgement. 'From there it takes little imagination to suspect the plane crashed somewhere and with your connections to American intelligence it would not be difficult to get pictures from their surveillance satellites of the track the plane followed, which would show it had crash-landed in this country.' Nothing from the ambassador but a cautious look in his eyes. 'I would suspect,' I continued, smiling disarmingly, 'judicious use of Google Earth could probably find a plane crash. So by saying "in this country" you had no "reports" of a plane crash is. . .' I tapered off at this point, looking at him.

'I believe,' he said, 'the word you're groping for is disingenuous.'

'Indeed,' I replied, 'though I did not wish to be seen to be rude or offensive.' His face remained completely impassive but those eyes indicated 'crafty'.

'So you are maintaining,' he said, 'it has taken you several months to get from the north of this country to the capital.'

'North?' I said. I looked puzzled. 'I have no idea what part of the country I was in.' I frowned and made out I was thinking. 'Ah, the north. That's where the plane *didn't* crash, is it?'

His body language indicated 'I do not know and I do not care' but his eyes belied this.

'If, as you say, you were on a flight from Louta to Wandaro then the flight path would be to the north of this country.' He paused to let it sink in. I wasn't fooled though.

He looked down at the papers on his desk as if consulting them and deciding what to say next. After a short silence he looked up and said, 'Our intelligence has indicated that there is a revolutionary group in this country being led by a white man. It seems as though this revolutionary group has had some success.' He paused and looked at me. He could obviously control the expression in his eyes when he felt he really needed to for they looked at me hard and deep.

'Oh come on,' I said. 'I am a lawyer. You can check that out. I have not been trained as a soldier. You can check that out as well. Do I look like a mercenary?'

'I do not know what a mercenary looks like,' he replied, 'but I have to say your face looks a little puffy as though you have been in a fight.'

'Frankly, I have no idea what my face looks like. I've not seen myself in the mirror for a considerable period of time. I'm not surprised at what you say though. If I am exposed to the sun for too long then my face often swells up; it sometimes gets a bit blotchy.' Pretty fast thinking on my feet here, I thought, and I hoped that the blotchy bit would cover the bruising discolouration. He grunted.

'What I would be asking,' I continued, 'were I in your position, was how I got past the embassy guard into the embassy.' One of the things learnt early in a lawyer's career is that it is wise to bring up and answer any weaknesses in one's case before the opposition does as this takes out the sting. His eyes instantly registered I had beaten him to the punch.

'And?' he said.

'I'm afraid this is an area where I am obliged to be cagey.' I smiled at him and adopted an extremely relaxed pose. 'You will find out, if you do not know already, I am an international litigation lawyer and I spend a large part of my time travelling around the world trying to solve problems or get evidence to solve problems. This means that I have learnt the type of people I need to contact or be aware of to get results. No matter what country, there is always someone who can help or at least point me in the direction of where I can get help. This country is no different. With no papers or other identification on me, I realised that if the local police stopped and questioned me I would be regarded as suspicious so I couldn't walk around the capital without papers. So I asked my escorts into the capital if they could find me someone who could arrange papers for me and they put me in touch with a man who put me in touch with someone else who eventually directed me to someone who did oblige.' His eyes were sceptical but by the same token if he had found out anything about me he must know I had a reputation for being rather resourceful.

'And you're not prepared to tell me who that someone is?' I shook my head. 'The difficulty I have in believing you is that these people do not work for nothing so you had to pay. How?'

I laughed. 'You are absolutely right. That was the big problem. However, I was lucky. The person I met who made the necessary arrangements for the papers was a die-hard Anglophile who believed what I said and took it on trust that once I was back in England I would send the money.

In a couple of weeks that person is going to send me an e-mail with bank details.'

The ambassador obviously thought this was a step far too far and I could see he was about to explode with incredulity. I put up my hand to stop him saying anything.

'I know what you're going to say. If this person could e-mail me then why couldn't I e-mail my office or even the embassy here to make arrangements to be picked up without any problems? The answer, sadly, is simple. I was told that government agencies monitor all e-mails in this country and it was highly likely they would act on any e-mail sent by me and pick me up, together with any person who let me use their e-mail, long before I could convince anyone in England or at the embassy I was alive and needed help. Quite frankly, I felt this person was being over cautious but that is what was believed so I could not use e-mail. Similarly, the tele-phone – but apparently the telephone system here is so awful the chances of me getting a call through to you were slim and England rather non-existent.'

'If what you say is correct, then surely to e-mail you with bank details would arouse the suspicions of the authorities.'

I laughed. 'Certainly not. As you are aware there is a constant stream of spam e-mails from this continent encour-aging people to send money to designated bank accounts in order to release vast fortunes to them with big profits. All my contact would need to do is to send one of those spam e-mails to a dozen or so people, one of which would be me.' To head off his next question I continued. 'The reason my contact has to wait for a couple of weeks before sending the e-mail is to make sure I get back to the office and switch off our spam filter otherwise the e-mail is likely to be rejected and I will never see it.'

'All very plausible.'

At that point there was a knock on the door and a young woman came in handing the ambassador a piece of paper.

She looked at me and I smiled. She smiled back. Number one rule in my business, be nice to the staff, for not only do they often have the best information, but they can screw you up big time if they don't like you. I guessed I needed all the friends here I could get.

The ambassador slowly read the piece of paper he was given and looked up at me.

'We have called the telephone number you gave my colleague and spoken to a young woman who was not at all surprised Nigel Turner was alive. She mentioned something about him being like the bad penny, always turning up sooner or later. When asked to describe Nigel Turner, she said,' he looked down at the piece of paper, 'sharp as a knife; as crafty as a barrel load of monkeys; plausible and difficult.' He looked at me hard. 'A most accurate description I would say, Mr Turner, wouldn't you?'

I tried to look nonplussed and made a mental note that Catherine and I would have a few words when I got back to the office. A long silence followed while the ambassador seemed to mull over his options. He accepted I was who I said I was, he must have known I was on the plane and I was as certain as I could be he knew the plane had crashed. After that I don't think he knew what to believe. If the official line was that there was no plane crash then he could hardly question me as to whether there were any other survivors. After a long while he said, 'Your story is,' he paused as he saw my raised eyebrow, 'rather,' he corrected himself, 'you have related facts that you were in the countryside for a long time and that because of the injuries sustained you spent a considerable part of that time in an unconscious or semiconscious state.' I nodded and he paused again. 'Now to be frank with you, our information and intelligence in this country is not of the highest order. Outside of the capital here it is very difficult for us to travel freely and so we know little of what is going on in the villages and what it is the people are doing. I believe you can help us with this.' I frowned, indicating that I could not possibly help any more than I already had but he was not put off his stride. He smiled a large, warm and engaging smile, leant back in his chair and put his fingertips together.

'You see,' he said, 'any information we can get, no matter how sketchy, will be helpful to us; to the British government. Therefore I would deem it a personal favour if you could spend some time with our Chief Security Officer and talk through everything you can remember. Just going through it slowly with an expert may well allow you to remember more. Even the attitude of the people you met would be nice to know. The fact that they helped you and were friendly towards you is a good sign. I'm sure you can help us more than you think.'

The last thing I wanted was a long session with an intelligence bod, which is what he meant when he referred to a 'chief security officer', but I could see any refusal would increase the ambassador's suspicion of me so I shrugged my shoulders in a resigned sort of way.

'Good,' he said, looking over the top of me, 'have you met our Chief Security Officer?'

I turned around in my chair and saw, standing in the doorway, a three-piece suit hanging on a six-foot skeletal body, above which was a black, fleshless skull beneath greying, almost white, close-cropped curly hair and from which the palest of pale blue, totally expressionless eyes, bored out, searing deep into my brain.

'Mr Turner,' the skeleton said, 'I believe we have met, just the once.'